ALSO BY HENRY BROMELL

The Slightest Distance

I Know Your Heart, Marco Polo

The Follower

Little America

Little America

A NOVEL BY

Henry Bromell

ALFRED A. KNOPF   NEW YORK   2001

Grateful acknowledgment is made to the following for permission to reprint
previously published material:

Hal Leonard Corporation: Excerpts from "One for My Baby (And One More for the
Road)" from the motion picture *The Sky's the Limit,* lyric by Johnny Mercer, music by
Harold Arlen, copyright © 1943 (copyright renewed) by Harwin Music Co. All
rights reserved. Reprinted by permission of Hal Leonard Corporation on behalf of
MPL Communications Inc.

Music Sales Corporation: Excerpt from "Catch a Falling Star," words and music by
Paul Vance and Lee Pockriss, copyright © 1957 (copyright renewed) by Music Sales
Corporation and Emily Music Corporation. International copyright secured. All
rights reserved. Reprinted by permission of Music Sales Corporation and as
administrator on behalf of Emily Music Corporation.

The Richmond Organization: Excerpts from "Fly Me to the Moon (In Other Words),"
words and music by Bart Howard, TRO copyright © 1954 (copyright renewed) by
Hampshire House Publishing Corp. Reprinted by permission of The Richmond
Organization on behalf of Hampshire House Publishing Corp., New York, N.Y.

Universal Music Publishing Group: Excerpts from "Interlude," words and music by
John Gillespie, Raymond Leveen, and Mary Elizabeth Paparelli, copyright © 1968 by
Universal–MCA Music Publishing, a division of Universal Studios, Inc. (ASCAP).
International copyright secured. All rights reserved. Reprinted by permission of
Universal Music Publishing Group.

ISBN: 0-375-40684-0
LCCN: 2001089764

For
Trish Soodik
&
Willie Bromell

I wish to be useful, and every kind of service necessary to the public good becomes honorable by being necessary. If the exigencies of my country demand a peculiar service, its claims to perform that service are imperious.

—NATHAN HALE

Survey the desert places and the rockiest islands—Sciathus and Seriphus, Gyarus and Cossura; you will find no place of exile where someone does not linger of his own desire.

—SENECA

Everything stated or expressed by man is a note in the margin of a completely erased text.

—FERNANDO PESSOA

One

1

One summer Saturday morning in 1957, almost five months before the events in question, the front door of a modest, two-story stucco house on P Street, in Georgetown, Washington, D.C., opened wide and out I stepped with my mother and my father. I was ten at the time, nursing a pompadour. We had been back from Syria for three years, and in five months we were to be stationed in Kurash, the subject of this story. My father was a spy, or, as he prefers to be remembered, an intelligence officer, with the C.I.A., from 1950 to 1978. He was recruited out of a Wall Street investment firm. He hated Wall Street, but, being a Wasp in good standing, he could only express his hatred indirectly and involuntarily. His neck used to lock in a rigid sideways staring position when riding the commuter train back and forth between Grand Central Station and Hastings-on-Hudson. We lived there—my father, my mother, myself, and a cocker spaniel named Winston—in a rented house on Clinton Street. I wouldn't say my father, once in the C.I.A., became a happy man; melancholia being, I now realize, endemic, deep in my family's genes. Rather, I'd say he swapped one kind of anxiety for another. His neck no longer seized on him, yet the acid drip of intelligence-gathering did eventually eat a sizable hole through his stomach and cause him to almost bleed to death.

On that hot summer morning, in 1957, my father and I headed off for Wisconsin Avenue at a leisurely pace. My mother waited for us to turn the corner, then gave chase. Up Wisconsin Avenue I walked. My father disappeared into People's

Drug Store. My mother hesitated, made a decision—she went after my father. A mistake. When she entered the chill relief of People's air-conditioning and looked around, she couldn't find him. He had vanished.

We were playing a game.

The game was called Spy.

My father and I were an agent and his control. He had to pass a message to me. My mother was counterintelligence. If she could catch us passing the note, she would win. If she couldn't, we'd win. We always won. My father always won. Even in the pretend version of his life, he had to win. Looking back , I now see that my mother had to assume on a regular basis the role of a kind of spy's whipping boy, losing over and over again to my father. But maybe this game, played on weekends since I was seven, helped prepare her for December 1958, when my father flew back to Washington for consultations and left her, to the consternation of all involved, in charge of the Hamra station.

I have several questions regarding what happened, exactly, in that year, 1958, in that place, Kurash.

Kurash was a small country wedged between the eastern border of Jordan, the rump of Syria, and the southwestern corner of Iraq. It no longer exists.

What happened, in history, inexactly, is this: in December of 1958, in Kurash, the young King, only twenty-three at the time, was killed as he stood in the garden behind Hamzah Palace smoking a cigarette. His reign, which lasted a mere five years, ended in the darkness of the garden, his body prone on the gravel, a shadow leaking from him, his own blood or his soul departing his body, shadow of himself, essence of himself, the Fallen King. The blood spread from his wounds, the shadow soon surrounded him, obscured him in the night of December 31, 1958. Three-thirty in the morning. Tuesday. He died instantaneously.

His kingdom collapsed. His branch of the Hashemite family flamed out and burned.

He had no children to suffer exile.

His little country, Kurash, vanished, consumed, like a snack, by Iraq and Syria, in 1965. Our State Department protested, sort of. President Johnson sent the Sixth Fleet to anchor in Beirut Harbor, just to remind people that the United States was still around, that we hadn't been totally distracted, that Vietnam was not our only concern, which of course it was, and gave the lie to our big gray boats bobbing uselessly in Beirut Harbor, the big gray boats I saw myself from the front lawn of the American Community School, where I was then a high school senior. When I say Kurash vanished, I mean vanished, gone, evaporated. On any map of the Middle East published after 1965, where there had once been a tidy triangle of earth labeled Kurash, there where the borders of Syria, Jordan, and Iraq once had to stop and circumnavigate that brave anachronistic kingdom, they now meet, unimpeded, grossly cheek by jowl.

Gone like a dedicated Politburo leader airbrushed out of a black-and-white photograph of Stalin and his henchmen. Gone like the great tribes of the Sioux and the Shawnee, the peaceful Pocumtucks, the animistic Mohawks.

Eliminated from history.

I know from accounts recently published in the *New York Times* of secret Congressional hearings in the seventies that a C.I.A. case officer in Hamra, Kurash, in 1958, carried to Hamzah Palace and delivered to the King once a month a briefcase full of cash. In his book *Pax Americana*, George Seal of the University of Iowa posits that the King was killed by agents of the United States, agents hired and handled by the C.I.A. My father was chief of the C.I.A. station in Hamra at the time of the assassination.

I'm interested in history, which I presently teach (Modern European) at Santa Monica College in Santa Monica, California—Robert Redford's alma mater. I'm interested in what happens inside history, what history hides, what gets left out and what is forgotten.

I'm fifty-two years old. My own son, Eli, like me an only child, is now twenty-three and a wizard at special effects in the movies, more specifically, in horror movies. If you've seen *The Third Spider* or *Crown of Blood*, if you've seen the robocyd's computer head explode in *Demon Grin*, if you've seen the mutation of the caryatids in *Time/Slash*, then you've seen my son's work. My wife and I live in a two-bedroom bungalow in Ocean Park, about five blocks from the Pacific. I want to state for the record that my wife is terrifically intelligent and looks twenty years younger than her age, frequently causing unemployed young actors to swivel and stare when she sashays by to get her morning latte at Coffee & Bean on Main Street. I wake up eager to bask in her kindness and brilliance; the last thing I see each night before slipping off to the world of dreams is her patient and forgiving smile.

I have before me a fairly comprehensive chronology of events, drawn from witnesses; some participants; memoirs, including Ambassador Tyler Burdick's *Cold War in a Hot Place* (Random House, 1961); newspaper reports; files released to me, under the Freedom of Information Act, by a reluctant C.I.A.; and, whenever possible, scholarly works. I say whenever possible because there aren't many scholarly works dedicated to the question of Kurash in 1958. Very few. In fact, only three: Thomas Polmar's massive *Heartbreak Arabia* (Praeger, 1963), the aforementioned *Pax Americana* by George Seal (Harcourt, Brace, 1962), and *Reluctant Imperialists: CIA and Postwar World Politics* by James O. Merrill and Eugene S. Fontana (Simon and Schuster, 1966). I do not, however, know what happened inside history, I do not know if Hamlet killed Polonius, I only know that Polonius died. I lack, so far, to date, regrettably, the evidence of an observer. I have no Mercutio to explain Romeo, I have no Enobarbus to teach me the sad secrets of Anthony, I have no one who has seen too much and can do too little except confess.

Truthfully, I think I've always been kind of scared to find out exactly what went on in Kurash in 1958. My father is, after all, my father—secretive, withheld, diffidence personified, but still, my father. I love him deeply, though we aren't close, and never have been close. I don't know if I trust him. I don't even know if I like him, as a person separate from my father, I mean, some man out there named Mack Hooper going about his business, the retired C.I.A. officer who was raised by Quakers, voted for Adlai Stevenson, and wrote poetry, for a period, which he later had the good sense to burn in shame. Imagine simple and innocent words— "Good morning, old chum" or "Have you seen my glasses?"— gathering about them mysterious significance, as if they were perhaps coded and in need of deciphering. Imagine a Waspish distrust of sentiment and self-exposure legitimized by an oath of silence, a holy promise never to reveal who he really is and what he really does. I don't know him is what I'm saying, and, to bring the espionage metaphor to its logical conclusion, it has occurred to me that the only way I can learn anything about my father is to spy on him, which is why I flew to Boston and am presently camped out in the guest room of my father's condo overlooking Boston Harbor.

At night, when he's asleep, I consult my books and the several hundred index cards I have collected, each one covered with scribbled tidbits of information gleaned from the hundreds of books and documents that I have read and left behind in the UCLA library. I also unroll, scroll-like, a long piece of heavy white paper on which I am constructing my chronology of the events of 1958, in Kurash, my chart of the various comings and goings of the principal players, a diagram of What Really Happened, I Think, on which I fully intend to connect all the dots and then fearlessly stand back and see what I've got. The last determining clue found, cipher deciphered, the mystery solved. The truth. Even though I keep reminding myself there is no such thing.

I told my father I was here because I wanted to ask him some questions for a book I'm researching about American foreign policy in the Middle East during the cold war as well as the cold war's culture of espionage. "What the hell is that?" he asked. "Us," I said. He gave me a funny look, reminded me of his secrecy oath. "All I want from you," I said, "is a feel for the time, the places, the people. You were there; you know what it was like."

I know better than to be direct. Instead, I feign this almost personal curiosity, a general interest in my childhood, just to get him talking. I ask him to describe something physical. My father loves the material world. The Hamra airport, for example.

"Oh, in those days it was just a one-story white limestone building straddled by two runways on the edge of the desert."

He says this as if offhandedly describing a beautiful woman he once seduced, then leans forward to blow into his cup of steaming Earl Grey. We're sitting in his living room, a big rectangle of a room facing the harbor, old Navy buildings of granite and brick, silent circling seagulls. He likes to sit here and drink tea and watch the boats in a kind of nautical trance. Spots of autumn sunlight fill the room, along with a vague and pleasant scent of old furniture and books.

He straightens, sips. "I wish I still smoked. I miss my cigarettes."

Yesterday, while he was wheeling his cart through Bread and Circus in search of our dinner, I found, in his study, prowling, digging, snooping, spying, a note scribbled in a woman's hand across a piece of yellow, lined paper: "O love, you could not know or do know the way I feel thinking of you as I stare out this window at the gravel driveway, the high garden wall, the palm trees and flat-roofed houses of the city. . . ." The note was folded inside a Penguin paperback edition of *Travels in Arabia Deserta*, orange cover now faded to a dim pink, a smear of suntan lotion on the back page. Inside the cover, in my father's microscopic, spidery scrawl, I read: "February 1958, Kurash." What does this love note mean? From whom did it come? Not my mother, it isn't her handwriting. A girlfriend?

I almost ask, but instead stick with circumspection.

"When did you first go to Hamra?"

"I arrived, alone, on January the third, 1958," my father replies. "You and your mother were still in Rome."

2

The Air Kurash DC3 taxied to the terminal and stopped. Through the window my father could see camels threading their way along the horizon. The crew opened the door; he disembarked onto the tarmac. He loved, immediately, the dry desert breeze.

"Did someone meet you?"

"Yes. Roy Sweetser, and a driver. Hussein. They had the biggest, brightest red Chevrolet you've ever seen. Brand-new. It looked like a spaceship. Do you remember Roy Sweetser?"

A picture comes to me of a thin, sorrowful man in a seersucker suit, sitting in the shadows of his living room surrounded by Bedouin carpets and brass trays and ebony and mother-of-pearl tables, puffing on his pipe while his wife, Barbara Sweetser, née Roberts, shy, small-boned, blond, fond of angora sweaters and penny loafers, served small cups of after-dinner Turkish coffee. The music coming from a Zenith record player was Nat King Cole singing "Cottage for Sale." The earliest reference to Roy Sweetser I have found is a single "confidential memo," released to me under the Freedom of Information Act, a year-end assessment report dated December 12, 1957, written by Milton Gourlie, C.I.A. station chief, American Embassy, Hamra, Kurash. It reads: "Strengths: loyal, honest, hardworking, no known vices. Weaknesses: limited intelligence, limited imagination, no guts. Advancement recommendations: None."

"I remember him," I say.

Roy Sweetser was thirty-one years old at the time, a career C.I.A. officer halfway through his first assignment in Kurash, ranked GS12 with a standard State Department cover as second secretary. The morning my father arrived, he stood watching, with some trepidation, the Air Kurash plane taxi to a stop. Indeed, the sweat trickling down his rib cage had more to do with nerves than the heat. His stomach churned, a bitter bile backed up in his throat, the sour taste of that morning's coffee and the half pack of Chesterfields he'd smoked since leaving the house. Milton, he felt, had been less than forthcoming about this new arrival, coy even, simply passing him off as "a welcome addition to our happy family." The "family" being, Roy surmised, the local C.I.A. station's four members: himself; Milton, the scholarly, bespeckled station chief; Renee Bartlett, everyone's secretary and arguably the only one around who really knew what she was doing; and Johnny Allen, the code clerk, so paranoid and dedicated he sometimes slept on a cot in the code vault, monitoring and protecting each transmission as if it were a love letter. And now they were five. . . .

But Roy knew better.

He knew that Milton didn't think much of him, and he knew, or at least suspected, that this new fellow, Mack Hooper, was arriving to usurp what little power Roy had. Hence the churning stomach. He tossed away his cigarette and watched the passengers descend from the airplane, looking for the man he had glimpsed only in a small black-and-white photo. There he was, at the top of the stairs, squinting in the sudden bright light, dressed in a gray summer Brooks Brothers suit, Oxford blue shirt, dark tie: his nemesis.

My father.

"We got in that damn bordello of a car and drove straight to the embassy." He suddenly stands, spotting something out on the harbor—a tugboat, battered red and black, moving ponderously toward land. His gaze dreamily follows the boat, then he glances back at me. "Anyway, Roy was pleasant and cordial without really revealing anything about himself."

Hussein drove like a blind man, leaning on the horn as he imperiously scattered pedestrians. My father mainly remembers the clamor, the noisy chaos of people and diesel Mercedes buses, kids clinging to the backs for a free if hazardous ride, the weird mix of camels and donkeys and cars and trucks.

"You'll like it here," Roy said, looking back from the front seat to face my father. "It's a good posting. We've got a nice club, swimming, baseball, that kind of thing. Plenty for the wife and kid to do. You have a kid, right?"

My father grunted, searching for a cigarette of his own. "A son. Terry. He's ten."

That's me. A first, tentative appearance on the stage, a name: Terry Hooper.

My father found his cigarette, lit it, gazed out the window at the colorful tumult, and said nothing for the rest of the drive.

"Did you miss us?" I ask.

"Excuse me?" My father looks genuinely puzzled.

"Me and Mom. Did you miss us?"

"Probably. I don't remember." A note of defensiveness creeps into his voice. "I had a lot on my mind."

Hussein finally pulled through a high metal gate, past two Desert Legionnaires posted as guards, and into a wide, gravel driveway in front of a two-story limestone building that had once been someone's house. He parked the Chevrolet, and they all got out, stretching. My father followed Roy up the stone steps and into a kind of reception area, threadbare couches underneath bright posters of American landmarks: the Grand Canyon, the Lincoln Memorial, the Manhattan skyline. A Marine Guard, so young that pimples blossomed on his cheeks, sat behind a government-issue wooden desk.

"Morning, Mr. Sweetser."

"Good morning, Sal. This is Mack Hooper. He'll be joining our happy family."

"Welcome, sir." Sal nodded, surprisingly bashful.

As he led my father down a corridor past quiet, busy offices—Agricultural, Military, Cultural—Roy hated himself for quoting Milton's pious, meaningless description of their supposed "happy family." Not that Sal had realized it was a quote, but it was, and that seemed to Roy infinitely sad, pathetic, the words of a loser trying to shore up his tenuous position in the world by wearing the same tie as his boss. Family my ass, he thought, approaching the thick metal security door and pressing the buzzer on the left side. A camera gazed down at them. Family you love, family you can trust. Renee buzzed them in; the security door clicked open.

"Can you describe the offices?"

"Sure." My father closes his eyes. "Directly upon entering you were facing Renee, who sat at her desk, eyes on the security monitor, a service .45 in her top drawer. To your left was Milton's office; to your right the vault room, Johnny Allen in there enciphering or deciphering. At the back end was Roy Sweetser's office, and next to that a room the size of a small closet. That was mine. A desk, a chair, a window."

"What was the view from the window?"

My father studies the dust motes swirling around his apartment. "The driveway. A wall. A couple of scraggly palm trees."

"Could you see the city?"

"Some rooftops, a mosque, that's about it."

And so there they deposited him, my father, thirty-two years old, in this office the size of a closet, alone with the view.

O love

Roy Sweetser was a fairly experienced case officer, but he wasn't a very good one, and he knew it. Part of that was due to incompetence, part to laziness. His meager list of assets included a few Kurashian, Egyptian, and Syrian functionaries of dubious value who supplied him with precious little that could be considered worthwhile. He assumed my father's arrival was directly linked to his own incompetence, and so he returned to his office in a sulk, brooding, calculating the angles. Renee entered my father's closet-size office in Sweetser's wake, gave my father her woeful, bug-eyed smile, and extended a welcoming hand. "My name's Renee. Don't mind him." A nod over her shoulder indicated Roy. "He's just jealous. He thinks you're going to take his job."

She cast a quick, expert glance around my father's tiny premises. "A few pictures on the wall, a plant by the window, maybe a rug on the floor, this place'll spiffy right up. Blinds. You're going to need blinds. I'll get you pencils, legal pads. Milton wants to see you."

She led him back across the central office to Milton's door, bumping into Johnny Allen, a stack of cables in his hand.

"Johnny, Mack Hooper."

The two men shook hands, Johnny protective of the cables, as if he suspected my father might grab them and flee directly to the Russians.

"How old was Johnny?"

My father thinks. "Early twenties."

"And the station chief, Milton?"

"Early forties."

He had glanced up from behind his desk as my father entered, light from his gooseneck lamp spilling into the lenses of his tortoiseshell glasses, two opaque orbs obscuring his eyes, so that for a moment he looked like a grinning blind man. Stocky, sandy-haired, dressed in blazer and chinos, he offered his freckled hand across the mound of papers. "Milton Gourlie. Welcome aboard, Mack."

"Thanks. It's good to be here." Or some such banality. My father's head was starting to whine with fatigue. He hadn't slept in forty-eight hours.

"I'm not going to waste your time with any bullshit, Mack. I'll get right to the point. Hodd has sent you to me for one reason and one reason only. He wants you to adopt the King. Our only potential pal within shouting distance is a twenty-two-year-old kid who won't talk to us. He only talks to our British cousins, who are about to go broke. I want you to become his friend, I want you to convince him that we're willing to support him after the British leave."

Unexpectedly, Milton smiled, almost chuckled, as if to a private joke. "Not, mind you, that I think it can be done. The squirt's a real piece of work. So good luck." Milton shuffled through some papers on his desk, pulled up a handful, studied them. "Says here Hodd was pleased with the work you did in Syria. Says here you have the gift of confidence. That true?"

Imagine Roy sulking in his office while twenty feet away, behind closed doors, Milton explained to my father that the King was an English-educated playboy, a speedster with a fleet of powerful sports cars and a heavy foot, a sybarite with a seemingly endless appetite for young women, preferably European or American, all of which my father already knew, from his own homework, from the briefings he'd received before leaving Washington. But he said nothing. He listened. My father was always a good listener. Roy scooped a few Miltowns from the glass jar on his desk, swallowed them like peanuts, bent his head toward the murmuring voice on the other side of the wall—Milton's voice, droning indecipherably. Roy was miserable. He'd be sent back to Washington within weeks, he was sure of it, sent back an abject failure and shuffled off to some demeaning paper-stacking job in Building C, never to be heard from again. No more hardship allowance, no more cook and houseboy. Barbara would have to get a job.

He wanted to shoot himself.

O love

3

"They had a car for me, a three-year-old Opel," my father remembers.

I remember, too. "It was kind of red, with a gray interior, right?"

"Yeah. Piece of shit automobile. Constantly overheating. Anyway, I finally got it started and drove with Renee over to our house. What was to be our house."

Outside of which, behind which, in a rocky field, dark-skinned men squatted *tap-tap-tapping* limestone into square blocks, building blocks, the stuff from which every house in Hamra was made, the tapping as musical and regular as church bells.

"The house was already furnished, pretty ugly stuff, functional, though I knew your mother would transform the whole place somehow. I met Eid, the cook, and Ahmed, the houseboy."

Eid, tall and thin, worried, big-knuckled hands willing dinner into existence; Ahmed smoking a cigarette at the kitchen table and chatting softly as day ended and the *tap-tap-tapping* gave way to the night sounds, desert sounds, wind whining over the flat roof of the house, sheep bells carrying across the stony field . . .

"Then I did something very smart. I drove with Renee back to the office, stuck my head into Roy Sweetser's office, and asked him if he wanted to have a drink."

Roy looked up, surprised, considered in what ways this might be a trap, a trick question, then shrugged, pleased despite himself: "Sure."

They drove in tandem, Roy behind the wheel of his own car, a black '57 Ford Fairlane, to the Hotel Antioch, one of the few colonial buildings in the city, built by the British in the early part of the century across from a Roman ruin, an amphitheater where, later that winter, I sat on cold hard stone and watched the Ice Capades, trim American girls with muscular thighs whizzing around the man-made ice, a blessed gift from our cultural exchange program.

They sat in the old-fashioned bar, nursing whiskeys.

"I did not come here to take your job," my father said. "I don't want your job. I want your help doing my job."

"Which is?" Roy asked innocently.

"I'm supposed to become the King's best friend."

"Ah." Roy nodded sagely, though in truth he was taken aback, perplexed. "That's it?"

"That's it."

"How are you going to do that?"

"I haven't a clue. Any ideas?"

Roy had none, could offer none, yet felt so flattered that my father had even asked that he became, from that moment forth, my father's most stalwart supporter. They had another whiskey, ate dinner together in the hotel restaurant, empty except for a few Arab businessmen dressed in Western garb, a visiting Danish soccer team, and what must have been a group of tourists, English, to judge by the pale, pink, baffled faces poised intently above their guidebooks. My father remembers nothing of what he and Roy said during dinner. The meal itself was passable. He drove home alone to our house, smoked a cigarette in the living room, and read for a while, *Travels in Arabia Deserta,* the same paperback, not faded yet, that I found forty years later in his study in Boston. Then he went to sleep.

"What's he like, this new guy?" Barbara asked Roy that night as they readied themselves for bed.

"Not bad, a straight shooter, I'd say. Went to Yale. Good man."

It was only as he was lying under the covers next to Barbara, inhaling the sweet fragrance of her skin and various mysterious lotions, that he realized his stomach no longer hurt. It had relaxed, like a squid releasing its victim. He belched pleasantly and fell into an immediate sleep, a smile on his weak, sunburnt face.

The next morning, a Wednesday, my father was introduced to the senior staff at the weekly staff meeting, up on the second floor, in Ambassador Burdick's corner office overlooking the embassy garden, the bougainvillea, bright *cannas,* a solitary date palm, an empty fountain. The office itself contained an American flag in one corner, a framed photograph of President Eisenhower on the wall behind the Ambassador's huge mahogany desk, a left-over piece of colonial extravagance, as well as several worn leather chairs and a couch where the senior staff now sat gathered together: the C.I.A. station chief, Milton Gourlie; the military attaché, Colonel Allen McCone; the political officer, Chester Boyden; the deputy chief of mission, Jeffrey Blake; and Tad Greenway, the economic counselor. The Ambassador himself, Tyler Phelps Burdick III, liked to stand for these meetings, perhaps because his lower back gave him trouble, perhaps because he felt it gave him some undeniable and appreciable superiority over his staff, much as Mussolini suffered his minions to cross a room the size of a football field before reaching his desk.

Six weeks later, my mother and I arrived from Rome, where we had been encamped in the Pensione Ruben on via della Croce. That's when my *troubles,* as my mother still likes to put it, began: an existential crisis, the sudden discovery, encouraged by disloca-tion, the vagaries of geography, and, I suppose, culture shock, that *nothing was stable.* Dense crowds of sour-smelling men and women shrouded in black, only their dark eyes and dark tattooed hands to distinguish them, clogged the narrow streets, their inco-herent babbling accompanied by shrieking taxi horns and spooky drifting minaret calls. Sleepless, I became a student of the long dawn shadows, hallucinated a palpable, crumbling world, the empire of termites, the habitat of disintegration. Books vaporized in my hands. Dogs with open sores populated by squirming maggots panted at the garden gate. Frightened by my bed, its tendency, when the lights were off, to swallow me, absorb me, liquefy me, I took to sleeping, or trying to sleep, on the cool hard substantiality of the tile floor. Next door, our neighbors sat outside at night, clustered before a TV perched on a chair, and watched an English program, *Robin Hood,* which for some reason I found singularly reassuring, the Merry Men in their long-ago romance swigging mead and gathering around their very own wife/mother Maid Marian, all played on the stage of the desert, watched with fascination by a family raised on dates and pomegranates and the merciless shifting sands, days so hot the night itself became a celebration, the shade of a palm tree more of a safe haven than all of Robin Hood's forest. I could share that with them, lying next door on the tiles, I could share that bright black-and-white window into another, parallel universe, the one from which I came and to which, borne along by the peal of English trumpets and the thud of horse hooves clattering across a wooden planked bridge into the verdant comforting gloom, I hoped I would soon return.

What I needed, of course, was my father to come to me and hold me and tell me that everything would be all right, but he didn't, partly because it never occurred to him to do so, and partly because he was already being sucked into the events I am now trying to piece together, forty years later, from memory, from interviews with as many of the principal players as I can find, from months of research, hours spent poring over fragments of C.I.A. material circa 1958, and of course from my conversations with my father and my mother, who after all were there, and who could, if they would, explain everything.

Or could they?

"Remember what I told you," my father reminded me yesterday, not in his condo overlooking Boston Harbor but out in the Public Gardens, on a cold gray day as we took a walk past the dormant swan boats. "When I joined the Glue Factory I signed a secrecy oath. I swore that I would never reveal what I knew. And I won't. Ever. I'll answer your questions as long as they don't tread on anything substantial. I'll give you a feel for things, tell you some anecdotes, but that's it. My personal opinion is that guys like me who retire and then go on to blabber in public, in their stupid autobiographies or in the boardrooms of multinational corporations, should be shot. I'd happily pull the trigger myself."

By Glue Factory he meant C.I.A. Why a factory where tired old horses are put to death and ground up into an adhesive paste should serve as a metaphor for the C.I.A., I can't explain. When I asked my father, he just shrugged and said it had something to do with the essential meaninglessness of life.

The next day, visiting the Boston Museum of Fine Art together, gazing upon one of Picasso's jokester masterpieces, a woman dissected into her several arresting selves, he muttered, "Anyway, what do I know? One thing I learned as an intelligence officer, the one thing those thirty years taught me, is that there's always another secret, the story is never, ever fully told. Lunch?"

I had yet to work up the nerve to ask him who had sent him the letter I'd found folded into his old Penguin edition of *Travels in Arabia Deserta*. Why was she crying out to him, and was she part of the story?

I had yet to confess the extent of my own spying.

The Saturday of my first week in Hamra my mother and father were invited to Ambassador Burdick's house for dinner and cocktails. They drove there in the Opel, leaving me behind in my second-story bedroom, listening to the wind howl across the flat roof. For consolation I played the Platters.

> *O yes I'm the great pretender*
> *pretending that I'm doing well . . .*

Hymn to loss and regret, American-style.

The Ambassador's residence, a modern rectangle of stone and glass, held over a hundred people that night, members of the diplomatic community; Kurashian government officials; significant businessmen, foreign and local; journalists; artists. They filled the large living room, spilled out onto the wide terrace and backyard beyond, sweet with jasmine. The Ambassador's wife, Kathy Burdick, made a point of greeting my parents at the door, ushering them to the bar, making sure they got the drinks of their choice, then taking my mother aside and introducing her to Barbara Sweetser; Milton's wife, Lorraine; Renee; and the rest of the embassy women, mostly wives, mostly eager to help their husbands do well, survive, succeed. They exuded a kind of glassy-eyed eagerness, brittle, confused, the earnest patina of Smith and Mount Holyoke not quite the shield they needed, here in the desert, in 1958. My mother did not want to be one of them; she was already, without quite realizing it, in search of another self. Knowing this, let's leave her for now, enfolded by Kathy Burdick, Barbara Sweetser, and Renee, in a corner of the crowded living room, and follow my father as he is steered by the elbow, Ambassador Burdick at his side, into the Ambassador's study. The door is closed, the Ambassador turns his two-martini attention to my father, a contented smile on his face.

"Everything going well, Mack?" he asked.

"Fine, thank you, Mr. Ambassador."

"Call me Tyler, for Christsake."

"Okay, Tyler."

"I'll level with you, Mack. The Glue Factory makes me nervous. Very fucking nervous. Know why?"

My father shook his head. "No, I don't."

"Because you know more than I do." Burdick grinned.

The grin faltered. He bore down on my father.

"So the little favor I'm going to ask of you is that you let me know if there's something I should know about that I don't know about." He was disturbingly close. "I'd rather not make a horse's ass out of myself in public simply because I haven't been informed of the fucking facts. And don't give me any shit about Milton Gourlie. Milton wouldn't tell me his phone number if he didn't have to." The Ambassador straightened. "That's it. Thanks for hearing me out."

He opened the door, waved for my father to exit the study first, followed him back out to the party without another word. Milton Gourlie watched anxiously from across the room.

4

Reconstructing those first few months in Kurash, those months when I was myopic with misery, awash in tangible alienation, but, in the final analysis, not part of the story, merely, at most, a gloomy onlooker, I have been able to set before me several facts, what must pass for facts in the interest of moving forward, discerning a narrative. These facts are: The United States, symbolized best by that big red Chevrolet that greeted my father when he stepped off the airplane, had hunkered down to fight the cold war and win it. The cold war was not simply a geopolitical extension of national hubris, though hubris did indeed rule the day. Rheumy Episcopalians and flinty Presbyterians from Yale and Wall Street held sway, projecting onto the world their own vision of churchly virtue versus the godless unwashed hordes. It was not imperialism, exactly, though American businessmen clamored for more markets and felt it their right and obligation to seize them when and where they could. We had, after all, just sent the Marines ashore in Lebanon, there to protect Things as They Are. Eisenhower was president. John Foster Dulles was secretary of state. His brother, Allen Dulles, former O.S.S. operative in Geneva, Switzerland, was director of the C.I.A. These men did not believe in containment. They believed in victory. Halfway around the world from their Chevy Chase driveways and Georgetown row houses, the King of Kurash, a mere eighteen when he assumed the throne after the assassination of his father in 1953, held tenuous dominion over a country summarily and arbitrarily carved out of the desert, along with Syria,

Lebanon, Iraq, and what was then called Trans-Jordan, by France and Britain following World War I. There was really no such place as Kurash. It was a piece of sand inhabited by Bedouin tribes and, in the city of Hamra, a small community of Jewish traders and a university staffed primarily by English and Palestinian scholars. France and Britain had selected the King's grandfather Ali to rule Kurash for the same reason they chose his brother Feisel to rule Iraq and his other brother Abdullah to rule Jordan, because they were all members of the Hashemite family, of the Kuraish tribe, one of the largest, most powerful, and therefore most respected Bedouin tribes in Arabia. They were descended in the male line from Muhammad's daughter Fatimah. The blood of the Prophet ran in their veins. Even the name given Ali's small new country, Kurash, was a clumsy, indelicate elision of the tribal name, Kuraish. Hamra was chosen as the capital simply because it was the biggest place around, an ancient trade route town, a former Roman colony, and, more recently, a military outpost for the British. The King's father, who inherited the throne from Ali, was shot in the head, at close range, by a mentally unstable patriot convinced that the King's father was an Israeli spy. He was not. The King, until that moment an eighteen-year-old schoolboy, found himself whisked one night from his dormitory in Surrey, England, to an RAF base outside London and then flown directly home to Hamra, where he was, by morning, crowned.

John Foster Dulles and Allen Dulles had dinner that night at the University Club on Sixteenth Street. It was summer, a hot, muggy Washington summer, and they were both momentarily depleted, drained. Martinis revived them. Their conversation meandered. They rued the recent closing of their secret tunnel carved out under East Berlin so that the C.I.A. could tap the East Germans' phone lines, a project that had given them both particular satisfaction. They discussed the unsettling rise of left-wing militants in Central America, and agreed that countermeasures should be taken. They stared for a baleful moment or two at the miasma of Africa, a postcolonial unraveling that had set loose age-old tribal animosities, family feuds so complicated no one could follow them, though both knew the Russians were in there stirring things up, hoping for chaos. Then they turned their attention to the Middle East. Nasser was a pain in the ass with his nationalist pan-Arab siren song, and they agreed that if possible he would have to go. Israel, they agreed, despite their residual anti-Semitism, was the bedrock upon which they must build and was therefore to be supported at all costs. Then they got to the question of Kurash. A small silence settled over their table.

"This new King, he's a mere boy," John Foster mused aloud, contemplating his silverware. "Who's the station chief out there?"

"Milton Gourlie."

Another impenetrable silence.

"Stability, Allen. A boy needs a father. Stability at all costs. That's how we're going to beat the Russians."

He was right.

More facts: Nasser, the Socialist, wanted the King, a monarchist, to go. His intelligence service, aided by the K.G.B., was already hard at work on various assassination plans. The Israelis didn't trust the new King because he was young and untried and a Hashemite. On the other hand, they had so thoroughly infiltrated Kurashian Intelligence and the Kurashian Army that they felt secure. Any move to hurt them they would know about in advance. The Russians had already decided that the novice King was a target they couldn't resist, an opportunity for them to undermine a reactionary government and close the pincers on Israel.

Fact: The King, his first week home, started buying cars. A Ferrari, a Jaguar, a Corvette, an Alfa, a Triumph, an MG. They were shipped out from Europe and America. He stored them at Hamzah Palace, on the outskirts of Hamra, each with its own garage and mechanic.

Fact: Even Elvis Presley was now part of the militant American crewcut vigilance, having been drafted, shorn, and sent off to West Germany, where, presumably, he would be among the first to fall should the armies of the Soviet Union and the East Bloc launch their expected attack on the rest of Europe. My point being that even Americans had a King who was expendable. In his absence, a compilation LP called *Fifty Million Elvis Fans Can't Be Wrong* was pressed and released. I bought it at the PX, took it home, played it over and over again on the little yellow Phillips record player given to me on my tenth birthday in Rome by my mother, music to accompany my gradually diminishing despair.

Won't you wear my ring around your neck . . .

Back home kids were making out in basements. I saw it in *Life* magazine. Why wasn't I making out in basements?
O love
Milton Gourlie sat at his desk in his office, tilted back in his chair, freckled hands clasped behind his head, and gazed morosely out at my father and Roy Sweetser. Behind him, on the wall, hung a map of the Middle East. My father could see Kurash lodged like a walnut between Syria and Iraq, ninety percent arid, ninety-nine percent Muslim, a sandy blotch miles from any port, a country smaller than Rhode Island with a population of less than two million, which would give it, he calculated, roughly the same specific gravity as Springfield, Massachusetts, a city he had visited every Saturday as a boy to have Dr. Bolton check on his braces. Roy looking much improved, an avuncular glint in the eye as he contemplated Milton's head and realized, for the first time, that it was an outsize head, a very large head. This insight seemed to lend to Roy a subtle advantage, and added to his feeling of well-being.

"The King ran amok again last night." Milton looked back and forth between them. "He crashed one of his sports cars into the statue of his grandfather in the middle of Jebel Hamra Circle. Not one but two girls with him. Swedish girls. Fifteen-year-old girls. Fortunately, Major Rashid got the King home and the girls onto a plane back to Sweden before this escapade became public knowledge. Mack, you should go over and introduce yourself to Major Rashid. He's head of Kurashian Intelligence. A good man. Anyway, this has got to stop. This kid is going to ruin us."

"Milton, I've asked Roy to help me figure out a way to get closer to the King," my father said. "I could use his expertise."

Roy beamed modestly, studied his shoes. Milton nodded.

"I've gone over everything we have on the King, and I don't think the usual channels will get us what we want."

"I've asked Ambassador Burdick to have the King over for dinner and arrange an introduction to you, Mack."

"No, that's what I mean, that won't work. You're right. He's a kid. He won't trust anyone he meets at a diplomatic reception."

"Well then, how the hell do we get to him? He avoids us like the plague. He's polite, distant, kind of like he's making fun of us. We've got friends inside his intelligence service, friends inside the palace, friends among his bodyguards even, but we never walk away with anything approximating hard news, and we sure the fuck have no degree of control or even influence."

My father hesitated a moment. He hadn't been there very long, and he knew what he was about to suggest would sound nuts. But he was also pretty sure it would work. He cleared his throat. "I want to start a go-cart club."

Milton and Roy turned and stared at him.

"A go-cart club?" Milton asked. "Little cars that go around and around?"

"Fast little cars that go around and around. Soup them up, really fast cars. We'll build a racetrack, we'll get everybody at all interesting to join, we'll have official races and official winners and losers and trophies, and then we'll wait."

"For what?" Roy was honestly confused.

"For the King to join."

And that's what they did; they started a go-cart club. Out in the desert. They rented some land, built a clubhouse and a few garages out of the ever-present Kurashian limestone, put on corrugated metal roofs, hired a bartender. My father personally supervised every detail, including the laying and grading of the racetrack. He ordered ten Class A fiberglass go-carts from Hartley's in San Diego. They arrived about a month later, on flatbeds driven across the desert from Beirut. I remember that day well; it was a Saturday, and my father took me with him to oversee the unloading of the go-carts. They looked spectacular to me, silver muscular toys gleaming in the bright sunlight, wonderful oversize toys magically released into the real world, if indeed this was the real world, which I was still having difficulty accepting. My mother and Barbara Sweetser and some of the other women had prepared a picnic for the event, and now we all sat around on blankets in the shade of a solitary palm tree and ate chicken sandwiches and English biscuits, the men sipping beers, the women and children lemonade. Before us, the ten go-carts absorbed the warm sun. My father had even found a mechanic to keep all these things going, a retired middle-aged RAF mechanic named Rodney who had first been posted to Kurash with the British Colonial Office thirty years earlier, his job being to keep the British command vehicles in working condition. He had fallen in love with a Kurashian woman, the woman who did his laundry, resigned his commission, stayed on when most of the British military withdrew following the close of World War II. He had a garage in downtown Hamra that kept Kurash's meager supply of Mercedes-Benzs on the road. He had blunt, oily hands, a shy, deferential way of listening to my father, one knee bent, his chin propped on his knee, pale, pale blue eyes resting on the go-carts. "Don't worry, Mack," I remember him saying. "They'll work." And I also remember the deep, unspoken respect my father had for this man, this Rodney, a shared, taciturn understanding of something I could never quite get and I could certainly never share with my father. I probably resented Rodney. Poor Rodney.

The honey trap was laid. In place. Every weekend, races were held. The ranks of the club swelled, five additional go-carts were ordered. My father won more than his share of the races.

"Was that part of the plan, to lure the King to you, or were you just better than everyone else?

"I was better than everyone else. Most of the time. There was a German there, I can't remember his name, a teacher at the university, little delicate guy but shit could he drive. No fear. Guts of granite."

"So how long did you have to wait before the King showed up?"

"About two months."

"Tell me."

"Well, it was toward the end of one of our Saturdays. The sun was going down. Sunsets on the desert are something. Red, red sky, the cold of night seeping up out of the sand like a fresh sea breeze. Really nice. We'd pretty much finished racing for the day. Visions of martinis danced in our heads. I was helping Rodney with the carburetor on one of the go-carts when I heard someone shout something like, 'What the hell is that?' So I looked up, and there, approaching us, closing fast, was a whirling cloud of sand. We all kind of nervously waited."

The swirling sand, shot through with crepuscular red and black, rose higher as it reached a dune, over which now appeared maybe a dozen Jeeps and Land Rovers, all painted camouflage beige. As they got closer it could be seen that they were bristling with Arab Legionnaires, Bedouin warriors trained by the British, dark faces wrapped in red-and-white-checked *kaffiyehs,* rifles held free and ready, as well as members of the Royal Circassian Guards, golden-haired, blue-eyed Russian exiles banished to the desolation of Kurash by the Czar a century earlier, ragpickers who had lived like beggars in the ruins of the Roman amphitheater across from the Hotel Antioch until plucked up and awarded their holy duty by the King's grandfather Ali. The entire procession descended, sliding down the side of the dune, and pulled up to the racetrack. All attention turned to a short, squat, broad-shouldered young man in the first Jeep.

The King, my father realized.

He wore plain military *mufti* and a Legionnaire's *kaffiyeh.* His restless brown eyes gazed upon the startled foreigners. Serious, diminutive, he dismounted the Jeep, stepped briskly to the nearest go-cart, gave it an admiring glance. A mere twenty-two years old, he looked like the precocious schoolboy he had until recently been, except for the neat black mustache he wore on his upper lip. When he smiled, as he did now, his white teeth revealed themselves like laughter, and it was hard not to smile back. My father did.

"I would like to race a go-cart." His English, down to the quiet aristocratic drawl, was perfect.

Before Milton blundered forward and ruined everything, my father spoke up. "I'm sorry, Your Majesty, but only club members can race the go-carts."

Both Milton and Roy Sweetser shot my father horrified looks. He ignored them. The King slowly, curiously turned his attention to my father. This was the beginning, this moment—the King moving a few paces closer, peering in the gathering gloom to see my father clearly, my father holding his ground, willing the King even closer, then finally stepping forward himself and offering the King his hand and his own version of a bright smile. "But of course, Your Majesty, we would be honored if you joined our club. My name is Mack Hooper."

The King shook my father's hand, still curious, somewhat amused. "Are there formalities involved, joining your club?"

"Yearly membership dues, that's all."

"And how much would they be?"

"One hundred dollars."

"Three hundred *dinars.*"

"Correct, Your Majesty."

"I accept."

"Great." They shook hands again. "Welcome to the Hamra Go-Cart Club."

5

I'm holding in my hand a black-and-white Agfa photograph of my father and the King standing behind a row of those shiny toylike go-carts, Roy Sweetser and Milton Gourlie and Rodney and all the other racing enthusiasts of Hamra, circa 1958, arrayed behind them like a grinning chorus. My father wears rumpled khakis, a white broadcloth shirt, sleeves rolled. The King is dressed as he was the twilight he first appeared over the desert horizon: military *mufti*, red-and-white checked *kaffiyeh*. His brilliant smile accented by the dark, bobbing mustache, his feet firmly planted on the sand, he stands at patriarchal attention, commanding, dignity personified, yet sublimely unpretentious, matter-of-fact, and, of course, boyish. Twenty-two, and a monarch. My father is a full foot taller than the King, his wiry, angular New England body still youthful, trim, and energetic. He hovers beside the King like a friendly missionary from some long-gone empire, quaintly, touchingly concerned. Almost exactly forty years ago.

These days, seventy-four now, living by himself in his condo overlooking Boston Harbor, my father is just beginning to experience the fragility, the mortality, of his own corporeal self. He has a pinched nerve in his upper back that sometimes renders him incapable of picking up a glass. Last fall he had a gallstone removed. His arms, once knotted with muscle, now look like an old man's, loose flesh on bone. I worry about him slipping on the unforgiving ice of Massachusetts winters, tumbling, something cracking. He's upstairs now, asleep in his monkish bed. I sit downstairs in the kitchen, sorting through old photographs while the embers in the pot-bellied stove glow and quietly collapse.

I discovered these photographs in the bottom drawer of my father's desk, an old-fashioned secretary that he inherited from his father. As I study them, one by one, each snapshot sends me tumbling back into the past, the past I can only half remember, the past I witnessed without knowing, without understanding. For example: My mother and Barbara Sweetser exploring one of the *tells* scattered about the desert outside Hamra, gentle undulations in the ground that signify lost cities, buried homes and temples, from which they usually returned with some fugitive object, a miniature bottle, votive figure, broken blade that came to line a shelf in the living room and that today occupy a bookcase with glass doors in my mother's apartment on Massachusetts Avenue, near Harvard Yard. Here's another photograph: My father returning home from work, wearing a gray suit, papers under his arm, cigarette dangling from his lips, an Ivy League gangster if ever I saw one. I can see behind him the corner of the stone wall surrounding our stone house where I once fell and cut my forehead, requiring eight stitches. He has a relaxed, almost jaunty smile on his face, so perhaps it's the Monday after his first meeting with the King at the desert racetrack; perhaps he's feeling a sense of triumph, or at least accomplishment, secure now in the knowledge that the first phase of his gambit has paid off.

And think, for a moment, what that has entailed. Weeks spent in his closet of an office, pouring over files. Field reports from any officer, including Roy Sweetser and Milton Gourlie, that might shed any light on the King's personality, his desires and fears and habits, his labyrinthine family. None did. Analytical papers from Washington, including a history of the Hashemites and a psychological profile of the King. Memos filed by diplomats who had dealings with the King, debriefings of American and English businessmen who had spent time with the King, trying to sell him weapons, technology, oil exploration expertise. All of this to realize one simple fact, a fact that had been staring them all in the face ever since the young monarch had been whisked away from his boarding school in England and deposited in the royal palace on the outskirts of Hamra. He liked fast cars. He liked *driving* fast cars.

During the course of this preliminary investigation, my father had taken Milton's cue and introduced himself to Major Rashid. He had called first, then driven over to a modern office building, not far from the embassy, where Kurashian Intelligence was headquartered. Major Rashid's office was on the third floor, a modest room with white walls and tile floor that faced, through a plate-glass window, a jumble of flat white rooftops and, in the near distance, the *souk,* where, at that very moment, unbeknownst to my father, my mother was looking for rugs to cover the bare floors of our house. Major Rashid greeted my father with a wary smile and a firm handshake. He was dressed, Western-style, in suit and tie. He had strong, blunt hands and wore a Rolex on his left wrist. My father had studied his file; he knew that Major Rashid was Palestinian, from an old and honorable family, that he had attended the American University of Beirut, where he had studied engineering, that he had joined the Kurashian Army after college and had risen to the rank of major, carving out a niche for himself in military intelligence. He was transferred to Intelligence in 1950, and by 1955 was running the show. His attributes included a quick, practical mind and a deep allegiance to the royal family. The King's father had, rightly it seems, trusted him, and now, in turn, his son trusted him, in fact relied on him to help fend off the myriad demons, domestic and foreign, swirling dangerously around him.

Tea was served in little glass cups. Major Rashid and my father both lit cigarettes. On the wall hung a portrait of the King.

"So you've come to spy on us," Major Rashid began.

"Yup, and I was kind of hoping you could save me a lot of time and pain and just tell me everything I need to know."

Major Rashid's smile tightened. "For instance?"

"His Majesty's army chief of staff, General Ali Abu Anwar, is Egyptian by birth. What are his ties to Nasser?"

"Egyptian Intelligence has several times approached the General with personal messages from Nasser, which the General has chosen to ignore."

"What kind of messages?"

"Invitations to meet."

"The General feels no sympathy for Nasser's brand of Arab nationalism?"

"He feels a great deal of sympathy. We all do, including His Majesty."

My father considered that one for a moment. Major Rashid was putting him on notice. The Kurashians had no intention of being American puppets.

"His Majesty's second cousin, Taji Mazzawi, who serves as an informal economic adviser, has ties to the New Dawn, a Baathist organization based in Baghdad."

Major Rashid shrugged evasively. "He does?"

"Yes."

"And that worries you?"

"No. It worries my superiors in Washington."

"Why?"

"Because Baathists are Socialists and Socialists are not much better than Communists, in their view."

"And in your view?"

"Unless someone's being paid and supplied by the Soviets, I don't really care what they talk about at the dinner table."

Major Rashid glanced down at his hands, folded before him on the desk, then back up at my father. His smile had softened. "Do you like movies?"

"What kind of movies?"

"American movies."

"Depends which one, I guess."

"*The Spirit of St. Louis* is playing at the Majestic. Jimmy Stewart. Directed by Billy Wilder. Have you seen it?"

"No."

"Would you like to?"

"Sure."

Thus began a monthly ritual, my father and Major Rashid going to the movies. Afterward, they would have dinner together, usually at one of the many restaurants located on the fringes of the *souk,* small, cramped places specializing in lamb. Invariably, my father was the only Westerner there, and it was there, scooping up rice with warm pieces of bread, that he learned what little Arabic he knew. He determined fairly early on that Major Rashid would not broker an introduction to the King. In fact, my father felt it unwise even to mention the idea to him. Instead, he focused on his own relationship with this earnest, honest man set with the unenviable task of divining for the King who was friend and who was foe.

My father and Major Rashid were, certainly, friends. He came to dine at our house a few times. I remember him, perched on the living room couch, smoking his Lucky Strikes and listening with particular pleasure to my mother's Frank Sinatra records.

> *Fly me to the moon*
> *and let me play among the stars;*
> *Let me see what spring is like*
> *on Jupiter and Mars . . .*

He drove a Mercedes-Benz, one of several entrusted to Rodney's mechanical care. He had a wife, but she never came to dinner with him, and my father says he never met her. No children. They had tried and finally resigned themselves to failure on that score. What struck me most about him was his reserve, an air of loneliness that surrounded him even when he was sitting smiling on our couch and listening to Sinatra. He took to bringing me small presents, English chocolates and, once, a model airplane. He was, I realize now, a kind man who wished he had a son of his own.

More photographs: A Fourth of July party in our backyard, my father flipping hamburgers on a grill, Renee sitting with a drink in her hand; Christmas morning, presents under the tree; my mother sipping coffee in her bathrobe at the dining room table, a dark-haired forties movie star with a Vassar smile.

After that first meeting with Major Rashid, realizing he was on his own, my father returned to his office, the stubbled view, the stacks of files, and stayed there until he came up with the go-cart scheme.

"Once the King had joined the Hamra Go-Cart Club, then it was a simple matter of waiting for him to trust me. He bought his own go-cart, came every Saturday, happily raced around the course. He was good, if a little reckless. Sometimes he won, but never because I let him. I drove to win myself. That way, he respected me."

Thus my father spoke as we drove home from dinner tonight. We'd eaten in a Greek restaurant he likes on Cambridge Street, a hole-in-the-wall with Grandpa cooking in the kitchen, his son greeting everyone at the door, *his* sons serving food. We split a bottle of *retsina*, devoured the *moussaka*. I plied him with more questions about those first few months in Kurash, but he was tired, he didn't really feel much like talking, so I let him eat in peace. Back at his condo, we parked the car, a rusting ten-year-old Toyota. He gazed up at the clear spring night. "Can I ask *you* something?"

"Sure."

"How come you're suddenly so interested in my relationship with the King?" he asked, eyes on Orion.

"I've always been interested. I've always wondered what really happened."

"You'll never know what really happened. *I* don't know what really happened."

"You wouldn't tell me anyway, right?"

"Right."

"So you raced go-carts and waited. For what, exactly?"

"For the King to summon me."

I too gazed up at the stars. "How did you come to join the C.I.A. in the first place? You've never told me."

"I got a phone call."

"From whom?"

He hesitated. "A friend. Someone I'd gone to Yale with."

"A close friend?"

"No. I hadn't seen him since we graduated."

"He worked for the C.I.A.?"

"Yes, though I didn't know that when he called. This was in 1949. The C.I.A. didn't get its charter until 1947. It was all still pretty new."

"What did he say?"

"He asked me out for lunch. We gossiped about Yale friends and then he told me about the C.I.A., what it was doing, and asked me if I'd like to join. I said yes."

"Just like that?"

"Just like that."

"What did Mom say?"

"She was excited. We were both excited. We got a little drunk that night. Why not? It was the beginning of a great adventure. That's what we thought at the time."

"And now?" I asked. "Do you still think that? Was it a great adventure?"

He contemplated middle distance, somebody parking halfway down the street. "Yeah, it was. I was lucky. I got to do something with my life. I hated Wall Street. I hated investment counseling. That phone call saved my life."

And with that, he entered his condo and went straight to bed, leaving me alone in the kitchen with these photographs.

More picnics in the desert.

Driving to Jerusalem with the Sweetsers.

My mother and father holding hands in front of our house in Hamra, grinning into the camera.

It was in Kurash that I decided my father was not normal.

With a child's sixth sense I knew he was up to something strange and different and vaguely dangerous. The phone would often ring in the middle of the night. My father would answer, mutter a few terse words, then dress and disappear into the darkness outside. Sometimes he would be gone for days. One time he didn't come back for three weeks. There was a large, complicated radio in his study that for some reason I decided was a clue, an icon of clandestine communication. He was dismissive of the regular diplomatic staff at the embassy, and they were suspicious of him. When I asked him what he did at work, he told me he pushed paper clips around. He told me he collected pencils. He told me he fiddled his thumbs. Finally, as he tucked me in one night, I confronted him. I don't remember the words exactly, but I said I thought he was doing something he wasn't telling me about and that it scared me, which it did. He sat down on the side of my bed and told me not to worry, that he was perfectly safe, that I was imagining things, and that he was exactly who he claimed to be. A midlevel diplomat with an interest in automobiles. "Good night, son." He kissed me on the cheek, which he rarely did, and made me feel even more uneasy. It was a gesture to cover a lie. Later in life, when I was about thirteen, he finally confessed and told me the truth, or his version of it. "I'm an intelligence officer. I collect information which makes it easier for the President to do his job well. But this is a secret, and now you must keep it, too." I blushed with serious pleasure. I felt I'd been initiated into the important world where the Real Decisions were made, unknown to the public at large, and I clung to that secrecy as though to a holy vow. Once, when another boy in school, whose father was a mere Aramco executive, asked me what my father did, I simply said, "Stuff." He said, "Like what, beat off all day?" Since I couldn't tell him what I took to be the truth—that my father was fighting a deadly and secret war so that people like his limp-dick dad could wallow around the golf course at some happy horseshit country club—since I couldn't tell him that, I broke the kid's nose. I was constrained by my own pledge of secrecy. I could tell no one what my father did. Of course, in reality, I had no idea what my father did. I was protecting a mystery. In college, I loosened up a little, no doubt because I discovered that "My father is a spy" was a great opening line with girls. Two out of three times it led right to the sack.

"So were you trained at Camp Perry?" I ask him the next morning as we eat breakfast—Grape-Nuts and orange juice. Outside the window, a light drizzle, pearled gray, obscures the harbor.

"Yes. Way out in the Virginia countryside."

"What did you do?"

"Our instructors were mostly British, old school guys from MI6. We learned about codes, hand-to-hand combat, weaponry. Leave a pot of geraniums in the window and it means . . . whatever. How to approach an asset, how to get him to cooperate. Blackmail, money, ideology. You'd be amazed how many people did it for fun, kicks. How to make contact. How to pass a message. How to get rid of a tail. How to follow someone, alone or with a team. How to plant bugs. How to tap telephones. One time we were dropped off in the middle of Richmond, two teams, one whose assignment was to pass a message, the other whose assignment it was to catch them doing it."

"Like playing Spy."

"Right. Only we all ended up getting arrested by the Richmond police for 'suspicious loitering.' We spent the night in jail." My father chuckles.

The rain has stopped outside, bits of sunlight poke through the clouds.

After Camp Perry, my father was assigned to Washington, K Building, specifically, part of the C.I.A.'s original headquarters, several prefabricated Quonset huts on the Mall lining the reflecting pool. Eventually he was sent over to Abu Dhabi, then Kuwait, where we had sizable oil interests, and where he distinguished himself by getting very close to the ruling family. Without their quite realizing it, they had found themselves turning to my father more and more for advice, until eventually he was the first person they sought out in times of trouble or even worry. When several tribes from the interior threatened to cut pipelines unless they were allowed to share in the sudden black wealth, it was my father who persuaded the Kuwaiti government to go along with the demand. When, within Kuwait City, a small Communist Party, aided ineptly by Moscow, tried to organize Palestinian workers, it was my father who alerted the authorities. He had spent four years in Kuwait. He knew it was time to go when, his last Christmas there, he had supervised a relief flight to the hungry of Aswad. The plane had dropped dozens of turkeys with little messages tied to their gristly feet: "A gift from the people of the United States." The next day, he requested a transfer.

Then he went to Kurash.

Set his trap, and waited.

While he waited, he spent time with me. Sort of. He helped me build the model airplane that Major Rashid had given me, a B-17 Flying Fortress with lots of neat little clear plastic gun turrets that swiveled. We did the work at a card table he set up in the living room. My mother sat in an armchair reading *A Passage to India,* sometimes aloud, sometimes putting the book down to chat with us while we worked. I'm not sure I've ever been happier, and I sometimes suspect it is as much to recapture that brief, illusory happiness as it is to find the truth that I now rummage around in the drawers of my father's past. He had brought his gooseneck desk lamp in from his study and put it on the card table. The Flying Fortress came together in a warm pool of light. Looking back at us all these years later, a father and his boy working on a model airplane at a card table, I can't imagine that the man who gently showed me how not to smear glue on the plastic windows of the Flying Fortress is in fact a bad man.

During that same period he took me to Oristibach's on Al Kifah Street in downtown Hamra, a three-story colonial building, British-built, that was a proper department store. We rode the elevator up to the top floor and he led me into a big room full of toys, back to a glass counter containing hundreds of brightly colored lead British soldiers, made by Britains, and all the military Dinky Toys, solid dark green metal trucks and Jeeps and camouflaged Hawker Hunter jets and Centurion tanks with working rubber treads. I think I swooned, discovered ecstasy, or the rapturous joys of solitude, as I stood there staring through the glass at the green and red uniforms of the marching Highland Guards and the tawny camels and fluttering lances of the Egyptian Camel Corps, rows upon rows of serious soldiers with dark black eyes and healthy pink cheeks, their rifles held smartly on their shoulders, their boots polished to a glassy shine. And the Dinky Toys, so solid, so sturdy, ready to roll across my bedcovers in campaigns worthy of Montgomery and Rommel, half-tracks, troop carriers, five-ton trucks, ten-ton trucks, armored cars, a flatbed tank carrier, each in its own yellow box—I gripped the edge of the glass counter in my excitement, glanced up to see my father gazing thoughtfully down at the toys, a small smile on his face, my own unbridled happiness reflected there, calmer, almost studious. He bought me my first Dinky Toy that day, a scout car, which, in a state of mute, blissful stupefaction, I carried home in the Opel and up to my room. I had a yellow, portable Phillips record player that my mother had bought me in Rome, and on this record player revolved, repeatedly, the few 45s I had: Pat Boone's "Catch a Falling Star," The Kingston Trio's "Tom Dooley," The Platters' "The Great Pretender." I stacked them on the spindle, sat down on the bed with my new scout car. I was making my peace with this odd, palpitating place, this land that seemed to exist only in my mind, or as part of my mind, a dream I could not simply dismiss, or walk away from, since I took it with me wherever I went: Kurash.

Imagine my surprise when my mother and father took me with them out into the desert to watch Kurashian military maneu-

vers, an annual event, a tradition established by the King's grandfather, and into view came rolling full-size versions of those same
tanks and Jeeps and armored cars, while overhead three Hawker
Hunters streaked through the sky. The entire diplomatic community was there, most of the ranking Kurashian bureaucracy, and,
of course, the King. My father pointed him out across maybe a
hundred yards of sand. He seemed too small to be a king, fragile
despite his stocky body. He stood under a tentlike pavilion, surrounded by Army officers, occasionally lifting binoculars to
watch more closely the nearby maneuvers. At one point, my
mother turned to my father and whispered, "Don't look, but he's
watching you." And she was right, he realized, glancing casually
in the King's direction. The King had his binoculars trained on
my father. It was just a moment, then he turned his attention
back to the tanks and shrieking jets, but it was enough to make
my father feel a flutter in his gut, and then immediate irritation,
as if he'd done something untoward. It was almost sexual, this
feeling, is my guess, and so naturally enough it unnerved him.
But the truth is, of course, that my father was indeed engaged in a
courtship, a flirtation, and he was therefore forced to play by a
flirtation's attendant rules.

Smile demurely.

And wait.

6

I⊂ had by now become clear to my father that Roy Sweetser was close to useless as an intelligence officer. After weeks of shuffling through Roy's field reports and chasing down each of his assets, my father knew no more about Kurash than when he'd arrived. He felt sorry for Roy and so avoided making this failure a point. Milton Gourlie, on the other hand, was pretty good. One of the original O.S.S. guys, with a Medal of Honor in his sock drawer, given to him by President Truman for his work assisting the Greek underground on Crete during World War II, Milton understood that the task before them was to gather accurate information from a swamp of rumor and misinformation, and he also understood that the best way to do this was by making the right friends. Here, however, his personality betrayed him. Milton was not good at making friends. He had tried, unsuccessfully, to recruit several interesting prospects, only to have them shy away from his straightforward Ohio charmlessness. He would walk right up to them, shoulders hunched in a battle-ready crouch, and hit them broadside with his pitch, much like the college linebacker he used to be slamming a running back as he came through the line. He lacked any feeling for the Semitic sensibility, the elaborate yet modest dance of manners born of the desert. In fact, Milton hated the desert, saw nothing in it but mind-numbing heat and cultural deprivation. "You can't live in a tent and create *The Magic Flute*," he was fond of saying. To which my father wanted to reply, "You can't create *The Magic Flute* and live in a tent." But he never did say that. He was too tactful.

Renee, he discovered, had a drinking problem. It was her only relief from her unremitting seriousness. Preternaturally single, everyone's favorite ugly sister, she lived for her work. She was the first to arrive and the last to leave. She was protective of Milton, of Roy Sweetser, of my father, even of Johnny Allen. She kept the .45 loaded in her desk drawer, daring anyone to threaten any of her men. She wore sensible skirts and blouses, smoked an endless succession of Kents, made sure the shredder devoured all loose scraps of paper floating around the office, made sure the files were neatly maintained and cross-referenced, made sure that all appointments were duly noted in her datebook and that each of them was met, on time. Her apartment, which my father saw but once during those years, spoke volumes of her isolation. Sparse Danish furniture, shelves of Agatha Christie mysteries, and a kitchen cabinet well stocked with vodka. She had a few friends, other single women who worked in the embassy, mostly as secretaries. They spent weekends together at the American Club, tanning themselves by the pool, and once a week they got together and played bridge. Renee drank at night, alone in her apartment, listening to the BBC World News and the American Armed Forces station on her glowing Grundig radio, inhaling Kents and vodka until she was numb enough to sleep. Hangovers greeted her every morning, painful, familiar as an old friend. She drank instant Nescafé, drove to the embassy in her battered Renault. It wasn't until she was inside the office, behind her desk, that she felt human.

Johnny Allen shared a house with the two Marine Guards, Sal and his buddy Max Struther. I can't imagine what they did at night, three American men in their early twenties. Except for a few British programs like *Robin Hood* broadcast from Baghdad, there was no TV in those days, and the movies in town stayed around for what seemed like months. Once, on one of their regular expeditions, this time to see *The Last Hurrah* with Spencer Tracy, my father and Major Rashid bumped into Johnny, Sal, and

Max in the lobby of the Majestic. An awkward overlapping of identities ensued, an encounter so out of the normal context that they weren't sure how to speak to one another, what to say, what image of self to assume. They milled inconclusively, all smiles and nods, then took seats on opposite sides of the theater, where, released from perplexing self-consciousness, they were each able to enjoy the movie, though my father found himself drifting, wondering when he would hear from the King, worrying, for the first time, that his plan might not succeed.

Then it happened. My father was summoned.

"When, exactly?" I asked. "How?"

We were walking up the steps to the Isabella Stewart Gardner Museum.

"On a Saturday," he said. "At the racetrack in the desert, the Hamra Go-Cart Club."

The King arrived in a Land Rover with his usual entourage, waved greetings to the assembled foreigners, approached my father with a bounce in his gait, and shook his hand. In retrospect, my father feels he should have appreciated the mischievous glint in the King's eye. He passed it off, at the time, to a good mood, figuring monarchs were as entitled to one as anyone else.

"What do you say, Mack, to a small bet?" the King inquired offhandedly, making his move.

"I asked him what kind of a bet, and he said, 'Well, how about that I beat you in today's first race?' 'And if you lose?' I asked. 'I'll pay you one hundred dollars,' he said. Of course, one hundred dollars was the cost of his admission to the Go-Cart Club, which, it suddenly occurred to me, he hadn't yet paid."

We paused at the front door of the museum, stepping aside as some fellow art lovers exited the museum.

"And if you lost?" I asked.

My father gazed benignly around at the mottled Boston morning, barren oak shadows dancing a merry dance in a breeze off the Charles, so far away from that scrap of sand in Kurash forty years ago. He shook his head. He was laughing, I realized, a full-throated chuckle. "If I lost, I had to eat sheep's eyes."

"Sheep's eyes? You're kidding."

"Bedouins consider sheep's eyes to be a delicacy. He was inviting me to dinner. I couldn't have refused, even if I'd wanted to. The greatest insult you can offer a Bedouin is to refuse his hospitality. And the King knew it, knew I knew it. The bet was just a challenge, the first time he'd let me know he wanted to be friends."

"So what did you do?"

"I accepted."

Word of the bet quickly spread, and by the time everyone was in his go-cart, engines revving, the first race about to begin, bystanders had started making bets on the bet, the odds leaning slightly in my father's favor. Rodney, in his customary role, lowered the green flag, wheels spun wildly in the sand before catching a grip and catapulting the go-carts forward. My father took the inside lane and held it, the King right beside him. Six times they circled the track, each holding his position. The others fell behind.

My father caught a glimpse of the King grinning at him as they rounded a turn into the seventh and final lap. My father pressed his gas pedal full to the floor and steered steadily toward Rodney and the waiting finish flag. The King relentlessly kept pace. "The strange thing is, I really wanted to win, I wanted to beat him. I'm very competitive, as you know. But I didn't want to run the risk of wounding his vanity, not with a bet at stake, not with everyone watching." Twenty yards from Rodney, my father reluctantly took his foot off the pedal, and in that brief instant the King surged ahead, Rodney waving him the winner. My father crossed the line a few seconds later. The King was already bounding out of his go-cart. My father rolled to a stop.

"Tonight, at Hamzah Palace," the King said to him before he could even switch off his engine. "Seven o'clock. I'll be waiting for you."

He gave my father a little salute and a huge smile, turned on his heel, and returned to the Land Rover in which he'd arrived.

Milton anxiously approached my father.

"What did he say?"

"He's expecting me at seven."

Milton shot my father an admiring look tinged with envy. "Congratulations."

They both turned to watch the Land Rover disappear back over the desert, a diminishing trail of dust.

That night I watched my father from my window as he left the house and got into the Opel, waving to the Kurashian sentry who stood in a small guardhouse outside our garden wall. I watched him drive away, the Opel getting smaller and smaller, and when I returned to my bed, which had become the Battle of Alamein, fought with my Dinky Toys, my initial scout car plus two tanks, a howitzer, and a Jeep, I felt a hollow place opening up inside me, unnameable anxiety, and I was afraid. Eid was cooking dinner downstairs in the kitchen; I could smell his quixotic version of Quiche Lorraine. Ahmed had smoked his last cigarette at the kitchen table, sipped his last glass of tea, walked to the bus stop, and now rode through the Kurashian night toward home, a tired brown face in the brightly lighted window.

Allen Dulles, five thousand miles and eight time zones away, was on the secure line with his brother. Through his window, he could see tourists on the Mall. He was telling John Foster the news, that one of his officers, by the name of Mack Hooper, had been invited to dinner by the King, and then he amused him with the story of the Hamra Go-Cart Club. John Foster chortled. Though not as adventurous as his younger brother, he knew a good tale when he heard it. As Allen hung up, his deputy director of plans, Frank Wisner, knocked and entered. Wisner looked like an untrustworthy professor, his suit rumpled and pitted with cigarette burns, his glasses held together with a paper clip, his long nervous fingers stained with tobacco. Wisner had just received a cable from their station chief in Saigon. There'd been an assassination, one of the rogue feudal lords shot down as he left his jungle cathedral. Dulles and Wisner rattled the change in their pockets and gazed together upon the tourists on the Mall, considering their various options, forgetting about Kurash, forgetting about the King, forgetting about my father.

It took my father less than twenty minutes to reach Hamzah Palace. The guards at the gate were expecting him, let him in, and showed him where to park. He was then escorted into a large waiting room, and from there a servant led him down a long hallway and into a living room, straight-back chairs arranged around a copper coffee table. In the chairs my father was surprised to see, beside the King, Major Rashid and two other men he did not recognize, both Arabs, both watching him curiously as the King rose to greet him.

"Welcome to my humble home, Mack. I believe you already know Major Rashid." Rashid nodded, revealing nothing. "This is my cousin, General Ali Abu Anwar, a good friend and adviser and my Army chief of staff." The taller of the two men stood and shook my father's hand. He was wearing a desert costume, a simple clean white robe. He said nothing, and my father sensed immediately a certain degree of hostility. "And this is Kumait al-Farid, professor of religion at the university." Kumait's elegant hand, a gold signet ring on the small finger, reached out for my father. He had a surprisingly firm handshake and a friendly, open smile. "Pleased to meet you," he said, settling back in the chair, faintly amused. My father felt studied, objectified. He fingered his tie, thought of my mother for reassurance. *For good luck.*

"My Prime Minister, Sherif al-Hassan, unfortunately cannot be here tonight." The King gestured to an empty chair. "Sit, Mack, please."

My father sat. More servants appeared. He was offered a Coke. He accepted, craving bourbon.

"Mack is a wonderful race car driver," the King offered. "Usually he beats me."

"He let you win, Your Majesty," said General Anwar.

Kumait turned to my father. "Why did you do that?"

Before my father could think of a response, Anwar spoke up. "Because he wanted to gain entrance into His Majesty's confidence. He didn't want to offend him."

"Is that true, Mack?" Kumait asked.

"Yes," my father said, surprising Anwar and making Major Rashid smile to himself.

Kumait stared up at the ceiling, studying my father from the corner of his eye. "He would have asked you to visit anyway. I don't know why, but His Majesty likes you."

The King abruptly stood. "Enough. It's time for dinner."

The next thing my father knew he was back in the circular driveway outside the palace. A large silver Mercedes 300 SEL purred quietly to a stop; a uniformed driver jumped out and opened the back door. The King silently gestured for General Anwar to enter first, then Major Rashid, then Kumait. He closed the door on Kumait, muttered something in Arabic to the driver, who climbed back in behind the wheel. The electric window rolled down, Anwar leaning across Kumait to worriedly address the King, also in Arabic. They had a brief exchange, and my father could see a sudden blush of irritation spread across the King's face. He waved the driver on, and the Mercedes pulled away and drove down the driveway to the gate, vanishing in a blur of red taillights.

The King turned to my father. "I'd like to show you something."

He headed off in the opposite direction. My father tagged along, cool as could be, at least on the outside, waiting for the true nature of this adventure to reveal itself. He wondered if he was being tested, and what it would take to pass muster. He found it hard to believe that they were all simply going to drive to a restaurant in downtown Hamra for dinner. The King rarely ate out, he knew, and never in public, except for state occasions. It was considered unseemly.

They walked along in silence, side by side, their shoes crunching on the gravel. The lights of the palace shone through date palms, casting long, spindly shadows. The air was light tonight, coming off the desert. The King gazed straight ahead, jaw muscles working.

"I apologize," he eventually said.

Sometimes he spoke so softly my father had to lean down, closer, to hear him.

"General Anwar had no cause to make you feel uncomfortable like that. You're a guest in my house."

The King stopped, put his hand on my father's arm, gazed at him with a touching anxiety, as if his only concern were my father's delicate feelings. "Do you accept? My apology?"

"Of course, Your Majesty."

Happiness returned to the King's face, and they continued their walk.

"I probably would have done the same thing, or something like it, if I were them," my father went on. "They want to protect you, and they don't trust me."

"I don't need their constant protection."

They approached a rectangular, single-story building with a row of garage doors, one of which the King slid open, reaching inside and snapping on an overhead light to reveal a gleaming black Corvette.

"Do you like it?" Again, that touch of anxiety, the desire to please.

"Very much," my father said. "It's beautiful."

"You drive." The King tossed him the keys.

They lowered themselves into the red bucket seats, my father turned the ignition. The V8 churned, a mighty roar, echoing in the garage.

"Straight out the front gate, then take a right," the King said.

My father dutifully steered the Corvette away from the palace and onto Al Qasr Avenue.

"Faster," the King said. "Take her for a run."

My father punched the gas and felt the car surge forward, pressing him back against the seat.

"Faster," the King urged eagerly.

The speedometer climbed up to eighty. My father, though usually confident of his driving skills, could not shake the notion that he had beside him a king, that one false move could leave this monarch smeared across the desert highway like so much road-kill. For that's where they were headed, out into the desert. The two-lane road they were on led, eventually, to the Iraqi border, and from there to Baghdad, almost six hundred miles away. He wanted to ask where they were going, but suspected that the King wanted to surprise him, and that it would be impolitic to question him. So he kept the Corvette running at eighty and followed his headlights into the desert. The King lit a cigarette.

"Did you really let me win?"

My father considered. "Yes."

"And the other races I won, all these weeks. Did you let me win those, too?"

"No. Don't forget, I beat you plenty, Your Majesty."

"Kumait's right. I would have invited you over anyway. I want a rematch. Pull no punches next time."

My father nodded.

Pretty soon they saw taillights up ahead. As they got closer my father realized it was the silver Mercedes. The King grinned.

"Pass them."

My father floored the gas pedal, pulled out, and sped past the Mercedes, catching a quick glimpse of Anwar's angry face at the back window. The King waved, naughty boy, practically giggling, gleeful. Christ, he really is just a kid, my father thought, slowing down and cruising through the night. He decided the best way to play this was straight.

"Your Majesty, I'm sorry for letting you win. I was afraid to scare you off, I guess."

"Apology accepted," the King said, pleased.

"It won't happen again."

"I believe you."

"I want you to trust me."

"Oh, I do, I do."

And he did. This boy, in an instant, for some reason, chose to trust my father, knowing full well that my father's interests were not his own, that in fact my father was the servant of a hugely powerful state that could squash him like a scorpion, at will. The King was far from stupid. He had learned, from his father, who had never been to school at all, let alone a posh English boarding school, that the only thing he could completely count on was his tribe, his clan, his family, the Hashemites, several thousand strong among a population of two million, these desert people my father guessed they were now driving to see. So why did he trust him? My own theory is that the King needed my father, without knowing it until they shook hands that first time at the Hamra Go-Cart Club. He had no father anymore; he had no brothers. He needed to rest his head for a moment, he needed to believe, in the shade of someone else's strength, that he could let sleep his vigilance.

Daddy.

And at that moment, my father, seeing the King looking like a little boy with a fake mustache dressed up in a soldier's uniform, vowed secretly to take care of him. This really is a kind of love story.

My father began his pitch, there in the Corvette, a swift American mirage streaking across the desert.

"My country wants to be a friend to your country. We want your reign to be a success. We think we can help you. My job, my assignment, is simply to tell you that, face to face, man to man. If you're not interested, I'll leave you alone."

"Help me how, exactly?"

"Well, for starters, with information. As I'm sure you know, I work for the Central Intelligence Agency. We would like to share with you our knowledge of Soviet intentions, Israeli intentions, Nasser's intentions, Iraq's intentions, Syria's intentions—"

"But my good friends the British see to all my intelligence needs," the King interrupted.

"Really?"

"Yes, of course."

"Then why aren't they here tonight?"

The Corvette hummed quietly along.

"Are you interested?" my father asked.

"I might be."

"I don't think it would be appropriate to get into much more detail without your advisers present."

"I agree."

Forty years later, my father turned away from a pilfered Florentine fresco in the Isabella Stewart Gardner Museum, in Boston, and shrugged, shook his head, clearing it of something uncomfortable, some burden that had crept up on him as he told me his story. "Let's eat. I'm hungry."

He turned and walked away. I followed him down to the cage, asking him what he and the King had talked about as they finished their drive into the Syrian desert. Baseball, he told me. The King had asked my father to explain the various positions on the field, the rules that governed play, and then had listened carefully as my father did his best to tell him, trying hard to make clear the insouciant beauty of the game, the bliss of sitting in the green bleachers on a Saturday night, hot dog and beer in hand, while out on the vibratingly brilliant green diamond small acts of skill and daring unfolded like a ritual dance. When he was done, the King said nothing for a while, gazing straight ahead through the windshield of the Corvette. Finally, quietly, he spoke. "We have no such games. I learned to play cricket when I was in school in England. They are related, I think, baseball and cricket."

My father wondered how difficult it had been for the King to leave his beloved father, his beloved grandfather Ali not yet dead, his beloved desert, and wake up on a cold damp foggy English morning surrounded by stone and moss, cruel Anglo-Saxon children with their haughty, abstract games, teachers who carried in their heads the entire history of that race, the long, intricate, bloodthirsty saga of a people whose destiny it was to arrive at the far shores of the world and plant their flag in the Kurashian sand. A boy, not a king, alone among the English, nibbling soggy high tea biscuits at his end of the long refectory table beneath the dining hall's high Gothic arches and windows. It must have been terrifying to return home and assume the crown at the age of eighteen, but it must also have been a relief. The King rolled down the Corvette window and inhaled the cool desert breeze rushing into the car.

"Take a left, up ahead."

My father squinted at the darkness beyond his headlights, could see nothing.

"There." The King pointed.

My father turned, on faith, and felt the Corvette bumping along a rough beaten roadway. They continued like this for about ten minutes, then came over a sudden rise and dipped down into a sandy valley toward shimmering lights. A cluster of tents, he saw as they got closer, black tents pitched under the clear dark sky.

"Stop here," the King said.

Shadows approached them, Bedouin men in long robes and *kaffiyehs*, daggers strapped to their belts, rifles in their hands. They flung themselves at the King's feet when they recognized him, kissing his hand and murmuring greetings. My father stood to one side, feeling a little out of place, embarrassed, while more desert fighters hurried to the King, their love and excitement reflected in the unbridled joy with which they welcomed him, their voices making a kind of singing sound. Across the desert behind my father came the silver Mercedes, disgorging Major Rashid, General Anwar, and Kumait. The King, enjoying himself, said something teasing in Arabic. My father saw the suspicion in their eyes as they silently glanced at him before following the King to the largest of the tents, a "house of hair" made from goatskins. They entered through an open flap. My father glimpsed carpets on the ground, thick, colorful pillows scattered about, brilliantly decorated camel saddles, oil lamps casting a baroque filigree of shadows. The King sat, the others followed suit, reclining against the camel saddles, in a circle, no man present worth more than any other man, everyone equal here on the carpet in the tent beneath the desert stars. My father was made to feel comfortable, the Bedouin manners considerate, yet he also felt himself being scrutinized. Servants instantly appeared, carrying food, platters of flat, round, unleavened bread and rice and roasted lamb that they set down in the middle of the circle. The King indicated that my father should start.

"Go ahead, Mack," he said.

My father realized that everyone else was waiting for him to begin. He scooped up a handful of rice and lamb, ate. To his relief, it was delicious, perfectly tender, tasting of the fire it had been cooked over, fire and herbs—thyme, sage, rosemary. As all present watched him, my father slowly finished chewing, turned to the King. "In all honesty, Your Majesty, that is the best lamb I have ever tasted."

The King smiled, nodded happily. Major Rashid gave my father an almost imperceptible wink of congratulations. The King translated, more contented smiles followed, and then everyone else started eating, digging at the rice and lamb with their fingers, drinking cups of sour goat's milk, reverting to Arabic, a pleasant drone soon filling the tent, stories told, jokes exchanged, business conducted. There sat my father, cross-legged on the carpeted ground, both legs falling asleep, a dull numbness turning to prickly pain. Servants kept bringing in more platters of food, and my father found himself wondering when the sheep's eyes would be presented, and how in hell he was going to get them down without gagging. Forty miles away, in Hamra, Johnny Allen, alone in the cable vault, was receiving and deciphering a message from headquarters, more specifically, from Division Chief Hodd Freeman, incidentally the old friend from Yale who had called my father up one day when he was working on Wall Street and taken him out to lunch and asked him to join the nascent C.I.A. The cable contained the substance of a meeting held that afternoon in Allen Dulles's office. At the meeting, beside Dulles and Freeman, was Deputy Director of Plans Frank Wisner. They were noodling around a small problem, namely, how to stem what seemed a rising tide of pan-Arab enthusiasm that threatened to swamp American foreign policy in the area. They studied a chart on the wall that traced this threat, starting with the establishment of the Baath Socialist Party in 1954, in Damascus, and spreading quickly to Egypt, where, in 1952, Nasser had come to power, himself a Socialist, if not overtly a Baathist. Little difference, in their minds. In 1956, he nationalized the Suez Canal, the single boldest attack on Britain and France's colonial hegemony the region had ever known. More recently, Camille Chamoun's government in Lebanon had asked for America's help in putting down a pan-Arabic so-called Free Officers' revolt, and Eisenhower had responded with U.S. Marines, who within weeks were landing on the beaches of Beirut. Soldiers and sunbathers had flirted on the white sands in front of the King George Hotel while waterskiers zipped frothily among the landing craft. What Dulles and Wisner and Freeman discerned was a disturbing trend: Arabs wanting to seize control of their national destinies, throw out the Europeans and Americans, combine forces to create a deeply harmonious and highly militaristic union, and then drive Israel into the sea. What worried Dulles and Wisner and Freeman is that they could easily imagine this trend succeeding. What to do? They hammered out a proposal, had it cabled to all Middle East station chiefs.

My mother was downstairs, absorbed in E. M. Forster. I was under the covers, moving military hardware across my sheet in the glare of a flashlight. Renee was on her second vodka of the night. Roy and Barbara Sweetser were at a cocktail party in the Russian embassy, and Roy, in one of his fitful attempts to be professional, had wangled himself a seat next to Vitaly Kedrov, a midlevel K.G.B. officer. Vitaly was drunk. He missed his wife and three-year-old boy. K.G.B. officers were rarely allowed to bring their families with them when posted overseas, the logic being that this would deter them from defecting. It worked, for the most part. But it also left them lonely and vulnerable in other ways. Six months earlier, Roy had had one of his contacts, a Kurashian in the Ministry of Culture, a Paris-educated and quite dashing young bachelor, invite Vitaly out to a dinner party and then take him to a fabricated fleshpot, a C.I.A. safe house on Musa Street in which waited two luscious French girls borrowed from the Beirut station. While the Kurashian bachelor enjoyed the gifts of one of the girls in one of the bedrooms, Vitaly went at it with the other girl in a second bedroom, his performance captured on film, of course. Soon Vitaly was regularly visiting the safe house, the unwitting but not unwilling star of his very own porno movies.

"Vitaly, have you enjoyed the ladies on Musa Street?" Roy asked casually.

"Very much," Vitaly replied, way ahead of Renee now, easily into his third vodka.

This was followed by a painfully slow realization, an inebriated double take: "How did you . . . ?"

He couldn't bring himself to finish his question.

"I was thinking today, it would be terrible if anyone found out about your dalliances in our safe house." Roy let his eyes wander across the room to Sergei Prokov, head of the local K.G.B. office and Vitaly's boss. "I mean, someone might get the wrong impression."

Vitaly fixed Roy with a wet, soulful gaze. "What kind of wrong impression?"

"Well, you know, that you were doing something in return."

Vitaly fought a fluttering panic, dread turning his eyes even wetter. Roy thought he was going to cry.

"My boss, he's putting pressure on me, Vitaly," Roy continued, glancing over at Milton now, who was deep in conversation with the Syrian Ambassador. "He feels strongly that it's only fair that we receive some gesture of appreciation for our help in the procurement of these tasty young ladies."

"Please, no," Vitaly whimpered.

"I'll keep trying to hold him off." Roy gave Vitaly a reassuring pat on the arm. "Don't worry."

This is how the story gets told; this is how the mystery gets unraveled. Bit by bit. Seemingly unrelated parts placed next to each other until, *voilà*, we get a picture.

Back in the "house of hair" my father's legs had pretty much atrophied. He'd forgotten all about the sheep's eyes. His main concern now was what would happen when he tried to stand.

"Mack, tell us, what do you think of our country so far?"

It was the King who spoke.

The tent grew quiet.

My father chose his words carefully. "I'm very glad I'm here, Your Majesty."

"Do you find us backward?" the King asked. "Compared to your country?"

"We have more cars and highways and factories, we have huge cities made of concrete, we've got some of the best hospitals in the world, we have the largest home-owning middle class in history, we have great universities where wise men teach our youth. But we don't have men of the same family sitting under the stars in a tent, we don't have warriors on camels crossing the desert exactly as their fathers and their fathers' fathers did before them, we have forgotten how to live alone and face our own demons, our own souls, we lose the language in which we sing every generation, we throw away more than we save, more often than not our code of honor does not live in our hearts but is handed to us from above.

I'm not at all certain which of us is more backward than the other."

He was bullshitting, of course, but he also meant it, and what he said carried a certain weight. The men in the tent judged it for a moment in silence.

"In my opinion, no offense to you or your government, the United States has three simple goals in the Arab world," General Anwar said. "One, to protect the oil fields in Iraq, Saudi Arabia, Kuwait, and the Emirate States. Two, to create markets for its products, Chevrolets and Coca-Cola. Three, to lend arms and material support to the Zionists in Israel. None of these goals benefits us. I am trying hard to understand why we should be friends."

My father decided to meet him head-on. "General, we should be friends because you cannot survive without a friend among the major powers, and you would be making a terrible mistake if you thought anyone else, any other major power, would be a better friend."

"We have Britain; that's more than enough."

"Britain is no longer a major power. Without our support, Britain would collapse. Without our support, you will collapse. We would like to replace our British cousins and take care of you. The British, by the way, are in agreement."

"You want to conquer us; you want to destroy our culture."

"No, we don't. Remember, we never asked to rule the world; we never asked to be the world's policeman. We were attacked, our allies were attacked, we honored our commitments and our national duty, we stopped Hitler, we stopped Emperor Hirohito, and now here I am, sitting with you. I thought I was going to be a lawyer in Ashfield, Massachusetts. That's a very small town with very simple legal concerns."

The King was listening carefully. "Then what do you want?"

"We want to stop the Soviets and the Chinese from turning the world into a labor camp."

The King looked around the tent at his silent friends, his advisers, then back to my father. "We appreciate your honesty, Mack. Thank you."

"I did have a question, Your Majesty."

"Yes, of course, go ahead."

"Am I really going to have to eat sheep's eyes?"

This cracked the King up. He let fly with a deep belly laugh.

"You already have," the King gasped, wiping happy tears from his eyes. "You already have."

7

My father and the King parked the Corvette on the gravel driveway in front of Hamzah Palace, the sky still clear, full of spanking new stars. They stood for a moment, side by side, and contemplated the heavens. It was by now two in the morning. Hamra slept below them, the barren hills in shadow. Sentries stirred in their guardhouses, patrolled the perimeter of the palace smoking cigarettes, cradling machine guns.

"When I was a boy, my father used to conduct all his business in a tent. In the desert, usually, where he felt most at home, but also here in Hamra. He would have the tent pitched right over there." The King nodded toward a shaded corner of the huge garden, pine trees and palms. "He didn't like the palace, except as a showpiece. He even slept out here."

So this boy-king, armed only with the desert knowledge his father had taught him in a tent, must now rule a nation of telephones and cities and jet airplanes. Again, my father worried for him, wanted to put his arm around the shoulders of the diminutive man standing beside him and reassure him that everything would be all right. He didn't, of course. It would have been inappropriate, presumptuous. It was not in his nature to do so. It was in his nature not to feel what he was feeling. Instead of offering any such gesture, therefore, he simply offered his hand and thanked the King for the honor of spending the evening together, an unspoken promise to aid the King. The King accepted my father's thanks, acknowledging his equally submerged instinct that he had met a man, a foreigner, he could trust. They bid each other good night; then my father returned to his Opel and drove back across Hamra to our house. The King watched him go, the red taillights disappearing. He stayed there for a moment, absolutely still, enjoying the solitude. Then he climbed the stone steps and entered the palace.

Two days later, Roy Sweetser strolled into my father's office and told him he had leaned on poor Vitaly Kedrov and that in total terror Vitaly had told him that there had been, recently, a great deal of cable traffic between Moscow and Hamra, concerning, he sputtered, when pressed, something called Desert Rose.

"What the hell's that?" my father asked.

"Not a clue," Roy said. "Nobody back home has ever heard of such a thing."

"Doesn't Vitaly see the cables?"

"No. His boss does the decoding. They don't exactly trust each other over there."

"So he says. Do you believe him?"

Roy shrugged.

Desert Rose was the name the K.G.B. had given to a clandestine operation, in support of the Egyptian Intelligence Service, whose desire it was to remove the King and put in his place someone more sympathetic to Nasser's pan-Arabic, anti-American crusade. The Russians were angling for a better relationship with Nasser, a relationship they could manipulate to their advantage—a goal they finally achieved, nine years later, in the aftermath of the Six Day War. At the time, in Kurash, in 1958, the C.I.A. had only a name, Desert Rose, and no idea what it meant. Three days later, on a Monday, the C.I.A. station in Cairo reported increased cable activity between Moscow and the local K.G.B. office. They also reported that the head of Nasser's Intelligence Service, one Colonel Saad Eddin Ibrahim, had been spending a lot of his leisure time in the company of the K.G.B.'s station chief, Nikolay

Pestryakov. Then came the big break, less than two days later. A young clerical secretary who worked for the Egyptian Intelligence Service in their headquarters on Tahrir Street, and for whom the C.I.A. had already purchased a beachfront apartment in Miami, walked out of the building with a handful of cables, coded, designated Desert Rose, stuffed into her purse. She got into a cab, was driven home, and as she paid the driver she handed him the envelope containing the filched cables. The cabdriver then drove to the *souk*. Carrying the envelope, he bumped into a foreigner. They both apologized. When the foreigner walked away, he had tucked safely inside his jacket the envelope in question. Which was sent to D.C. and the contents decoded.

One week after the King and my father drove into the desert, five days after Roy Sweetser first mentioned the existence of Desert Rose, Milton Gourlie, Hamra station chief, received the following cable from Washington: "It is now clear, based on all available data, that a plot to assassinate the King is under way by the Egyptian Intelligence Service, abetted, at a safe distance, by the K.G.B. They're also going after Hussein of Jordan and Feisel of Iraq. Nasser cannot tolerate independent monarchies in the midst of his pan-Arabic fantasy. What is not clear, however, is: (a) the nature of the assassination plot, viz. how and when, and (b) whether or not any Kurashians are involved, and if so, who they might be. Freeman."

Milton felt sick. The cable swam before him, murky, undefined catastrophe. If the King was killed, on his, Milton's, watch, then he, Milton, was fucked. If, on the other hand, he told himself, brightening, he were able to penetrate the plot, undo it, save the King, then he, Milton, would be a hero and destined for one of the larger stations, maybe Berlin, or even Istanbul, with its prickly array of listening devices marshaled along the Soviet border. He lit a cigarette, studied the cable, tried to clear his head. For the next few hours he remained sequestered alone behind his office door, making careful notations on a yellow legal pad.

That night he had dinner with my father, in the dining room at the Hotel Antioch. He explained the situation. My father gazed through the dining room window at the broken columns of the Roman amphitheater across the street. He was intensely, painfully, aware of the fact that he might not be able to protect the King, that like his father the King could be destined for an early death, death by assassination. The idea of destiny bothered my father, removing, as it did, any chance of change. What if it was futile even to try to protect the King? On the other hand, my father reasoned with himself, what if the King's destiny was to live, to survive, to rule until he died, years hence, of natural causes, in bed, contentedly asleep? Then it still didn't matter what my father did; the course was set, the King would triumph. My father rejected destiny, that night, in all its forms, knowing that if he accepted it he would be paralyzed. At the same time, of course, he implicitly accepted the rule of chaos, embraced it as the friend of action. Which, he would discover, leads to a different kind of futility.

"We've got to find out if any of these assholes is planning to kill the King."

Milton handed a piece of paper to my father. My father glanced at it. Milton had listed various organizations—the Communist Party, the Muslim Brotherhood, the Baathist Party—that could be considered a threat to the King, organizations outlawed but still alive and kicking, organizations benignly ignored by the King.

"I was thinking you, Roy, and I could each take a group, focus on them, see what we come up with."

My father nodded, his eyes drifting back to the Roman ruins across the street. In the daytime, under the bright, indifferent light, the broken stones assumed an almost peaceful aspect, certainly they spoke most poignantly of sleep and rest, a centuries-old *siesta,* lizards flicking over granite, moss shadowing the crevices, history here marked by a succession of lazy, almost pleasant subjugations. But at night the cool darkness pressing down on the shattered theater spoke to my father of a more violent memory, cold hard facts, maybe, or an absolute futility that rendered him weak with despair: this small oasis, this haven of shade, conquered by the Sumerians, conquered by the Babylonians, conquered by Alexander, conquered by the Romans, conquered by desert Arabs rising up from the southern deserts, bringing their message of Islam, conquered by the Ottomans, colonized by the British, passing now into the American sphere of influence . . . What was one king among so many dead and lost, entire languages gone forever? And what was one intelligence officer among so many advisers to the court but a dry skull picked bare by the wind and the sand?

My father called Rashid, using the phone behind the bar. Leslie Smythe-Jones, MI6, attached to the British embassy, was having a drink with a Kurashian my father did not recognize, an elderly man in a neatly pressed gray suit, starched white shirt, club tie, his upper lip sporting the ubiquitous local mustache.

"Hey there, Mack," Smythe-Jones intoned, vaguely amused, as always, and slightly condescending. "How goes the world of skullduggery?"

"Just fine, thanks, Leslie."

"This is my good friend Abdul Kilani." Leslie waved a hand in the Kurashian's direction, who nodded politely. "He's a Commie."

My father gave the man a second, more interested look.

"Thought that might catch your attention."

My father and Abdul exchanged smiles and a handshake. Then my father turned his back to them as Rashid answered the phone. "Hello?"

"It's me, Mack. We need to meet. It's important."

They chose a coffeehouse in the *souk* and hung up.

The *souk,* in Hamra, in those days, hadn't changed much over the years, still very much a stopover on what remained of the ancient trade routes, a shadowy maze of stalls and narrow alleys, goatskins stretched overhead for shade, where caravans stopped on their way from the Red Sea or Persian Gulf or Trucial Coast or

Baghdad to Damascus and Beirut, delivered their goods, stayed for a few days, then moved on, camels swaying drunkenly under the weight of fresh goods. When my mother and I first flew from Rome to Hamra, via Beirut, to join my father, we passed over just such a long meandering line of Bedouin traders and their camels, bright splotches of color on the sand below, each trailing its own desultory shadow. And then, months later, there they were again, this time preserved in lead and enamel paint, five perfect toy reproductions of Bedouins riding camels lying in a dark red shallow cardboard box marked BRITAINS in the glass counter of Oristibach's. The *souk* itself, which my father now entered, suddenly conscious, again, of his foreignness, his gray summer suit and drip-dry shirt and creaking shoes, moving as he was into a world made up exclusively of dark-skinned men wearing desert garb hawking their wares at earsplitting decibel levels, spices and metals, clothes, radios, books, pomegranates and olives, goat cheese, Indian teas, medicines . . . the *souk* itself seemed to my father an absolutely magical place, and he often spent afternoon hours there alone, wandering from stall to stall, finding and bringing home odd assortments of Arab life: a long-barreled flintlock rifle, a beautifully tooled camel saddle, a complicated brass samovar. These found their way into the living room, next to the small stone birds and shards of pottery my mother brought home from her expeditions to the various *tells* surrounding Hamra, and which I would study, intently, as I roamed our house on empty afternoons, waiting for my parents to come home from wherever they were, wherever they'd gone. I can close my eyes and see, distinctly, the books piled up next to the armchair in the living room where my mother liked to read, brand-new books either sent to her in the diplomatic pouch by friends back home in Washington or bought downtown in the English Bookshop on Al Kifah Street: *A Death in the Family, Dr. Zhivago, The Ugly American, Voss* . . .

Rashid and my father met, shook hands, settled onto simple kitchen chairs while a boy brought over a brass tray containing coffee and small cups. They sipped the thick, sweet Turkish brew, then got down to business.

"Nasser's trying to kill the King," my father said.

"I know," Rashid replied sadly, peering into the bowels of his cup, reading the coffee grinds.

"You know?"

"Yes."

"Why didn't you tell me?"

"I didn't know it was my job to tell you everything I know." He smiled at my father, lit a cigarette. "Anyway, I have no real information. Who, when, how . . ."

"We'd like to help you."

"How do you propose to do that?"

"Pool our resources."

"You don't have any resources, Mack."

Rashid, of course, was right. My father acknowledged this with a resigned nod. He was not a salesman. The two men contemplated the imponderable for a while. Around them, the *souk* continued its loud and colorful business. Still in silence, Rashid pulled an envelope from his jacket pocket and laid it on the table before my father. My father picked up the envelope, opened it, and retrieved six grainy black-and-white photographs of a naked middle-aged man, unmistakably Caucasian, in bed with two young, naked Arab boys. The boys he did not recognize. The man was Ambassador Burdick. In one of the photographs he had one of the boys' dicks in his mouth and his own dick buried to the shaft in the other boy's asshole. His eyes were closed in pleasure. Jesus Christ. My father put the photographs back in the envelope, lit a cigarette.

"Are these real?"

"Unfortunately, yes."

"Who took them?"

"That's not important. What's important is that I got ahold of them before any damage could be done. I have the negatives."

My father studied Rashid carefully, waited for the rest.

"They're also in the envelope."

My father looked. They were.

"Do with them as you will," Rashid said, too bashful to look my father in the eye. He was embarrassed, my father realized. Embarrassed by the incident, embarrassed by the photographs, embarrassed by his own implicit power in the discussion.

"I don't want the damn things," my father said.

"I'm sure you don't, Mack." Rashid stood, offered his hand. "I'll let you know if anything develops regarding the Egyptian threat to His Majesty. Good night."

They shook hands. Rashid turned and walked away into the depths of the *souk,* looking very small and tired.

8

I stayed up late last night in the guest bedroom of my father's condo, in Charlestown, and arranged, in as orderly a fashion as possible, on a yellow legal pad, the most basic facts I know, what we call history, the chronological overview, the Big Picture that we crave so intensely and that tells us so little. Yet, as an organizing principle, it will have to do. My father snored gently in his room next door.

The Baath Socialist Party, with its anticolonial and pan-Arabic agenda, was established in 1954, in Damascus, Syria.

Two years later, in 1956, Nasser, a declared pan-Arabic nationalist and anticolonialist, nationalized the Suez Canal. By defying Great Britain and France, principal investors in the canal, and their much loathed coconspirators, the Israelis, Nasser became a hero to millions of Arabs.

In 1957, Egypt and Syria formed an alliance, the United Arab Republic, thereby encircling the more traditional desert monarchies of Jordan, Iraq, and Kurash.

In 1957 the United Arab Republic formed an "economic and military partnership" with the Soviet Union, thereby aligning the nationalist, pan-Arabic, anticolonial movement of the Middle East with the International Communist Movement, i.e., not only the Soviet Union but also all of Eastern Europe, China, North Korea, North Vietnam, and Cuba.

In 1957, in response to what was beginning to feel like something frightening and inevitable, like inertia, like what Marx called history, Washington, paranoia settling as gloomily as permanent bad weather, declared the so-called Eisenhower Doctrine, by which the United States promised to come to the aid of any country in need of military help in its fight against Communism.

In 1958, three months after Major Rashid handed my father those incriminating photographs of Ambassador Burdick, a nationalist cadre of Army officers staged a coup against King Feisel of Iraq, our King's cousin. Feisel and his various cousins and uncles and servants were shot in the garden of the Baghdad palace. He was holding a Koran in his hand.

In 1958, King Hussein of Jordan, also cousin to the recently executed King Feisel of Iraq, found himself quelling a conspiracy of young nationalist Army officers who wished to repeat their fellow officers' success in Iraq. They almost succeeded.

In 1958, most weekends, you could find Allen Dulles, my father's boss, at his Georgetown brick rowhouse on Q Street, hosting get-togethers with his top officers, foreign policy wonks, selected journalists, and concerned intellectuals. Sucking cigarettes and swilling martinis, they spread out before them an imaginary representation, a mental map, of the world as it then existed, and this is what they saw: Since the end of World War II, the Soviet Union had added seven hundred million people and five million square miles to its already considerable empire. Communists had won wars in China, Vietnam, and Tibet; they had fought the Yankee Imperialists to a standstill in Korea; their political parties were on the ascendancy in Italy, Indonesia, Egypt, Cambodia, Laos.

In 1958, every Arab intellectual and artist under the age of forty held tight within his heart the fervent belief that any moment now the Arabs would unite, rid themselves of the Israeli humiliation, grow flowers in the desert, grow poems in the desert, never drink another Coca-Cola, never drive another Chevrolet. Ali Ahmad Sa'id, aka Adonis, Syrian poet living in Beirut, wrote, in 1957, in "Resurrection and Ashes":

*O Phoenix! This is the moment of your new resurrection
The semblance of ashes has become sparks, a starry flame
Spring has crept in the roots, in the earth
The past is awake from its slumber . . .*

In 1958, *Annie Get Your Gun* opened on Broadway.

In 1958, Ricky Nelson's "Poor Little Fool" was displaced from the number one spot on Billboard's Hot 100 by "Volare," a song that made me want to be back in Italy, back on a leafy *trattoria* terrace overlooking the sleepy Mediterranean, a song whose words I could not understand because it was in a foreign language. Tongue of the unsaid. Voice of the never spoken.

In 1958, my father arrived in Hamra.

"So what did you do about the photographs?" I asked.

Last night, in his condo, dark Boston Harbor outside the windows.

My father looking so old . . .

When Odysseus finally got home, he was recognized by no one but the blind old family dog, who saw not by sight but by smell. If I were to study my father in 1958, leaving the house for work one cool spring morning, Chesterfield in one hand, papers in the other, sauntering across the stony garden, past the smiling Kurashian sentry to the red Opel, and if I were then presented, forty years later, with the man before me now, stooped, thirty pounds lighter, nothing of the strength left except a suggestion of power in the shoulder muscles, white-haired, weak-eyed, would I have recognized him, my father? Maybe the hands, the lean, veined fingers, still steady. But that's about it.

"Dad?"

"Hmm?"

"The photographs? Of Ambassador Burdick? What did you do with them?"

He turned then from the bookcase, where he was hunting

down some obscure information on the crankcase of a 1926 Bentley, and gave me a long, thoughtful look.

"Dad? The photographs?"

"I don't want to talk about this anymore," he announced.

"Excuse me?"

"I don't want to talk about Kurash, 1958, the Glue Factory, Ambassador Burdick, the King—especially the King."

"Dad, you can't just stop now."

"Sure I can."

"It's a story. Dirty pictures, the King of Kurash about to be assassinated. Come on."

He fixed me with his over-the-glasses tough-guy look, which since I was a child he's used to freeze me in my tracks. "Remember what I told you, about assholes who swear an oath, a goddamned *oath,* of secrecy, then cash in on services performed?"

"Yes, I remember."

"Well, we've reached that line."

That was it. He clammed up. I tried everything I could think of, appealing to his vanity, his sense of history, my psychological and emotional needs as a son, but to no avail. His notion of duty had returned to him full force, and I could tell that he bitterly regretted every word he had already uttered, each word, in his mind, a betrayal.

"Why do you want to know?" he kept asking me. "Why is it so important to you?"

"I told you, it's for my book," I said. "And I'm curious."

I had known this moment would come, that he would eventually stop talking. My father may be self-involved, but he's not unobservant, he's not a fool. Walking through his darkened condo to the kitchen, past the closed door of his bedroom, through the living room with its beautiful Roberts etchings of mid-nineteenth-century Petra, moving through all those invisible layers of loneliness, I'm acutely aware of the sensitivity he can bring to bear when it suits him. He must have been a good spy, or intelligence officer, as he still prefers to think of himself. And so with a survivor's instinct saving him from the soul's gilded mirror, he has raised his head and sniffed the air and asked himself why the hell his son wants to know so much about Kurash, about 1958, about the King.

That year, 1958, was the last year I lived at home.

After that, I went to a succession of boarding schools in England, Switzerland, and, finally, New Hampshire.

Those endless evenings gazing out the blackened windows at my own reflection, the Kingston Trio singing "Tom Dooley" on my yellow Phillips record player, form the final chapter of my childhood.

You grow up fast in Little America, or not at all.

Little America as in, referencing New York City, Little Italy, or, referencing Los Angeles, Little Saigon, a miniaturized and to some extent bastardized version of a real place far, far away.

Our stone house in Jebel Hamra lay in a row of five almost identical stone houses all occupied by Americans, most with a new Chevy or Ford in the driveway. Honest. You could get milk shakes and hamburgers on the third floor of the American embassy. As already mentioned, current movies were shown every Saturday night, and within the licensed shadowy ardor of our corrugated tin hut, the Hut, young boys like myself felt for the first time the exhilarating palpitating softness of young American female flesh, pressed cheek to cheek and awash on the musical fumes of Fabian and Elvis. Friday nights Renee and Johnny Allen and the Marine Guards went bowling at the American Club, the Sweetsers and the Gourlies and my parents and even Ambassador Burdick and his wife, Kathy, sat in the bar upstairs in overstuffed armchairs scarfing gin and tonics, Planters peanuts, Luckies, Chesterfields, Camels, a veritable orgy of chemical indulgence.

> *Hang down your head, Tom Dooley,*
> *Hang down your head and cry.*
> *Hang down your head, Tom Dooley,*
> *Poor boy you're bound to die . . .*

I boil water in my father's kitchen, sip tea at his table, aware of so much that isn't here, that used to be here, so much that my mother has taken with her to her perch above Mass Ave.: cookbooks, pots, pans, wall decorations, various oriental knickknacks, twigs of rosemary. There's another mystery at the heart of the mystery, my parents' baffling decision to live apart in their twilight years. I make a bet with myself that if I look closely enough I will find, somewhere in this kitchen, a remnant of 1958, and sure enough I do, on a shelf by the window, back behind a box full of old picture frames my father has found in garbage cans and brought home: another one of those boxy black-and-white Agfa photographs with serrated edges, this one of me, ten years old, sitting under a pine tree on the edge of a rocky Kurashian field, stones and sand stretching unbroken to the horizon. I have my hand stretched out to shake a dark-skinned, wrinkled old man's hand, the hand of an Arab squatting beside me, grinning gap-toothed into the camera. I'm wearing a *kaffiyeh* on my head; I'm squinting in the bright desert light, my eyes, what I can see of them, dull testimonials to acute shyness. Snatches of memory assail me there in the Charlestown kitchen: the Naugahyde red interior of the station's Chevrolet, the back of Hussein's head as he drives, the scent of his cologne . . . a picnic under the pine trees, this man who wandered over to say hello, a shepherd perhaps, a farmer of the hopeless soil. My mother there, off to the left, a peripheral blue, pouring soup from the Scotch-plaid thermos bottle, slicing bits of fruit and holding them out to us on the edge of the knife. My father . . . where? Behind the camera? Is my shyness aimed at him? Has he turned, for a moment, his professional eyes to me, wondering, Who is this boy; what makes him tick? No, such questions remain unasked. My family treasures most the feelings we've never expressed and assumes feelings that, in fact, I doubt ever existed, but the assumption of which, the invention of which, on my part anyway, pressed flat to the cool tile floor listening to Robin Hood and his Merry Men in the garden next door, fighting off the great emptiness crouched at my door like a bloodthirsty cutthroat, meant the difference between hope and despair.

Mom and Dad love me, they think about me, they care about me, they will protect me.

The essential myth, the necessary lie.

It was a world of spies, then, spies and their Vassar wives with big smiles and healthy white teeth and red lipstick and packs of cigarettes, spies and their bowls of Miltowns and shakers of very dry gin martinis, spies and their redoubtable families from Cincinnati and Hartford and Santa Barbara, spies and their cotillions and boathouses and summer nights on the lake with fireflies and overgrown tennis courts, just that instant of twilight and the brief flash of tan thighs and white shorts as the laughing girl lunges for the tennis ball spun like a bullet into the dank foliage. Spies who answered the call to duty, spies who answered the call to adventure, boys from Yale and Harvard and Princeton and the University of Virginia, boys who joined the O.S.S., boys parachuted in blackface Behind Enemy Lines, boys smuggling belts of gold to resistance groups in Poland and Hungary, boys waiting one hot Greek morning to pull the trigger that will explode the head of the German officer now leaning down to wipe some offending speck from his gleaming boots, his last act, his last gesture of orderliness, his last thought itself a fragment, something like, The way the evergreens lose their snow in great whooshing thumps—BLAM, curtain down, the American boy, the American spy, smiling to himself with satisfaction, grateful to his father for teaching him how to skeet shoot, those miserable freezing winter mornings in Greenwich. *Pull.* BLAM.

We were on our way to Jerusalem, in that black-and-white Agfa, I remember now. We would soon cross the border into Jordan, drive the length of the holy valley to the holy city, a city so old it seemed to me, at ten, to be, literally, haunted, thick stone walls sweating beads of moisture a backdrop to weird neon hallucinations, ethereal crypt-o-visions, my own private Technicolor, a nightmare's big screen presentation of . . . everything. So we had stopped under the pine trees for a picnic, the smiling gap-toothed man had introduced himself. I was wearing a *kaffiyeh*. The King had given me the *kaffiyeh*. The King had come to our house, to visit. I remember my mother and father being nervous, being calm, tidying the living room, putting plenty of Cokes on the bar, just a regular American spy and his family getting ready to receive a king. His Majesty. I don't remember his arrival; I don't remember his departure. Was he alone? Were there guards? And why, exactly, was he there? Did he and my father discuss business? Was it a purely social visit? He came, he went, a vanishing act, and left behind in my hand the soft luxuriant red-and-white-checked *kaffiyeh,* a gift I do remember him handing me, that shy, almost diffident look playing across his face as I said thank you and he nodded with pleasure. My second sighting of the King, first at the military exercises, now here, in my living room, a mustache bobbing above the friendly smile—he slips into my consciousness as quietly and unobtrusively as he slipped into our house. *"Marhaba."*

Hello.

Lambent sacred Cocktail Hour, clink of ice against glass, the steadily rising good vibrations emanating from the increasingly salubrious grown-ups, laughter in the next room, all is well in the next room, lipstick on the crumpled cigarettes in the next room . . . this is how spies relaxed, in 1958. They knew a thing or two that you and I do not know, their relationship with the stone wall and the bougainvillea, the traffic roundabout, the mysterious Mercedes at night, the black one purring like a contented cat as it pulls away from the palace, the harem. If you know a secret, others look like fools. If you protect that secret, your duty is holy. Gin and nicotine, tranquilizers and go-carts, picnics in the desert and charades on Saturday night: ancient rituals of the far-flung empire.

Upstairs the children listen to music and move regiments of toy soldiers across the floor. The children of spies. Children of Little America. C.I.A. brats.

Catch a falling star and put it in your pocket
Never let it fade away . . .

Penny and Carolyn, blond and blue-eyed, daughters of Roy Sweetser and wife, Barbara, future horse-riding, bomb-throwing debutantes, Radcliffe revolutionaries, eleven (Penny) and thirteen (Carolyn) at the time, prim and proper and solemn in their party dresses, listening as to familiar winds bringing word of a home they barely remember. The Gourlies' son, enthusiastic Chipper, who would come back from Vietnam a heroin addict, crouched on my floor directing armies across an imaginary mountain range.

There were others, in my life, who shared this deniable existence, this overseas childhood, those early tutorials in invisibility, but these three—Carolyn, Penny, Chipper—were there that night, those nights, riding the nimbus of Cocktail Hour.

We grew up in places like Georgetown and Alexandria and Chevy Chase; we were flown in great thumping silver Pan American airplanes all the way to Rome, all the way to Greece, Beirut, Damascus, Baghdad, Hamra, Cairo; we went to American Community Schools; we spent weekends swimming at the American Club, we watched American movies (*Love Is a Many Splendored Thing, Jailhouse Rock, Cheaper by the Dozen*) at the embassy on Sunday nights; we had dances; we groped each other, at the Hut, a corrugated tin room across the embassy garden, the inconclusive view from the Ambassador's window . . .

If you can't find a partner
Grab a wooden chair
Let's rock . . .

Poems sung in exile by boys and girls for whom the deepest, truest significance of life lay in a fully faded pair of denim jeans, preferably Levi's or Lees . . .

Sweatshirts worn inside out . . .

Desert boots . . .

Meanwhile our fathers were toppling governments, or propping them up.

A case in point would be Hamra, Kurash, in 1958.

While we explored the tricky formalities of Close Dancing, the C.I.A. was secretly spending a whole lot of tax money on the King of Kurash. I know this from internal C.I.A. memos I have read, memos released to me, as I believe I've mentioned, thanks to the Freedom of Information Act. In those days, a measurable amount of the financing of American foreign policy was actually conducted through the good services of the C.I.A., for the simple reason that the State Department, A.I.D., and the Pentagon had to submit to Congress an itemized foreign aid budget, a budget that was then chopped to pieces by various interest groups, whereas the C.I.A. did not, the C.I.A. simply received a yearly check and could spend it as it saw fit, no questions asked. Approximately three million dollars was siphoned to the King in 1958, in monthly installments, delivered, in a briefcase, by a C.I.A. case officer, that is to say, by Milton Gourlie, or Roy Sweetser, or my father.

My father the spy.

My father the spook.

My father the silent, gray-skinned man delivering a briefcase full of money at midnight.

Two

1

My mother opened her apartment door, gave me a startled look, as if I were a not-so-friendly ghost. "Why, hello, darling."

"Yes, it's me. I'm alive. Hi."

I entered, dragging my two duffel bags behind me, one filled with dirty clothes, the other with weighty books and index cards, the pulp of my research.

"Is everything all right?"

"Just fine, thanks." I dropped the bags and looked around at her exotic but constipated quarters, two large rooms filled with things Middle Eastern: Persian carpets, a couch from Baghdad, a Kuwaiti door transformed into a coffee table, brass lamps, mother-of-pearl and olive-wood cigarette boxes and side tables, wall hangings from Isfahan of dainty men with curling shoes, the artifacts from Kurashian *tells* in the glass-fronted bookcase, more shelves lining the walls and sagging with books: Ouspensky, Patrick White, Freya Stark, *A Death in the Family*, the cover long gone, the binding faded to a warped pastel blue.

"What happened?" my mother asked.

She was giving me her bemused look, a brief direct stare followed immediately by a scattered opacity, as if, having asked the question, she was no longer interested in the answer. She was wearing jeans and a long gray sweater, her hair, white now and parted in the middle, hanging like a boy's to her shoulders. She wasn't wearing her wedding ring, I noticed. A new development.

"Dad happened," I said. "Remember him? The quiet narcissist who used to be your husband?"

"He's still my husband. We're not divorced."

"You know what I mean."

"No, actually, I don't know what you mean. I think we should have some tea."

She disappeared into the small kitchen off her living room. I could hear the rattling of crockery and silverware, water running from the tap into the tea kettle. I collapsed on the Baghdadi couch, settled back into the tough, scratchy pillows, tried to chill. Oddly, I must have slept, because the next thing I knew my mother was placing a tray on the coffee table and pouring us both cups of tea. I sat up groggily, my limbs heavy.

"Now, what did your father do?" she asked.

"He stopped talking."

"Altogether?"

"No."

"Selectively?"

"Yes."

"He's good at that." She blew on her tea, much as my father had, days ago, in his condo overlooking Boston Harbor.

"He was telling me a story, and then he just stopped, right in the middle, and refused to go on."

She studied me. "He was telling you a story?"

"Yes."

"How unlike him. About what?"

"The King, Kurash, 1958."

"You mean you were asking him questions."

"So?"

"He'll never tell you what you want to know. You know that."

I sighed, took a swallow of the hot tea. "Why aren't you wearing your wedding ring?"

"It broke."

"How symbolic."

"I'll tell you what's symbolic: It can be mended."

A long, intricate silence followed, my mother busying herself with pouring us both second cups of tea. I glanced at my bag of books on the floor, remembering that it contained my father's faded Penguin edition of *Travels in Arabia Deserta,* the yellow piece of lined paper and its plaintive plea folded within. *O love, you could not know or do know the way I feel . . .* I almost asked my mother what she knew about this incomplete missive, then thought better of it.

"What do you want to know?" she asked.

"Everything."

"Why?"

"I'm writing a book. I want to know what happened."

"What kind of book?"

"History."

"History?"

"Recently, on the front page of the *New York Times,* I read an article about Kurash, in 1958. It mentioned, in passing, that every month a C.I.A. officer attached to the local C.I.A. station carried a briefcase full of money to the King, in his palace."

"That's why your father won't talk to you anymore. He's scared of you."

"Scared of me?"

"Yes. He told me."

"When?"

"This morning. He called."

Even separated they form a conspiracy into which I can never gain entry. "Thanks for telling me."

"I just did."

"Mom, we're talking about forty years ago. No one gives a shit what happened forty years ago, in Kurash."

"Watch your language."

"I promise I won't ask about any secrets, okay? There will be no breach of national security in this house."

"I don't know anything. I was the dutiful housewife, blind as only a dutiful housewife can be."

"Tell me about Hamra. What's the harm in that? Please."

After a pause, she leaned forward to blow into her own cup of steaming Sleepytime. "Hamra in those days wasn't much more than a small town."

She went on to describe Hamra's main boulevard, Al Kifah Street, with its trolley tracks running down the middle and its sidewalks lined with shops and eucalyptus trees; the two movie theaters, the Majestic and the Odeon, that Rashid and my father frequented, with their fare of mostly American movies; the *souk,* a hot, crowded scramble of voluble shadows; the English bookstore, where my mother got her novels; the colonial Hotel Antioch, with its garden of blue fountains and fig trees. Mostly Hamra was a smattering of single- and two-story limestone buildings, slender, needlelike minaret towers rising high above the flat rooftops, and a thin foliage of pine trees covering the barren, surrounding hills. The indigenous population, all two hundred thousand, included the Bedouin, with their black goatskin tents scattered about the knolls and *wadis.* Hamra was a small town made smaller, for my mother, by the implicit boundaries of Little America. To escape our ghetto's horrifying innocence, the false and claustrophobic reassurance, that weird Yankee version of colonial vanity, weird because it had more to do with homesickness than aggrandizement—to escape this Little America my mother plunged, all alone, deeper into the *souk,* intentionally lost herself among the smells of cardamom, cinnamon, *zatar,* nutmeg, coriander, turmeric, cumin, and cloves, the gleaming brass trays, the hieroglyphic, incomprehensible chatter, she dragged Barbara Sweetser with her to the *tells* outside Hamra, digging, scraping dirt, burrowing among the ruins of forgotten cities looking for something substantial, she brought home books and got herself a tutor, a student at the local university who had spent two years studying at MIT and spoke passable English, with his help learning the rudiments of Arabic, lonely, lonely, lonely, lonely as the King in Hamzah Palace.

"What can you tell me about him?" I asked.

"The King? He was very nice."

"That's it? 'Nice'?"

She shrugged, cupped her hands around her warm cup of tea. "He was young."

"Twenty-two when you arrived."

"That young?" She seemed surprised. "I can't believe it."

"Believe it."

"But he was just a boy. A child."

"An emotionally needy child. Who turned around one day and bumped into his long-lost older brother, Mack Hooper, my father, your ex-husband."

"He's not my ex."

"Yes, he is."

"He's not. Don't be snide."

"Mother, you live in separate domiciles. You endure separate days. Your spooning nights are over. By the way, why?"

"Why what, dear?"

"Why did you split up?"

"We didn't split up. Don't be so dramatic."

"Why did you do whatever it is you did that resulted in your living apart from each other?"

My mother did her little vanishing act, disappearing back behind her eyes, a cloudy confusion left for me to contemplate, wait upon.

"The King was a religious man," she finally allowed.

His day always began early, before light, when he would cross the garden behind Hamzah Palace to the small mosque his grandfather Ali had built among a grove of pines. Chill, sweet desert air brought to him the scent of rosemary and jasmine. He inhaled deeply, seeking contentment, brief peace before the rush of duty and responsibility.

God is great.
I testify that there is no God but Allah.

The *muezzin's* call to morning prayers, a guttural, singsong chant, deep-throated, floated across the rooftops of Hamra to the garden where the King now paused, delighted, and listened.

I testify that Muhammad is God's Apostle.

It was coming from the Daraa mosque, he guessed, in the northeast corner of Hamra, near the truck stops, corrugated tin huts where huge Mercedes trucks hesitated on the edge of the desert, drivers disembarking for gossip and coffee.

Come to prayer, come to security.
God is most great.

Three more prayer calls pearled the morning, *muezzins* holding forth from the tops of Hamra's other three mosques, prayer overlapping prayer, rippling echoes of the greeting of the day to the Holy One reverberating from house to house, street to street, as all across the city men who felt nothing for the desert, who distrusted the desert, who hated the desert, knelt and prayed, bowing to Mecca, as out in the desert itself, the palace of sand and dreams from which the King and his old family had sprung, the Bedouin, who mistrusted the city dwellers, who mocked them as weaklings, knelt and pressed their foreheads to the cool ground, memory of night—the Ruwalla in the East, with their seven thousand tents, the Huweitat in the South, the Beni Atiya, the Beni Sakhr with their three thousand tents. From this the King must weld together a country. A country that had absolutely no significant economic force—no oil, little agriculture, no industry. A country that, until now, had lived on a subsidy paid by Her Majesty's government of Great Britain. A subsidy, including "development" programs, that amounted to thirty million dollars per annum. Money that within a few months would be gone.

Growing increasingly edgy as the morning, and consciousness, progressed, the young King entered the small mosque. Servants had already lit the five oil lamps in anticipation of his coming, a morning ritual, and discreetly withdrawn. He faced the semicircle of the *mihrab,* opened his hands and touched the lobes of his ears with his thumbs.

"Allahu Akbar . . ."

He murmured his intention, five *rah'as,* or bowings, then began to pray, reciting each prayer in a distracted stupor, words he knew so well, words he had recited so many times, that often, certainly this morning, he hardly heard them. He tried not to let anything but his contemplation of the Holy One enter his mind, he tried banishing, in a kingly way, all other thoughts, but, as was so often the case, he failed. He was preoccupied, bent there in supplication in the garden behind the palace, the little mosque dark except for the guttering lamps, by the American, Mack Hooper, my father, for it seemed to the King that he, my father, had offered the King a deal, his handshake a proposal, presumably official. But the King had no idea, really, what that deal might be, what was being, exactly, proposed. He thought of Americans as blunt, sometimes crude people, believing everything they said, which made them good salesmen, but, as his father had once warned him, dangerous friends. The King's personal experience was limited, having spent far more time with the British, whom he had inherited from his father, who, in turn, had inherited them from *his* father. The King had studied Homer and played cricket with the children of the British ruling class. Over time the King, like his father, like his grandfather, had come, if not to understand, then at least to have a feeling for the British. But the Americans, Mack Hooper, my father, remained a mystery to him.

"Bismillah il Rahman il Rahim."

In the name of Allah, the Compassionate, the Merciful.

The King bowed his head, touched the soft carpet with his forehead, remembered walking to this very mosque years and years ago, his father's voice even and thoughtful in the predawn coolness. "You will be surrounded by those who wish you ill, by those who seek to use you to their own ends, for that is the nature of man." Brought here by his father those long-ago early mornings to kneel between his father and his grandfather and recite these same prayers, to learn—they had been teaching him, those mornings, he knew now, much as they taught him when they took him out to the desert to shoot a rifle, or ride a horse, or celebrate the end of Ramadan with the Bedouin. They were teaching him how to behave, what to do, how to lead, and they were teaching him who he was, where he came from, what it meant to be an Arab and a king. Sadness descended upon the King. He suddenly and intensely missed his father. This was emotional territory he rarely let himself visit, so he shied away, relegating his sadness to a corner of the room, where it sat in the sputtering shadows, head bowed, watching him.

May God grant me guidance, may God grant me good judgment, may God forgive me my lapses of judgment, for example, perhaps, allowing myself to even consider trusting the American, Mack Hooper...

The King's grandfather, an imperial old man in desert robes and *kaffiyeh,* had been taken from him when he was only eight and exiled to Rome by the British, who no longer could countenance his spendthrift ways. He preferred to call it desert courtesy, the paying of largesse to the Bedouin chiefs. The British could see nothing but their quickly emptying coffers. He had died in exile, in Rome, keeling over of a heart attack on the via Veneto, a Cairo newspaper in his hand. Yet it was his honoring of the old ways, his careful dispensation of respect and money, that had fashioned of the disparate, feuding, distrustful Bedouin tribes a semblance of order and the beginnings of a national consciousness. The Crazy Old Man, the British had called his grandfather, in their clubs, over drinks, bloodshot eyes restlessly roaming the rattan room, hideous pale pink legs crossed in starched khaki beneath the slowly revolving overhead fans, *whirr-whirr-whirr,* the musical tattoo of empire, barely audible beneath (above) the genteel grunts of colonial self-assurance. How they had managed to have the Arabs see themselves through English eyes, and so, in one swift accepting plunge, see themselves as quaint artifacts of a primitive world, alienated from themselves . . . that, the King mused, was perhaps the most insidiously effective of all the accomplishments of the British Empire.

The joke was, the irony was, that once the King's father was firmly in control, advanced to the throne by the British, he reverted to the same ancient practice, passing out money to the Beduoin chiefs, which the British now reluctantly, belatedly, realized was a necessity.

Lowering his hands and folding them together, the left within the right, the King recited the *Fahtiha,* the first chapter of the Koran.

> *"Praise belongs to God, Lord of the Worlds,*
> *The Compassionate, the Merciful,*
> *King of the Day of Judgment . . ."*

Maybe he missed his father, especially, that morning, because, fighting an uneasy sensation of incipient threat, a sensation that until now, this moment, he had not even admitted to himself he felt, he wanted someone to turn to, someone to confide in, someone whose judgment he valued, someone he could trust, completely. He understood exactly enough to understand that he had no such person, except perhaps for Major Rashid, who after all was only a minor official, a trustworthy cog, and could not help him with matters of policy. General Anwar he valued but did not trust, nor Kumait, whom, perhaps, he loved. They both suffered from enthusiasms, the voluptuous tyranny of ideas, drawn to the secret gathering of an inner circle of true believers, in Socialism, in Nasserism, in Communism, in the secret and unspeakable inner heart of Islam. . . .

The British had been bankrupted by World War II, their empire was disintegrating. The Americans were filling the vacuum created by British withdrawal, but they were tainted by their colonial affiliations, the cut of their suits, the color of their skin. The Soviets, bearish men sweating vodka, whom, like his father before him, he despised and feared, were able to assume the radical high ground, though anyone with half a brain knew this could not possibly be right, that the Soviets were even more dangerous than the Americans. The Israelis wanted him dead, Nasser wanted him dead, the Saudis wanted him dead, the Palestinians flooding his small country with their refugee camps of shacks hammered together from tin barrels and license plates and advertisements for Coca-Cola wanted him dead, or at least wanted his crown for themselves. Who could help him pick his way through this minefield?

> *"Say, God is One, the eternal God*
> *Begetting not and unbegotten*
> *None is equal to Him . . ."*

The King bowed from the hips, hands on his knees. He decided, then, whimsically, almost hopefully, that what the Americans were offering him, besides intelligence, was money, money to replace the thirty million dollars per annum that the British were withdrawing and without which the King, his country, his people, would be doomed. He knew that the Americans would expect something in return for their money, as the British had done before them for nearly thirty-eight years. The next question, then, was, What did they want?

"I extol the perfection of my Lord the Great."

He straightened, eyes closed.

"Allahu Akbar."

He sank gently back to his knees, placed his hands on the ground, his nose and face also to the ground, repeating the invocation.

"Say, God is One, the eternal God
Begetting not and unbegotten.
None is equal to him."

He rested back on his haunches, pronounced the credo, glancing over his right shoulder.

"Peace be on you and the mercy of God."

Over his left shoulder.

"Peace be on you and the mercy of God."

"What I often wonder is how the King survived at all," my mother said, coming out of her kitchen carrying little Italian cakes on a plate, which we dipped into our tea. "Did you know that someone once poisoned his toothpaste?"

"Who?" I asked.

"I don't know. Your father never found that out. He thought it was the Israelis, but he couldn't prove it. Not that anyone really cared. Not yet."

"How did the King know?"

"What?"

"That his toothpaste had been poisoned. I mean, it seems to me, if you're brushing your teeth, by the time you figure out the toothpaste's been poisoned, it's too late to do anything about it. Pretty much a gargle-and-die type of situation."

"A little bit fell from the tube onto the edge of the sink and immediately ate through the enamel. Don't be so glib."

The March sun that morning in 1958 was well into the pale blue sky by the time the King left his grandfather's mosque and returned across the garden to the palace. He stopped to examine the new irrigation ditch he had ordered Yusuf, the palace gardener, to dig. It ran the length of the garden, less than a foot deep, soil dark from the fresh water recently absorbed. The sun, hot already, beat down on the King as he stooped and studied a straggling line of ants working its way across the ditch and into the damp shrubbery beneath the fig trees. Though a king, he felt that morning no greater than an ant, struggling blindly along through an obstacle course of arbitrary and meaningless impediments. He stood, squinting toward the back wall, where he could see Yusuf pruning the oleander trees, and softly cursed himself, his weak, adolescent fearfulness. He had no father to help him, not anymore; his father was dead with a bullet hole in his head; his grandfather was dead on the via Veneto, his last sight on earth a bright red-and-white Cinzano ashtray that toppled from the tin-topped table as he, and it, tumbled to the pavement. Three tables away, Federico Fellini, sipping espresso, heard the commotion and glanced up to see three freelance news photographers rush toward the crumpled body and start snapping pictures in a flashbulb-popping frenzy; he saw the exiled King; he saw his bodyguards chasing away the photographers, and felt, beneath the irascible surge of curiosity, a deeper, more exultant stirring: *La Dolce Vita* (1960). Just a footnote.

The King stood there a moment longer in the harsh sunlight, shading his eyes with his hand and watching Yusuf prune the oleander trees, deliciously postponing the real start of his day. He knew only that he was alone.

Basimillah il Rahman il Rahim.

In the name of Allah, the Compassionate, the Merciful.

2

O n the famous afternoon my mother first tried to explain shepherd's pie to Eid, his eyes dull with something like panic as he tried to comprehend the concept of such a thing, my father walked into the kitchen, dressed in one of his three identical gray suits, home early from work. My mother, startled, practically jumped. My father never came home from work until it was dark. He was often the last to leave the embassy, except for devoted Renee.

"Mack, are you all right?"

He glanced at her, distracted. "Can we talk?"

He cocked his finger, nodding outdoors, and she followed him into the patch of dirt behind our house. The ever-present workmen were in the field beyond the wall, *tap-tap-tapping* chisels into stone, a Sisyphian task that was starting to grate on my mother's nerves. My father had brought her here because he assumed, he had to assume, he had reason to believe, that our house was bugged. He proceeded to tell her of Ambassador Burdick's sexual indiscretion, sparing her the visual details, the photographs themselves, but not the intent, the inclination. She stared at my father, shook her head, lit a Chesterfield. "Tyler?"

My father nodded, lighting his own Chesterfield. "Tyler."

Any gesture, in 1958, unaccompanied by the lighting of a cigarette, was, by common cultural consent, not authentic. A dove cooed plaintively, palpitantly, in a tree next door.

"Have you told Milton?" my mother asked.

"No."

"Anybody?"

"You. That's all."

This was, they both knew, a sticky wicket. They spent the next several hours kicking it around. It was inevitable, it seemed to my father, at the time, that sooner or later the news would get out, become public, an embarrassment. The Arab boys, the photographer, the photographer's girlfriend, brother, pal, whoever developed the photographs, anybody in Major Rashid's office, Rashid himself . . . Worse, before it became a public issue, a problem of perception, which at least had the virtue of not being real, any one of these same participants could leverage for themselves something along the lines of blackmail. That was conceivable, even though my father's sense of the Ambassador was that he was an honorable man, because my father also knew that it was always and everywhere unwise to submit anyone's honor to certain tests, foremost among them survival. That just wasn't fair. But my father also knew that if he submitted the photographs, the information, the implication, to Milton, no matter how discreetly, the Ambassador would inevitably be ruined, his wife would inevitably find out. For some reason he did not fully understand or even question, my father liked Tyler Phelps Burdick III. The question remained, however: What to do?

"Go see Tyler," my mother suggested. "Alone."

They had moved to the downstairs bathroom by now, the one next to their bedroom, and they were sitting on the edge of the tub with the shower curtain closed behind them and the shower itself flowing full blast to drown out their voices, because, again, remember, the house was bugged, everything they said, everything we said, was recorded and listened to; that was the assumption, that had to be the assumption, though no one told me about it because it was assumed I had nothing to betray. That's how I found them, that afternoon, coming home from school with a full bladder, dropping my books in the living room and running straight to the downstairs bathroom, flinging open the door to see them both sitting there, on the edge of the tub, smoking Chesterfields, the shower hissing, their faces flushed and sweating, steam and tobacco clouds billowing out into my face.

This was one of the moments that suggested to me, even then, that there was something odd about my family.

About my father.

About what he did.

According to my mother, who I guess can be trusted, my father decided to approach the Ambassador by simply showing up, unannounced, at his residence. He did so that night. A servant wearing a starched white coat answered the door, showed him in. Mrs. Burdick appeared first, offering him a warm smile, accepting his apologies, leading him to the study and waiting with him until the Ambassador showed up, fresh from a shower, scrubbed and glowing. Then she politely withdrew, pleading domestic duties, and left my father and Ambassador Tyler Phelps Burdick III alone in the study.

"Drink, Mack?"

"Please."

"Martinis sound about right?"

"I wouldn't say no to a martini."

My father never said no to a martini in his life.

The Ambassador rattled around at the bar, pouring, shaking, all the while keeping up a pleasant drone of inconsequential yak: a leak in the embassy plumbing, the dreaded arrival of a visiting congressman next week, the Ambassador's ceaseless lobbying for more money to help Kurashian farmers, all twelve of them . . .

"Here you go, Mack." The Ambassador handed my father a martini, lifted his own in a brief toast.

They drank, settled in green leather chairs.

"So, Mack, is this about our little heart-to-heart?"

For a moment my father went completely blank. He had no idea what the Ambassador was talking about.

"Is there something I should know about that I don't know about? I'm speaking, of course, about the fucking facts."

And then my father remembered, their talk here in this study three months ago, the Ambassador's meaty hand firmly planted on his shoulder, the squeeze of authority, asking, ordering, him, my father, to be his, the Ambassador's, own personal spy. He had forgotten the meeting, pushed it aside, knowing it was never going to happen, he would never stoop to being a State Department informant, and yet here he was.

"Actually, yes, there is something you should know about."

Puzzled, the Ambassador watched my father stand and cross to the hi-fi, arbitrarily pick a record, Frank Sinatra's *Only the Lonely*, put it on the turntable, touch needle to vinyl, ease the volume knob upward, then return to the Ambassador and draw his chair closer. A sudden beaming smile illuminated the Ambassador's freshly scrubbed face.

"You fucking spooks, you really do this kind of shit, don't you? Hot damn."

He happily slapped his knee. Up close, he smelled of Ivory soap and aftershave.

It was a strange attitude, my father leaning close, as if to whisper in the Ambassador's ear, and yet speaking at a normal level, his words lost to the world within the swelling sadness of Frank Sinatra's late-night lament. Perfect security.

It's quarter to three, there's no one in the place . . .

The Ambassador's face shifting from conspiratorial chuckles to confused bafflement to crimson shame to stone-cold stillness, listening, tilted toward my father, listening, absorbing, the bones in his big proud body going liquid, everything pouring out, leaking, escaping, evaporating. He sagged in his green leather chair, watched my father pull the envelope of photographs and negatives from his suit pocket, watched the flame of my father's Zippo ignite the evidence, the proof, the charges, black-and-white blurry limbs curling into embers, bright blue opaque film flaming in the ashtray Kathy Burdick had filched from the King George Hotel in Beirut last winter. His life.

He resigned that week, citing health reasons, retired with his wife to Guilford, Connecticut. He taught one semester a year at Yale, a seminar in third-world diplomacy. He wrote his memoir, *Cold War in a Hot Place,* published to some acclaim by Random House in 1961. He served on the board of directors of several corporations, including Revlon, Westinghouse, and Texaco. And then he disappears from the public records.

So set 'em up, Joe . . .

Parties were thrown almost every weekend that year, 1958, afternoon barbecues or cocktail parties or charades with buffet or sit-down dinners in candlelight. As full spring grew closer, riper, a moist heaviness came in on the desert air, like a hint of the distant Mediterranean far across the Kurashian plains, the craggy hills of northern Lebanon, cedars rooted to rock that once looked down upon the red sails of Phoenician boats. When the wind shifted to the east, it brought with it the amber dampness of Iraqi marshes, too ripe, spoiling, the harsh, pitiless decadence of the Tigris and Euphrates, plump pomegranates spilling their glistening seeds upon the sand.

We went down to the Hut, Friday nights, Carolyn and Penny Sweetser and Chipper Gourlie and myself, across the embassy garden.

Put your head on my shoulder, whisper in my ear . . .

The sound track of our lives, inner and outer, was decidedly American that spring. 1958. The children of spies. We formed our own special corner of the Hut, across from the others, separate from the others, drawn hence by what force, what distinction, what self-consciousness, I cannot now say, but there we huddled, proud and insecure all at once. When I broke the circle, when I stepped out and approached Carter Greenway, eleven-year-old daughter of the economics officer, and asked her to dance, when I returned from our squeamish, hesitant fox trot, nervous sweat granting me an embarrassing, premature mustache, I was welcomed back like a traitor, silence greeting me in the eyes of Carolyn, of Penny, of Chipper.

Renee, in desperation, increased her intake of vodka to three stout glasses a night, and yet she still could not sleep, the Penguin mysteries blurred before her eyes, the records spinning on her record player made no more sense than any other scratchy cacophony, say a ten-car pileup, or the breaking of a thousand bottles in the great alley behind the one true bar in heaven, the interior of which she more than glimpsed, worn leatherette red booths and dim lights and a leering paternalistic jukebox winking at her from the end of the room, near the pay phone, the bathroom door. She took the Marine Guard, Sal, as a lover, briefly, because of course, once sated, he left her, crawled from the window and greeted her the next day at work as if it had never happened, as if he had not removed her clothes and roughly clasped her untouched body, her nipples so eager she convulsed in orgasm the first time his tongue, thick with beer, touched them.

Roy and Barbara Sweetser took a ten-day trip to Venice, their first leave in three years, and my father realized with some ruefulness that it was hard to tell that Roy was gone, there was no appreciable difference at work. Or so he told my mother. The Sweetsers sent a postcard, a reproduction of a Carpaccio painting, Saint Jerome in his study, visited by invisible illumination, watched by his cat. My father and Milton put in fourteen-hour days. Using a *Baltimore Sun* correspondent as a willing front, they rented a safe house on Jaffa Street, near the soccer stadium, swept it thoroughly for bugs, and there met on a regular basis with their pathetically few agents, focusing on Desert Rose. Of course Major Rashid knew exactly what they were up to, where, when, and with whom, but politely said nothing. The Soviets paid no attention to them; they were too busy leading the local Communist Party by the nose, eager university students, upper-middle-class Palestinians, children of doctors and lawyers involved in their own Oedipal, suicidal adventures. Nasser's agents, and there were many, some known, some unknown, existed in a twilight world my father could not penetrate, could not even get close to.

"It made him crazy," my mother said, remembering. She had taken me out to the beach on Plum Island and we were walking along the edge of small, frothy waves. Trees to our left offered armfuls of golden-yellow leaves for our admiration. Children in sweaters chased a dog across high dunes feathered by weedlike foliage. "He'd come home every night depressed and irritable, and we'd sit in the damn bathroom with the shower running and he'd tell me over and over how much he feared for the King's life."

With good reason, as it turned out.

A new ambassador arrived from Washington. Donald Muir. Forty-six years old, lean as a minaret, over six feet tall, career officer, Arabist, with a wife, Tootie, and a child, a daughter, at Brown. I remember him as a shy, vague figure in flannel pants and blue blazer smiling down at us from what seemed a great height. This was in May, Easter, egg-hunting on the embassy lawn, Hamra, 1958.

And my mother went to a wedding.

The wedding at which she met Kumait.

The wedding of Dina Husseini to Ahmad Dulak. My mother had been invited by Dina's mother, Hindi Husseini, and Kumait was there because he had been Ahmad Dulak's tutor in classical Arabic literature at the university. Mrs. Husseini and my mother had become friends through their work at the State Palestinian Orphanage, a collection of former barracks on what had once been a British Royal Air Force base ten miles outside of Hamra. Almost five hundred parentless, homeless children were housed there. They attended school, they played soccer on the dusty parade grounds, they prayed to Allah, and they waited, they dreamed, they prepared themselves for the day when they would return to the plangent fertile fields of Palestine, the shady orange groves of Palestine. Even as a kid I remember thinking, But where will all the Jews go?

Into the sea, into the sea.

"But that's not going to happen," my father would say, lighting yet another Chesterfield. "It's never going to happen."

"Why not?" Major Rashid would ask, prim and shy as a bridesmaid, on the sofa.

"Because Israel is a Western creation, the culmination of a Western problem, the historical solution to a Western problem, and the West will never let you or anyone else drive Israel into the sea."

"Then the Soviets will help us."

"That's bullshit, Rashid, and you know it. The Soviets will help you destroy yourselves, period. That's what they're good at. That's all they're good at."

"We cannot accept Israel as an uncontested fact," Major Rashid said, becoming somewhat heated, his face flushed and his hands anxiously picking at the crease of his careful wool pants.

"You're going to have to," my father responded, with his usual second-martini toughness, stern dad to idiot child.

At this point my mother would tactfully interject some piece of cheerful news, like: "I heard today that Duke Ellington's going to play in the Roman amphitheater."

Which he did, by the way, his piano right in the middle of what in winter had been the skating rink for the magical if hallucinatory Ice Capades, there in the Roman ruins, butts cold on hard stone seats. In our house, those nights, in the silence following my mother's diplomatic change of subject, Major Rashid would glower into his whiskey and my father would suddenly get petulant, racked with guilt because he had been too harsh with his friend, wielding the sword of logic a little too mercilessly, a little too unkindly. "Why would Duke Ellington ever come here for Christsake, Jean?"

"It's part of the USIS cultural exchange program," she replied calmly.

As if to prove it, as if, by foreshadowing his arrival she could guarantee Duke Ellington's eventual presence, my mother left her chair and crossed to the huge Zenith cabinet and put "Mood Indigo" on the turntable, and sure enough Major Rashid was soon tapping his polished toe with pleasure and my father, his head tilted back and his eyes on some distant Harlem Renaissance on the ceiling, was whistling along. They both loved Ellington, also Ella Fitzgerald and Thelonious Monk. I could always tell things had gotten really nasty, and Major Rashid was really frustrated, when I heard him hiss at my father: "How dare you lecture us, Mack. Just look at the way you treat *Negroes.*"

"In point of fact, my family lost eighteen men on behalf of the Northern effort in our Civil War, which as you may remember *freed* the Negroes." And then, depending on how much he'd had to drink, he might offer a final, telling riposte, one that also happened to be the truth: "Anyway, who are *you* to lecture *me*? The greatest slave traders in the world were *Arabs.*" Madagascar would then settle in the room like a shameful relative, hands covered in blood, and my mother would once again have to change the subject.

At the State Palestinian Orphanage, outside of Hamra, in 1958, children in clean white shirts lined up every day in rows under the staggering sun and sang songs about their lost orange groves and date trees and grassy riverbanks, their lost cool stone farmhouses with grape arbors and flower gardens and plashing fountains, flocks of sheep dotting the hillsides, the small bells at their luxuriant, fleecy necks ringing gracefully through the hypnotized twilight: *"I-am-not-lost, I-am-not-lost. . . ."*

All of the Middle East, in 1958, had a huge chip on its shoulder.

"Israel, like the United States, is living proof that even the greatest national achievements usually start with a crime, " said Kumait to my mother, later that day, the day of the wedding. "In your country, the Indians were in the way. Here, the Palestinians were in the way."

They were standing at one end of the large reception room, and had just been introduced by the bride's mother, my mother's friend, Mrs. Husseini, who had then wandered away to attend to the many servants and aunts and grandmothers working in the kitchen on, among other things, three lambs trussed and cooked whole. Kumait, slim and effortlessly elegant in his lightweight gray suit and white shirt, *sans* necktie, buttoned to the top, regarded my mother with a pleasant, noncommittal smile before announcing: "I know your husband."

"You know Mack?"

"Yes. Not very well, but I do know him."

She asked him where they'd met, and he told her, and she remembered my father's having described to her the neat, silent, thoughtful man sitting beside General Anwar the night he'd first visited Hamzah Palace.

"So you're a teacher at the university."

"Yes, sad to say."

"Why sad?"

"Because I have nothing of interest left to think or write or teach. I'm bored." He said this with an ironic sparkle in his eye, contradicting his own words, or at least not hating himself for his restlessness.

She liked him immediately, this small, dapper man at her side, a full three inches shorter than she, with his surprising rogue's grin and fine, graceful, almost feminine hands. They stayed together for the duration of the wedding, mostly watching, Kumait sometimes explaining odd rituals. My mother noticed, and Kumait confirmed, a fashion schism between the older women and the young women present, the former wearing tradi-

tional tribal robes, their heads covered, the latter cheerily rambunctious in chiffon and satin and pearls, Parisian dresses and
Italian high heels. Everyone drank fruit juice and nibbled pista-
chio nuts and small sweet cakes, admired the bride's recent
hairdo, a lacquered imitation of the grotesque jazzy bouffant currently in style Stateside. When the handsome bridegroom arrived,
much was made over him by the assembled celebrants; they rever-
entially touched his sleeve, his cheeks, greeting him.

"A terrible student," Kumait confided to my mother as they
watched Ahmad shake his new father-in-law's hand, casting a
quick, flashing smile toward the blushing Dina Husseini. "But a
very nice boy. A good heart. A big heart. He wants to be a doctor
and tend to the poor. I'm sure that's exactly what he'll do."

One of the older women, carried away by the excitement, let
loose with a startling, high-pitched warble, a quick vibrating
clucking of the tongue at the back of the throat, the ancient ululation
of desert women welcoming their men back from battle.
Kumait seemed a little embarrassed by this demonstration, this
reversion to the old ways, for when he glanced again at my
mother, his smile was gone.

About a week later, my mother called Kumait at his university
office. She asked him if he'd be at all interested in joining her,
Barbara Sweetser, and Tootie Muir on one of their excursions to a
neighboring *tell*, and then, halfway through the invitation, she
found herself apologizing, because, after all, he was an expert on
Kurashian antiquities and probably had better things to do than
spend the day with three well-intentioned but ignorant American
women. To which, laughing, he responded that no, in fact, he
didn't have anything better to do, and that if she would allow
him he would like to suggest a special destination, Qeseir Arbah.
Had she been there? No, she hadn't. Excellent. How about
el-Khirmeil? She hadn't been there, either.

A date was set, the ladies packed a picnic lunch, my mother
requisitioned Hussein and the bright red Chevy.

3

The drive to Qeseir Arbah, and thence to el-Khirmeil, due east across the desert following the old Roman road, took about an hour and a half. It was hot—the metal of the Chevy too hot to touch. Hussein kept the windows up and the air-conditioning blasting full. Sand leaked into the car, within minutes a fine mist of the stuff covered the dashboard, the red vinyl seats, their skin. My mother, Barbara Sweetser, and Tootie Muir shared the backseat, Kumait sat up front next to Hussein. He spent the entire drive facing them, his arm across the back of his seat, grilling them on, as he put it, the "history of our conquestations." He was surprised by how much they had managed to glean from the books they had read, though until he pointed it out my mother had never thought of Kurash's history in terms of conquests, but that, she realized, is exactly what had happened: first the Persians, then Alexander the Great, then the Nabataeans, the Romans, the Byzantine, the southern Arabian tribes of Muhammad, followed by the Crusaders and then four hundred years of Turkish rule, followed, finally, by the British—for two thousand, five hundred years Kurash was ruled by someone else. "It never ends," Kumait said ruefully, then with a quick, self-deprecating smile: "We have made politics of the art of friendship. We have had no choice."

"But surely that's over now," Tootie Muir said. "You're independent at last."

"I don't think so, my dear Mrs. Muir. No, sadly, I don't think so."

By which my mother, alone among the ladies in the backseat, took him to mean that the United States was playing the age-old role of regional bully. She took exception.

"Having an interest in an area is hardly the same as conquering it," she responded.

"If I am convinced that more than anything in the world I want a television, a nice red car like this one, a fine drip-dry suit, bottles of cold Coca-Cola in my new Westinghouse refrigerator, and if, to attain those things, that image of myself, I give up, I turn away from, I abandon my own life, my own culture, then I have been conquered, it seems to me, my dear Mrs. Hooper."

"That's a choice to be made or not. If you want, you can read nothing but ancient Arabic texts, ride a camel or a donkey or a horse, wear Bedouin robes, and drink rosewater."

"I'm afraid you're both getting a little above me now," Tootie Muir said, confused.

"They're having a political debate," Mrs. Sweetser chimed in.

"Oh. How rude."

Qeseir Arbah, their first stop, was a stone castle of mortared walls, stone and brick, built by one of the early Omayyad caliphs at the beginning of the eighth century A.D. While Hussein stayed by the car, smoking a cigarette, Kumait led the ladies through what had once been a hunting lodge and bathhouse, vaulted rooms arranged around a courtyard. "Most likely this was a springtime residence for princes who lived primarily in Damascus. Prone to sudden fits of nostalgia, missing the desert, they would come here to go hunting, to bathe and rest and amuse themselves with poetry, astronomy, philosophy, song, wine, and women." They stared up at ceilings decorated with paintings of dancing bears wielding musical instruments and plump, startlingly lifelike Rubenesque nudes.

A blanket was spread in the shadows cast by the domed castle, and there they ate hard-boiled eggs and cheese sandwiches. My mother watched Kumait as he entertained Barbara Sweetser and Tootie Muir, detecting now a disdain that she'd missed at first, hidden as it was by his charm and erudition and vague sexual allure, a mask, she thought, worn as effortlessly and elegantly as his dapper English clothes. Did he hate himself, she wondered, and was that why he hated them? Despite their having locked horns, briefly, on the subject of Coca-Cola colonialism, she continued to like the man, to be drawn to him, to sense something within him that could help her find her place here in the desert, in this strange, small corner of Arabia. At the same time, he, Kumait, circling my mother, resenting her placid American good nature and eagerness to please, perhaps even taken aback by her genuine desire to learn more about Kurash—he must have realized he was letting himself like her, admire her, and that to do so could be risky.

"So, what, you had an affair?"

"You have the mind of a journalist," my mother retorts, disdainfully tossing the word "journalist," the whole cheap, ironical concept, back over her shoulder, a nasty rebuke, a hand grenade.

She's on her way into the kitchen to check on the lasagna, vegetarian, of course.

"Sounds like a yes to me."

"We did not have an affair," she calls from the kitchen, clattering things around.

"But you were attracted to each other, right?"

"We liked each other. We respected each other." She reappears in the doorway. "We were friends."

"Mom, what did you do all the time while Dad was out peeping through keyholes?"

"I kept busy, don't you worry about me."

"How? Doing what?"

"Well, studying the culture, learning the language . . ."

"But weren't you lonely?"

"Yes, I suppose I was. But so what? Isn't everyone?"

I can sit here now and gaze down upon those two figures, Kumait and my mother, at a picnic in the desert in 1958, and shout aloud, "Go ahead, please, kiss each other. Make each other happy." But there's no point, they can't hear me, and anyway, they're both too well bred to break that particular rule. Instead, they said it all with imploding smiles as my mother offered a slice of apple to Kumait, held out on the blade of a knife, an offering of love such as she had once, on our way to Jerusalem, during another picnic, given to me.

El-Khirmeil turned out to be an ancient settlement built on the side of a dry *wadi* covered with basalt pebbles and boulders. Kumait pointed out an empty cistern, which he called a *birkeh,* and then showed them several small rooms made of stone that had inscriptions carved on their lintels. "These are cells, for monks," Kumait said. "This was a Christian monastic settlement, dating from the sixth century A.D. Here, look." He pointed to the inscriptions. "This is Arabic and translates, roughly, as 'In the name of God I made this cell.' That's a Maltese cross." He straightened, gazed around, eyes obscured behind sunglasses. "For centuries caravans stopped here for water. The monks lent aid to the travelers and tended to the sick."

Kumait then showed them, about a hundred yards away, several massive basalt slabs that were covered with what looked like graffiti, spindly scratches carved in the stone, childlike rock drawings of human stick figures and animals, oxen, birds. "These are prehistoric," Kumait said. "Thousands of years old. We know almost nothing of the people who lived here then."

My mother leaned closer, the heat suddenly intense, her head throbbing, sweat stinging her eyes, and stared at a rock drawing of a man and a woman in a seated position, holding each other in a tight embrace. A passion celebrated in stone, thousands of years ago. Lovers? Man and wife? Dizzy, my mother reached out and touched the stone, traced the fine lines with her fingers.

"Are you all right?"

It was Kumait, at her side, tentatively resting his hand on her elbow.

"I'm fine. Just a little hot."

"Sit down for a moment. Rest."

"No. I'm fine. Really." She pointed to circles surrounding the couple carved in the stone. "What's that?"

"Hard to tell, exactly. The remains of an older drawing underneath. There are layers of time, layers of art, each new generation simply adding their pictures to what was already here. They didn't save the old."

My mother was suddenly overwhelmed by something like pure joy as she glanced past Kumait to Barbara Sweetser and Tootie Muir, who were examining a nearby boulder, then to Hussein beyond them, small in the distance, leaning against the Chevy and patiently waiting. Evening was coming on, the air had a crisp clarity to it, everyone stood distinct with his own shadow in lucid attendance, each pebble and rock also with its own reflection, deep, motionless shadow. If there had been a bird around, a crow or a raven or a buzzard, it would have ceased flight, then, still as an echo, frozen overhead. But there was no bird. There wasn't a cloud in the sky.

Kumait asked again. "Are you all right?"

"Yes, yes, I'm fine, Kumait," she said, using his name for the first time, with a grin wide and unprotected. "Absolutely fine."

That's how it happened, there in that desert, at that moment, in 1958, to my mother, a healthy American pragmatist.

"An epiphany?" I asked.

"Sort of," she replied. "I guess."

We had been strolling along the Charles, the imposing red brick buildings of Harvard to our left, and were now sitting on the cooling grass and gazing out at the sculls skimming lightly over the water, a delayed *slap* reaching us each time the oars made contact, bright, evanescent sparkles of twilight.

"But what did you see? I don't understand."

"It wasn't what I saw, I don't think, it was the way I saw it. I just felt something, very clearly."

"What?"

"God?" She gave me a look. "Is that too corny?"

"Yes."

Have you noticed that my father was, is, damn near invisible?
I have. No matter how hard I try to see him there, in Hamra, in
1958, doing whatever it is he did, I can't quite get him in focus. He
really must have been a very good spy, a very good intelligence
officer. He barely exists, yet he's always there, lurking around
the heart of things, the first cop at the accident, the shooting, the
domestic dispute, as if he'd known it was going to happen, where
it was going to happen, when it was going to happen. Nothing
about him drew attention to himself, which is quite a feat when
you think about it. Not his close-cropped already-graying hair,
not his institutional tortoiseshell glasses, not his never-changing
outfits: suits-flannels-blazers-loafers. He wore a Timex wristwatch.
Milton was right, my father was good at listening, he liked to
listen, listening gave him the slight but all-important critical
distance he needed to Stay Aloof. Talking, he always felt, was con-
fessing, a messy affair. He preferred his monkish silence. "Gathering information," is the way he puts it: "That was my job, and I
was good at it." Notice the testy athletic posturing, as if one had
to be convinced that my father in fact was good at It, or that It
was even what he in fact did. The secret thing. Spying. According
to my dictionary (*American Heritage*), a spy is "an agent employed
by a state to obtain secret information concerning its potential or
actual enemies." Fair enough. God knows we've all got enemies.
It's probably a good idea to know what they're up to. In Kurash,
in 1958, while my mother was out having epiphanies, my father
and Milton and Roy and Renee were doing their best to figure
out what the Soviets were doing, what the local Communists
were doing, what the local Baathists were doing, what Nasser was
doing.

For example, when would Desert Rose bloom?

When was someone going to take a crack at the King?

Who might that someone be?

Gathering intelligence.

Sounds so innocent, doesn't it? Gathering intelligence . . .

I think the key to understanding what my father really did is to be found a little farther down in my dictionary, where it says that a spy is "one who secretly keeps watch on another or others."

Well, you can keep watch by hiding in the bushes and looking, or you can keep watch by *overseeing* "another or others." You can be someone's watcher, someone's handler, in which case your job is not so much to gather information as it is to control events.

Which brings us to that monthly briefcase full of crisp American dollars.

According to those recently published articles in the *New York Times,* the first delivery, to the King, by the unspecified C.I.A. officer, was made that April. April fifteenth. Tax day. 1958. The British had notified the King, through their ambassador, Sir James Straithorn, that Her Majesty's government could no longer keep Kurash on the dole. Her Majesty's government was itself broke. The shortfall Kurash faced would have been in the neighborhood of thirty million dollars. That's a lot of glue, as my father would say. Without which Kurash's nonexistent economy would completely founder.

Our foreign aid package to Kurash, if approved by Congress, would total approximately twenty-seven million dollars. This figure included the projected cost of men and material, advisers and tractors, to be ministered by A.I.D. and the State Department.

Question: Where would the other three million dollars come from?

Which brings me to the two things I learned from my mother this week.

The first thing I learned from my mother this week was that on the night of April 15, 1958, my father had come home from work carrying a locked briefcase that he made her sit and watch while he showered and changed. He then handcuffed it to his wrist, next to the Timex, and disappeared, only to return for breakfast. He did not tell her where he had been, a fact she noted, since he usually told her pretty much everything he did. She thought. When I asked her if there had been any meetings between my father and the King, that she was aware of, before my father disappeared with the briefcase handcuffed to his wrist and after that initial get-together at Hamzah Palace and later in the Syrian desert, she said yes, once.

"When?"

"I don't remember."

"Try, Mother."

"It was forty years ago."

"How long before Dad disappeared with the briefcase hand-cuffed to his wrist?"

She thought: "A week?"

"So maybe around April 7, 1958."

"Maybe."

The second thing I learned from my mother this week is that it had been my father's idea that she call up Kumait and ask him to join her and Barbara Sweetser and Tootie Muir on their *telling* expedition.

"Why?"

"He thought we'd like each other, that I could use a friend."

"That's it? That's all?"

"Yes. Don't be so suspicious."

And off she went down the produce aisle of Bread and Circus, noiseless traffic outside on Prospect Street leaving plenty of aural space for Cambridge Muzak.

> *Hey, Mr. Tambourine Man*
> *Play a song for me . . .*

4

The King approached his mother's quarters on the second floor of Hamzah Palace with a heavy heart. He had quarreled that morning with General Anwar and Prime Minister Sherif al-Hassan, and the encounter had left a tight knot palpitating in his stomach, a bitter taste of doom stuck in his throat. Passing an open window, he heard a dove coo, stopped for a moment, and gazed down upon the garden, Yusuf at work near the new irrigation ditch. Lucky Yusuf, he thought. One pair of khakis, torn T-shirt, bare feet. Moving from flower to flower, pleasantly lost in the minutiae of gardening, at ease among the ants and the doves. The King envied Yusuf, would happily, that morning, have exchanged places with him. Leaving the window, continuing along the hallway, the King, now irritated on top of everything else, irritated at himself for his ongoing lassitude, inertia, ennui, envy—the King suddenly felt the ghostly presence of his father and grandfather walking beside him. Indeed, they had both often walked this hallway while alive, on their way to visit their women, their wives. Now their invisibility seemed, to the King, accusatory; he felt mocked by the imaginary echo of their footfalls beside his own. He felt, as both Sherif al-Hassan and General Anwar had also made him feel, like a child, hopelessly inadequate. How was he, a twenty-two-year-old playboy with a puppy's mustache, supposed to know how to save his country? His father had walked this same hallway to visit the King's mother, his father's first wife, but also his second wife, who had lived in the east wing with her own set of servants and who had died, just in that room over there, while giving birth to a stillborn daughter, the King's mother holding her head and sobbing openly. The two women had been very close, and the King suspected that his mother's perpetual state of lugubrious widowhood had more to do with her lost partner in wifely duties than her dead husband. It was in this wing of the palace that the King himself had lived until he was ten, before his father pulled him out, taught him how to ride a horse and shoot a gun, and then sent him off to boarding school in England. He remembered that his father had usually summoned his mother to his own quarters when he'd felt the need for her, but that at times he could be heard approaching along this same hallway to his mother's rooms. Afterward, she would prepare him tea, put hashish in his pipe, listen as he spoke quietly of his troubles. Listen and, his father had once admitted, advise. His father with his two wives, his grandfather with his five wives . . . The King stepped toward his mother along the loud tile floor without a wife to his name, for which, he knew in advance, he would suffer during the coming visitation. His trepidation at seeing his mother was as much due to his dread of chastisement as it was to his creepy sense of intruding into his parents' private life, retreating into the bloody pulp and loins of his history.

He reached the outer door, knocked.

"Enter."

Beyond the door, his mother, a sixty-five-year-old woman wearing a loose black robe, looked up from her seat by the window and shot him a piercing, questioning look. She was smoking a pipe, and for a moment the King had trouble accepting that; he could not quite believe what his eyes were telling him. He stepped closer and saw that it was his father's hashish pipe.

"What are you doing?"

She ignored him. "Have you found a wife yet?"

And so, he sighed, it begins. "No."

"Have you even looked for a wife?"

"No."

"Do you have any intention of ever looking for a wife?"

"Yes."

"When?"

"Soon. Right now I have bigger problems to solve than where to find a damn wife."

He'd raised his voice, startling even himself. He lit a cigarette. His mother puffed on the hashish pipe. He sniffed—it wasn't the thick, moist Lebanese drug she was puffing, it was regular tobacco.

She saw him staring. "Nicotine for an old lady. A queen, ha-ha. A few puffs, that's all it holds. Not like you. You're going to kill yourself."

It was true. He smoked as many as three packs of Lucky Strikes a day.

"What's the matter?" she asked.

He sat down next to her, took her small, gnarled, arthritic hands, stroked them.

"Why do you stay in here all day long?" He gave her a smile. "Why don't you go somewhere, Beirut, Rome? Do you remember the time we all went to Rome and stayed in the Grand Hotel and I dropped water balloons out the windows onto people's heads?"

She was still watching him quizzically. "Your father wanted to turn you in to the Italian police when the management complained. Teach you a lesson, he said."

"Go to Rome. Stay at the Grand Hotel. Enjoy yourself."

"I never did feel comfortable there. People stare. I like it right here in these rooms." She looked around at her entire world, the thick rugs on the tile floor, the brazen, gold-leafed, faux Empire furniture that had seemed elegant thirty years ago when his father had imported it from Harrod's. Now, to the King, it all looked like the slightly shabby imitation luxury offered in any second-rate, third-world furniture store. It depressed him.

"Why don't you let me get you some new furniture?"

"What are you talking about?" His mother was horrified. "Your father gave me this furniture. When I die, you can pile it into a pyre and burn my corpse. Until then, it stays right here."

She placed his father's hashish pipe on the nearby olive-wood table and sat back, waiting for the King to speak.

"I don't know what to do." He felt so weak, confiding in a woman, and had to remind himself that his father had done so, too; he had confided in this very woman now patiently watching him with her head tilted thoughtfully to one side.

"About what?" she finally asked.

"The British are abandoning us."

He could see, in her eyes, that this was information difficult, if not impossible, to process. It was the British, after all, who had helped create the Hashemites as rulers of Kurash. It was the British who, for three generations, had sanctioned them and supported them and protected them, three generations of tall, chalky, mustached, starchly uniformed, prickly efficient administrators and advisers with a love for Arabic, the throaty roll and flow of the language, a love for the Bedouin, the bracing simplicity, the firm and fundamental code of honor that ruled the desert, a real love for the place, the people, all this and of course a keen feeling for British rule, Pax Britannica. He would, strangely, miss them.

"They've run out of money and the will to run an empire," the King said gently. "It's over. Now, I believe the Americans are prepared to fill their shoes. I believe the Americans have made a proposal to take up the slack."

"Money?"

The King shrugged.

"Enough to support us? As much as the British gave us?"

The King shrugged again.

"You have to find out."

"When I proposed that to Sherif al-Hassan and General Anwar this morning, they both scolded me like a child."

"Why?"

"Well, they each had slightly different reasons. Sherif al-

Hassan feels we must walk a balancing bar between the West and the East, between the United States and Russia, Capitalism and Communism. That we cannot commit ourselves too far in either direction. Otherwise we will be caught in their war and destroyed. Sherif al-Hassan is a practical man. His are practical objections."

"And General Anwar?" his mother asked.

"General Anwar feels that it's a question of destiny, and honor. That we must align ourselves with Nasser because only Nasser can offer a Third Way, an Arab Way. He feels that the United States wants nothing more than to subjugate us and support the Zionists in Israel. He feels it would be a profound betrayal on our part to accept American subsidy."

The King stubbed out his cigarette in a small brass ashtray on the table, immediately lit another.

"So they don't want you to take money from the Americans."

"No."

"Where do they suggest you get the money if not from the Americans?"

"A little from the Americans, a little from the Russians, a lot from Nasser."

"Nasser doesn't have any money."

"I know."

"And the Americans won't pay you for only part of your friendship. Nor will the Russians."

"I know that, too."

"You cannot play a coquette, flirting with both sides, committing to none. Sooner or later your suitors will get angry and crush you." She picked up the empty hashish pipe, put it down again. "What is Sherif al-Hassan thinking?"

Once again, the King shrugged.

"What about Nasser?"

"There is a man I trust, a Major Rashid of the Intelligence Service, and he tells me that Nasser can only offer Nasser's Way."

"What is General Anwar thinking?"

This time the King lifted his hands, palms upward, tucked his head slightly and jutted out his lower jaw, then shrugged, a gesture as old as the *souk*. He was aging before his mother's eyes, atavistic resignation welling up within him, and he knew it, which made him feel even older.

"First of all, don't trust the Russians. That is what your father always said. The Russians and the Turks."

The King lit another cigarette.

"Second of all, don't listen to Sherif al-Hassan and General Anwar. Clearly they are idiots."

"But if I align myself with the Americans, I align myself with the colonial powers, the Europeans, not our Arab brothers."

"Let me tell you a story. In 1926, when your grandfather Ali was king, the Wahabis looked north from the desert of southern Arabia and saw his fields of fruits and rows of growing vegetables and decided to take them. They invaded our small country. Our *brothers*. As they advanced toward Hamra, other Bedouin tribes, more *brothers,* smelling blood, joined them, until finally there was no one left to stand with your grandfather except the Desert Legion and of course his Circassian bodyguards. The Desert Legion was commanded by an *Englishman.* Colonel D. Anthony Parson. Colonel Parson never even considered abandoning your grandfather. It was the *British* who helped your grandfather Ali drive the Wahabis back into the desert. So remember this: Your brothers would as soon see you dead as embrace you. Maybe the Americans today will stand by you as the British did your grandfather."

The King remembered this story well, though he hadn't heard it, or even thought about it, in years, not since he was expelled from these same rooms to study with his father and grandfather. Ali liked to sit in the garden in the evenings, drinking tea, and it was there that he told the future King stories about Hashemite history, including this one. In 1926, no longer young himself, Kurash a British protectorate, Ali had advanced with Colonel

Parson against the thousands of Wahabi warriors streaming across the desert toward Hamra, a great camel army heralded by the fluttering red-and-green banners of the Ikhwan and afloat in a great seething moil of swirling desert sand that could be seen from miles away, an approaching apocalypse. Colonel Parson and King Ali, besides several hundred well-armed, brave but terrified men, had at their disposal one aircraft and two armored cars secured from the Royal Air Force base near the Hamra airport. The airplane dropped stick bombs along the front lines of the Wahabi troops. The armored cars swooped down from the nearby dunes, machine guns spitting bullets into the encroaching camels. The battle lasted less than fifteen minutes before the Wahabis retreated in disarray, leaving behind the bloody corpses of four hundred fellow tribesmen. Another five hundred were taken prisoner. The Wahabis never invaded Kurash again.

The King decided he would meet with the American, Mack Hooper, my father. Tonight. Sherif al-Hassan and General Anwar could go fuck themselves.

A huge weight lifted from his shoulders, the King brought his mother's hands to his lips and kissed them gently. She demurred, the habit of a lifetime, withdrawing her hands and kissing them, then folding them quickly within the folds of her black robe. Her look, when she cast it upward upon her son, was shy, loving.

5

Alone in my mother's apartment, in Cambridge, near Harvard Yard, I went prowling, rifling through her books and papers, shelf by shelf, looking for clues or even mysteries, I didn't care, I just wanted a *clearer picture*. I'd forfeit, for the moment, meaning, context, understanding. Just give me a crisp snapshot or two and I'd be happy. Example: The King, after he left his mother in her wing of Hamzah Palace, went down to the garages, took out his Porsche Speedster, and sped through the gate before anyone could stop him, before any of his blue-eyed Circassian bodyguards could leap into their Land Rovers and follow him. He drove out into the Syrian desert at a hundred miles per hour. Ten minutes outside city limits, he saw a Mercedes truck hurtling toward him in the wrong lane, itself traveling at close to a hundred miles an hour. The King grinned. The driver of the truck was playing chicken, a favorite highway game of the Kurashians. Who would chicken out first and swerve aside? The King bore down on the accelerator, unflinching. Closer and closer the Porsche and the Mercedes truck approached each other, screaming across the desert. The Mercedes blasted its German horn. The King drove on. The Mercedes truck yodeled again. The King drove on. At the last possible second, in a deafening roar of down-shifting diesel, the truck veered away, swaying precipitously into the other lane, the ashen yet smiling gold-toothed driver glancing down, shocked when he recognized his young king shooting by in the other direction. Example: Back at the palace that night, the King, knowing he had a few hours before my father arrived for their meeting, called for a woman. He had several, stashed around Hamra. After some thought, he asked for the English girl, Esmerelda, a recent arrival who worked in a downtown travel agency. He'd met her at the Hamra Go-Cart Club one Saturday. She was about his age, lanky, small-breasted, far from the prettiest, but he liked her open-faced, lusty good nature, the simple honesty with which she applied herself to the task of granting him great physical pleasure. A phone call was made, a car was sent, an hour later she was ushered into his rooms.

"Hey, there, Your Majesty." She sashayed toward him, plopping her purse down on an armchair, that big friendly smile, shockingly lewd, playing across her pale glowing face.

"Hello, Esmerelda." They kissed, politely, cheek to cheek.

He poured her a whiskey, neat, as she preferred. They sat; she talked, he listened. Her seemingly simple young life was in fact unbelievably complicated, involving as it did an insane father in Bristol, a mother who had run away to Majorca with the wife of the next-door neighbor, a brother who was a commando in the Royal Army, numerous local suitors of various nationalities, and her own unerring instinct for trouble. By the time she had finished her stories and her second whiskey, the King was deeply aroused. Laughing bawdily, she pulled him to the bed, yanking off their clothes. "How I love to do it with a king," she chortled. Soon that rapt, studious expression told him she was beginning her thoughtful and tender ministrations. He lay back and let her.

I flipped through my mother's books of the period, 1958, hoping to find a matching note to the one I had found in my father's copy of *Travels in Arabia Deserta: O love, you could not know . . .* I found a receipt or two from the English Bookshop on Al Kifah Street. I found a shopping list written out in my mother's neat, childish block printing for Ahmed. I found the torn-off top half of a book of matches, advertising Halim's Happy Laundry, stuck as a marker at page seventy-one of *On the Beach.*

The phone rang. I considered it, then answered. It was my father.

"Is your mother there?" he asked in his deeply pitched, conspiratorial voice.

"No."

"Please remind her we have a date tonight."

"A *date*?"

"Yes."

"You guys *date* each other?"

"Yes."

"Where are you going?"

"The symphony."

"What are they playing?"

"Beethoven's Violin Concerto."

"Don't know it. I'm a rock-and-roll man myself. Care to answer any questions?"

"No, thank you."

He hung up.

April 7, then. 1958. One week before my father made his first visit to Hamzah Palace with the briefcase full of money. He was summoned by the King. A call came to him at his office, in the embassy. He had just lighted a Chesterfield and was enjoying the soothing onrush of death as it tingled his blackening lungs and coursed through his nicotine-addled body. He answered.

"Hooper."

"Good afternoon. This is General Anwar. His Majesty requests the pleasure of your company tonight. Ten o'clock. A car will pick you up. Where will you be?"

"Here. At work. The embassy."

"Fine." The phone clicked dead.

Summoned. My father contemplated the ash of his Chesterfield. Then he stood and walked over to Milton's office, knocked, entered. "He bit."

Milton, surrounded by pieces of paper, tense with the frustra-

tion he seemed to feel whenever he had to write field reports to
headquarters, looked up in a daze. "Who bit what?"

"His Majesty. Our bait."

"He did?" Milton sat up slowly, trying to feign some kind of
excitement. "He wants to see you again?"

"Tonight."

Milton settled back in his chair, hands clasped in that familiar
way behind his head. Roy Sweetser, in his office next door, heard
Milton and my father talking, once again an indistinct murmur,
and felt anew that pang of fear and jealousy. This time, however,
he was able to reason it away. Hadn't my father included him in
everything so far? Hadn't he even told Milton that he, Roy, was an
indispensable member of the team? Assuming assuredness, Roy
stood and wandered over to Milton's office, stuck his head casually in at the door. "What's up?"

"The King wants to see me," my father said.

"Wacko," Roy exclaimed, all energy and enthusiasm. "What's
next?"

"Mack visits him tonight," Milton told Roy. "Then we see."

"Milton, you should cable headquarters and verify the amount
I'm to offer tonight," my father chimed in.

"Right." Milton dragged a legal pad toward him and started
composing, calling out for Renee.

She appeared, bleary-eyed, beside hovering Roy.

"Renee, give this to Johnny and have him send it to headquarters," Milton said, ripping off a sheet of paper and handing it
to Renee.

Without a word, she left.

Johnny Allen took the paper into the code room, enciphered
it, sent it flying into space. Within an hour the answer came back.
Johnny glanced at it, whistled, handed it to Renee, who, still
without a word, took it in to Milton, who was by now sitting
with his feet up on his desk and his tie askew, chatting with my
father and Roy about Some Ideas He Had for snarking the Soviets. In particular he liked the idea of bringing American farmers

over to Kurash and letting them teach the Bedouin how to irrigate and plant, thereby showing the Kurashian masses that Americans had masses, too, to wit, farmers, and that they were smarter and more caring masses than the Soviet masses, who you never saw anyway, it was just their allocated henchmen you actually saw, Dimitri This and Vladimir That, sourpusses with three chins and vodka for sweat. My father was lost in the view from Milton's window, minarets and rooftops, a bright-colored sky punctured by thin, weak-kneed palms, black in silhouette. Roy was half asleep.

Milton took the cable. "Thank you, Renee."

He waited until Renee had left, for no good reason that my father could think of, then read the cable. He too whistled.

The ubiquitous black Mercedes picking my father up at the embassy might account for my not remembering him leaving, that evening, approximately nine forty-five. When he left from the house, I always watched him go, usually from my bedroom window. On the other hand, think what I've forgotten. He was driven directly to Hamzah Palace, escorted into the same room as before. There sat General Anwar, Kumait, the King, and, this time, Sherif al-Hassan, a cagey man in his early sixties who sat back behind his many plump wrinkles and waited for someone else to commit himself. My father noted the absence of Major Rashid, wondered if it signified anything, decided not. Kumait's fretful gaze was filled, or so it seemed to my father, with a lover's newfound curiosity, in fact he almost blushed, as if they now had, through my mother, an illicit personal relationship, which, come to think of it, is probably exactly what my father had hoped for when he suggested she contact Kumait in the first place. My father the spy. My father the intelligence officer. My father the collector of information. Not bad, Dad.

I call him at his condo, his condo overlooking Boston Harbor.

His gruff voice answers, clearing its throat: "Hello?"

"Was Kumait one of your agents?"

"Don't be stupid." *Click.* The phone goes dead.

To resume: Kumait glanced away, slightly red-faced, like a man introduced to his mistress in front of his wife, while General Anwar gave my father the evil eye. He was pouting. Sherif al-Hassan rose with considerable natural elegance and offered his soft, well-groomed hand. "A pleasure to meet you, Mr. Hooper. His Majesty has told me all about you."

The King, looking particularly boyish tonight, positively buoyant, laughed. "I hardly know the man, Sherif al-Hassan. He's as much a mystery to me as he is to you. Mack, please, sit. Whiskey?"

My father sat, nodded. "Thank you, Your Majesty."

A servant whisked away.

"How have you been since last we met?" the King asked cordially. But it was more than a polite question. He really wanted to know. My father wondered again at the King's gentle concern, the sadness he would feel if Mack Hooper had been having anything but a grand time.

"Splendid," my father replied, giving it a little British twist that he hoped might make the King feel at home.

And again, the radiant smile: "Good, good."

The servant returned, my father took his whiskey, enjoyed a good, hard pull, realized too late that he was the only one drinking. He put down the glass and didn't touch it again.

"Has Your Majesty given any more thought to our previous conversation?" my father asked, getting right to the point.

The four men exchanged startled glances. Kurashians were used to spending half an evening together before getting to the point. The King nodded to Sherif al-Hassan.

"May I take it you speak on behalf of your country?" Sherif al-Hassan asked my father, hooded turtle eyes barely moving.

"Yes, you may."

"When last you met, you said something to His Majesty about 'taking the place of our British cousins.' I believe those were your words."

"They were."

"Would I be correct to take that as an offer of help?"

"You would, yes."

"Military help?"

"Yes. Plus pertinent intelligence, as I mentioned to His Majesty."

"Financial help?"

"Yes."

"Enough to replace what we have lost due to the regrettable withdrawal of British assistance?"

"I think so, yes."

Once again Sherif al-Hassan, the King, General Anwar, and Kumait exchanged glances. Anwar leaned forward. The King lit a cigarette. My father lit a cigarette.

"How much?" Anwar asked.

"Thirty-two million American dollars per annum."

No one blinked. They considered that sum as you might consider a fresh avocado at the supermarket. Interesting.

"That should more or less cover your shortfall, if our information is correct," my father concluded.

"It is," Sherif al-Hassan said. "More or less."

For the first time he smiled. A small, possibly ironic smile, but a smile.

"Of course we also realize that you will need somewhere in the neighborhood of another three million to meet all your expenses, especially your regular payments to tribal leaders and the cost of maintaining His Majesty's office at an appropriate standard."

"Congress will approve the aid package?" Sherif al-Hassan asked.

"Yes."

"They will never approve the extra three million." General Anwar snorted. "The Zionist lobbyists will make sure of that."

My father laid down his trump card. "Congress doesn't have to approve. We'll take care of it."

"We?" It was Kumait who spoke. "You mean the C.I.A.?"

My father said nothing.

"In what form would we receive this extra money?" Sherif al-Hassan asked.

"Cash. Twelve monthly payments. Roughly three hundred thousand dollars each payment. I will personally deliver it to His Majesty the first week of every month."

That was it. My father had played his hand. He sat and waited.

"What would you expect in return for all this?" General Anwar asked.

Here came the hard part. "Very little. This is not a quid pro quo situation for my government."

"What, exactly?" Anwar pressed.

"Permission to discreetly build and maintain electronic monitoring stations along your northern border."

Everyone looked to the King. He lit another cigarette, nodded. My father lit another cigarette.

"What else?" Sherif al-Hassan asked.

"Permission to discreetly build and maintain a small air base in the Bswan desert. By small I mean large enough to handle Phantom jets and troop transport planes."

Anwar laughed, sardonic, bitter, angry. "A *discreet* air base?"

"Would we receive Phantom jets for our Air Force?" the King asked.

"No. But we will guarantee your protection with our Phantom jets."

Anwar shook his head, glared furiously at his glossy back shoes. Sherif al-Hassan gazed at my father unblinking. The King hesitated, nodded his head.

Sherif al-Hassan turned to him. "Your Majesty—"

The King motioned him to be silent. He then looked at my father.

"Anything else, Mack?" he asked.

"Yes. We would like to help you build up your own intelligence service. We would like to assist Major Rashid with money and training."

The King nodded, waited.

"That's it."

"That's it?"

"That's it."

The King smiled, offered his hand. My father shook it, a grin spreading across his own face, he could feel it.

One week later my father delivered the first briefcase of cash to the King. April 15, 1958. Deliveries continued on a monthly basis.

Using an American contractor, the air base was begun in the Bswan desert. By the end of April four monitoring stations were under construction along Kurash's northern border. Major Rashid, somewhat taken aback by the flurry of attention, suddenly had enough money to recruit ten new young officers, directly from the university or seconded from the Army. They were sent to Camp Perry in Virginia for a six-month course in the art of espionage. My father, Milton Gourlie, and Roy Sweetser kept careful track of their money's disbursement, as, for that matter, did the King. Besides being used to bolster the military and cover general governmental expenses, the funds were used to kick-start a much-needed antimalarial program and a water development project for the central plains. A hospital took shape in the center of downtown Hamra, several clinics were hastily thrown together in the provinces. Doctors arrived from the United States. Engineers arrived from the United States. The King personally approved business ventures proposed to him by petitioners with various, mostly wacky, ideas. A cement factory, a tannery, two canneries, a plastics factory, a battery factory, several tobacco farms, and, the King's own favorite, a pencil factory were all given the go-ahead in that first month. Most efforts failed, usually due to lack of experience. Some, including the pencil factory, succeeded.

Hodd Freeman reported all the good news to Allen Dulles,

who in turn told John Foster Dulles, if for no other reason than to cheer his brother up. John Foster was not feeling well— depressed, enervated. With the shining exception of Kurash, the entire world seemed to be continuing its downward spiral into godlessness and existential servitude. The story of the young King's compliance even made its way into President Eisenhower's morning briefing book, which he liked to read over cornflakes, fresh orange juice, and coffee, black. I've seen copies of that day's briefing. My father is praised, but indirectly, not mentioned by name.

The Hamra Go-Cart Club flourished. My father and the King and Rodney could be spotted there of a weekend, bent above their go-cart engines, tinkering thoughtfully. Behind them, the women, heads protected from the heat by bright Italian scarves, sat smoking cigarettes on picnic blankets while their kids, including yours truly, played disorganized soccer on the blazing hard sand.

My mother and Kumait returned to the desert, visiting more ruins, notably Tell el-Kharaq, featuring several Moabite stone fortresses, and the Nabataean tombs, temples, houses, cisterns, aqueducts, and altars carved into the sandstone cliffs of el-Meshffar. They explored the crumbled remains of what Kumait swore was a first-century A.D. monastery where holy martyred monks had once lived among the scorpions, where fragments of the New Testament had been found in clay jars, scribblings, memories, tall tales, hallucinations, dreams, nightmares, desires . . .

Stories of the holy man walking out from the desert to save the world . . .

Stories of the kind man with infinite love in his dark, crazy, melancholy eyes . . .

"They plotted, and God plotted. God is the supreme Plotter. God said: 'Jesus, I am about to claim you back and lift you up to Me. I shall take you away from the Unbelievers. . . .' "

My mother read the Koran, in bed at night next to my sleeping father.

"On that day of Resurrection the heirs of Paradise will be busy with their joys. Together with their spouses, they shall recline in shady groves upon soft couches."

6

Meanwhile, the law of inertia made itself felt with some force in the geopolitical fandango of the time. What passed for American foreign policy, cobbled together and set in motion by high-minded Protestants in an atmosphere of paranoid nostalgia, did not, would not, of its own accord, stop. Every day, all over Washington, throughout that spring of 1958, meetings were held to discuss ways in which Communism, by which was meant a conspiratorial evil force spreading across the globe like a creeping liquid black shadow in an old movie, could be stopped. Imagine doctors gathered together in emergency session to ponder a growing plague. That was pretty much the mood in those rooms. Everyone took himself very seriously. So when Nasser in late April of 1958 announced that Egypt and Syria had formed a pact of lasting friendship and dubbed this pact, portentously, the United Arab Republic, Hodd Freeman developed arhythmical heart palpitations. Doctors decreed that he'd suffered a mild heart attack. On their orders, he suddenly went from half a fifth of Johnnie Walker a night to zilch, and that almost killed him, sucked the spirit out of him, made him question the meaning and wisdom of life and hallucinate corpses along the side of MacArthur Boulevard as he drove to work in the morning. The Dulles brothers took one of their strolls, circumscribing the Reflecting Pool, by the Mall, ghostly figures with their nocturnal pall wandering unseen among the tourists. They had very little good information on exactly what Nasser was up to, the C.I.A. having failed in this regard, and so they were forced, they felt, to assume the worst, that this United Arab Republic was but a front for some devious, Soviet-inspired conspiracy to dominate the Middle East, destroy Israel, confiscate all Western oil syndicates, and in general gather together the howling unwashed hordes and unleash them upon us all.

The law of inertia said that action would be taken to counter this demoralizing trend.

The law of inertia said Fuck You to Nasser.

About this time my father had an interesting encounter with Leslie Smythe-Jones, outgoing head of local MI6, last seen in the bar of the Antioch Hotel. He caught up with my father at the American Club one Saturday afternoon less than a week before he was due back in London. Smythe-Jones was then in his early fifties, ruddy-faced, something of an intellectual, with an abiding interest in late-Nabataean culture. He collected artifacts and was a friend of Kumait's. They had even worked together on a monograph for the British Institute, one of the earliest attempts to systematize Nabataean linguistics. I was in the pool with Carolyn and Penny and Chipper, midway through a game of Marco Polo, when I happened to glance over toward my mother and father sitting under an umbrella at one of the poolside tables. They both wore sunglasses and were laughing. Leslie Smythe-Jones, Mr. Smythe-Jones to me, on the two occasions when we had met, approached my parents' table, a little shy, awkward in his peeling English skin, ridiculous in his khaki shorts and leather sandals.

"I say, Mack, could I have a word with you? Hello, Jean. How are you? The boy? Good, good."

Not listening, moving off with my father, leaving my mother alone at the table, all expression hidden behind dark glasses.

"Marco Polo, Marco Polo, Marco Polo . . ."

O to taste again the happy exhaustion of those afternoons at the American Club, brown skin sweet with chlorine and Coppertone, the heady fragrance of potato chips and burning imported cow flesh wafting over the sunburnt thighs of sharp-eyed, indolent mothers! O to gaze again upon the earnest dads in Bermuda shorts and madras shirts, hair scalped in severe militant crewcuts, as they chuckled together near bowls of salted peanuts at the bar!

"Well, Mack, I'll get right to it, I know that's the way you like things, close to the bone." Smythe-Jones rubbed his raw cheek, cracked a crinkly smile. "Take care of him." The smile vanished, replaced by an open, vulnerable look of total sincerity. "Please take care of him."

"Him?"

"His Majesty."

The King, of course. Until recently, Smythe-Jones had been his caretaker. Had been so since the King assumed the throne. Before that, for close to a decade, he had been the King's father's caretaker. Almost fifteen years of his life had been spent in this small hot desert country. A complex web of wrinkles now spread out from each eye, a permanent squint now creased his face, the legacy of those years. "Will you promise me that, Mack?"

"I'll do my best, Leslie."

"No, no, that won't do; that's not good enough. You must *promise* me."

This was a passing of the torch, my father didn't realize but I do, from one man to another, from one colonial power to another, there by the pool filled with squealing, splashing children.

"I promise," my father said, after some thought.

"Good. Thank you. I feel much relieved. It's your show now," Smythe-Jones went on, visibly grateful. "I understand that. I accept that. For all I know, you chaps will do a much better job than we did, though I doubt it. No, what matters to me now, the only thing I care about any more, is that the young lad be seen to properly."

"His Majesty?"

"His Majesty."

My father found it curious and moving that this man so clearly cared so much about his former ward.

"He's a good boy, Mack. A little rambunctious, of course. I'm afraid we did spoil him a bit, but a good boy and not stupid, Mack, not stupid. He's not as crafty as his father, I'll grant you that. In no way wily. But he's got a good head." Smythe-Jones respectfully tapped his balding pate. "Plenty of brainpower."

A glint of fear then slivered through my father's heart, for he saw in Smythe-Jones's kindly eyes a reflection of his own growing love for the King, and it scared him.

"One more thing, Mack." Smythe-Jones pulled a piece of paper from his pocket and handed it to my father. "You might remember Abdul Kilani. I introduced you at the Hotel Antioch bar not too long ago."

"I remember."

"That's his home phone number." Smythe-Jones nodded at the piece of paper. "Give him a jingle."

He straightened, glanced around, very much a man running down a list of to-do items and checking them off, one by one, so he could leave this place with a clean heart.

"Well, that's that, I suppose. Good luck with everything. Cheerio."

They shook hands and then Leslie Smythe-Jones walked away and out of my father's life forever.

Soon thereafter Johnny Allen handed a cable to Milton Gourlie. Milton read it, then read it again. He opened his office door and called in my father and Roy Sweetser. They sat facing his desk; he sat behind his desk, the cable spread out before him. He flattened it fastidiously several times. He was developing a small tic in his left eye, my father noticed, and glanced to Roy to see if he saw it, too. But Roy saw nothing, he was too busy trying to read the cable surreptitiously and upside down, to no avail. Milton cleared his throat.

Across town, the King was in his chambers with Army chief of staff General Anwar and Prime Minister Sherif al-Hassan. They had before them the full text of Nasser's statement announcing the creation of the United Arab Republic, in particular, buried amid the anticolonial Yankee-bashing rhetoric, the following: ". . . remembering especially the enmity we feel for those desert dogs the Hashemites, ruling despotically over our Arab brothers in Kurash, Iraq, and Jordan, doing the bidding of English and American warlords, who have armed them and advised them . . ."

Milton cleared his throat and one more time pressed his palms upon the open cable, moving his hands evenly outward, concentrated as a child on his task, lips pursed.

The King stopped reading Nasser's statement and looked up at Anwar and al-Hassan.

Milton stopped his ministrations and looked up at my father and Roy Sweetser.

"What is Nasser trying to prove?" the King asked.

"Washington wants us to, uh, create our own Arab pact," Milton said.

General Anwar was the first to speak. He proceeded very, very carefully. "Nasser wants to unite all Arabs under one banner. Syria has agreed to join him. That's all that's happened."

"Surely my good friend the general is understating the case." Sherif al-Hassan's lizard eyes barely flickered, but his words practically hissed. "Nasser wants to unite all Arabs under *his* banner, and with this treaty he has taken his first solid step toward achieving that goal."

The King was thinking about his grandfather chasing the Wahabis away from their dead and into the desert, his grandfather high on his horse and swinging wide his bloody sword and calling out praise to the One True God as the wounded lay dying at his feet and he showed no mercy. . . .

"What kind of new pact?" my father finally asked. "And with whom?"

"Arab solidarity, that kind of thing," Milton improvised, peering down at the cable with a gentle, puzzled look on his freckled face. "With Jordan and Iraq. The kings are all related, after all. Hashemites, don't forget. First cousins, am I right, Mack?"

"They hate each other, Milton. Their fathers hated each other."

"I will form my own pact," the King announced, startling Anwar and al-Hassan. "I will form a pact with Baghdad and Amman." His eyes flashed fury, quick, imperious, and dangerous. "The Hashemites led the great Arab revolt. The Hashemites are the leaders of Arab unity, not Nasser; Nasser's *not even an Arab.*"

He slammed his fist down on the table, smashing his coffee cup, sending his ashtray flying, ashes and cigarette butts scattering to the floor.

"My grandfather washed his face in his enemy's blood, and I will do the same."

When my father asked for a meeting with the King, when he got together with the King that week, the next day, in fact, such is the power of inertia, the King interrupted him before he could lay out the brilliant if incomprehensible Washington Idea with the news that he, His Majesty, the King of Kurash, had decided to form a pact with his Hashemite cousins, the kings of Jordan and Iraq, which, of course, in essence and detail, was the Washington Idea, so that all my father had to do was take a moment's deliberation before nodding assent, and then drive back to the embassy and announce to Milton the whole thing a done deal, *fait accompli,* nicely wrapped and delivered by hand, thank you very fucking much. Cables flew, a veritable flurry, between Hamra and Washington. At some point it was deemed wise to inform the Ambassador. Milton disappeared upstairs to do so. (Historical note: The Ambassador still had no idea that my father was secretly delivering to the King almost three hundred thousand dollars a month in a briefcase.) The King flew under cover of night to Amman, where he had to set aside his jealousy of King Hussein, and then to Baghdad, where he had to set aside his dislike of Feisel, and convince them both of the wisdom of creating their own United Arab pact, which they would call, they decided after some debate, the Arab Federation. Back in Hamra, Kumait was called in to help the King draft the announcement. Kumait was excited, Kumait was reluctant, Kumait was confused. Kumait agreed to help. At two in the morning the phone rang in our house and my sleepy father was summoned to the palace to read and comment upon the announcement. Coca-Colas were lifted in a toast as the sun rose, throats hot and hoarse from a thousand cigarettes. At noon that day, May 14, 1958, the King addressed a press conference in the palace, carried on national radio. "I wish to announce today the formation of the Arab Federation. . . ."

Within twelve hours President Eisenhower made an announcement of his own, this one informing the world that the United States was ready and able to stand beside any country in the world needing assistance to resist the forces of Communism. He then took a few minutes to praise the efforts in this direction of the kings of Jordan, Iraq, and Kurash and their recently formed Arab Federation. He specifically offered them United States largesse. The King and the Americans were now linked in the public mind.

The American Imperialists and the Hashemite Monarchies.

Radio Cairo hurtled invective across the Sinai at the King.

General Anwar seriously considered resigning. Instead, he called a friend he knew to work for Egyptian Intelligence. They met and talked.

Major Rashid was called to the site of this conversation by the officers he had tailing the friend who worked for Egyptian Intelligence. They called Rashid because they could not quite believe their eyes. The site was a roadside coffeehouse about sixty miles from Hamra. Rashid watched General Anwar exit the coffeehouse with the friend who worked for Egyptian Intelligence. He watched the two men embrace and get into their respective cars and drive back to Hamra. He lowered the binoculars. He had a headache.

At Kumait's weekly meeting with his favorite students, in his apartment on Nahas Street, there was no debate that night, no general discussion of the Role of Intellectuals in the New Arab World, instead there was only anger, and disillusionment, a deep and intractable sense of betrayal. Their king was resisting the forces of history.

Their king was subject to a greater force than history. Their king was subject to the law of inertia, about which young people know nothing.

7

WAITING for my mother to return with my father from the symphony, Beethoven's Violin Concerto, I sat in the small bay window and stared down at sluggish rusted traffic slicing through a sudden autumn rain on Mass Ave. There was a bar across the street I used to frequent in the early seventies, one of those railroad car places, long and narrow and dark, with a bar on the left, a few tables crowded together on the right, and, in those days, a tiny stage at the far end, near the bathroom door, where a group I then admired, Lothar and the Hand People, often performed. Were they any good? I wondered now. Who knows? Sitting in the bay window, pleasant memories returned of raucous evenings in the arms of various dangerously sloe-eyed coeds, down there where a current batch of patrons, three young men with retro-punk spiky hair, now stumble out of the bar and vomit on the sidewalk. In my time, a synaptical confusion so far back in our foreshortened history that it seems a quaint hallucination less real than World War II, in my time we were too stoned to get that drunk; I was, anyway, positioned in a corner of the bar, a superior vantage point for viewing lithesome undergraduates coming and going, puffing chastely away at a joint, sipping the occasional cold, cold beer, watching Lothar and the Hand People do their stubbornly midsixties thing on the tiny stage, already outdated, already mired in fleeting, crumbling, imploding historicity, their thin flowered hands waving them away into darkness and oblivion. Where were those dancing coeds now? Fifty-year-old women scattered about these greater United States, busy on a thousand thousand errands, existential and otherwise, everyone pulled apart, flung from the bar down there on Mass Ave like fragments of exploding nebulae spinning out into black, cold, meaningless space. Everyone waving goodbye, passing out souvenirs, childhood photographs . . .

I rummaged around in my mother's kitchen, rooted among the health food grains and vegetables for something damaging. . . . Ah, fair *vino,* a nice Chianti, shades of Hannibal Lecter. I am, after all, dismembering and devouring the past. I unscrewed the cork, poured a generous glass, paced the small apartment, sipped the drink of the gods feeling less than godly myself.

Any good theory of history would have to include the notion that we can never really know anything, that life is lost as soon as it's lived, that even as we eagerly move forward through one frangible certainty after another we're forgetting each one as it shatters behind us, our wake of broken glass, detritus, junk.

The same wake where, if we poked around long enough, we might find the corroded remains of the King's Corvette, his father's splintered hashish pipe, a little oil painting of midday weekend Hamra that my father had picked up somewhere and left propped in a corner of his so-called study, where I would of an afternoon sit and ponder the misty heat-induced pastels— beige, green—shimmering up from Wadi Rum.

The same wake that washed to shore the lost objects of unknown cities out in the desert where my mother and Barbara Sweetser and Mrs. Gourlie searched in the heat like treasure hunters, objects now arrayed on a shelf in my mother's small apartment on Massachusetts Avenue. I bent and peered, Chianti in hand. Perfume bottle? A dove? Clay bowl? No way to tell, that's the point, and even when we think we know, no way to tell what it was like to be the woman who raised that perfume bottle to her neck two thousand years ago, thinking in a language we no longer remember of a man, or a woman, blinked out in time and history like a dead star.

We cannot know. We do not know.

I was on my third glass of Chianti and well beyond saving, in the full grip of this meditative funk, when I heard the key at the front door and looked up to see my mother, giggling like a schoolgirl, enter and call back out into the hallway: "Call me tomorrow."

I pounced, drunkenly, leaping over the couch, knocking a lamp to the floor, yanking the door all the way open, and collared my surprised father, dragging him into the apartment, slamming the door closed, and standing there, my back to the door, panting, determined, and slightly dizzy.

"How was Beethoven's fucking Violin Concerto?" I asked, or mumbled.

"Lovely," my mother said, watching me curiously.

My father had his back up, ready to fight. I addressed him.

"Why won't you talk to me?"

"I told you. When I swear before God to do something, then I godamn well do it."

"I'm your son."

"So what?"

"You're supposed to confide in your son. Share secrets. Not hide everything from him."

He looked suddenly tired. I could tell that he missed, once again, maybe always, at moments like this, his beloved cigarettes. He absently patted his pockets, searching for something that was no longer there. He looked around, as if he might have misplaced them somewhere. "Why don't we all just have a drink and call it a night?"

"No drinking for me. I'm going to sleep. Good night, darling." She kissed my father. "Thanks for the symphony."

She turned to me and graced me with one of her friendly smiles, forgiving, almost bemused. "Good night, dearest one."

She vanished, an apparition, into her bedroom, closing the door behind her. My father and I regarded each other, then he headed for the kitchen, came out with the bottle of Chianti and a glass for himself. Without a word, we both sat, assuming positions at either end of the Baghdad couch, my father pouring wine into his glass, my glass, then settling back against those hairy, prickly, uncomfortable Bedouin pillows and giving me another long look.

"One question. That's it."

"Did you or did you not carry a briefcase filled with money to the King on the first week of every month in Hamra in 1958?"

"Forget it." He sipped his wine.

"Was it or was it not your job to handle the King and make sure he did pretty much what we wanted him to do, in Hamra, in 1958?"

"He was my friend. I spent half my time *not* doing what the blockheads in Washington wanted me to do."

"What is it exactly that you *didn't* do?"

"Try another question."

"What was your interest in Kumait?"

"Next."

"Fuck you, Dad. You're not answering anything."

"My prerogative, remember?"

"Tell me about the riots."

"Riots?"

"May 16, 1958."

He stared into his empty glass, refilled it, finishing off the bottle.

"All right," he said.

Virgil, in the *Aeneid,* employs a simple metaphor to describe the way rumor spread among the population of Carthage: wind rippling across a field of wheat. So it was, according to my father, with the riots of May 16, 1958, in Hamra, Kurash—a riot being, after all, a rumor of revolution, an impromptu, anticipatory excitement preceding the storm. A mild spring breeze gathered force until it was a gale bending the strongest date palm to the ground. It started in the Bakr District, among the slums of displaced Bedouin and exiled Palestinians, a trickle of angry noncitizens making their way from their mud and tin hovels carrying crude, homemade signs calling, in vivid dripping reds, for the dismemberment of the King. Behind them, in the single, kerosene lamp–lit, low-ceilinged rooms where they lived, radios tuned to Radio Cairo spit out venom like a deranged Greek chorus: "The King's Arab Federation is a Monarchist Imperialist plot to subvert the will of the People. The King is an American spy, the King works for the Israelis, the King steals the flowers of Arab maidenhood and subjects them to copulating with dogs and horses, the King smokes hashish and applauds, his pudgy little clapping fingers atwinkle with priceless jewels as profligate gifts are showered upon him by American and British oil corporations, the King spits on the People, the King drives his fancy Rolls-Royce while you languish destitute and debilitated. . . ."

From this initial series of indignant, hot-faced puffs the breeze spread, gathering force in the narrow, cramped, crooked alleys of the Bakr District, breaking out into the open air of Faisel Square, gathering more force from the unemployed workers milling on the sidewalks who joined the angry, chanting procession, the breeze now a roaring wind as it swept up more and more people into its inevitable flow toward Hamzah Palace and the American embassy.

The law of inertia at work once again in the name of history.

About which we know nothing if we were not there, and even then we know only random fragments.

My father was there, on his way home from work, when he saw the mob approaching from the far end of Al Said Street. For a second, he hesitated, torn between the desire to get home and make sure my mother and I were all right and turning around to warn the embassy. He decided we were probably safe, spun the Opel into a U-turn, and sped back through the embassy gate, jumping out of the car and telling the Desert Legion guards to close and lock the gates behind him. To nervous Sal, the Marine Guard on duty, he reeled off instructions: Get all the Marines up on the roof, fully armed, pronto. He raced into the C.I.A. offices, instructed Renee and Johnny Allen to start shredding everything they could get their hands on. Renee blanched and solemnly got to work. Johnny disappeared into the code room. Milton and Roy hurried from their offices, rushed to the roof with my father as he explained the situation. They were joined by the Ambassador, who gazed down at the encircling shrieking mob with admirable equanimity.

"Do we shoot?" he asked, with what seemed like idle curiosity.

That's when my father realized the Ambassador wasn't just preternaturally calm, he was in shock. My father put his hand on the Ambassador's shoulder and said, "Sir, I think we should call for help."

"Yes, of course, right away." The Ambassador turned to Chester Boyden. "Chester, get some help over here."

Chester disappeared downstairs as the first volley of rocks hit the embassy with a loud clatter. Everyone ducked and took cover. Down below, in the street, the crowd surged against the gate, people were crushed, trampled underfoot, teenagers ripped up the pavement and flung chunks of concrete toward the embassy. The women, many of them hidden behind black veils, clucked their tongues in that high-pitched wail, desert salutation, desert lament. Some young men hoisted one of their own up onto the wall surrounding the compound. Sal tossed my father a frantic, ashen look. "Fire, sir?"

Before my father could answer, before he could even decide, before he could even decide if it was his decision to make, they all jumped at the repeated loud staccato sound of gunfire. The Desert Legionnaires had opened fire, the young man on top of the wall tumbled back into the arms of his friends, a sack of blood. The wailing reached higher, became more frenzied, insistent, rage sending the mob in a concerted charge against the gates again, the gates this time bending inward, sagging dangerously on their hinges. The Desert Legionnaires fell back a few paces, assumed firing positions, their officer, a man in his twenties, wild-eyed, laughing as he bellowed orders.

My father lit a cigarette, inhaled as if it were his last. Nicotine lucidity swelled his heart with the jagged illusion of well-being.

I couldn't help interrupting: "Were you worried about us?"

"What?"

"Were you worried about me and Mom?"

It took him a few seconds to process the question. "Why are you always asking me that? Of course I was worried about you. But I wasn't exactly in a position to do anything about it. Right?"

Right.

At Hamzah Palace, less than a mile away, the storm had also reached the outer gates, closed now against the mob, Desert Legionnaires holding position but not yet firing. On the roof of the palace, the Circassian Guards set up machine guns and contentedly prepared themselves to go to heaven. Dying for the King would be a pleasure, an honor. Pity that crowd if it broke through the gates.

The King gazed down at the roiling mayhem outside his palace from a second-story window. He was dressed in his army uniform, had hurriedly strapped on his pistol. He too lit a cigarette and, in the momentary rush of his own delusional narcotic calm, contemplated his situation. He could feel Sherif al-Hassan standing beside him, saying not a word, also watching the riot below. Behind al-Hassan, for the moment silent, stood an impatient Colonel Bitar, General Anwar's second-in-command. The phone rang. Sherif al-Hassan answered, listened, grunted, hung up.

"Lieutenant Kamal reports that the mob has started burning and looting on Al Kifah Street. He also reports that his police officers are powerless to stop it."

"Where is Anwar?"

"We can't find him."

"Let's just hope these people don't find him before we do," the King said softly. His eyes looked purple, bruised with fatigue and worry. He crushed out his cigarette in an ashtray, immediately, thoughtlessly, lit another.

The phone rang again. Sherif al-Hassan answered again. He listened, replaced the receiver. "They're scaling the walls of the American embassy. Desert Legionnaires have fired on the crowd, killing at least one. The American Marines are on the roof and preparing to fight."

Colonel Bitar spoke up. "Your Majesty, my troops are ready to move. Please give me the order."

"Not yet, Colonel Bitar. Not yet. We must wait for Anwar. He is my chief of staff."

"Your Majesty, I humbly suggest we don't have the time to wait."

The King whirled on him. "I say we will wait and we will wait."

He paced away from the window, indecision making him slow-witted, thick-limbed, cotton-mouthed. Remember, he was very, very young—he had just turned twenty-three the previous week. Though he wore a uniform, he had never served in the armed forces, had no military training, had never commanded troops in battle. Having made a decision to shake hands with the Americans, having made a decision to stand up to Nasser, he had never considered the possibility that the consequences would overwhelm him. He was not at all sure what to do. It was as if, having steeled himself to climb an impossibly steep mountain, he now found himself, not on the top, but facing an even higher and more dangerous mountain. Sherif al-Hassan and Colonel Bitar watched him circle the room, two experienced, tough, pragmatic grown-ups waiting for a child to make up his mind. The King imagined his mother upstairs watching the mob through her window, terrified, perhaps preparing herself for death.

In the name of the One and Only God . . .

"Your Majesty." It was Sherif al-Hassan, moving with his slow weight toward the King. "You must make a decision. Now. In ten more minutes, those people down there will be climbing the palace steps. They will be overrunning the American embassy."

He leaned in close, taller than the King, a small brutal smile on his hooded, mottled face. "All great men begin by making two or three very hard choices. They are baptized in blood. They rise up victorious because they are feared. They are respected. Your Majesty, it is time to fight for your kingdom."

The King felt himself nodding. Sherif al-Hassan turned to Colonel Bitar, also nodded. Colonel Bitar quickly left the room.

Here's what happened, in fairly rapid succession, according to my father that night, according to all the accounts I have read, though we will never really know:

As the storm breached the embassy wall, more young men waving sticks and World War I rifles spilling into the compound, the Desert Legionnaires, so well trained by the British, fell back in orderly fashion, firing as they went, killing five, six, ten, twenty of the rioters. Once inside the embassy itself, front door bolted, they took up positions at the windows and continued firing. Up on the roof, the Marine Guards kept wary watch, at the ready, but did not themselves fire. After approximately half an hour of this stalemate, the mob having achieved little except to trample the well-tended embassy garden, tanks were spotted rolling down Al Said Street. Cheers went up from the rooftop. The mob hesitated midsurge, then fled, leaving twenty-two corpses behind, including a ten-year-old boy. On Al Kifah Street in downtown Hamra, tanks had rolled right over the running demonstrators like bulls running over drunken fools at Pamplona. Up on Jebel Hamra, at Hamzah Palace, more tanks had lumbered into view just as the Circassian bodyguards opened fire on the mob, dozens falling in the first barrage.

By nightfall smoldering order was restored, a curfew imposed, tanks patrolled the city, crunching over broken glass like giant mechanical insects.

"You better believe the martinis flowed that night," my father concluded, forty years later, in the apartment of my mother, the apartment of his wife from whom he is not divorced but with whom he no longer lives. "Christ, I had a hangover the next morning."

He gazed regretfully at the empty bottle of Chianti on the Kuwaiti coffee table, then at me. "And that is the last thing you'll get out of me."

I quickly changed the subject. "Dad, why are you and Mom living apart?"

"I haven't the foggiest. One day she simply told me she wanted a place of her own, that she had been looking and found this apartment. I helped her move in that week. I think it's a test."

"What kind of a test?"

"To see if I can live without her. To see if I can shop and cook for myself, keep the house clean myself. To see if I can sleep without her next to me."

"Are you failing or passing?"

He shrugged. "I'm getting maybe a C. I live on peanut butter and Campbell's soup, but she doesn't know that. I sleep okay if I have at least two drinks and some wine."

For the first time in my life I felt sorry for him, sitting there so woebegone on the old couch, missing his cigarettes, wishing he had another bottle of wine, gazing dumbfounded toward the closed door of my mother's bedroom.

"Why would she test you like this?"

"She thinks that I think that I don't really need her. She thinks that I think that I'd rather be alone. She thinks I'm wrong, and wants to prove it." He paused for a moment, considering. "Of course, there is another possibility."

"What?"

"Maybe she just doesn't like me anymore."

Before going back to his place, he told me something I've been turning over in my mind ever since. "We all start out thinking, if that's the word, and I'm not sure that it is, we all start out *feeling* that some kind of orderly life, some kind of happy life, is attainable, and then, slowly, inexorably, without our really realizing it, that feeling becomes an expectation. Most of us end up feeling that happiness is our God-given right. Well, guess what, it isn't. I haven't learned much in my time on this earth, but I have learned that. Good night."

And then he was gone.

Three

1

Midnighт. Dumbarton Avenue, the Gourlies' Federal manse in Georgetown, up the twelve brick steps and through a dark green wooden gate that always creaked. I was on the second floor, in the guest bedroom, the same bedroom my father stayed in when he was called back to Washington for consultation in late December of 1958. I stared at the bed—there are two—in which he lay for his nap the afternoon he arrived, knowing the meetings were going to be difficult. On the second bed of this guest room in Georgetown lay the reference books and the several hundred index cards I had emptied from my duffel bag. I also had the notes I took while interrogating my mother and father in Boston, as well as my father's faded Penguin edition of *Travels in Arabia Deserta*, which I now opened and from which I gently removed the unexplained love note: *O love, you do not know . . .*

Across the hall, Mrs. Gourlie was dying of cancer.

Mr. Gourlie walked the walk of the insomniac all night. I could hear him moving back and forth, back and forth, restless sentry on the walls of his wife's diminishing life.

Chipper Gourlie, according to his father, lived somewhere in the Maryland suburbs of D.C. and drove a cab for a living. He was fifty-two years old. The last time I saw him, in the summer of 1968, he had just returned from Vietnam with a terrible junk problem. He told me stories, right here in this house, upstairs on the third floor, in his boyhood room underneath the eaves. Stories of American helicopters being shot down by punitive American jet fighters, stories of ranking officers only visiting jungle bases surrounded by bodyguards lest one of their own assassinate them, stories of a brave, frightened first lieutenant ordering Chipper's platoon to take a hill that they had already taken and then abandoned, according to orders, a few weeks earlier, losing in the process half their fellow soldiers and the previous first lieutenant, to which Chipper had responded by placing the end of the barrel of his M16 to the temple of the first lieutenant and pulling the trigger.

I have explored this house until I know every secret it contains. . . .

I spent Christmas Eve here as a kid, after my family returned from Kurash, listening to *My Fair Lady* and playing The Game, our riotous charades; I came here on Easter to sip lemonade in the huge high-walled back garden; I came here when my parents were overseas again and I had no place else to go; I came here when I was down to torment the government; I came here while I went to summer school at Georgetown one year; I prowled the rooms, I searched through drawers and cabinets, as if maybe I could find my father here.

I was getting closer, even as Mrs. Gourlie lay dying nearby.

I had caught a glimpse of her when I arrived, through the open door of her bedroom, so frail and pale and white-haired I couldn't recognize her at first; she looked ancient, eviscerated, skeletal. It's the cancer, replacing each cell with anticell, destruction mutating with such greed from corpuscle to corpuscle. I don't think she saw me. Later, she came down for dinner, dressed nicely, her white, white hair brushed back, and took her place at the head of the table, across from Mr. Gourlie, who by then had had three martinis and was coasting along in a state of even-handed beatitude. He ate, smiling and mute, while she entertained me the way she had once, in this same house, at that same table, entertained ambassadors and undersecretaries and foreign correspondents and all those early C.I.A. boys in their easygoing loose-boned seersucker radiance.

"Well, now, you must absolutely tell me everything you have been doing," she said, turning to me the warmth of her Tennessee smile, her southern belle smile, so that for that one moment I was alone in her eyes and important. The effort that must have cost her, the pain in her body, in her bones, that she must have willed aside, stifled, in order to bless me with her charm. "Have we been good? Have we behaved ourselves? And what *are* all those mysterious boxes we've been accumulating upstairs? Have we reverted to type and become a spy?"

Yes indeed, though I couldn't tell her that.

And on it went, throughout dinner, anecdotes about Mr. Sumner pissing in the gladiolas during last year's Georgetown spring garden tour, guileless jokes that, on the third echo, you realized were probably racist or anti-Semitic, uttered with all innocence even as Mary, the elderly black maid who had been with them since I was a boy, wandered quietly in and out serving and clearing the table. Every now and then Mrs. Gourlie would let her eyes settle on her husband at the other end of the table. "Milton, darling, you're dribbling." Or: "Milton, my eternal love, could you pass me the rolls?" Or: "Milton, sweetness, what was the name of that scandalous young man we met at Lyford Keys last summer, the one who used to be the Princess of Glouchester before the, er-um, operation?" When dinner was over, coffee served and carried away by Mary, Mrs. Gourlie had stiffly stood, graced me with a final brilliant smile, and excused herself, sheer willpower escorting her up the stairs and back into the dark cave of her room, where the pain must have welcomed her.

All quiet now on the second floor.

Several weeks ago, before leaving Los Angeles and flying to Boston to interrogate my father, I received a cordial letter from the C.I.A.'s general consul, one Edmund P. Lawrence, inviting me to visit C.I.A. headquarters in Langley, Virginia, at my convenience, to review the relevant files. The only real ground rule he laid down was that I could take notes but I could not remove the files from the building. Thus I found myself, this morning, an overcast, moist morning already heavy with late Indian summer's foreboding heat, leaving the Gourlies' house in Georgetown and driving to Langley in my rented red Taurus. Edging my way through rush-hour traffic, I felt definitely that I had spread myself too far over too much time, for I was at once myself, nervously approaching the arsenal of C.I.A. headquarters, and I was my father, driving to work for a debriefing, back for consultation from Syria or Lebanon or Saudi Arabia, his various postings after the Kurashian debacle of 1958. A soft Virginia rain started to fall on the windshield as I crossed Key Bridge and moved west along the grassy banks of the Potomac and its steady stream of jogging bureaucrats. By the time I pulled up to the C.I.A. gate at Langley, I was having an out-of-body experience. The guard smiled pleasantly; I managed to give him my name, recited from memory, and the next thing I knew I was parking the Taurus in a massive parking lot full of cars and walking past what looked like a sizable white geodesic dome, an auditorium where, on special occasions, the assembled spooks are addressed by the Director or even, occasionally, the President, as was the case, for example, after the Bay of Pigs, when Kennedy fired Allen Dulles and then came out here to this auditorium and spoke enchantingly, charmingly, manfully of what secret glories they could revel among as clandestine warriors as long as—he made it clear—they never forgot that their job—he made it clear—was to win. Not lose.

In 1958, Allen Dulles was still winning, or at least convincing himself, and his President, that we weren't losing.

Appearances matter.

For example, in the matter of Kurash, and our investment in the young King, certain dividends were paying back handsomely, or so it seemed.

The Chevrolet division of General Motors had recently

landed a contract with the Kurashian government to open a dealership in Hamra. Said dealership would not be taxed by said government. And said government agreed—unofficially, of course—that other dealerships by other car manufacturers would be superfluous.

IT&T won a contract to build and maintain for the Kurashian government an efficient telephone system. Thirty Americans had already arrived and were working on the project.

IBM won a contract to equip all Kurashian government offices with new typewriters, adding machines, and so forth.

Ford Motor Company and Boeing Industries won a joint contract to replace all outdated British military vehicles, including airplanes, effective immediately.

Coca-Cola signed a contract with the Kurashian government to open a bottling plant in Hamra, again, with favorable tax conditions and an understanding that rival soda companies would not find themselves welcome in Kurash.

Imagine someone like General Anwar, chief of staff, studying these figures. Imagine the Soviets studying these figures. Imagine the Egyptians studying these figures.

A heavyset, jovial man in his mid-forties met me at the bottom of the steps leading up to C.I.A. headquarters. According to the laminated tag that he wore on a little chain around his neck, his name was Bob Easton. "Welcome to the center of the known universe," he said, first shaking my hand, then clapping me on the back, boisterous as an old college pal. "You better wear this." He handed me a chain like his, with a tag that said VISITOR.

His game was public relations, he continued, starting briskly up the steps with me close behind. I would not believe the amount of work there was for him to do in a typical day. Requests by scholars, like me, that warranted serious attention, and many, many requests by journalists from all over the world, many of which warranted no serious attention whatsoever—we were through the main glass doors and crossing the granite-floored lobby, our feet pitter-pattering across an American eagle and scripture from Matthew: "Seek the truth and the truth shall set thee free." I don't think the C.I.A. is what Matthew had in mind, and almost say so to Bob Easton, but I don't have the heart to interrupt his endless flow of public relations chatter as he bounds into an elevator, grinning like crazy, and punches buttons, rocking back on his heels as we rise upward, hands jingling change or keys or both in his pants pocket. "Used to be this place was paranoid, I mean really paranoid. The cold war guys, they were spooky, let me tell you. A bunch of them were still around when I first joined up. Booze and paranoia, that was their daily diet. They died of liver disease and high anxiety, all of them. Angleton, you've heard of James Angleton? In charge of counter-intelligence? Find the mole before the mole found us? I used to see him wandering the hallways muttering Ezra Pound poems to himself."

Ding—the elevator door slides open; Bob Easton strides out and away. I'm getting a stitch in my side just trying to keep up with him.

"Place is completely different now," Bob informs me as we sweep past bright red office doors, a cheerful, industrious energy evident in the faces of the men and women we also pass, men and women who come each day here to the C.I.A. the way others go to hospitals or law offices or classrooms. "Sure, we still got some male, white, Protestant Ivy Leaguers, but they don't run the joint, not anymore. Here we go."

He ushered me into this room, this Research Library, it said on the red door, where the file folders were waiting for me on the desk.

"What you got there," Bob said, nodding toward the file folders, "is all that we got, pertinent to your area of inquiry, Kurash circa 1958. Gotta love that Freedom of Information Act. Have at it. Enjoy yourself."

With a chipper wave, he disappeared.

I sat down, nervous, and opened the top file folder.

From the folder I pulled . . .

Inside the folder I found a typewritten . . .

. . . dated April 18, 1958, three days after my father handed the first briefcase of cash to the King.

Reading in part: "I believe all effort should be made to track not just the activities of the left-leaning conspirators in our midst, most notably Egyptian Intelligence and the Soviets, but the activities of the Muslim Brotherhood as well, for common sense would tell us that the threat to the King, when it comes, as it surely will come, might just as well come from the right, from the historical sentimentalists, as from our Socialist friends. The Arab mind I encounter every day, in all walks of life, is looking for a racial identity, the Arab equivalent of an indigenous nation-state. It is also looking for a way back into the Koran, true belief and a kind of purity that we in the West cannot contaminate."

Signed, at the bottom: "M.H."

That would be Mack Hooper.

My dad. Ever vigilant.

2

The day after the riot, Kumait wandered down Al Kifah
Street in a kind of shaken trance. His world had just
taken a violent, jarring tumble. He stopped in front of
Oristibach's Department Store, the gilded Royal English crown
carved above the double mahogany front doors, and stared in disbelief at the shattered glass windows and tattered ashes of gray
flannel clothes and pink Caucasian mannequins, the burnt and
bent Mixmasters and Schwinn bicycles tossed out onto Al Kifah
Street like so much useless rubble. He soon found himself, to his
amazement, grinning, or rather, he sensed, then acknowledged, a
happy tightening at the corners of his mouth, a mirthful, anar-
chic glee burbling up into a brief, choked laugh. He wanted to
break a few windows himself. There was something sexual to this
happiness, this longing, an arousal he could not and did not want
to deny, though it did feel illicit, dirty, secret. As he hurried
guiltily away, past the broken windows of the English Bookshop,
he could see, inside, the gleaming hardbacks in their happy rows,
a dimly lit well where he had spent many a serene hour pouring
over the novels of Dickens, Hardy, Melville, Hemingway. He
stopped, stooped, retrieved a half-scorched, waterlogged book,
turning it over to read the title: *Light in August* by William
Faulkner. He let it fall back among the shards and pebbles of
glass, the splintered wood, the ripped stuffing of a European armchair. He continued home, self-conscious under the watchful
gaze of soldiers positioned in groups along Al Kifah Street. Tanks

poked out from the side streets, gun turrets probing blindly, side
to side, up and down, looking for enemies, victims. He kept up
a quick pace, his eyes on the littered sidewalk before him, until
he finally reached his own street, Nahas Street, more of a lane, or
an alley, off the main boulevard. His building, four stories tall,
built in the late nineteenth century by a French trading company,
faced a small café, The Oasis. Normally, no matter what the time
of day, the three or four metal-topped tables outside would be
crowded with men in *kaffiyehs* absently playing out and flipping
back their strings of amber worry beads while they sipped endless tiny cups of thick, sweet Turkish coffee and argued vocifer-
ously over politics and soccer. But today the tables were empty.
Kumait pressed the button on the side of his building's front
door, heard the distant buzz as the door cracked open, entered,
and climbed the old marble stairs to the second floor, where he
lived, facing the street, in two small rooms.

He heated water in the old kettle that wobbled, made himself
some tea, then sat at his desk by the balcony and smoked a cigarette, gazing out and down at Nahas Street. He was tired, drained.
In the thirty-six hours since the riots had started he had lost
something so essential to the way he thought of himself that, for
the moment, he felt aimless, boneless, a shadow-person with just
enough personality to throw a feeble reflection, no more. Belief
had been replaced by the disquieting pornographic thrill he'd felt
out in front of Oristibach's. He could conceive of nothing more
satisfying to do tonight than visit Madame Apollinaire's and lose
himself in fleshly pleasure. And yet his country was teetering pre-
cariously on the edge of ruin, his beloved King was in despair, and
the jackals were circling the capital, yapping maliciously, Nasser's
fools, Nasser's idiots, Nasser's morons. They had died like fools,
too, thirty-five of them altogether, most of them young, children of the dispossessed and overeducated (several students had
participated), shot down in the midst of their vainglorious posturing by the King's nervous soldiers. Kumait sipped his cooling

tea, watched his cigarette smoke spiral upward toward his high, grimy ceiling. He could not imagine preparing for classes tomorrow. He could not imagine teaching tomorrow. He was too agitated, too depressed, too aroused. Without giving it much thought, he reached down and freed his cock from his trousers, stroking it large and stiff, pushing back against the chair, arching his back, eyes closed but hardly blind, for he saw most vividly a score of young men and women offering, opening themselves, to each other: girls to girls, men to men, men to girls, girls to many men, kissing, caressing, exploring, guiltless and glassy-eyed. He came quickly, surprising himself, grunting, gasping, opening his eyes as his come shot up in quick, mucous white spurts onto his chest. Panting, aching, Kumait lay there for a moment, then hobbled up and into the bathroom, where he cleaned himself with toilet paper and took a shower.

Feeling pleasantly depleted, and still somewhat without an identity, he changed into clean clothes, his usual uniform of crisp white shirt and dark wool pants, then returned to his desk by the balcony. The tea was cold. He lit a new cigarette, watched the shadows stretch across Nahas Street below. Schoolchildren, leather schoolbags dangling from their narrow, uniformed shoulders, hurried past, sandals clattering loudly, idle carefree laughter rebounding between the walls. Kumait sighed deeply, stretched, relaxed. He could get used to having no names for his feelings. The excitement of the past twenty-four hours, as it receded, left him feeling empty, content. When he saw General Anwar, dressed in civilian clothes, round the corner from Al Kifah Street and approach his apartment building, he had to struggle to remember that this was expected, arranged, and that he, Kumait, was part of it, part of the movement that had stupidly set the riots in motion, that he indeed did have an identity which, if revealed to the world, could cost him his life.

He stood, buzzed Anwar in, waited while the General climbed the steps, opened his door, and stood aside as the burly soldier, out of breath, wheezed into his apartment, immediately glancing around in distaste at the mess of papers and books and lighting a Marlboro.

"When are you going to clean this place up, eh?" Anwar looked around again. "You live like a student."

"Would you like some tea?"

"No, thank you." The General finally looked him in the eye. "Well? So?"

Kumait indicated the tattered armchair by his desk. Anwar sat, holding his cigarette like a scepter, as if it might bring him luck, or at least protect him. Kumait took his hard desk chair, leaned forward, elbows on his knees. Anwar's face was sallow, drawn. He probably hadn't slept for a couple of days.

"Our agreement was that there would be no riots until the Islamic Action Front agreed it was time," Kumait began.

"I could not stop them," Anwar said, a little defensively. "They had a life of their own. These people are frustrated, Kumait. They're angry."

"They were pushed by you; you were pushed by Nasser. I heard the broadcasts from Radio Cairo."

Anwar nodded reluctantly. "The Egyptians have no patience."

"Remember, my old friend, the goal is to pressure His Majesty, not overthrow him or kill him. The Egyptians have their own goal, and we will let them think what they want to think, but we are clear about what we're doing, correct?"

"Correct."

Kumait studied Anwar closely to see if he meant it. He couldn't tell. They had known each other since their student days at the American University of Beirut, more than twenty years now, and yet Kumait still had trouble reading Anwar sometimes. The man withdrew into a well-protected mental redoubt, his smile, even his gaze noncommittal. Kumait leaned across his desk and clicked on his lamp. Anwar blinked. He hadn't shaved; his short, dark hair looked dirty; his black eyes, pupils retracting, continued to reveal absolutely nothing of what he felt. For the first time it occurred to Kumait that maybe he could not trust Anwar. He was returning to himself, he realized, the free-floating nonbeing of the hours just after the riot was indeed gone; he knew all too well who he was now, and the thought of this lack of trust between two old and very close friends, two friends who had shared the same passions as young men, the discovery of the great classical Arabic poetry, the all-night discussions and arguments about Colonialism and Nationalism and Socialism, even, sometimes, the same girls, the same brave coeds from Palestine and Damascus who had ripped off their veils in Beirut to seek the sun—Kumait did not like this person he was remembering, himself, who could mistrust and suspect someone he loved, his friend, Anwar.

It was all so complicated, too complicated, Kumait suspected, to end well. Over the years, after returning home to Kurash to serve the King's father, and then, after the assassination, his young son, the King himself, Anwar had secretly aligned himself with President Gamal Abdel Nasser of Egypt, Baathist Socialism, and the dream of Arab unity. Kumait had quite naturally, being a scholar, drifted toward the pull of history, and more than a decade ago joined the Muslim Brotherhood, the local political wing of which was the Islamic Action Front, of which he was a clandestine leader. The Brotherhood had been started in 1928, in Egypt, by one Eid al-Banna, as a youth club dedicated to moral and social reform. Its heart was rooted in the Koran. It was as much a religious as a political movement. By 1958, it boasted almost a million members in seven Arab countries. Kumait had almost left the Brotherhood in 1954, infuriated by the executive committee's decision to oppose secular education, women's rights, and land reform. He stayed, however, because he believed that without context no reform has meaning, that even Arab unity would be pointless if it simply increased political and economic leverage and encouraged individual liberties. He was an intellectual who believed in Allah. Anwar was a practical man who believed in earthly justice. Now they were intent upon bringing their two ways together, here, in Kurash, in 1958.

"Anwar, tell me, can you control Nasser?"

"Nasser is not the enemy, Kumait. He is the only man with a vision of what we must do and the means and determination to do it. Tell me, can you control the Muslim Brotherhood? Will the priests appear with their swords and holy self-righteousness and slay all those who think differently?"

Kumait did not know the answer to that question.

He changed the subject. "Please tell your friends in Egyptian Intelligence that this is Kurash, not Egypt, and that here we will do things our way. No more riots until we're ready. No harm to the King. Otherwise, the Brotherhood will withdraw its support. We will oppose. Do you understand?"

"Of course I understand," Anwar said with an irritated, dismissive wave of his blunt hand. "I'm not an idiot."

Kumait smiled. His old friend and he might pull this off yet. The idea was simple enough: Free the King from the gravitational pull of the Americans, force him to see that there was another way. Then, balancing the demands of Nasser's pan-Arabic Socialism and the Muslim Brotherhood's well-meaning atavism, steer the King toward a position of independence, self-reliance, spiritual honesty. The trick, the deciding point, was going to be the Army. They had to have the Army with them, or at least a significant portion of it, and to that effect they now focused their energies on the Third Tank Division, Anwar's old command before he had become chief of staff.

"I appointed General Ali Mazzawi to replace me," Anwar said. "I trained many of the junior officers. I can expect a certain degree of loyalty."

"Yes, but do they share our beliefs, our goals?" Kumait asked.

Anwar shrugged. "We'll find out, won't we?"

3

Consider the fragments.

After the orgy of the riot everyone gathered up his clothes and tiptoed home, a little shame-faced, exhausted, pleased to discover the next day that no one had to face hell's burning rage. God, it seemed, was not angry with them. Allah, it seemed, understood, forgave. The dead bodies were quickly buried in shallow paupers' graves out by the city dump, on the road to Damascus, quickly buried and quickly forgotten. Feeling better, everyone got back to work.

In Little America, Milton Gourlie's anxiety had not yet made itself evident; Renee went on the wagon; and Johnny Allen met a nice girl his age, Pansey Poesy, who worked as a secretary at the British consulate, and they were soon spotted hand in hand going to the movies at the Majestic. Roy and Barbara Sweetser became regular bridge players at the weekend games in the bar at the American Club, a development my father viewed with distaste, all card games being *a priori* a complete waste of time, but which in fact vastly improved the Sweetsers' sex life. They would return from these games of mental parry and thrust enflamed with desire, horny as rabbits, ripping off each other's clothes as they stumbled to the bedroom. The new Ambassador and his wife were not as social as Ambassador and Kathy Burdick. They both moved through life with a slightly baffled, nearsighted squint, more academic than diplomatic, yet the embassy sailed along on an even keel. Milton Gourlie rarely told Ambassador Muir everything that was going on, but he didn't categorically exclude him,

either; in fact, he included the diplomatic officer and the economics officer in his nonclassified briefings, not at all a common
practice in those high-handed days of imperial espionage, when
spy was king. My mother continued what she now called her
"studies" with Kumait. They would traipse out into the desert
together to wander among the wind-blown *tells,* sometimes with
Barbara Sweetser and Tootie Muir, sometimes, preferably, alone.
General Anwar started inviting junior officers of the Third Tank
Division to his house for long dinners, by the end of which
he would be speaking quietly, passionately, to a half circle of
already half-convinced converts about the need to free Kurash
from the Americans and achieve the reality of national sover-
eignty, a true Arab identity. The dark eyes of the young officers,
mostly Bedouin boys who had grown up among the black
goatskin tents and wandering herds of sheep, bells jingling softly
on the hills as, again and again, regular as clockwork, this day and
forever, the sun sank into the cool upcoming desert night—the
dark eyes of these boys glowed excited and daring above their
cigarettes and Turkish coffee as they listened to Anwar softly
recite their deepest desires. And the King, well, the King convened meetings at the palace every morning, after prayers,
increasingly cheerful as the threat of political dissolution seemed
to wane, as the American money began to make itself felt in the
pencil factory, the village irrigation system, the country clinic.

"Let me begin," my father's memos began . . .

"A fair summation would be," he proposed . . .

From a cable dated May 30, 1958, declassified June 1998:
"What's confusing, of course, is that Nasser is mythomaniacal,
narcissistic, and profoundly anti-democratic, yet he has convinced a majority of the Arab world that he is the opposite, which
I guess says more about the ability of man to fool himself, that he
sees what he wants to see, than it does about Nasser's or any other
leader's actual abilities."

Whereas up until now the political parties in Parliament had
been limited to the National Party, headed by Sherif al-Hassan

and supported by the King, and the Muslim Brotherhood, condoned because it was (supposedly) a religious party, the King let it be known that he would look the other way should more parties feel an imperative to express themselves in the next election, set for eight months hence. The Communists surfaced, the Baathists raised their unruly heads, an Egyptian-supported United Arab Party came into being, even a small, somewhat militant Coptic Party declared itself. Campaigning was limited to speech making at Faisel Square. The National Party controlled the only newspaper in Kurash. The National Party controlled the only radio station in Kurash. There was no TV in Kurash, at the time, late spring, 1958, though the Americans were working on that problem, too. The squawk of loudspeakers bolted to trucks inching their way through tangled downtown traffic accompanied by bleating impatient horns became a familiar lunchtime distraction.

Consider the fragments.

Sand settled on the palm leaves, on the metal-topped tables, on the balcony outside the King's bedroom, overlooking the garden, his grandfather Ali's small mosque, where the King continued to go every morning to pray, to clear his head before the day's buzzing confusion began.

At the Hamra Go-Cart Club, in the desert, permanent pavilions were built, little blocks of fluttering shade along the periphery of the racetrack. The King once sat with us on our blanket and ate cold chicken, a broad smile on his face, cracking bad jokes that even he knew were bad. I saw my father gazing kindly at the King, saw there the thoughtful, concerned gaze of an older brother, pure as the desert air.

O love

Rodney, at the King's request, relinquished his Mercedes business downtown and moved up to Hamzah Palace, in charge of the King's many cars, his salary doubled.

Chipper and Penny and Carolyn and I sat bored witless in our American Community School classroom listening to Miss Webster drone on about . . .

. . . *chip-chip-chip* went the stone masons outside my window, all day, every day, day after day after day . . .

We saw, Friday night, at the embassy, *Run Silent, Run Deep,* a World War II submarine movie depicting considerable but modest American ingenuity and courage. We bought it all, breathless.

We shuffled, Saturday night, at the Hut, to Paul Anka's "Put Your Head on My Shoulder," lament to baroque suburban barbecue moonlit innocence already vanishing.

The King asked for weekly updates on the progress of the pencil factory.

The Dulles brothers took a stroll in the Virginia woods, following a leafy path along the Potomac, enjoying the inducements of spring: honeysuckle, jasmine, rutted blossoming cherry trees, silent fragrant floral fireworks of pink and white. Allen sneezed. He suffered from allergies, hay fever, had since childhood. His eyes looked out, bloodshot, bleary, at the late May profusion.

"Hay fever acting up?" John Foster asked.

Allen nodded, blowing his nose on a monogrammed handkerchief.

They both wore blue suits, by the way, as they picked their way delicately through the bramble and briar.

"I hate spring," Allen muttered. "Though it is pretty, I'll grant you that."

"It's what I call the False Hope," John Foster mused. "That there could be anything waiting up ahead except the sweltering suffocation of summer, then the quick brilliant death of fall, followed by the burial, beneath snow, we call winter."

Both men's minds, left to their own devices, gravitated toward the melancholy. They resisted daily. It was a question of discipline. So odd now to look back at these two straight-back reformers walking in the woods and realize that much of American foreign policy at that time had its roots in depression.

"How are things with Kurash?" John Foster asked, picking a cherry blossom and sticking it in his lapel.

"Stable." Allen sneezed again.

"Gesundheit."

"Thank you."

"Our young king doing nicely?"

"Very nicely, yes. Milton Gourlie has things well in hand. Your man Muir knows enough to let things take their course."

On they went, thick-soled Abercrombie brogues squelching in leafy mud.

"John Foster, do you ever wonder . . ."

"Wonder what?"

"What if we lose?"

"Lose?" The thought was inconceivable to John Foster Dulles.

Allen, the spy, the introvert, could not be stopped. "What if the Communists just keep winning? What then?"

John Foster fixed his younger brother with a look to kill, exaggerated by the vengeful glint of bright May sunlight on the lenses of his steel rimless glasses.

The King, who would never meet either of the Dulles brothers, took to visiting his mother in her wing of the palace on a weekly basis, seeking her advice and trusting it more as each week went by. Less than two weeks after the riots, he horrified Sherif al-Hassan by going to the Bakr slums. Once again, his mother's idea. He simply drove there with his entourage of Circassian bodyguards and bulletproof Land Rovers, walked into the first hut he came to; there he found an old woman cooking over an open fire, several naked children crawling around, a stench of sickly human flesh. Word spread; within minutes hundreds of the slum dwellers pressed about the King, touching him, touching their foreheads, grinning gold-toothed greetings, reverential, then ecstatic. The bodyguards tried to keep the King within a tight protective circle, failed. He launched out on his own with outstretched hand, swallowed up by crowds of pushing, clambering poor people, an undulating organic tidal wave. General Anwar had been visiting military installations in the north at the time of the King's journey to the Bakr District. He was incredulous that the King would have done such a thing. Kumait, who was with the King for this venture, later described it to Anwar.

"At first he was afraid," Kumait told him, over coffee, after dinner, at The Oasis. "He had to force himself to get out of the Land Rover, force himself to enter that first dark smelly little hut, but when he saw how the people appreciated it, when he felt them touching him, instead of feeling repelled, or even more frightened, which, if you ask me, would have been the natural reaction, he felt instead some kind of emotional tug; I saw him smile in a way I've never seen before, and he just waded in further. I'm telling you, it was fantastic. I had tears in my eyes."

Anwar finished his coffee, wiped his thick mustache, lit a Camel cigarette with his gold Ronson lighter and settled back, peering off through swirling plumes of smoke. "Think of this, Kumait. Maybe he's changing, on his own."

"Yes, I think he is. He asked me this morning to collect for him the best of classical Arabic poetry. 'The kind of stuff my grandfather used to read.' That's what he said. Can you believe it? Our little king?"

It was now close to midnight. Atop Jebel Hamra the King was feeling lonely, awake in the dark palace, pacing the red-and-white squares of tile floor, wandering out to the terrace and the garden, while down in the city Kumait and Anwar finished their coffee and cigarettes. Rediscovering classical Arabic poetry had also been his mother's idea. "Find out who you really are," she'd admonished the King. "Read the words your grandfather Ali read." Unspoken was the fact that Ali's son, her husband, the King's father, had enjoyed Cole Porter as much as any ancient desert bard. Cole Porter and Gilbert and Sullivan. The King remembered fondly traveling with his father once a winter to London to stay at the Dorchester and attend productions of *Pirates of Penzance* and *H.M.S. Pinafore.* He lit a cigarette of his own, sat in a wicker chair, inhaled the garden smells, allowed himself to feel a quiet moment of satisfaction. His kingdom slept around him peace-

fully. Today construction had begun on the roof of the pencil factory. He had spent the week dispensing to various Bedouin chiefs
the loot carried to him in a briefcase by my father.

Consider the fragments.

Down the hill, in Hamra proper, Kumait and Anwar were taking a midnight stroll along Al Kifah Street. Most of the cafés were
still open and fairly crowded. A bell clanged behind them; they
jumped out of the way of a trolley car clamoring its way down the
middle of the boulevard.

"What if we're wrong?" Kumait ventured.

"Wrong?" Anwar asked. "About what?"

They were as close as brothers, despite the different paths they
had taken, certainly as close as Allen and John Foster Dulles plod-
ding the soggy banks of the Potomac in Virginia.

"What if His Majesty doesn't need the prodding we think he
needs?" Kumait asked.

Anwar was quick to answer. "He is in love with the Americans.
Mack Hooper is the big brother he never had. He's already
addicted to the money. No, he needs prodding."

"If we simply told him how we felt?"

"We've already done that, Kumait. A hundred times. He
doesn't listen to us."

"That was before. We've agreed, he's changing. Maybe he'd
listen to us now."

"No."

"I think we should try."

"That would jeopardize everything."

They continued along the street in unresolved silence, smoking their cigarettes.

Behind them, Major Rashid's agents kept pace.

From a report filed by Roy Sweetser, August 23, 1958: "On the
evening of May 11 Major Rashid's agents followed the subjects
Kumait and Anwar to the corner of Sidon Street, where they sat
and enjoyed several glasses of *arak* and several hours of intense

conversation. This was more than a month before we had any idea they were in collusion."

Consider the fragments.

Up in Hamzah Palace, the King stood abruptly from his wicker chair on the terrace, flicked away his cigarette, and strode inside to a telephone. He glanced at his watch. Almost twelve-thirty. He hesitated, then picked up the receiver. What the hell. He was a King. He dialed. The call was monitored by Johnny Allen and Philip Merrill, a special operations officer flown in from Germany two weeks earlier. They had finished their tap of the palace lines just that afternoon. Their listening post was one of three Hamra C.I.A. safe houses, a four-room rented limestone house about three blocks from Hamzah Palace.

Johnny and Philip Merrill heard the line ring once, my father answer at the other end. "Hello?"

He was in bed, reading, next to my sleeping mother.

"Mack?"

My father, startled, recognized the King's voice. He sat up straighter. "Is everything all right?"

"I'm fine."

"What's wrong?"

"Nothing's wrong. I can't sleep. I was wondering if you could come over."

"Now?"

"If it's not too much trouble."

"I'll be right there."

The line clicked dead. Johnny glanced at Philip Merrill, logged the call.

From a declassified cable sent from the American embassy in Hamra to C.I.A. headquarters in Washington, D.C.: "Telephone intercepts of the week May 12–May 19 revealed no contact between King and Egyptian or Soviet agents. Of twenty-nine personal calls logged, twelve were to Sherif al-Hassan, eight to his chief of staff, eight to various females, most notably Esmerelda

Tweedy of the Borges Travel Agency, and a single call to Mack Hooper. From these and other observations the King would appear to be clean." This memo is initialed "M.G." Milton Gourlie. Station chief, about to be upended.

Indeed my father was good. Up and dressed in a matter of minutes, he leaned down and gently shook my mother awake. She came to consciousness with a gasp of fear. "What's wrong?"

"Nothing. I have to go out, that's all. He called."

I heard him leaving, since I was still wide awake, up in my bedroom. I heard his footsteps downstairs, then the sound of the front door opening. I slipped from bed and hurried over to the window, looked out in time to see him crossing to the gate and saying something to the sentry, who came clumsily awake in his little guardhouse. My father got into the Opel and drove away, across Jebel Hamra, past all the houses dark and quiet.

The next day, a Tuesday, Kumait spent the afternoon with the King, in the garden, in the shade of the pine trees. Yusuf moved in slow motion down by the hyacinth, trailing his hose, black as a lizard.

"The poetry of our ancestors can be divided into two categories, Your Majesty," Kumait began, spreading before him the text. "The *qasida*, or ode, and the *qit'a*, or occasional piece. The *qasida* is far and away the dominant form; in fact, it is considered by experts to be the only valid form of classical poetry. I must confess, however, Your Majesty, a particular fondness for the *qit'a*, especially those of Abu Tammam, who died about one hundred and fourteen years after the Flight, or, by the Christian calendar, A.D. 846. Little is known about the origin or original purpose of the *qit'a*. It has been speculated that they are fragments remembered of lost longer poems. . . ."

All that is remembered.

Fragments of the whole, of what we have forgotten or lost, misplaced facts, in memos, in files, in boxes, spread across the second bed in the second-floor front guest room of the Gourlies' Federal mansion on Dumbarton Avenue.

The King, too, over time, developed a fondness for the *qit'a*.

That night, after arriving at the palace, my father and the King sat out on the terrace facing the cool, dark cave smell of the garden and talked. The small mosque at the far end was the shade of a shadow. It was now one o'clock in the morning. Servants brought tea and withdrew. The King lit a cigarette; my father lit a cigarette. They both enjoyed the ritual. It made them feel at ease, among like-minded men. They sipped their hot tea. English tea. Remnants of empire. Earl Grey.

"So what do you think, Mack?" the King asked.

"About what, Your Majesty?"

"The state of our affairs."

"Improving, I would say, cautiously."

"You're a cautious man, aren't you, Mack?"

"Yes, I suppose I am."

"My father was cautious."

That sounded, to my father, suspiciously like an aspersion. Did the King think less of his father for his caution?

"You can miss a lot in life, being too cautious," my father said. "High passions will pass you by. The thrill of great risk sometimes. On the other hand, you will make fewer mistakes, being cautious, and that would appear to be our primary concern, yours and mine, at the moment. No?"

The King nodded, drew on his cigarette, listened.

"I'm no genius, Your Majesty. The only way I'm going to win is by thinking more carefully than the next guy."

"Does being right play no role?"

"Being right *is* the role. I heard about your going to Bakr the other day. In my opinion, that was the right thing to do *and* the smart thing to do, the cautious thing to do. It assumes nothing."

"I'm their king, too."

"Exactly."

A comfortable silence went by while they finished their cigarettes, squashed them in a brass ashtray.

"Are you sure everything's all right?" my father asked.

"Yes, I'm sure."

"Do you miss Captain Smythe-Jones?"

"He was a good man, but no, I don't miss him. He was also a worrywart." The King glanced benignly at my father. "I feel I'm in good hands."

This pleased my father, more than it should have. It spoke of a personal interest. "Good. I'm glad."

"I'm sorry I dragged you out of bed this time of night."

"I was awake. Reading."

"What were you reading?"

"One of my son's books. I found it in the bathroom. *The Famous Five Take a Holiday.* A detective story of sorts. English. Pretty good."

"Do you read much?"

"No. My wife does."

"I'm having Kumait teach me classical Arabic poetry. We're starting tomorrow."

"That's way beyond me, I'm afraid."

"My grandfather Ali loved this poetry. He knew much of it by heart. He could recite it beautifully. 'Fate proceeds on its way, and both doctor and patient depart . . .'" A shy shrug. "That's all I remember. I have no idea what it means."

Consider the fragments.

They talked until the King finally allowed fatigue to conquer him, and then my father stood and said goodbye. The King walked him to the front door. Before my father left, the King said, matter-of-factly, "Mack, from now on, why don't you give me my weekly Intelligence briefings."

He meant instead of Milton Gourlie.

It wasn't a request. It was a command.

4

Chipper Gourlie finally showed up, last night, in the doorway of the guest room of his parents' house, unannounced, shy, or respectful of my solitary, scholarly activities. His smile, when it came, was as broad and mischievous as ever.

"Terryster," he said, with great and genuine affection, head cocked forward, inviting me to join a gleeful conspiracy. "Wanna get stoned?"

He'd lost a lot of weight since I saw him last, his hair was white, his eyebrows were white, otherwise he looked pretty much the same, dressed, as through time immemorial, in pressed khakis, Weejuns, and white Brooks Brothers shirt with the sleeves rolled exactly four times. His gloriously restored black London cab, circa mid-1950s, was parked in his parents' driveway. We got in and headed out Wisconsin Avenue, Chipper driving as fast as he talked, a steady stream of intense, often incomprehensible chatter that was at once both intimate and bombastic, conversational and highly rhetorical, his tongue tripping from one to the other without a slip, felicitous as nitroglycerine.

"So what I'm saying, Terryster, is that when you get right down to it, down to the cruddy corrupt soul of things, we've got no business telling anyone else what to do, how to live their lives, who or what to worship, because, I mean, Terryster, after all, who are we to speak? Who the fuck are we to presume anything about anything? Know what I'm saying? God it's good to see you, old man. Damn good. Jolly fucking good. We've all been spread to the four corners, haven't we? Scattered by the winds of Imperialist time. O, I could rue the day . . ."

And here he drifted off to a moment's silent thoughtfulness tinged with sad regret, a cluck of the tongue and shake of the head, until, snapping out of it, a visceral shudder running up his back and along the twitching muscles of his shoulders, he fixed me with a bright-eyed grin, all those perfect teeth, the best money can buy, as yet undamaged by the massive amounts of drugs he obviously continued to take. "We had some good times, though, didn't we, Terryster?"

He was thinking of someone else, I thought, maybe no one in particular, but certainly not me, unless, of course, he meant our gloriously fucked-up childhood.

"O halcyon days of yore," he remarked bitterly to himself.

Did he remember rooting for Easter eggs in his mother's garden? Did he remember putting me on his shoulders and covering us both with a grown-up's overcoat, so that, as one, as a tall One, we could be . . . who? Frankenstein? In a game of charades, on a night of The Game, in his parents' living room, circa 1958, our parents and the Sweetsers all around us clapping, happy forgiving gin laughter carrying us upward on wings of melting wax. The next day, in the glare of brutal parental hangovers, we crashed back to ground, stunned and bruised.

"Chipper," I ventured, screaming over the nostalgic death moans of Jimi Hendrix, "what happened to all the toy soldiers?"

"I've got 'em." He winked, once again inviting me to join the conspiracy. Which conspiracy, exactly, and what its purpose, I could not say. "In my house."

"Where we're going?"

"Where we're going."

We rocketed by the old Soviet Union embassy on Sixteenth Street, a walled compound the size of a small university, rooftops still bristling with disused jamming devices and satellite discs. In its heyday there must have been several hundred K.G.B. officers in there, masquerading as diplomats of one kind or another. Those involved in the Middle East must have known of my father, Chipper's father, Penny's father, their names, in fat files, must have cropped up once in a while, in the course of K.G.B. ruminations here and elsewhere.

Chipper braked and the London cab screeched to a halt at the curb of a dark, suburban, middle-class street. He leaped out, all business, brisk and purposeful, and came around to my side of the car, yanking open the door for me. "Home is where the heart is." He giggled.

He escorted me to the front door. I noticed tin foil blocking the mail slot. He rattled many keys, turned them in many locks; we entered. It was stuffy inside, airless. He flicked on a light, shut the door, turned all the locks the other way. Looking around, I saw that thick curtains covered all the windows. There was something vampirish about the place, about Chipper himself as he now led me through a modest living room that appeared to have been designed by a motel decorator in 1964 and left untouched ever since. Down we went into the basement, Chipper busily turned on more lights, and here I saw a sight that truly took my breath away, made my heart go pitter-patter and my pituitary gland overheat with metabolic enthusiasm. I was smack dab in the middle of a toy museum. Chipper had transformed the basement, with a master impresario's hand he had made it theatrical, magical, shelves of lead soldiers lining the walls, Scottish Highlanders and Lancaster Gunners and Bengal Lancers, all dutifully marching toward harmless, happy battles in some imperial land of Oz. More shelves, stocked with Britains military vehicles, half-tracks and howitzers, and Dinky Toys, the green metal tanks, tank carriers, scout cars, jeeps, troop trucks . . . I stood there trembling at the brink of childhood, stepped closer, touched a Bengal Lancer, carefully lifted a Hawker Hunter and—I couldn't help it—flew it in graceful circles around the room in my hand. Chipper, grinning, like a host who has successfully surprised a guest, introduced him to a woman of exceptional charms, withdrew to the far end of the basement where, I saw, he had neatly shelved thousands of records. No CDs down here, no tapes even. Like a scholar, Chipper considered the many choices, pulled out an LP, with reverential fingers removed the black plastic disc itself, and placed it on a turntable. A turntable! Music soon thereafter rumbled forth from speakers as big as coffins. Sarah Vaughn.

I live in a dream for a moment . . .

Looking more closely, I noticed that many of the lead soldiers and metal vehicles were dented and dinged from our wars on the bedroom floors of our houses in Kurash. A World War I foot soldier was missing an eye, a Scottish sniper an arm, a few Confederate cavalry riders their horses. Suddenly the innocence seemed to have an inner, darker life. These mute toys were the veterans of our childhood, the survivors, maimed and wounded and half dead, buried forever in their memories of misery, mud and thunder and cold steel and screeching shells. I flashed on the Kurashian Army circa 1958, still driving its British tanks, identical except in size to the hefty solid Centurion I now held in my hand, the same few Hawker Hunters flying overhead, small, in perspective, as these toys, semblance of an air force. A toy army, a toy air force, led by a toy king. All to amuse the children of empire, the children of Little America. Us.

But I never knew at the moment . . .

Chipper appeared at my shoulder and handed me a glass water pipe, which I lifted to my lips as he flicked a Zippo, another whimsical artifact. The water bubbled as I inhaled the strangely tasteless pot. We sat, Chipper and I, in armchairs I now recognized too, for they had come from his room on Dumbarton Avenue, and passed the water pipe back and forth and listened to Sarah Vaughn bemoan so beautifully the beauty of so much pain.

I'd thrill as your arms would enfold me...

All the while, Chipper was talking, tripping, rambling, free-associating. "Government hasn't much more than currency to justify the . . . Televised sports transfixing the world, stupefying the world, hypnotizing the world until what we've got is a massive global delusional trance. . . . Surrealism is alive and well, oh yes it is, just take a gander at advertising. . . . Clinton's the one man our age capable of seeming to be who he isn't and making us feel guilty for knowing that, as if we were betraying the leader of our generation, the fucking toothless asshole. . . ."

Puff-puff, gurgle-gurgle, went the water pipe, still oddly tasteless, or rather and more exactly, tasting of some kind of mentholated airiness.

Love's a passing interlude...

"Chipper, let's talk about our fathers."

"What about 'em?"

"What they did."

"In the world?"

"Exactly."

"Undermining duly elected democracies? Assassinating long-haired angels of visionary politics? Laying waste to enemies of the corporate American juggernaut? That kind of stuff?"

"Right. Did they do that, do you think?"

"Know they did, Terryster. Saw some of it myself, with these mine very own eyes, in that little faraway poem called Vietnam."

"No, I mean, do you think our fathers did anything like that? Specifically, our fathers. Yours and mine?"

He mulled this one over, ear cocked to Sarah Vaughn, hypothetical intruders, the whispers of the toy soldiers on the shelves. "Haven't a fucking clue. Probably. Yes."

"In Kurash?"

He turned his eyes, pupils now dilated fiercely into points of concentrated, refracted light, on me. "You think they're friends, your father and mine?"

"Of course."

His immediate smile, leering close, was sadistic. "Let me tell you a story."

And he did.

About the night in Kurash in 1958 that my parents and the Sweetsers were having dinner with his parents, no children invited, about the game of charades they played after dinner and how Chipper saw it all from the top of the stairs, where he was hiding, where, like all of us a victim of genetic coding, he was spying.

His father and mother were sitting side by side on the couch that night, his father unusually quiet and somewhat morose. He had been acting odd, Chipper had noticed, for several weeks, coming home early from work and taking long naps, staying up late at night alone listening to his favorite musicals, *Oklahoma!* and *My Fair Lady*, over and over again on the record player. He started smoking, which he never used to do, and once or twice Chipper heard him yelling at his mother, also an unheard-of event—his father was, normally, very gentle, very considerate. He seemed now to be struggling to contain himself, to not explode, tight and anxious as he paced the house lecturing Chipper repeatedly about the virtues of an organized life, a disciplined life, a life with clearly defined objectives, a life approached with *focus*. "I'm no smarter than the next guy, Chipper," his father would tell him. "Hell, I'm a lot dumber than some of them, say Mack Hooper, who thinks he's pretty damn smart, and I suppose is. But the reason I'm successful is that I know how to stay *focused*." Until that moment, Chipper had not known that his father was successful. He had not even known that such a concept existed—success—and that with it came its shadow self, its dark twin: failure. He was watching his father unravel and succumb to failure's sad nourishment and even as a thirteen-year-old kind of realized it. He saw it most clearly, most frighteningly, perhaps, in his mother's eyes those weeks, the way her Memphis drawl with its funny, teasing flourishes became more and more frantic and inane. She was worried, and Chipper knew it.

So there they were, his parents, sitting side by side on the couch, with my parents and the Sweetsers arrayed before them in various armchairs, the men straddling leather ottomans. *Clink-clink* went the ice cubes, *glug-glug* went the delicious-looking drinks, gin and tonics for the most part. *Puff-puff-puff,* everyone sucked on cigarettes, the living room downstairs was tumultuous with smoke. That, and laughter, joyous, intimate laughter rising as they played The Game, our charades. A time when these otherwise repressed Wasps kicked off their shoes and threw themselves so entirely into mute dramatic renderings that casual observers, visiting Kurashians for example, could be forgiven for thinking something was wrong, that maybe Americans were a little crazy in unexpected ways. While we're on the subject of repressed Wasps, I think it's important to get one thing straight: Wasps, My People, as I lived among them in 1958, were not repressed in their behavior, as purveyors of popular culture seem to believe. In fact, these Wasps were often highly eccentric and flamboyant in their behavior, for example my father that night in the Gourlies' house leaping about like the village idiot, yanking on his tie, tongue lolling, bent double and dragging his hands on the floor. All this accompanied by gales of laughter and wild applause, from everyone but Mr. Gourlie, who was slumping deeper and deeper into his funk. No, these Wasps were repressed only when it came to their deepest feelings, so susceptible were they to being overwhelmed, laid waste, by joy or terror or hurt.

Chipper watched from the top of the stairs as Mr. Gourlie, Milton Gourlie, his father, lumbered reluctantly from the couch and assumed his place in front of the crowd. My mother handed him a small, folded piece of paper, upon which had been written, by the opposing team, the subject he must enact. He pondered it for quite a long time, long enough for Mrs. Gourlie to become concerned.

"Milton? Are we there? Alive and breathing?"

He looked up, slightly dazed, took a deep breath, and made a weird circular motion with his hand.

"Milton, how many words?" his wife, Chipper's mother, interrupted.

He thought deeply, held up five fingers.

"Five words," everyone recited, relieved.

He nodded vigorously, then again made that strange circular motion with his hand.

"A movie," my mother said.

He held his forefinger to the side of his nose.

"A movie with five words in the title," my father said.

Chipper's father again held his forefinger to the side of his nose. He seemed, in the process, to glare at my father.

"First word, darling?" Mrs. Gourlie asked.

He pinched his fingers together.

"Small word," Mr. Sweetser called out.

"Of, an, the—"

Frantic waving from Mr. Gourlie.

"The Something Something Something Something."

He held up three fingers.

"Third word."

He pinched his fingers together.

"Another small word."

"An, of, the, it, and—"

More hopping.

"The Something and Something Something," his wife mused.

He held up four fingers.

"Fourth word?"

He pinched his fingers together.

"An, of, the, it—"

He was jabbing his finger at Mrs. Sweetser, who had started the recitation.

"It?"

He shook his head.

"The?"

He touched his nose with his forefinger.

"The Something and the Something."

"A movie."

He held up two fingers.

"Second word?"

To their absolute astonishment, and Chipper's, up on the staircase, his father proceeded to disrobe, ripping off his shirt, prying off his shoes, hopping from foot to foot as he yanked away his socks, stepping out of his trousers, pulling down his boxer shorts. Mrs. Sweetser screamed. My mother was laughing so hard she had tears in her eyes.

"Naked?" Mrs. Gourlie ventured.

Her husband touched his finger to his nose, then whirled on my father. "You think I don't know what's going on, Mack? Do you really think I'm a total idiot? Don't answer that. Fuck you. Suck my dick."

He fondled himself.

"The Naked and the Something," Mr. Sweetser said, trying to get The Game back on track.

"Dead, you morons," Mr. Gourlie practically screamed. "The Naked and the fucking Dead."

At which point, he collapsed to the floor, writhing and clutching an imaginary wound so realistically that everyone gasped. A profoundly uneasy silence fell upon the room, broken only by Milton Gourlie's slobbering gasps and writhing naked contortions. Chipper's mother rose from the couch, squatted down beside him, placed her hand gently on his forehead. He let himself be calmed, until he was still, and then she eased him upright by the elbows and led him away to their bedroom. He turned around only once, at the doorway, and hurtled these words back at my father: "You want my job, Mack? Take it. It's yours."

The Sarah Vaughn record had come to an end, the stereo, the

basement, as silent as my parents' shock forty years earlier. Chipper was for the moment consumed and distant and, I suspect, sad. Sad for his fallen father those many years ago, sad for his white-haired mother now dying in her room on Dumbarton Avenue. I, in my armchair, my head oddly calm and lucid, felt only a painless guilt, more knowledge than feeling, just an awareness that my father had, inadvertently, I hoped, somehow caused Chipper's father great pain, a paranoia that had finally brought him down.

"That was his nervous breakdown?" I asked.

"That was his nervous breakdown."

"I'm sorry."

Chipper shrugged, handing me the pipe. "Another cold warrior bites the dust."

"What kind of pot is this anyway?" I asked him, sucking down the ethereal smoke and passing the pipe back to him. "It doesn't have any taste."

"Pot?" He looked around the room, searching for such a thing, the meaning of such a thing. "This ain't pot, Terryster."

The Zippo sparked; he sucked at nothingness.

"What is it then?" My face was already flushed with panic.

"This here is grade-A crack."

"Goddamnit, Chipper." I stood, furious.

My heart was hammering. Was this it? Was I going to OD in the basement of Chipper Gourlie's house? "Whiskey," I gasped.

With concerned and gentle attentiveness, he poured me a stiff shot of Glenlivet. I downed it, then another, and another. It took a fourth to calm my heart, to slow down the palpitating anguish in my chest. Now drunk, I asked Chipper to take me home to his parents' house.

Good middle-class boy to the end.

Citizen of Little America.

5

The day following Milton Gourlie's performance of *The Naked and the Dead,* he did not come to work. Nor did he communicate with anyone. My father, Roy Sweetser, and Renee all covered for him, though they never had a discussion about it, they drew up no battle strategy. Protecting their own was instinctive. Three days passed, four days. The Ambassador came down for a visit, a very rare occurrence, seeing as how the station offices gave him the "willies," as he put it. He peeked into Milton's empty office, sought out my father.

"So, Mack, I haven't seen Milton around lately," the Ambassador began.

"Milton? Really? He's here somewhere."

"He missed the staff meeting this week."

"To tell you the truth, he's been pretty busy."

"Ah. Good. Tell him to stick his head in to see me, would you?"

My father called the Gourlies' house. Mrs. Gourlie answered.

"How is he?" my father asked.

"Terrible. He won't get out of bed."

"I'll come over."

"I don't think that's a good idea."

Finally my father felt he had no choice but to cable Hodd Freeman with the facts and to ask for advice, knowing full well that this would end Milton's career. The Gourlies were immediately flown back to the States. After a short delay, my father was promoted to station chief.

My parents celebrated downstairs in the living room, candlelight and champagne, more Frank Sinatra.

My father continued carrying the monthly briefcase full of American cash to Hamzah Palace.

The best time to try and talk to Milton Gourlie, I discovered, was in the morning, over breakfast, gentle Mary padding in and out with orange juice and coffee. This was a beautiful old room, the "small" as opposed to the "formal" dining room. It had a low ceiling, a fireplace, and an uneven polished brick floor. A bathroom door at one end was graced with a half model of a black-and-white steamer, THE HEAD painted in white on the hull. A French door opened out to the flagstone patio and garden. Mrs. Gourlie was upstairs in bed, locked in her losing battle with cancer, shades drawn against the light, the heat, the buzzing cicadas, memories of her annual Easter party in that garden, brightly painted eggs hidden by her the night before among the boxwoods and discovered the next day, Easter, by Chipper and his little friends in their Sunday best as they ran beneath rolling peals of music from nearby church bells. Milton Gourlie seemed to me to be in a permanent state of shell shock, the effect no doubt of his wife slowly dying next to him. He had visibly softened, as if his bones had lost some of their vitality.

"Mr. Gourlie?" I began, on a hopeful note.

I still called him Mr. Gourlie, as I still called the dying, white-haired hostess upstairs Mrs. Gourlie.

He looked at me, friendly, brain-dead. "How's your old man these days?"

That's the twelfth time he'd asked me that question.

"He's fine," I said. "That's actually what I wanted to ask you about. My father. And you. In Kurash."

He narrowed his eyes thoughtfully, touched by a vague, not-altogether pleasant memory.

"In 1958," I finished gamely.

"Ah." A noncommittal puckering of the eyebrows. He picked at his sectioned grapefruit, Mary's handiwork.

Subject broached, I pressed on. "When you left, in June, what happened? I mean, why did you leave?"

"I wasn't cut out for that game," he said. "So I retired. I'm rich."

"What, exactly, weren't you cut out for? What made you quit just then?"

"Poor health."

"Was my father in any way responsible?"

"For my leaving? Not at all."

"You didn't feel threatened by him?"

"Good God no, why should I?"

"Because it must have been clear fairly early on that he was going to take your job away from you."

Mr. Gourlie fixed me with an angry look, then shook his head. "Your father had nothing to do with it. My health failed me; that's all."

Since talking to Chipper, I'd found a few relevant cables in the Research Library at Langley. Though the term "nervous breakdown" is never used, "high anxiety," is referred to, as well as "work-related stress . . . a growing realization among his co-workers that he had reached the edge of his limit and must be helped." A memo from the embassy doctor in particular pointed out the "eight unrelieved years of seriously demanding work Milton Gourlie has put in, first in Berlin, then Rome, and finally here in Hamra. He is physically and mentally exhausted, and I highly recommend an immediate leave of absence." My father, when I called him on the phone and asked him what had happened, said simply that Mr. Gourlie had "fallen to pieces." My mother could add only that Mr. Gourlie had "just sort of unraveled; I could see it happening, we all could, but we didn't really understand what it meant until it was too late to do anything about it. We were very naive in those days. Psychologically, I mean."

Now Mr. Gourlie rose a little shakily from the breakfast table, wandered into the study. I could hear him making himself a gin and tonic, then settling down before the TV, a loud and imbecilic game show. He would remain there, except for a two-hour siesta, until dinner, the fragments of what he knows lost forever within his drifting consciousness.

There's enough sadness in this house to crush the bravest of men.

I escaped to my Taurus and drove over to Renee's apartment on Wisconsin Avenue. She lived in one of those attractive, European-style apartment buildings not too far from the National Cathedral flung up during the thirties to take advantage of all the bright young men and women coming to Washington to manage that great national rescue mission known as the New Deal. I called Renee last night, told her I was here, that I wanted to see her. "Come on over," she'd commanded in that gravelly voice of hers, musical with Salems and Smirnoff. I parked about a block away, walked along the sidewalk buckled by the roots of oaks and elms. It was a clear, cool day, sky blue, and as I walked I wondered what exactly I expected to learn from Renee, for it's always been clear to me that her loyalty toward my father has never slackened, that she would as soon die for him today as forty years ago. I hadn't seen her in over a decade, and so when she answered her door and I saw that she had shrunk at least a foot, her hands curling into small arthritic claws, I was a little taken aback. She looked like a troll. But her bulbous eyes, magnified by the thick lenses of her glasses, gazed at me as lucidly and skeptically as ever. "Is that you?" she asked. "It doesn't look like you."

"It's me."

She let me in with a halfhearted smile and a proffered cheek, which I kissed. A squirming worm of a dachshund, toenails clicking across the old parquet floor, leaped at me and started humping my leg. "Get off, you horny old goat," Renee ordered. He ignored her. She did nothing about it, turning and heading toward an armchair in the living room. I pried the beast off me, held him at bay as best I could, and joined Renee, sitting across from her on a ratty couch. The dachshund sat staring at me accusingly, mournfully. I'd jilted him.

"Poor Bertie," Renee sighed. "He's damn near as old as I am."

She fixed me with that unsettling, magnified look. "Goddamn, it really is you. I can see it now. I'm glad you're here. I'm glad you came to call. First of all, how're your mom and dad? I haven't heard from them in a long time. Still living in Boston?"

"Yes, though not together."

"What do you mean, not together?"

I told her. She listened, shook her head. "How odd."

"I agree," I said.

"And they go to the symphony?"

I nodded. "Plus every Sunday they walk to the Museum of Fine Art, look at some paintings, have lunch. Tuesday is movie night. They prefer foreign movies. Mom says she likes subtitles. They give her something to read."

Renee digested all this. Bertie started humping my leg again. "Stop it, you disgusting animal," she hissed, kicking at him.

I gently pushed Bertie away.

"What are you doing in Washington?" Renee asked me. "Where are you staying? Do you need a place to stay? I don't have much room, but you can always use my couch."

I told her I was staying with the Gourlies. She looked grave.

"I hear Lorraine's not doing too well."

"No, she's not. I think she's dying."

"Not much to say about that, is there? I always liked Lorraine. How's Milton bearing up?"

I shrugged, thinking to spare her a description of his decrepitude. She had, after all, known the man when he was young and strong. Then I asked her if she knew where I might be able to find the Sweetsers.

"Mr. Sweetser's dead, honey. Lung cancer. Mrs. Sweetser moved south somewhere. South Carolina? Don't know what happened to Carolyn. Penny lives here, though. You should give her a call. She's listed. I'm sure she'd love to hear from you."

Penny, who, smiling sweetly, took me into the shadows of a corner of the Hut where we slow-danced alone, her forehead resting on my shoulder, her hands around my waist, my cheek pressed to the top of her thick blond hair, which tickled my nose, my hands around her waist, our bodies touching. We kissed, once, with the studious intention of ten-year-olds learning fractions, she pointed me innocently into the lascivious thicket of sexual desire from which I have never escaped.

"So tell me what you're doing here?" Renee asked again.

"I'm researching a book," I said. "I'm an historian, Renee. I specialize in relatively esoteric subjects. Modes of Diplomatic Deceit, Methodologies for a Late Millennium Corporate Self-Questioning, stuff like that."

As I'd hoped, her eyes had grown glassy with the effort of feigning interest. "Do you teach?"

"Yes, in California, Los Angeles."

"What a strange place to teach history. They don't have any."

"I know. It makes everything very hypothetical. I've gotten used to it. I even kind of like it." And now, with great skill, masterful sleight of hand, I hoped, I began. "What I'm researching is Kurash in 1958."

"Whatever for?"

"To understand what it was like to be a part of the American overseas subculture during the cold war."

"You expect people to buy this book?"

"Libraries, mainly," I extemporized. "And students. Sure. Why not? It's interesting stuff. Details of a vanished life."

"If you say so. I spent most of my time being a drunk, so I can tell you that the bottom of a vodka bottle looks pretty much the same anywhere in the world. Is that helpful? Bertie, stop licking yourself, for godsake." She nudged the offending dog with her toe. He continued slobbering. "I'm in AA now," Renee went on dreamily. "If you were to ask me what the present is like, as opposed to the past, I would say it's an AA meeting. I guess you could say my life, from beginning to end, has been pretty limited."

"Not true, Renee. Think of all the things you've done, the places you've been."

"Twenty years of boozing, twenty years of talking about boozing."

"You worked for the C.I.A., Renee. That's pretty cool."

"Not a fact to broadcast in this day and age. It's like saying you worked for the S.S. or something. Overthrowing happy innocent peasant governments, assassinating well-meaning nonaligned Socialist saints, opening your grandmother's mail, listening on your grandmother's telephone line . . ." She trailed off, angry, exhausted.

"Renee, what were you doing, really? People should know. The story should be set straight."

"I wasn't doing anything. It was people like your father who were doing things. People like your father who took all the risks while everyone else flipped hamburgers and drooled over the latest Chevy, never even asking themselves how all this material plenitude could be possible in the midst of a goddamn war."

"The cold war?"

"The cold war. Yes. Only it wasn't so cold in places like Kurash."

"Tell me," I encouraged her.

"I didn't *do* anything, I already told you. I answered the phone. I ran the shredder. I drank."

It was time to risk getting a little more specific. "Tell me about the King."

"A lovely man. Short. Head too big, lots of teeth when he

smiled. He had a good soul, you could tell. And he was so young. A boy, really. I saw him maybe twice."

"He and Dad spent a lot of time together, right?"

"A fair amount, yes."

"Doing what, exactly, if you remember?"

She gave me a funny look, the dawning of doubt. "They liked to race those little race cars, what were they called?"

"Go-carts."

"Right. Go-carts."

"What else?"

"Have you asked your father any of these questions?" she asked me, eyes quite focused behind those thick lenses.

"Oh, yeah, absolutely. Of course. But an historian has to get everyone's point of view. The Whole Story. The Big Picture."

"And what did he tell you?"

"I'd have to look at my notes, Renee. Something about extending our intelligence presence in Kurash, if I remember right. Helping the King keep Nasser at arm's length."

"Well, that's more than I know." She settled back in her chair, lit a Salem, inhaled deeply, coughed violently, recovered. Bertie watched this all from the floor, furry eyebrows arched quizzically.

"What can you tell me about the briefcase full of money Dad took to the King every month?" Might as well be direct at this point, I figured.

Renee tapped her cigarette ash into one of those small bean-bag ashtrays on the arm of her chair. "I don't recall a briefcase full of money."

"Do you recall a man named Kumait al-Farid?"

"No."

"General Anwar?"

"Of course. Everyone knew about him. He was chief of staff or something, right? Betrayed the King, the bastard. Worked for Nasser. Right?"

"Major Rashid?"

"Kurashian Intelligence. A nice man, your father always said."

"Did he work for us, or the King?"

"What has any of this got to do with American overseas subtitles, or whatever you called it?"

"Subculture. It's the context, Renee. The surrounding circumstances. What you saw when you peeped over the wall of your Uncle Sam ghetto."

"I saw empty bottles, like Faulkner." She stubbed out the Salem, labored to her feet. "Time to take Bertie for a walk. If I don't, he'll pee all over the place. His bladder's shot. Old age, poor thing. He's falling apart. Just like me."

She was already moving toward the door, picking up a leash draped over the doorknob, Bertie thrashing his way across the parquet floor in a slippery-footed frenzy of excitement. *Click-click-click.* "Stop slobbering, Bertie. Hold still."

I went with them out to the shady sidewalk on Wisconsin Avenue. Bertie, whimpering and straining against the leash, tugged Renee forward, practically pulled her off her feet. I tagged along. Renee granted me a sidelong glance.

"Was it hard for you, all the secrecy?" she asked.

I found myself fighting tears. "Yes."

This was not the way things were supposed to go. The pain Renee touched so easily irritated me; I shoved it back down my throat, surreptitiously dried my eyes with the back of my hand.

"Your father was always very proud of you," she persisted, as if to drag, with this patent falsehood, the pain right back up and reduce me to bawling idiocy. "He always showed everyone in the office your report card."

"My report card?" This was new information.

"You always got such good grades. Years later, when you got into Harvard, he sent me a postcard."

He never said anything to me about my grades, about Harvard, where, by the way, I was miserable, almost never leaving my room in Adams House, except to throw tomatoes at the visiting secretary of defense, Robert S. McNamara, and, several times, to drive down here to Washington to protest the Vietnam War. Why was Renee telling me this? I watched her hobble along next to me. She wanted me to forgive him, my father, to see him as she sees him, in a more favorable light, a damn near heroic light, a quiet shadow of a man lighting a cigarette on a foggy street corner, alone with himself and his knowledge, fighting a war he can never win and for which he can never be publicly honored.

The truth is, what she forgot is, my father never let doubt of any kind creep into his lucid brain, he was a simpler man than that, they all were, those prep-school warriors, those gee-whiz kids let loose upon an unsuspecting world, more dangerous than cynics, capable of murdering someone with the same offhand cruelty with which they casually discouraged outsiders from joining their clubs—a mere shrug of their blue-broadcloth shoulders extinguishing a life.

Have I got that right? Is that it?

Tell me, Renee, please. You were there.

But she lurched along beside me in silence, tending to Bertie, who delicately lifted a hind leg and pissed on a tree.

"Why did Mr. Gourlie quit?" I asked her.

"Nerves," she said, without hesitation.

"Did it have anything to do with Dad?"

"Call me next time you're in town." She reached up and kissed me on the cheek. "Goodbye, sweet boy. Give my best to your parents. And good luck with your book."

Off she toddled, yanking at Bertie's leash.

6

July 11, 1958. Three o'clock in the afternoon. My father was returning from a meeting with Major Rashid in Rashid's office, a meeting in which they had reviewed together Roy Sweetser's work as C.I.A. liaison, which was deemed satisfactory, barely. They had also gone over the cases they had in common, most especially what they called the Question of Egyptian Intelligence. My father and Rashid were at this point convinced that the Soviets were close to ineffectual in Kurash. From their sources within the Russian embassy and the local Communist Party, it seemed clear that the Soviets commanded very little power or respect. "Who the hell wants to be a Russian?" was the way Rashid summed it up, a question my father could have answered by citing close to half the globe. He didn't, afraid he might jinx things. It was pure dumb luck for him that Soviet Communism had a hard time sinking roots into the desert sands of Kurash. Egypt, Syria, Iraq, and Palestine were a different matter—especially Palestine. The Soviets were training the disenfranchised of the Jordan Valley in the fine art of terrorism. The Israelis, no mean terrorists themselves, continued to leave Kurash alone. They had no cause for serious worry here, and a lot of serious problems elsewhere.

That left the Question of Egyptian Intelligence, and their presumed role in Desert Rose, the presumed but still unverified plot to assassinate the King.

Major Rashid had drawn a diagram on a blackboard he kept

in his office, a breakdown of the command structure of Egyptian Intelligence. It was full of gaps, blanks, no-knowledge. They knew only that the Egyptians could not run operations from their embassy, since neither Egypt nor her new ally Syria had an embassy in Kurash, diplomatic relations having been severed the previous February. "It would have been easier if His Majesty had let them stay in their damn embassy," my father muttered. "At least we'd know where the bastards are." Rashid concurred with a distracted nod. My father was frustrated, and getting a little scared. For months Rashid's people had scoured Kurash for more concrete evidence of a clandestine Egyptian presence. They had intercepted trucks crossing the border from Syria filled with Russian-made weapons, machine guns, hand grenades, bazookas. They had caught several junior-grade Kurashian officers and bureaucrats meeting with members of Egyptian Intelligence who produced diplomatic passports when arrested, claiming immunity and flying back to Cairo. They had arrested and interrogated, to no avail, five Kurashian businessmen who often traveled to Egypt and were purported to have Nasserite sympathies. Nothing had led to anything. The leads went nowhere.

Rashid did not mention General Anwar's meeting with a member of Egyptian Intelligence, nor the existence of this agent, nor Anwar's subsequent meetings with the same unmentioned agent, meetings that Rashid's men had monitored.

"What about the Muslim Brotherhood?" my father asked.

Rashid shrugged. "I don't think they're a threat to the King."

Returning to the Opel from this desultory meeting, sunlight and heat blasting off the white limestone buildings and mirror-like windshields of passing cars, my father felt a familiar depression start to push its way up from his bowels. It was too early for a drink, so he fought it as best he could, distracting himself by stopping in at Oristibach's and buying me a box of English soldiers—a box I remember him bringing home that night and handing me in my unexpected happiness, the familiar red lettering, the five French Foreign Legionnaires gleaming sleepily within. Leaving the cafeteria. We sat and ate off our orange plastic trays and talked about sports. The Washington Bullets having become the Washington Wizards caused Bob infinite grief. "What kind of basketball team is called the goddamn Wizards?" He stabbed at his quivering Jell-O. "What's wrong with Bullets? Too violent? You know what's going to be the death of us? Political correctness, that's what's going to be the death of us." We never discuss my work, what I've been reading, although he did bring up my father. "Didn't mean to shoot off at the mouth about the Old Guard," he said, blushing slightly. "I heard your father was one of them and I just want you to know I meant no disrespect. Things have changed, that's all I meant."

"I understand. Don't worry about it. But thanks."

"So what was it like, growing up the son of a spook?"

I had no way of telling him. I just shrugged, smiled. "Confusing."

"I've got a kid, he's eight, and I know I could never do that to him, move him from place to place. But then that's easy for me to say, I'm a humble public relations man, they're never going to send me overseas. I hope."

Nights, I drove back to the Gourlies' house on Dumbarton Avenue. Mrs. Gourlie never came down for dinner again. She was in too much pain, Mr. Gourlie told me. He and I ate together in the breakfast room, Mary serving. Chipper never appeared again, and when I called the number he gave me, no one answered. Several times I asked Mr. Gourlie how I could get ahold of Chipper, and his response each time was the same. "How, indeed? That's the question. Where is old Chipper? I don't know, I'm afraid. He bought a house, but he won't tell me where it is. His mother would like to see him before she dies, so I hope he shows up."

"You don't have a phone number?"

"Nope."

After dinner, he retired to his huge Sony Trinitron in the

study, the TV an intrusion that signifies, to me anyway, the fall of this particular House of Usher. No way, when I was a kid, would there have been a TV in this house, or any of our houses, for that matter. TV was "a waste of time." It was the Idiot Box. Watching TV was like eating at McDonald's, not something "we" did. Yet here he was, all these years later, rendered insensate by his sadness and his tired body and his once-beautiful wife dying of cancer upstairs, and the only time I saw him happy was when he sat grinning in front of that TV. Actually, Mrs. Gourlie was never beautiful, she had kind of a horsey face, full-fleshed, a little coarse. But she carried herself with such innate good grace that she always seemed beautiful, to me, as a kid. I waved good night to Mr. Gourlie and walked around Georgetown, stopping in at Clyde's for a beer, gazing up at yet another TV screen, *Monday Night Football,* the pleasant drone of Al Michaels's voice as comforting as ten-year-old malt whiskey. There I reviewed, in my increasingly befuddled mind, all that I had read in the Research Library at Langley, adding whatever facts of history had emerged clearly and truthfully from the swamp of ancient paperwork to my enlarging chronology of the time, 1958, in Kurash.

Roy Sweetser's performance review, dated December 12, 1957, previously cited: "Strengths: loyal, honest, hardworking, no known vices. Weaknesses: limited intelligence, limited imagination, no guts. Advancement recommendations: none."

Initialed by MG, Milton Gourlie.

Three weeks later, January 3, 1958, my father flew in from Rome. The heir apparent.

A cable from Milton Gourlie, at that very moment cackling in front of *Third Rock from the Sun,* regarding important supply issues, namely, how the hell was he supposed to run an efficient station without proper supplies? And by supplies he meant, I discovered, reading further, just that: stationery, pens, pencils, erasers, typewriter ribbons, paper clips, staples, rubber bands, glue. This particular missive was dated January 5, 1958. My father had been in Hamra two days. My mother and I were still in Rome.

That would have been a time, those weeks my father was alone, when something could have happened, my father could have met a woman, sought out a woman, maybe he was alone at an embassy cocktail party and she spotted him and worked her way over to his side, offering a nice smile, a glimpse of soft mammaries, the quick tip of a pink, moist tongue that might well have led his mind from one thing to another, his body following closely, obediently, behind.

On the other hand, to fuck another woman would have been, for my father, a serious breach of security, a breach I could not see him committing.

The Big Picture, the Overview, is hard to pin down.

When I came back from Clyde's, Mr. Gourlie was still sitting in the blue light of the TV in the study, watching the Nature Channel. I bid him good night, climbed to the second floor, which creaked and moaned under my feet as I tried to steal quietly to my room and bed.

"Terry? Is that you?"

Mrs. Gourlie called me from the depths of her room. The door was open a crack. I peered within, saw that she was awake in the big bed, supported by many pillows, the bedside lamp casting a muted amber glow. Her face looked more cadaverous than ever beneath her wild white hair.

"Terry, please, come in. I want to see you."

I entered. There, in the corner, I saw her Victorian writing desk, a delicate construction of many tiny drawers. That's where she paid the bills, wrote letters to friends all over the world, delightful notes that said absolutely nothing but were a lot of fun to get, all bright chatter and malicious gossip. I'd read the ones she sent, over the years, to my mother.

"Come here." She motioned me closer.

I went and sat down beside her on the bed, taking her frail, unbelievably light hand in mine. Bones, hollow with air. She smiled at me, morphine eyes glimmering. "When I first met your father, he was twenty years younger than you are now. Think of that."

Think of that.

"I've had a good life," she said, and meant it. "I've been very, very lucky. I know that. I may be a stupid Memphis girl, but I'm not a fool."

Again, the bright, brave morphic smile. "I wanted to give you this."

She opened her free hand and held out to me a small box. I took it, examined it in the unhelpful light. It was made of olive wood, intricately patterned with inlaid mother-of-pearl.

"Open it," she said.

I did. Inside lay a little bronze figure, a reclining lion.

"Your father gave that to me. In Kurash. 1958. For my thirty-fourth birthday. I want you to have it."

I looked from the lion to Mrs. Gourlie, flustered, not at all sure how to respond. Was she the mysterious writer of the fragmentary love letter?

O love

Could that be? Mrs. Gourlie?

. . . you could not know or do know . . .

"Thank you," I said. "Thank you very much."

I leaned down and kissed her soft cheek.

"Mrs. Gourlie, do you recognize this line: '*O love, you could not know or do know the way I feel without you . . .*'? Does that ring any bells?"

"No, I'm sorry, it doesn't. What is it?"

"It's from a letter, written to my father, in Kurash, in 1958. By a woman, I'd guess. You wouldn't happen to know who that woman was, would you?"

Mrs. Gourlie was suddenly tired. It was as if the question itself exhausted her.

"I'm sorry. I'll go. Thank you again for the gift."

She held on to me for a moment longer. "Why do you want to know?"

I realized she was talking about the letter writer.

"It's important, for my research," I said idiotically.

"She lived in Rome. That's all I know. Don't tell your mother. It would break her heart."

"I think she already knows."

7

They set the potted geranium in the window; they mailed the postcard of Paris, France; they made a phone call, asked for Ernesto, and when told he didn't live there, apologized and hung up. They then, both of them, separately, Roy Sweetser and my father, headed off to one of three various safe houses: the suburban limestone place, one bedroom of which was still being used to monitor the phone tap of the Hamzah Palace; an apartment in a brand-new granite-and-glass catastrophe my father dubbed "a fine example of late Homosexual Aztec"; and another house, even smaller, located on a date farm about twenty minutes outside of Hamra. On their way, they each did everything they could to make sure they weren't being followed. They did exactly as they had been taught by their MI6 instructors at Camp Perry, Virginia, only this was no longer downtown Richmond, this was downtown Hamra, where it was a lot harder for two lumbering white men to disappear. My father entered Oristibach's, took the elevator to the second floor, browsed among British bathrobes for a few seconds, suddenly bolted up the stairs, at the third floor suddenly about-faced and returned to the second floor. There was no one behind him. He exited a service door, jumped down from a loading platform, hurried up the alley, and walked three blocks to a cab stand. He took a cab across town to Feisel Square, got out in the midst of the usual pandemonium, hundreds of Kurashians scrambling for buses, jumped into another cab, had it drop him off four blocks from the safe house, then walked the rest of the way, making sure, again, that no one was behind him.

The three agents were referred to only by their cryptonyms: Emerson, Alcott, and Thoreau. Someone with a literary sensibility, not my father, must have named them, probably one of the eggheads back in Washington who had majored in English. "It doesn't matter how well you know the history of the Baathist Party or speak the goddamn language if you can't tell shadow from act," I remember my father ranting, to my forbearing mother, in the evening, over martinis, during sacred vanished Cocktail Hour.

Emerson was a midlevel functionary in the Agriculture Department. He also belonged to the Communist Party, with which he had become deeply disenchanted, realizing that their goal was to oppose all fellow Socialists, including Nasser, who might challenge Soviet hegemony. It was from him that my father had determined that the local Communists did not pose much of a threat to the King or to United States interests. They were too disorganized.

Alcott seems to have been an Army officer, young, from a Bedouin tribe, who seriously resented what he saw as preferential treatment extended to Army officers from the city, from Palestinian families, better-educated officers who had graduated from the American University of Beirut. He was convinced that they were all, at heart, Marxists, secretly plotting the overthrow of the Hashemite family. In this Alcott was not entirely wrong, as we have seen. It was from him that Roy Sweetser learned, during the course of their meeting at the date farm safe house, that of late there had been increased nighttime maneuvers involving, especially, the Third Tank Division. Alcott was incensed that he and his fellow Bedouin officers had been excluded from a series of meetings with senior officers including General Anwar, the King's Army chief of staff.

Thoreau, interviewed by my father in the Homosexual Aztec

penthouse, appears to have been a member of the Muslim Brotherhood, maybe even a leader, for I have found in the files at Langley detailed reports on the monthly convocations of the Islamic Action Front. He had also been approached on several occasions by a deep-cover Egyptian intelligence officer, acknowledged in the files by the cryptonym Whitman, the eggheads, I guess, having run out of Transcendentalists. Major Rashid kept round-the-clock surveillance on Whitman. In fact, it was in the course of following Whitman that Rashid's men had first seen him meeting with General Anwar. About which my father still knew nothing, Rashid having decided, for reasons I don't yet understand, to keep this information to himself. My father felt fairly confident that Whitman had never succeeded in recruiting Thoreau, not so much because Thoreau was ideologically committed to the United States as because, in my father's words, "I judge him to be too anxious for his own well-being to play a game of doubles. Anyway, we pay him a lot of scratch." Thoreau, it seems pretty clear, was in it for the money. "Impecunious fuck," the division chief had called him in another cable. The division chief, Hodd Freeman, was himself heir to a perfume fortune. How self-righteous the rage of the rich.

My father and Roy Sweetser floated to each agent the possibility that Egyptian Intelligence and the Muslim Brotherhood, two unlikely coconspirators, could in fact concoct a scheme to overthrow the King. Emerson was skeptical. Alcott believed it perfectly possible, and suggested that the unexplained Army maneuvers and secret meetings might be relevant. Thoreau said only that he did not think the Egyptians would instigate or support an uprising they could not control.

None of them could know that the plot was born of love, at least on Kumait's part, not to overthrow the King but to save him from himself, from his weakness for the West. None of them could know that the plot was born of two men who had known each other since they were eighteen, students at an American university where, during the late thirties and early to mid-forties, anti-Western Arab nationalism had been born, irony of ironies. None of them could have known that of these two old and close friends, one of them, General Anwar, had lost faith in his ability to influence the King and had decided to betray the other, Kumait, by secretly conspiring with Egyptian Intelligence not only to rise up in protest but to overthrow the King and murder him as well. Anwar was a Baathist, he wanted a Baathist government in Hamra. The Egyptians far preferred Baathists to monarchic Hashemites. It was agreed. The Army would act alone, led by the Third Tank Division. The Muslim Brotherhood would be kept in the dark, and later, after the revolution succeeded, they would be eliminated, as they had been in Egypt.

This is what Anwar agreed to. This is what Kumait did not know.

On July 18, 1958, my father parked the Opel in the same spot near Oristibach's, at the same time, as he had the week before, when the envelope had first appeared. He left the car unlocked, walked away. On the passenger seat was another envelope, inside it a note written by him. It said: "We don't know who you are, we have no reason to believe you or trust you, and after some reflection have concluded that you have no idea what you're talking about. So please stop leaving envelopes in my car." The idea, of course, was to provoke this guy to such a degree of indignant wrath that he would contact them again, give them more information, ultimately reveal his identity. Roy Sweetser was on a nearby roof with binoculars and cameras. Major Rashid's men were deployed around the Opel: a waiter in a café, a taxi driver absorbed in his newspaper, a shoeshine man . . . Major Rashid sat in an unmarked car across the street. Three hours went by. Nothing happened. No one approached the Opel. Five hours, six hours. Finally, when it was dark and the street semideserted except for the occasional trolley car screeching and rattling by, Rashid called it a day. My father, who had been impatiently waiting in a restaurant around the corner, retrieved the Opel and drove home in a foul mood. The next morning, when he got in the car to drive to work, he saw an envelope on the passenger seat. Once again, as was his habit, he'd left the car unlocked. Glancing at the smiling guard in his guardhouse, my father knew without asking that he'd slept soundly most of the night.

This note named names.

Kumait, Anwar.

It was almost five o'clock, my head so dull and thick with facts I buzzed for Bob Easton. Within minutes he was there in the red doorway, hands in pockets, rocking back on his heels, collegial as ever. "All done for the day?"

"All done."

"Find anything helpful?" he asked, curious.

"Yes. Very. Thanks."

"Good, good. I'm glad."

He walked me down to the main entrance, retrieved the laminated visitor card from around my neck, shook hands good night. Then he retreated back into the building, a shy man in a gray suit, worried about his son. I was growing fond of Bob Easton.

I couldn't stand the thought of spending another evening in the Gourlie house, so on my way back into Washington I pulled over at a 7-Eleven, looked up Penny Sweetser in a phone book, then dialed her number at a pay phone. She answered on the third ring, sounding slightly harassed. "Hello?" It was a musical voice, chiming up, dipping down. "Hel-lo?" I could hear a kid crying in the background, and cartoon music coming from a TV.

"Penny?"

"Yes?"

"It's Terry Hooper."

A moment passed while Penny silently grappled with this information, cartoon music continuing in the background.

"Terry?"

"Yep."

"Well, my God, where are you?"

"Here. Washington. I was wondering if I could stop by and see you?"

"Tonight?"

"Well, if it's not a good time . . ."

"I'd love to see you, Terry, I really would, but things are kind of crazy around here right now. I'm sorry."

"No, no, I understand. Don't worry about it."

"How long are you going to be in town?"

"I don't know. Not too much longer. I'm staying at the Gourlies'."

"I haven't seen them in years. How's Chipper?"

"Strange." I decided to spare her the details. "Where's Carolyn?"

"New York. She teaches religion at Columbia. Very distinguished. Listen, Terry, I've got to go. Please call again, okay? Visit me. Promise?"

"Promise."

"Bye." She hung up, but not before I heard her say, crossly, "Jason, sweetheart, you've got to do your homework."

I drove the rest of the way to Georgetown in a mild funk, suddenly confused by the reality of Penny as a fifty-year-old woman with a husband and a kid. After our moment in the Hut, when she took me to her corner and showed me the curves of a girl's early adolescence, Ricky Nelson singing encouragement from the record player, the spinning 45, Penny and I had reverted to our prekiss selves, good friends and occasional playmates. After Kurash, we rarely saw each other until our senior year in high school, when the weird logic of chance and fate put us both at the American Community School in Beirut. ACS, as we called it, at that time, which would have been 1965, was fast becoming a haven for fun-loving kids from all over the Little America diaspora, from the Aramco oil fields of Saudi Arabia to the general consulates of Afghanistan and Kuwait. Penny and I saw each other around the campus, which by the way wasn't too far from the campus of AUB, the American University of Beirut, where

Kumait and Anwar had matriculated almost twenty years earlier. I often passed AUB on my way down to the hashish clubs of Beirut. Once I took Penny to one of those places, a narrow dark room below street level in the Arab Quarter, opaque with hash and cigarette smoke. Fifteen minutes and three tokes later, Penny, eyes bloodshot, coughing violently, made me take her back to school. "That was awful," she said. "Terrible. My head hurts. I can't believe you took me there." She didn't speak to me again for many weeks. After graduating, we both went off to Cambridge, she to Radcliffe, I to Harvard. I bumped into her once in the Blue Moon Café off Harvard Square. She was deeply into radical politics and was dressed like a drill sergeant for some third-world Socialist dictatorship in olive-green military pants and black military boots. She captured my heart all over again. I took her to a Nina Simone concert. She fell asleep during the third song, "Put a Little Sugar in My Coffee," which I had been hoping would have an aphrodisiacal effect. Instead, Penny's eyelids slowly closed, aflutter with revolutionary dreams.

Put a little sugar
in my coffee . . .

Time passed. We lost touch.

I parked around the corner on R Street, walked back to the Gourlies' on Dumbarton. Mr. Gourlie was in the study, watching the evening news and nursing a drink.

"Terryo, your Dad called," he sang out when he saw me.

I climbed the stairs to my room and dialed my father's number.

He answered, the usual scratching and coughing at the other end, trying to get it out: "Hello?"

"Dad?"

"There you are. What the hell have you been saying to Renee?"

"Nothing. Why?"

"She called me today in a complete dither. Said you must be working for the Soviets. I had to remind her that the Soviets don't exist anymore. She said, 'That's what you think, Mack. That's how damn devious they are.'" To my father's credit, he laughed.

I sat down on the bed. "Dad, I'm getting closer."

"To what?"

"What happened. In Kurash."

"Good. I'm sure it will make an interesting book."

"Why didn't Major Rashid tell you what he knew about Kumait and General Anwar?"

Silence.

"Dad?"

"I'm here."

"Why?"

More silence. I heard, distinctly, ice cubes rattling in a glass— sad, meager remnants of Cocktail Hour, like the tattered, smoke-stained banners of glorious battle brought out to view in VFW halls all across America, Saturday nights. Relics of finer days.

"Dad?"

"What?"

"Sooner or later you're going to have to talk to me about this."

"Whatever you say, kiddo."

"Okay, answer me this." I took a deep breath. "Did you have an affair with a woman in 1958?"

Rattle-rattle, glug-glug.

I pressed on. "A woman from Rome?"

"None of your damn business."

"I've got to know."

"Why?"

"It's a story. I need to know how it ends."

"You keep saying that. I don't care. Tough luck. You'll have to live in suspense. I told you before, I'm not talking anymore. I took an oath. Good night."

8

The note deposited on the passenger seat of my father's Opel outside our house in Hamra, Kurash, on the night of July 18, 1958, has not survived. At any rate, it wasn't in any of the files given to me by the C.I.A. I knew it named names because in a series of cables starting the next day, my father refers several times to the fact that Kumait and General Anwar had been explicitly identified by their unknown informant as co-conspirators in a plot to overthrow and assassinate the King. My guess is that the informant was either someone among the young Baathist Army officers or inside the Islamic Action Front of the Muslim Brotherhood.

When told of this second note by my father, Major Rashid still did not say anything about General Anwar's continued contact with the Egyptian Intelligence Service or about Kumait's involvement with the Islamic Action Front, the executive committee of which had recently convened behind the closed doors of Mohammed Riyadh's Star Line Import-Export Corporation, Ltd., on Al Banna Street near the *souk*, not far from the cafés where my father and Major Rashid used to have their post-cinema dinners. Present were: Mohammed Riyadh, middle-aged, voluble, epicene; Jamil al-Amir, a Palestinian lawyer trained in Cairo and Paris; Nasr Abu Tantawi, prematurely creaking (he was only sixty-one) and infuriatingly slow of speech, a banker; Laith Saleh, very small, hunched, in his forties, an engineer with his own general contracting business, one of the few in Kurash—it was he who had just finished building the pencil factory; and finally, of course, Kumait, our Kumait. What did they discuss? Their grotesquely naive plan to force the King to face Political Reality? Their imaginary relationship with General Anwar? Whatever it was, they were at it for three hours, and when Kumait finally emerged from the warehouse, he looked, according to Rashid's field report, "exhausted." Heading off to the nearest trolley stop, Kumait did not notice the two men at the café across the street who stood and followed him.

All that summer Radio Cairo kept up its steady stream of hysteria and loathing, Nasser's invective hurled across the air waves day and night.

I wish I could play for you the music coming from those same radios, in the *souk*, between polemics, when I would go there with my mother, afternoons after school, through the stripes of light and whirling dust motes, smells of coffee and cigarette smoke and spices, sounds of bartering and debate and of course those sweet, quavering voices and thrumming instruments on the radios rising and falling along a scale of sharp angles, dangerous memories, and hip-shaking lust. The King continued his studies with Kumait of classical Arabic poetry. Occasionally, he would come across a line or two that he recognized, that he had first heard falling from his grandfather's lips years earlier, when he was a child, and then he would always feel the same thrilling joy, qualified sometimes by a fractional sadness, for he missed the old man. When Kumait wasn't studying with the King, or writing speeches for him, or teaching his class at the university, or crafting his careful essays on pre-Islamic Kurashian culture, or attending the bimonthly clandestine meetings of the Islamic Action Front of the Muslim Brotherhood, he met with my mother and helped her with the Koran, which she was reading in an English translation. He steered her toward an interest in the mystical branches of Islam, especially Sufism. Heretical by nature, even in a religion not her own, my mother latched on to Sufism and never let go.

Her shelves in Cambridge still sag with slim volumes of Sufi wisdom bought in the English Bookshop on Al Kifah Street.

"You liked him, didn't you?"

I was calling directly from C.I.A. headquarters in Langley, on a pay phone in the lobby, believe it or not.

"Who?" my mother asked.

"Kumait."

"Don't be cheap."

"Tell me about your little excursion to the Crusader castle in Abirta."

"Excuse me?"

"August 23, 1958."

"Where are you getting all this?"

Abirta lay at the southern tip of Kurash, a three-hour drive from Hamra, all the time it took to transect Kurash from stem to stern. Wild black irises bloomed in the tawny desert. Hussein drove the red Chevy, Kumait beside him in the front seat, my mother in back. They passed caravans of gypsies who had come all the way from Turkey, tangle-haired children with long hostile stares at the roadside watching them go by; they passed the more open, curious glances of Bedouin, a long train of camels clinking and clanking its way toward Saudi Arabia; they passed, going the other way, columns of Army trucks full of waving troops rumbling north toward Hamra.

Maybe Kumait should have taken notice of those troops, those trucks. On the other hand, the Army often conducted maneuvers along Kurash's two main highways. Those British Bedford trucks, camouflage green, were a frequent sight. Nothing unusual about them. Hussein, driving, watched them disappear in the rearview mirror.

The Chevy continued south to Abirta, which could be reached only by leaving the highway and taking a dirt road several miles into the hills, then climbing upward until the castle came into sight, perched atop the highest hill with a wide, unobstructed view of the dry, yellow valley below and, in the far distance, the ribbon of highway, misty blue in the heat, mirages shimmering to life down there like ghosts of the Crusaders riding home to their castle.

"Do you notice anything odd?" Kumait asked.

My mother looked around, saw nothing strange, shook her head.

"Where are we?" he asked, smiling, ever the pedagogue.

"On a hill."

"More than a hundred miles from Jerusalem, more than a hundred miles northeast of the nearest Christian holy site. What were the Crusaders doing here?"

My mother had no idea. "I don't know," she confessed.

"No one does. This was a significant castle, too. It was built, as best we can tell, during the second great crusade of 1147. From artifacts found inside the main hall, from the existence of fairly extensive barracks for soldiers, we know that it was well stocked and well fortified." He pointed. "See that well? It's dried up now, but at the time it provided all the water these Crusaders needed to be self-sufficient. They irrigated and planted terraced fields of fruit and vegetables. They raised sheep and goats who grazed on the hillsides. By the way, women's earrings and bracelets were also excavated. These men wanted for nothing."

My mother looked around at the wind-worn, lichen-mottled walls carved with slots for archers to fire their arrows.

"There has been, over the years, some speculation that the Crusaders were here because they were protecting the Holy Grail." Kumait glanced at my mother, who seemed to be holding her breath.

I interrupted. "The Crusaders were there, they built that castle, to protect the Holy Grail?" I asked incredulously.

"It's possible, yes," my mother replied.

"Mom, you're talking about the *Holy Grail,* which exists only in a *story.*"

"Archaeologists, digging in the late 1920s, discovered a tablet with a Latin inscription which read: 'Knights of Christ, Defenders of the Faith, sworn to lay down their lives for the Holy Cup herein . . .' The tablet was found in a thick-walled antechamber, almost a vault, that had the appearance, inside, of a small chapel, with an altar. Kumait showed me."

He led her down from the wall and into the dark room, clicking his lighter to life and holding the flickering flame aloft, scanning the stone altar, a flurry of shadows.

When my mother spoke, her voice echoed. "They found no cup?"

"No." Kumait's lighter faltered, went out. He shook it, but it would not light again. In darkness, then, he said, "Whatever happens, Mrs. Hooper, I want you to know that I respect and admire you and your husband."

"Kumait, please, call me Jean. Why should anything happen?"

He said nothing.

To her credit, she made a mental note to pass on to my father Kumait's cryptic remark.

They drove to the nearest village to have lunch, the Chevy broiling. They sat at a simple wooden table under a grape arbor, served lamb and rice by a solemn little boy. Hussein ate in the kitchen. My mother could hear him in there, talking softly with the boy's mother, who cooked. Not much was said by my mother and Kumait. They were both tired, and my mother had a headache. Big black birds that looked like buzzards circled lazily overhead, floating on uplifting drafts of desert heat. Far away, a column of dust rose from the road. Kumait studied my mother, wondered how much exposure to history she could take in one day. Americans were not as tough as the British, Kumait speculated, not as enthusiastic in their assumption of protective coloration. There was something vulnerable about these Americans, and yet, or maybe for that very reason, something dangerous, too, something he could not understand, and feared, like the lethal, playful blow of a huge spoiled child.

"Jean, do you remember expressing to me once an interest in visiting a Palestinian camp?"

They were sipping Turkish coffee. Fed, my mother felt stronger. She lit a Chesterfield, and the nicotine drove away the remainder of her headache.

"Yes," she said.

"There is such a camp near here," Kumait said. "We could stop on the way back to Hamra if you wished."

"I'd like that very much, yes. Thank you."

But she was in no way prepared for the sight, coming down into a shallow valley in the wallowing, jolting Chevy, that now rose to greet her, a pile of tiny shacks made from bits and pieces of plywood and plastic and tin signs and oil drums split open and spread into warped rectangles, children with swollen brown bellies swarming around the car with outstretched begging hands, high-pitched voices chattering incomprehensibly, like insane sewing machines, big dark eyes peering at her with desperate curiosity through the dusty window. Kumait knew immediately that he had made a mistake, miscalculated. He ordered Hussein to turn the car around. But it was too late, the children had been joined by adults, men and women draped in black, obscured in black, dark eyes pressed to the windows, staring in animal bafflement. Hussein managed to maneuver the car into an open space in front of a building made of mud bricks and flying the Kurashian flag. The crowd pressed closer, surrounding the Chevy. Kumait gently forced his way out and stood in the stultifying heat, hand shadowing his eyes as he squinted around for help. It came from an unlikely source, a cocky young man in torn American blue jeans and a New York Giants T-shirt, who appeared from among the tin huts carrying a machine gun. His hair was thick, curly, wild. When he smiled, it was the smile of the simpleminded, someone who could torture with a grin as easily as crack a joke. Or so it seemed to Kumait. But remember, for him almost as much as for my mother, there was a foreignness to the Palestinians, a frightening Otherness that as a desert Arab he could never quite overcome. Hussein considered reaching for the loaded pistol he kept in the glove compartment, as per my father's orders, but decided against it, for he knew that even if he could get it out in time it would be useless; in fact, it would inflame the situation. The young man swaggered up to Kumait, leaned down, and glanced into the Chevy at my mother, who was sitting there remarkably calm; in fact, she nodded politely and offered him a friendly smile. Kumait noticed that and was impressed. Straightening, the young man looked Kumait in the eye and said, his smile in place and masking his words, "Are you crazy? What are you doing here with her?"

Kumait summoned his dignity. "She's a visiting American. A concerned American."

"Today of all days?" The young man glanced around at the silent, sullen faces surrounding them, then spoke urgently to Hussein. "I'll try and clear the way. Get her out of here now."

"What do you mean, 'Today of all days'?" Kumait asked.

"Turn the car around. Now."

Both Kumait and Hussein got back into the car. With a show of great authority, waving his machine gun when necessary, the young man cleared a path for the Chevy to follow. Hussein deftly but nervously, sweating, eyes small with worry, worked the car through the crowd. As he finally pulled away and the Chevy lurched its way up the rutted incline, my mother was startled to hear a sudden loud spattering on the roof, as of a harsh summer squall, hard pellets of rain clattering on the car's metal. It wasn't rain, she saw, looking back through the rear window. It was rocks, hurtled by angry children with arms like brittle sticks. Hussein gunned the car and they gained the summit, speeding through dust to the highway, then north toward Hamra.

9

Major Rashid sat in his office with a view of downtown Hamra and gazed vacantly at a cigarette smoldering in the black plastic ashtray on his desk, papers neatly arranged in perfect stacks. The shadows lengthened in the room. Darkness was creeping in around him, settling on the couch, the Bedouin rug, the portrait of the King on the wall, a smiling, broad-faced young man in a khaki military uniform and red-and-white-checked *kaffiyeh*. Rashid's gaze lingered a long moment upon that portrait, and then he reluctantly stood, picked up the spool of audiotape he had been holding in his hands, slid the tape into a manila envelope. As an afterthought, he pushed out his still smoldering cigarette in the ashtray. Straightening his tie, brushing back his sparse, graying hair, he glanced once more about the room, clasped the manila envelope to his side, and walked out the door, past his secretary, Suha, to whom he tossed a diffident "good night," past the junior officers, who nodded diligently if not obsequiously in his wake. He rode down in the squeaking elevator, crossed the echoing modern lobby where soldiers lounged with machine guns cradled in their arms. Finally, gratefully, he gained admittance to the cool twilight air. He stopped and breathed deeply. He was sweating, he realized, sweat that now vaporized in the desert breeze. The lights of Hamra blinked on prematurely before him, the bells of the trolley cars rang loudly, cars and pedestrians jammed the streets and sidewalks, the European cafés were open and filled with life. To Rashid this all seemed to be happening very far away and to have very little to do with him.

Over the hill, across Jebel Hamra, Little America pulled in its sails for the night.

Hard to describe this place out of time, except to say that it was at its core deeply American, or maybe that was more desire than accomplishment, maybe the view from my bedroom window as the sun set was more hallucination than actuality.

Picture an American village then, at twilight, identical tidy modest homes arranged in a pleasing suburban pattern along the straight ribbon of a road, each with its own patch of bright green lawn, most with a new Chevy or Ford (we're the only ones with a foreign car, I'm not sure why) parked at the curb, each with a barbecue grill nodding by the back wall, a tricycle upended in a walkway, a baseball bat left out among the daffodils. See the mothers calling their kids from the kitchen doors; see the kids, the girls relentlessly roller-skating, the boys religiously flinging a baseball back and forth through the impending, deepening dark, see them reluctantly pull apart and move off to their respective homes, their voices drifting behind them in the still air. " 'Night, Terry. See ya, Chipper. Stop pickin' your nose, Penny." See the men, the fathers, still wearing their office suits, minus the jackets, the sleeves of their luminous white shirts rolled high, see them out watering their tiny green patches. One of them is my father, and he seems for the moment peaceful, lost in the quiet necessary ritual of holding the hose above the roses, the jasmine, the roots of the olive tree. When he hears the sound of a car approaching, he looks up and watches Rashid's Mercedes pull over and park behind his Opel. Major Rashid gets out, holding something in his hand. The sun disappears the last quarter inch, horizon blinking to black, candle snuffed out, and suddenly it's night.

The King, meanwhile, was busy visiting the new pencil factory, which had finally commenced business, clambering like a child from machine to machine while a nervous Laith Saleh explained what each did. "This one here carves the wood into pencil-thin rods. This machine chops them into pencil-length pieces, like so. Now they move along this belt until they get here, where a hole is bored through each pencil. Can you see? Next the lead is injected. . . ."

The King reveled in the smells of wood shavings and machine oil, felt, within himself, a soaring optimism take hold, a real conviction that Kurash could and would create an economy for itself. Money was freedom, he ruminated, eyes on the first batch of finished pencils as they came shooting out of the last machine. The beaming Laith Saleh handed the King a pencil, then indicated a nearby pencil sharpener. The King inserted the pencil, briskly turned the handle until the blades were chattering smoothly, pulled out the pencil, now tapering to a point, and wrote on a pad of paper handed to him deferentially by Saleh: "To Laith Saleh and all the workers of the Jerash Pencil Factory, with many thanks and congratulations." He then signed his name. Saleh, reading the message, blushed with pleasure. He read it aloud to the workers, who cheered.

My father was by now sitting with Rashid in his study at the back of our house, first floor, staring unhappily at the spent tape spinning noisily on his reel-to-reel. He leaned forward and turned off the tape.

"Every time you visit me like this, it's with bad news," my father said.

"I'm sorry."

"You've had them under surveillance for how long?"

"Three weeks."

"You should have told me sooner, Rashid."

"I wanted to be sure. They are my friends, too."

My father nodded. He wasn't going to argue with Rashid over procedure. In fact, he thought Rashid had acted properly, intelligently. He would have done the same thing.

"I miss our moviegoing days," my father said with a smile.

"Me, too, Mack."

"I saw in the newspaper that *Vertigo* is playing at the Majestic."

Rashid looked blank.

"Alfred Hitchcock," my father clarified.

"Ah."

My father gazed at the reel-to-reel. "We should tell him."

"Yes, I think so. He should be back at the palace by now."

My father gestured toward the briefcase in the corner. "It's that time of month anyway. He's expecting me at eight."

They both glanced at their watches. It was eight-thirty.

"I was wondering, Mack. Would you mind going alone? I'm not sure I can stand to see his face when he finds out."

My father nodded, reluctantly.

About now, the King returned from the pencil factory.

About now, the King found Esmerelda in his bedroom, sitting on the little settee, smoking a cigarette and leafing through a women's magazine, *Vogue,* he saw, stepping closer.

"You look beautiful this evening, Esmerelda." He anointed her with his happy grin.

"You look pretty smashing yourself, Your Majesty."

And so they fell to bed, her throaty giggle making him nuts, his mouth grasping at her belly, her slippery sweetness on his tongue as he dove between her legs and she moaned emphatically, grunted is more like it, lifting her haunches and thrusting her pelvis against his lips, her strong fingers tugging at his head. Her breasts greeted him when she hauled him back up, trying to taste herself on his mouth. "Fuck me, Your Majesty," she whispered in his ear. "Fuck me, please." She spread her legs wide as he rose and entered her, slipped in and reared high and hard, fast, as he felt her fingers beneath him furiously rubbing her clitoris, also hard and fast, quick little movements that brought forth a stuttering series of gasps, her whole body coiling backward, her knees now riding his shoulders, her ankles clasped behind his back. "Come inside me, Your Majesty," she hissed, her hot breath in his mouth almost fetid, dank, issuing all the way up from her bowels, shit-taste. He came, slamming them both back against the headboard, draining himself into her, way up, way deep.

When he awoke, someone was knocking. He sat up in bed, groggy, weak. He had no idea what time it was. Esmerelda cast him a smile from where she lay sleepily next to him. "There's someone at the bloody door."

"Who is it?" he shouted. "I'm sleeping."

The meek voice of Mabud, one of the domestic servants, filtered through the closed door. "The American is here, Your Majesty."

"The American?"

"Mr. Hooper, Your Majesty."

Then the King remembered. It was Tuesday. The briefcase.

"Damn. Just a minute."

My father, standing in the hallway about five feet behind the servant, heard fumbling noises and a girl's giggles coming from inside the King's quarters and realized what was going on. He chuckled, said to the servant, "I'll be back." He was just starting away when the door was flung open and the King, flushed, hair disarrayed, looked out and smiled. "Mack. Come in."

"Your Majesty, I can wait for you down in your study—"

"No, no, don't be absurd, come on in."

My father could smell the sex on the King as he stepped aside to let my father enter the bedroom. A girl wearing blue jeans and a gray sweatshirt watched him curiously. She had short dark curly hair, tousled at the moment, and eyes pleasantly bloodshot.

"Hi."

She was English. He felt he'd seen her somewhere before. At the American Club? Or a party? "Hi." he said.

It was awkward, with the briefcase. He looked around for someplace to put it. He saw the girl noticing the handcuff. She turned to the King. "Should I go?"

"I think it might be best," the King replied. "My apologies. I'd forgotten I had an appointment. By the way, this is my friend Mack Hooper. Mack, this is Esmerelda Tweedy."

My father and Esmerelda shook hands.

"Nice to meet you," she said, somehow mischievous. To the King: "Toodleoo, Your Majesty."

The King laughed, clearly delighted. She left with a little wave, closing the door behind her.

"Sorry to interrupt," my father said when they were alone.

"God save me from this girl," the King said.

My father would have made a mental note to check up on this Esmerelda Tweedy.

Using the King's copy of the key, they unlocked the handcuff. My father handed the briefcase to the King, who without looking inside stashed it behind the bed.

While the King sipped Coca-Cola and my father sipped Jack Daniel's, the King excitedly told my father about the pencil factory he had visited that evening.

My father lit a cigarette.

He would have wondered, idly, if the girl, Esmerelda, posed a security risk.

Dreading it, he told the King that he had unfortunate news to share.

According to the cable he sent Washington the next day: "I explained to the King that during the course of routine investigations into the activities of suspected Egyptian Intelligence operatives, Major Rashid and I had stumbled upon a few unpleasant facts. I told him the facts. I showed him the surveillance photographs. I played him the tape Rashid had made of conversations between the two principals. I laid out for him the daily schedules of each man. I told him that it was my and Rashid's firm conviction that Kumait and General Anwar were involved in, were the leaders of, a plot to overthrow and assassinate him."

The King stood, walked across the room, opened the window, and looked out into the darkness of the garden below. Without turning around, he asked, "When?"

"We don't know, Your Majesty. We've had warnings that it could happen as soon as this week. Our suggestion is that you arrest both men now."

"No."

My father didn't like this at all. "Your Majesty—"

"No, Mack." When the King turned and once again faced my father, he had tears in his eyes. "No."

O love

"Where are they?" he asked, fumbling for a cigarette.

"Kumait is with my wife, visiting the Crusader ruins in Abirta. They should have been back two hours ago. General Anwar is with the Third Tank Division, on maneuvers, I'm not sure exactly where, which to be honest makes me very nervous."

"Find them both; tell them I want to talk to them. Tomorrow."

My father drove straight to the embassy and cabled Hodd Freeman the King's response. He was still trying to track down General Anwar's exact whereabouts when tanks from the Third Tank Division struck Hamra from the north. The First and Second Infantry Brigades moved in from the west and the east. They met little resistance. After a brief firefight, they overran the National Police Headquarters. Soon tanks and soldiers were circling Hamzah Palace.

Out on the southern highway, the gaudy Chevy streaked toward the city, headlights picking bright holes through the night. My mother heard Kumait say something to Hussein, who nodded and clicked on the radio, which he kept low, humming quietly along with the plaintive, singsong music. Suddenly the frivolity fell away and was replaced by an excited, almost hysterical male voice speaking in Arabic. Hussein turned up the radio, pulled the car over. He and Kumait exchanged glances, listened intently.

"What's he saying?" my mother asked, cursing her ignorance. "What's going on?"

Kumait was white. "The Army has rebelled. They've attacked Hamra."

His pale face, in the Chevy, with my mother and Hussein the driver, pulled to the side of the road listening to the hysterical broadcast from Radio Hamra, was due not only to his shock that the Army had acted alone, without his knowledge. It was due also to his immediate and clear understanding that this could not be happening unless he had been betrayed by his friend, his old friend, his best friend, General Anwar. None of which he could explain to my mother. He could only sit there listening to reports of the Third Tank Division firing on Hamzah Palace, gazing out the Chevy window at the darkness, something precious broken forever inside him.

Four

1

1 WAS in my room, listening to Dion and reading *The Famous Five Take a Holiday*, when the tanks started rumbling past our house. My room shook, vibrated, the windowpanes rattled. I got up and looked out. Since it was night, and the nearest street light was halfway down the block, I couldn't see much, just these huge predatory shapes oozing mechanically down the street. I counted three, four tanks. Then the telephone rang downstairs, and soon Ahmed was at my door, excitedly trying to explain something to me in hurried Arabic and broken, stumbling English. I gathered that I should pack a little bag, get my toothbrush. Where was my mother? I asked. Ahmed didn't know. Downstairs, Eid, his English better than Ahmed's, explained that Mrs. Sweetser was going to pick me up and take me to her house. Again, I asked, where was my mother? Eid didn't know, either. Mrs. Sweetser, when she picked me up and loaded me into her black-and-silver Ford Fairlane, told me not to worry. My father and Roy had called her fifteen minutes earlier from the embassy, explained to her what was going on, that my mother was south with Kumait, and asked her to get me and keep me until they figured out what to do next. She scooted me into her house, and we sat together in the living room with Penny and Carolyn, waiting, listening to distant gunshots pepper the night, single little pops and the more sustained rattle of machine-gun fire. Several loud explosions coming from the direction of downtown made us jump.

"What's happening?" I asked Mrs. Sweetser.

"They're fighting," she said.

She got up and poured herself a drink.

"Who's fighting?" I asked.

"The Army."

"Who are they fighting against?" Penny asked.

"I don't know."

"Good guys or bad guys?"

"I don't know."

"Are we going to die?" Carolyn asked.

"No, we're not going to die, sweetheart."

At which point there was a particularly loud explosion outside, sounding closer. We all flinched.

"Is my dad going to die?" I asked.

"No. He's safe."

"What about my mom? Where's my mom?"

"I don't know, exactly," she said. "But she'll be here soon. Don't worry."

My mother was in fact at that moment ten miles outside of Hamra, hunched forward in the backseat of the Chevy, urging Hussein to drive faster. The luminous green speedometer already read eighty-five. Hussein reluctantly notched it up another five miles an hour. Kumait kept fiddling with the radio, trying to get accurate news, but all he heard were shrill voices heady with bloodlust and what they said told him nothing. "In the name of Allah and all the Arab people, the Baathist Party of Kurash hereby assumes control of the country. . . . In revenge for the massacre of May 16 . . . In rage the People have spoken . . . In consort with our Palestinian brothers . . . The King is on the run, cowardly mongrel that he is. . . . The lackey of the bloodsucking Imperialists is surrounded in his palace. . . . The King is dead. . . ."

Wandering down to the kitchen of the Gourlies' Federal mansion, I made myself a cup of tea. My own reflection gazed back at me from the black windows. The clock on the wall said midnight. I dialed my mother in Cambridge.

"Hello?" She answered promptly, alert. "Who is it? Mack? Are you all right?"

"It's me again, Mom."

"What's wrong?"

"Nothing's wrong. I just need to ask you a question."

"What time is it?"

"Midnight."

"You called me up at midnight to ask me a question?"

"When the Third Tank Division rebelled and you were in the Chevy with Hussein and Kumait, did you realize that's what Kumait had been talking about when he mentioned 'if anything happens'?"

"I had an inkling. How do you know I was in the Chevy with Hussein and Kumait?"

"It's a matter of semipublic record. August 23, 1958. You'd just visited a Palestinian refugee camp. That had not gone well."

"What do you mean?"

"There was a threat of violence. To you. Being an American Imperialist warlord and all."

"I don't remember it that way. I remember a very nice older man who showed us through the camp, and then having tea in one of the houses, people generous as could be despite their terrible, terrible poverty."

This gave me a moment's pause. "So you do remember?"

"I remember the camp, yes, of course; it was the first time I saw one, and you don't forget something like that, trust me."

She was now wide awake and didn't want to hang up, I could tell. I stood there in the Gourlies' kitchen wondering what more I could ask her.

"Mom?"

"Yes?"

"Is Dad a good man or a bad man?"

A thoughtful hesitation, then: "A good man, I think."

"You think?"

"Yes."

"But you don't know?"

"I should get back to sleep. I've got to get up early tomorrow. Good night, darling. Call me again soon."

According to weather records I examined, it was clear and warm that August night in 1958, graced with many high bright stars, Orion in particular standing out in clear and bold relief. For two hours, starting around ten p.m., tanks from the Third Division fired repeatedly at Hamzah Palace from a distance of less than fifty yards. The impact was devastating. Small arms fire was returned, increasingly sporadic as the 75mm guns of the tanks pounded away at the thick palace walls. A fire started on the second floor. Soon thick black smoke, and then crackling red flames, were seen at the windows. An errant shell hit the small mosque the King's grandfather had built in the garden, leveling it.

General Anwar observed from a command car, watching through binoculars.

The First Infantry arrived on the scene around midnight and immediately attacked the palace. The Royal Circassian Guards and the Desert Legionnaires fought tenaciously, but they were pushed back, relinquishing first the front garden, then the gravel driveway and the fourteen garages, then the first floor of the palace. It took two more hours to take the second floor, at one end of which the fire still raged. No defenders were left alive.

General Anwar inspected the palace once it was secure, walking through the rubble of rooms where only days before he had sat with the King governing the country. He noticed an ashtray he had used now shattered on the tile floor.

Soldiers searched the rest of the palace, the grounds. They reported back to Anwar.

The King's mother was nowhere to be found.

The King himself had vanished.

My father decided it was time he leave the embassy and venture out into the city to see for himself what was happening. He had talked to my mother on the telephone, at the Sweetsers', where she had gone after finding the note Mrs. Sweetser had left on our front door. When my father asked about Kumait, she said only that he had left with Hussein in the Chevy. Soon thereafter Hussein arrived back at the embassy. My father thanked him for taking care of my mother and then asked him where he had dropped Kumait. "His apartment," Hussein said. "On Nahas Street." My father called Major Rashid. They agreed to meet at Kumait's apartment in half an hour.

Though they had prepared for the worst, piling sandbags onto the roof, behind which crouched Marine Guards, with orders this time, from the Ambassador, to return fire if fired upon, those inside the embassy did not again see the mob clambering over the walls. Instead, it was eerily silent on Al Said Street: no cars, no people, no trolleys, just the crackle of distant gunfire. Nor was there rioting on Al Kifah Street; it was as if, thinking that segments of the Army were taking care of their business for them, the legions of disaffected had felt content to stay safely protected behind the locked doors of their slums in Bakr. My father surmised in a cable the next day that they had acted according to orders from whoever lay behind the putsch, Nasser's agents and Baathist Free Young Officers, most likely—and my father was right, as evidence later unearthed would show. Renee reported that Radio Cairo was strangely silent on the subject of this coup d'etat, another indication that something was up with the Egyptians. When the tanks first rumbled into Hamra, my father had immediately called Sergei Prokov, K.G.B. chief in the Russian embassy, who swore he was as surprised by this turn of events as my father, and for once my father was inclined to believe him. The duty officer in Washington had summoned Hodd Freeman, Frank Wisner, and Allen Dulles, who met in one of the conference rooms with a view of the Mall for a full update, which came in fits and starts, cables from my father stating what little he knew in the order he learned it: National Police Headquarters capitulated after brief firefight; Army detachments assumed full control of Radio Hamra and imposed news blackout on all local newspapers; borders were sealed, the airport closed; Hamzah Palace was surrounded by tanks of the Third Division and pulverized for two hours, but the King escaped; no one knew where the King was; General Anwar went on Radio Hamra at one-thirty in the morning and declared himself head of a provisional Kurashian government, details to follow; a curfew was imposed; soldiers and tanks patrolled the streets of Hamra.

"Where's the King?" Wisner demanded of Hodd. "Find the damn King. Protect the King at all costs."

"With what?" Hodd asked politely.

The Ambassador held a meeting in his office with senior officers, and after some debate decided not to move all dependents onto the embassy compound. My father protested, was overruled. When the meeting ended, he left the building, hurrying past Marine Guards, got into the Opel, and drove through the gate onto Al Said Street. It was still empty. The abnormal quietude of the dark city must have added to the fearfulness my father surely felt as he crept along in the red Opel. Around him, tanks were assuming strategic positions, soldiers were erecting roadblocks. He was stopped twice, questioned by nervous officers who spoke no English, boys with fingers curled expectantly on the triggers of their guns watching curiously, waiting for orders, my father fumbling with his few words of Arabic and his atrocious accent. Somehow he talked his way through both roadblocks and continued on to Nahas Street. He parked, got out, approached the door of Kumait's apartment building. Rashid was already there, brooding, smoking a cigarette. He hadn't shaved, his clothes were rumpled, there were dark greasy stains under his eyes. He had the aura of a condemned man, which struck my father as strange, since if anything his role would be that of executioner. Reflexively, my father glanced up at Kumait's windows on the third floor. It was impossible to tell if anyone was in there. Behind Rashid, leaning casually against the wall of the building, stood four young Kurashian men, armed, eyes alert.

"Have you heard from the King?" was my father's first question.

Rashid shook his head. He really did look like a man about to be executed. He was that dejected.

"Where would he go?" my father asked. "Where would he feel safe?"

Rashid thought, shrugged. "The desert."

"Where in the desert?"

"I have no idea, Mack. I have no idea how he got out of the palace in the first place."

"Who would he call? Who does he trust?"

"The two men who started all this. But I don't think he's going to call them, do you?"

"We have to find him."

"I'm looking."

It was my father's turn to light a cigarette. It hurt his throat to inhale. For the first time it occurred to him that he could die if he kept this up, this smoking.

"Is the entire Army in this goddamned thing?" my father asked irritably.

"As far as I can tell, only the Third Tank Division and the First and Second Infantry Brigades."

"Only."

"That leaves two infantry brigades that do not appear so far to be engaged. Both of those brigades are Bedouin, as is the First Armored Car Regiment, also not participating." Rashid was exhausted. He rubbed his eyes. "The Third Tank Division that attacked this evening is entirely non-Bedouin. The same goes for the First and Second Infantry Brigades."

General Anwar, in his recent reorganization of Army command hierarchy, had appointed his cousin, General Ali Mazzawi, to command the Third Tank Division, and a good friend and fellow Nasserite, Zaid al Bahri, to head up the First and Second Infantry Brigades. He had planned this well. My father had only two more questions.

"Where are the Bedouin troops now?"

"I don't know. I've sent men out to try and find them."

"Where is General Anwar?"

"He's set up GHQ in the Hotel Antioch."

They both looked up at Kumait's windows.

"Let's go," my father said.

Rashid glanced at one of his men and nodded, stood back. As the young man began to fire his machine gun at the door, blowing out the lock, I was struggling mightily to enact *The Bridge on the River Kwai,* winner of that year's Academy Award for Best Picture, in a game of charades. The Game. My mother's idea, of course. Her version of Grace Under Pressure. Outside, the battle for the King's palace over, flames still sputtered at the windows of the second story.

"First word, small . . . A? At? Of? The . . ."

A finger to my nose.

"The!" my mother exclaimed, clapping her hands in glee.

Mrs. Sweetser smiled appreciatively.

"Go on," my mother exhorted me. "It's a movie. Six words. First word, 'The.' Go on, sweetheart."

I held up five fingers.

"Fifth word?" Mrs. Sweetser ventured.

A tug to the ear.

"Sounds like . . . you're cold?" ventured Penny.

"Sick? Feverish?" suggested Carolyn.

"You're shivering?" My mother this time.

A pinch of the fingers.

"Shorter? You mean . . . shiver? Sounds like shiver? The Something Something Something Sounds-Like-Shiver Something . . ."

Fire played across the glass of the Sweetsers' living room windows, behind my mother guessing, silent star systems in convulsion, red and yellow universal chaos in a whirlpool of ecstasy.

2

Kumait took down the hand-painted red box from the top of the bookcase, carried it gently to his desk. It was dark outside his windows overlooking Nahas Street. He clicked on his old gooseneck desk lamp, opened the box, pulled out three black-and-white photographs, of a certain age, curling somewhat at the corners, and studied them closely. All three were of two young men, both wearing starched white shirts and sleeveless sweaters, what looked like gray flannels and sturdy English walking shoes. Both had mustaches. In one photograph they stood before the sea, their arms around each other, grinning into the camera. A seagull observed from the rocky beach beside them. In another photograph, taken the same day, for they were wearing exactly the same clothes, the two dark-haired young men, for they were dark-haired, both faintly Semitic-looking, with prominent noses, jutting chins, and melancholy eyebrows, these two good friends, for such they seemed to be, by their attitudes, were sitting at a table under a Cinzano umbrella on a terrace, sipping coffee, smoking cigarettes, and, for the moment at least, oblivious of the camera, for they were their own subjects, unaware of anything save the conversation, clearly of an eventful kind, that drew them both to lean toward each other in debate over the table. The final photograph showed them walking across a lawn, the buildings behind them unmistakably institutional, academic. They carried books under their arms and they were laughing.

Question for future investigation: Who took the photographs?

The two young men in the photographs were of course Kumait and Anwar. The educational institution was of course the American University of Beirut. The year was approximately 1938, twenty years before the incidents of this story took place, and, to that extent, ancient history. Kumait, scholar that he was, found that adamantine fact the most startling of all, for it was indeed clear as a diamond and difficultly true that his friendship with Anwar, his love for the man, rooted so in the past, their past together, their youth together, was just that, of the past—ancient history. Finished. Over. It troubled his mind for the first time that maybe Anwar did not feel as he felt, that Kumait alone carried this passion, this sense of loyalty and shared fate, destiny. Perhaps, indeed, most likely, given the course of recent events, the events of the past twelve hours, Anwar had not given even a moment's thought to Kumait before betraying him and their King.

Kumait now placed the photographs on his desk, reached back into the red box, and came out with a pistol, a revolver. He turned the chamber. It was fully loaded, six bullets. He undid the safety, wondering who would come to get him, Anwar's men or the King's? Which of the two men he loved and admired the most in the world would be his executioner? Or rather, he thought, remembering his own gun, which of them would it be who found his bloodied corpse, and would either care? Fool, he cursed himself. Fool, fool, fool—the accusation echoed in his head, as the knocking on his door echoed in the room.

"Kumait?" It was a voice he didn't recognize, though it was familiar—a young man's voice, hoarse and tired. "Kumait, open up."

More knocking. *Fool, fool, fool.*

"Kumait?"

The sentimentalists always get outflanked by the realists, he thought, not moving. The romantics always betray themselves because they love life more than any one particular way of living it. They are at heart sybarites, Epicureans, sensationalists, just as they are perennially amateurs, dabblers, daydreamers—he, Kumait, was living proof of this, wondering now if that was not in fact the crowning achievement of his Western education, to desire everything and believe in nothing. No, no, they too have their crushing faith, he reminded himself, lowering his revolver and placing it on his desk.

Another voice spoke through the door. "Kumait, let us in, please." It was the American, Mack Hooper. Mrs. Hooper's husband. He could not escape these people. Maybe he did not want to. He stood and crossed the room, opened the door.

Four young men carrying guns rushed into the apartment, two of them pushing Kumait against the wall and frisking him for a weapon.

"It's on the desk," he said.

They retrieved it, clicked the safety back on, pocketed it. Kumait looked and saw my father standing in the doorway, and behind him the young intelligence officer Major Rashid. The other voice, Kumait figured, correctly. They entered, cautiously, looked around. The frightening young men assumed tactical positions about the room, one sitting casually on Kumait's desk, eyes on the street outside. My father and Major Rashid approached, Rashid closing the door behind them. Their skin looked yellow, taut with anxiety, and they both smelled a little. Kumait realized, when they drew closer, that they smelled of stale sweat and clammy clothes and too many cigarettes. They drew up chairs. Rashid motioned for Kumait to sit on the end of his bed.

"Were you going to shoot us or yourself?" Rashid asked.

"Myself."

"Why didn't you?"

"I started to feel sorry for myself. A form of self-love, I suppose. Pity can be a governing life force, and in this case it robbed me of my determination, my courage. I believe that's what Nietzsche had in mind when he castigated the Christians."

My father and Rashid exchanged glances.

Kumait smiled. "Now you can shoot me, correct?"

"We're not doing your dirty work for you," my father snapped.

Rashid straightened in his chair, gazed upon Kumait for a while without speaking. When he did finally say something, it was in such a soft voice that Kumait had to lean forward to hear him.

"Please explain all this to us."

"All this?"

"The tanks and soldiers. Your friend General Anwar. The collusion of the Baathists and the Muslim Brotherhood. Desert Rose."

Kumait was afraid to ask, but did. "Is the King dead?"

"No," said my father. Then: "We don't know."

"He wasn't in the palace?"

"He was. But he isn't." Rashid made a magician's gesture. "He's gone."

Kumait felt such a surge of relief flowing through his body, warm and forgiving, that he almost lay back on the bed and closed his eyes. He would have fallen immediately into a deep sleep, he knew it. No dreams. And he would have awoken thinking this was a dream.

"The Muslim Brotherhood is not involved in this uprising," Kumait said.

"Kumait, the uprising is a conspiracy between Free Officers and Muslim Brothers. We know that."

"It was supposed to be a protest. Not an uprising, not a revolution."

My father and Rashid regarded him carefully.

"You didn't know tonight was the night?" Rashid asked.

"No."

"Anwar betrayed you?"

"Yes."

My father, agitated, stood, lit his umpteenth cigarette of the day, glanced at the windows.

"They'll be coming for him." He was speaking to Rashid. "Anwar will arrest them all."

"At least," Rashid replied.

Rashid also stood, spoke quickly to the gunmen, and within seconds Kumait was being hurried down the stairs and out onto Nahas Street. He was pushed into a car and raced away, tires squealing too dramatically, he remembered, later, thinking, while behind him my father jumped into the Opel and followed Rashid's car and the tail car hurrying through the narrow byways of Hamra. They avoided the main avenues and boulevards, and were stopped only once, by a very young tank officer who was browbeaten by a tumultuous, intimidating Rashid into believing that they were on official business for General Anwar and the provisional government. *"That,"* he shouted, pointing through the windshield at Kumait, "is an Enemy of the People." The officer waved them on.

From my father and Rashid's interrogation of Kumait, which took place in the American embassy and was recorded by Johnny Allen and transcribed by Renee, then cabled directly to C.I.A. headquarters in Washington:

Question: You are an executive committee member of the Islamic Action Front of the Muslim Brotherhood.
Answer: Yes.
Question: For how long?
Answer: Five years.
Question: Since when did you become a devout Muslim, Kumait?
Answer: It was a cultural identity I was seeking.
Question: Arab identity.
Answer: Exactly.
Question: Did it not strike you as improper to be a confidant

of the King, a sometime adviser to the King, and yet at the same time belong to a secret organization outlawed by the King?

Answer: I was aware of the conflict, yes.

Question: When did General Anwar turn his services over to the Egyptians?

Answer: About five months ago.

Question: Why?

Answer: He became frustrated with the King's policy.

Question: Which aspect of the policy, exactly?

Answer: The King's inability to tear himself away from, first, the British and then you—the Americans.

Question: Is Anwar a Communist?

Answer: No, no, not at all. A Socialist, yes. He admires Nasser greatly. Too much.

Question: You don't admire Nasser?

Answer: Oh, yes, I admire him all right, but I think he will lead us to destruction.

Question: So what happened? Did Anwar approach you?

Answer: Yes.

Question: When?

Answer: Six months ago. He proposed that the Army and the Muslim Brotherhood work together to convince the King to alter his policies.

Question: How?

Answer: By stirring things up and making him see how desperate many of his people were.

Question: There was no intention to overthrow the King?

Answer: Not by the Muslim Brotherhood, no.

Question: You were unaware that Anwar would attempt a coup?

Answer: Yes.

Question: Do you think it was his intention to betray you from the beginning?

Answer: I don't know.

Question: Do you think he is in fact working hand in hand with the Egyptians?

Answer: I don't know that, either.

Question: He never intended to form an alliance with you, Kumait.

Answer: Then why did he pretend to?

Question: To control you.

Answer: Was it his intention all along to assassinate the King?

Question: I think that's a safe guess, yes.

Back on Nahas Street, an armored car pulled up, three soldiers leaped out. They hesitated, puzzled by the blown-away door, before charging up the interior stairs to Kumait's apartment. Finding it empty, they rushed back down to their patrol car and drove away. General Anwar had better luck finding the rest of the leadership of the Muslim Brotherhood. Nasr Abu Tantawi was dragged out of bed, Laith Saleh was found eating breakfast in a café on Feisel Square, Mohammed Riyadh looked up from his morning accounting, hot coffee in hand, to see the guns of jittery boy-soldiers wavering in his direction. His warehouse was searched, a Muslim Brotherhood membership list discovered in a safe, and by lunchtime another fifty arrests had been made. Anwar was not about to let reactionary religious sentimentality ruin his Socialist revolution. Anyway, as postmortem investigations revealed, the Egyptian Intelligence Service was at this time leaning heavily on Anwar to purge any and all potential challengers to his rule. In this spirit, he also arrested Abdul Kilani, head of the minuscule Kurashian Communist Party, as well as Kilani's senior lieutenants. He also arrested the president of the university, the editor of the *Kurash Today* newspaper, and every cabinet official in the King's government except Prime Minister Sherif al-Hassan, who was nowhere to be found. Those arrested were taken to the soccer stadium on the northwest edge of Hamra, deposited near center field, and watched over by armed soldiers. Men who in the normal course of things could not bring themselves to acknowledge one another, let alone speak, were soon huddled in small anxious groups, discussing the day's events. All believed the King was dead.

Anwar's zealots missed one member of the Islamic Action Front besides Kumait, and that was Jamil al-Amir, who was in his country house near Lake Ramadi, a euphemism for the stagnant little pond at the west end of the marshlands that made up Kurash's southeastern border with Iraq. He, like Kumait, heard the news on the radio, first the babbling inconsistencies on Radio Hamra, then a more measured report on BBC, measured but also inaccurate—it too insisted that the King was dead, killed in his palace by troops of the Third Tank Division. Jamil knew instantly that he would be in danger, and so left his wife and two children and mother and uncles and aunts and disappeared in his Mercedes with three bodyguards, all loyal and devout Muslims. That he had been tricked and betrayed by General Anwar was bad enough; that his beloved King, whom he had wanted only to nudge back in the right direction, was dead, that was even worse, a disaster, a tragedy. But the simple fact that it was obviously Kumait who had betrayed them from within, Kumait working in consort with his old and good friend Anwar who had helped assassinate the King, himself a good Muslim, and put in his place godless Socialists and Egyptians—this seemed to Jamil the most egregious aspect of this entire odious plot, and he vowed, as his Mercedes drew away from his family through the reeds and marshes of southern Kurash, that he would avenge his friends and Allah, as was his duty, as an honorable man.

At noon that first day after the night of the revolution, Allen Dulles authorized a high-altitude flyover by a U2 spy plane based in Turkey, and by three that afternoon C.I.A. and military analysts had determined that the missing Kurashian Army brigades had assembled in the desert at Zahawi, fifty miles from Hamra and were now advancing toward the capital city. The U2 also caught within its photographs a fact, aspects of a fact, three aspects of a fact, that no one had thought of, no one had remembered, and which, upon reflection, by anyone who knew or remembered their history, suggested the next turn this story would take: three creaky old Hawker Hunters baking in the desert.

My father and Roy Sweetser received this information at three-thirty p.m. Kurashian time. Renee handed the cable to my father as he sat at his desk contemplating the three black-and-white photographs he had taken from the desk in Kumait's apartment, photographs of a young Kumait and a young Anwar, university students, Beirut, circa 1938.

Who took those photographs?

At the time I was not thinking about Beirut or old photographs of old friends, I was on the second floor of the Sweetsers' house, in Penny and Carolyn's room, the three of us having taken off all our clothes and standing there pure and brilliant for a free exchange of ganders and gawks. This fit of exhibitionism was, if memory serves, Carolyn's idea. Downstairs, our mothers were deep into their second gin and tonics. Occasional tanks rolled by outside, rattling the windows. Sporadic gunfire punctuated the night. I stared at Penny's boyish nipples, Carolyn's genital-absence, a kind of sexual black hole that baffled me, confused me, and made me laugh. My pecker, the size of my little finger today and bald as a baby, made them laugh.

My mother and Mrs. Sweetser, downstairs, lulled to relative calm by the clatter of ice cubes, heard our laughter upstairs and smiled, happy to know we were happy, happy to share what they took to be, and I guess was, the innocence of our giddiness, unrehearsed, unmeditated joy.

My father and Rashid left Kumait alone with Renee and Johnny Allen and a wary Marine Guard, Sal, in fact, who was still having a hard time looking Renee in the eye. They climbed into Rashid's car and drove from the embassy compound, followed by the car full of Rashid's men. They headed southeast to meet the advancing remnants of the King's army.

It was six o'clock in the evening of the first day of the revolution, twenty-four hours since General Anwar's troops had attacked Hamra.

3

Any theory of courage, it seems to me, would have to include a depiction of the King of Kurash, age twenty-three, realizing one night that the main forces of his Army had turned against him, that in all likelihood he would be dead by morning.

My father, driving into the desert with Rashid, reviewed, in his mind, compulsively, the fragments of evidence that now, clearly, added up to this event, this night: General Anwar reorganizing the Army command structure and placing friends and relatives in charge of most important units; an unconfirmed report from the station chief in Damascus that Anwar had met with the Egyptian military attaché while visiting that city the previous Christmas; Thoreau's insistence that the Bedouin elements of the Army were being isolated, that unexplained nocturnal maneuvers were taking place; Rashid's observation that some senior officers were spending a lot more money on themselves than their Army salary could justify. . . .

They'd even been warned: Desert Rose.

If espionage is the art of gathering disparate fragments together in such a way as to suggest the truth of what will soon happen, then my father and Roy Sweetser had failed, miserably. Of course, Roy had his third-rate brain as an excuse. My father had no excuse, or at least none that he could find, none that he could accept. The headlights of Rashid's car bored holes through the night, holes my father wished he could crawl into, like a cartoon character, zipping them up behind him and disappearing.

How had the King escaped?

From my father's postmortem of what he called the August Coup, several long and detailed cables sent to Washington that fall, we learn that after my father left the palace on the night of August 23, the King went out to sit in the garden, trying to absorb what my father had just told him, that Kumait and Anwar had turned against him. One of his Circassian guards approached and announced that a Captain Mohammed Majali, of the First Armored Car Regiment, had unexpectedly arrived and wished to see the King immediately. Curious, the King had him admitted. Captain Majali, a Bedouin, told the King that his regiment, made up completely of Bedouin, had received orders that morning to retire into the desert some fifty miles from Hamra. The same was true for two Bedouin army brigades. Not only that, but both the armored car regiment and the infantry brigades had been ordered to travel unarmed, leaving all ammunition behind at base camp in Al Zabib. At the same time, Captain Majali went on, they had heard that the Third Tank Division, made up completely of non-Bedouin, had been ordered, fully armed, into Hamra. The officers of the First Armored Car Regiment and the Bedouin infantry brigades had met among themselves and decided that a coup was in progress, and that it was their sacred duty to warn and protect the King. It was a question, Captain Majali said, of *sharaf*. Honor. If His Majesty would accompany him, there was an armored car waiting for him in front of the palace.

The King wanted to believe that what he had just been told was impossible, that this spindly, nearsighted armored car officer was paranoid, delusional, misinformed. How could he deny, however, the force of what the man said when the King added it to what my father had already told him about Kumait and Anwar? Anwar was, after all, Army chief of staff. He had recently put his cousin General Ali Mazzawi and a good friend, Zaid al Bahri, in command of the Third Tank Division and the First and Second Infantry Brigades. Neither was a Bedouin. So much for Arab nationalism, the King thought sadly. Tribal mistrust runs deeper than any dream of unity.

The King called Sherif al-Hassan, warned him, asked him to alert the other cabinet members. He then dragged his protesting mother down from her lair on the second floor. She clutched his father's old hashish pipe and wouldn't let it go. Rodney was roused from his quarters above the garages; the servants were gathered. Several of the Circassians and roughly half the Desert Legionnaires on duty volunteered to stay behind and protect the palace. The King and his mother climbed into the armored car, Captain Majali nodded to his driver, and the odd entourage drove away, Majali's armored car followed by the Ferrari and the Porsche and the Jaguar filled with servants and soldiers. Even the Corvette was used, driven cautiously by Rodney.

An hour later the first tanks arrived and opened fire on Hamzah Palace.

The King drove west, toward the Jordanian border, into the desert. His mother peevishly stuffed tobacco into the hashish pipe and smoked it, silently defying anyone to tell her to put it out. No one did. She hunched beside the King, puffing irritably, while the armored car roared and clanked around them. It didn't have much in the way of shock absorbers, and so when they left the highway they were jounced violently from side to side, pitching headlong into each other, clinging desperately to their seats. Captain Majali contacted his regiment by radio and, using a primitive code, let them know that the King was safe and on the way. It was over the crackling, indistinct radio that the King heard for the first time that tanks had indeed attacked his palace. Was it really Anwar in command? he wondered. And what role did Kumait play in all this? What would the Muslim Brotherhood do? Why would they align themselves with their opposites, the secular Socialists in Cairo? At some point he stopped thinking about it. He stopped wondering, worrying. He felt none of the indecision that had momentarily paralyzed him at the time of the riots three months earlier. He was in no way fearful. His hands and voice, when he addressed a few questions to Majali, were steady.

"What exactly is the deployment of Bedouin troops?"

"We have all withdrawn to Zahawi, together. We have formed our own, separate command structure. General Samir al-Rahal is in charge."

General Samir al-Rahal, career soldier, a Bedouin, trained by the British. A good man.

"Are you armed?"

"Yes indeed, Your Majesty."

"Good."

What the King felt, without realizing it, was hurt, hurt that Anwar and Kumait had refused to give him a chance to fulfill his obligations to history. He was a Hashemite, after all, directly descended from the Prophet. It was his great-uncle Feisel who had led the Arab Revolt in 1919, who had first defined the goal of Arab nationalism, not some ambitious, social-climbing junior officer in the Egyptian Army. They would do all this without the past, without Allah? They were worse than fools, they were traitors, and like traitors they would now be dismissed. The King's jaw clenched tight, he grimaced and twitched, hands seeking revenge, the blood of his enemies, an involuntary twinge that only his mother noticed, and appreciated. She had seen it on the face of her husband, on the face of his father, and she pitied those who caused it.

"Where is the Air Force?" the King asked.

Captain Majali had to reflect a moment to understand what the King was talking about. To his way of thinking, Kurash had no air force, any more than it had a navy. Then he realized the King was referring to the three dilapidated Hawker Hunter jets left behind by the British and presently languishing at a disused British air base.

"In Khudra, Your Majesty."

"That's what, thirty miles from Zahawi?"

"Approximately, yes, sir."

Soon thereafter they arrived at Zahawi, the armored car slowing to a stop and Captain Majali opening the metal door. The King stepped out and down. He was greeted by General Samir al-Rahal, a small, stout fifty-year-old who pulled himself up to his full height, erect as a statue, and snapped a smart salute, British style, palm out, then knelt in the desert sand and kissed the King's hand. Behind the King, his sports cars disgorged his remaining Circassian bodyguards and Desert Legionnaires, while behind the proud and supplicating General several thousand infantry and armored car troops broke into a lusty cheer and pressed closer to the King, surrounding him as the poor of Bakr had surrounded him, touching him reverently, joyously, flinging themselves to the ground to kiss his hand, his feet. He moved among them in a daze. He felt a grin implant itself upon his face. He embraced these soldiers, one by one, embraced their scratchy uniforms and three-day beards, their rough thick shoulders and callused hands, their deeply male smell of coffee and sweat and cigarettes. Guns were fired into the air, the crowd surged as one toward a tent pitched and waiting in the dark, into which General al-Rahal and his officers and the King disappeared. Then the men sat and smoked cigarettes, embers like fireflies twinkling in the night, while within the tent their fate was decided.

"First, gentlemen, I want to thank you on behalf of your country and the Hashemite family for your unswerving devotion. It shall be remembered in heaven, if not on this earth, tonight, when we launch our counterattack." The King smiled around at the listening faces, faces worn with heat and sunlight and general exhaustion, to say nothing of frayed nerves, faces eager for him to tell them what to do. "General al-Rahal, I wish to activate the Air Force. Have the three Hawker Hunters accompany us when we return to Hamra. Can they be armed?"

"I'm not sure they can even fly, Your Majesty," the General replied.

The King turned to Rodney, at the back of the tent. "Can you get them aloft?"

"I can try," Rodney said stoically.

"Find the pilots, General al-Rahal," the King ordered. "And make sure the planes are armed."

"Yes, sir." The General whirled on an adjutant, sent him off to Khudra, accompanied by Rodney.

"We will counterattack in four hours," the King said.

The General was taken aback, but he hesitated only a second. "Yes, sir."

"The Hawker Hunters will disable the tanks of the Third Division. The armored cars will overrun the artillery, a difficult task, I know, but it must be done. Our infantry will follow. I want General Anwar captured by noon tomorrow. General al-Rahal, do you have a map of Hamra?"

One was produced. The King identified four primary targets: the Hotel Antioch, Hamzah Palace, Government House, and the National Police Headquarters. General al-Rahal and his officers immediately got to work, hurrying from the tent to organize their troops. The King was left alone. He sat down in a canvas chair. His whole body was suddenly shaking, quivering uncontrollably, as wave after wave of adrenaline roiled through him. He was still grinning, now a kind of idiot grin, he felt. He couldn't wipe it off his face. He laughed aloud, stood, relieved to find that his legs held him. To the tent he said, "Father and Grandfather, be with me tonight." Then he exited.

Outside, a plump moon had risen above the sands, turning the desert itself into a moonscape, every man and vehicle standing out sharply in crisply shadowed relief. Captain Majali appeared at his side, blanched white, reported that all was going well, everyone would be ready to move out on time.

"My mother?"

"She's resting, Your Majesty. Don't worry, we'll take care of her."

Spoken with such apparent and simple concern that the King did not know what to say. He nodded his thanks. Captain Majali wandered off.

It was then that the King saw, or thought he saw, his father approaching him across the bright moonlit sand. It was certainly his father, dressed in his military uniform, much like the King's, only with a few more medals, all of his own invention. He too wore a red-and-white-checked *kaffiyeh*. The question is: Was the King really *seeing* him? In short: Was this real? In some curiosity, and fear, the King waited, watching his father get closer, until, when the man was upon him, and had stopped, gazing thoughtfully at his son, the King could no longer maintain his composure. He glanced away, at the soldiers readying themselves, campfires doused, tents folded, General al-Rahal conferring with his officers. When he looked back, hesitantly, his father was gone. Put another way, his father was not there. The King was relieved, and disappointed. He found his mother, lying on a cot in another tent, smoking the hashish pipe, and told her what he'd seen, or thought he'd seen.

"It worries me," he said. "That I'm hallucinating, seeing things. Now of all times, when I must remain clearheaded."

She snorted. "Seeing things? No, no, that was your father, all right. He's worried. He can't help it. He's that kind of man. He came to me earlier, right here in this tent. He told me to stop smoking, and to tell you to say your prayers."

She's crazy, he reflected. There must still be hashish in that pipe, the black resinous hashish of Lebanon he remembered his father breaking free from a thick block and warming over a candle flame, then crumbling with his long fingers into that same pipe, a slow, graceful ritual followed ineluctably by the flash and flare of a match, the flame inhaled downward into the bowl of the pipe, smoke dribbling to the ceiling as the King's father took the rest

into his lungs. Soon he was smiling kindly and slightly withdrawn, quoting Gilbert and Sullivan. The King kissed his mother,
returned to the troops, secretly believing her—the ghost of his
father was with him, tonight.

Three hours later and ten miles away, approaching fast, my
father and Rashid peered into the darkness beyond the windshield of Rashid's rattling Land Rover.

"You're sure about this?" Rashid asked worriedly.

"I'm sure what I was told," my father responded cautiously.

Rashid wondered how the Americans could possibly know
exactly where the missing elements of the Kurashian Army were
located. He also knew better than to ask.

My father spoke again: "These troops, how do we know
they're friendly?"

Rashid shrugged behind the wheel. "They're Bedouin. They've
been excluded from Anwar's attacking forces."

My father was silent, pondering the darkness ahead.

"We don't," Rashid admitted. "Know. It's a guess."

Where was the King? Was he even still alive? Roy Sweetser had
gone off to try and find Sherif al-Hassan, hoping he might know
something. Renee had been told to stick with the Ambassador, in
case he was contacted by Sherif al-Hassan, or any other Cabinet
member, for that matter. Which was unlikely, my father reflected,
but worth a shot. He and Rashid had left the main highway and
were bouncing their way over hard-packed sand, maybe an
ancient camel track. His butt ached and there was something seriously deleterious happening along the length of his spinal cord,
cartilage compacted with jarring, repetitive fury. Rashid twisted
hard on the wheel, left, then right, then quickly, urgently left
again. Sometimes my father seemed just to be hanging on for
dear life as the Land Rover roared through the desert with a mind
of its own.

History roaring through the desert with a mind of its own.

The Inertia of History, deadly and unstoppable, coming your
way at eighty miles an hour . . .

My father and Rashid in their jittering Land Rover held on for the ride; the King now back in his speeding armored car held on for the ride; Anwar in his appropriated grand suite at the Hotel Antioch, with its views of the Roman ruins, sipped his tea and held on for the ride; Kumait, confined to Milton Gourlie's office, lit his zillionth cigarette and held on for the ride; Renee took her ninth clandestine nip of vodka and held on for the ride; Johnny Allen saw her and pretended not to notice and held on for the ride; all the soldiers clasped their guns in one hand and held on for the ride with the other.

In the desert in the moonlight from a great height, say the height of a U2 overflight, you would have seen the teeny headlights of a single car moving through the night toward many teeny headlights spread in strategic protective alliance and watched skyward by three teeny shadowed shrieking airborne Hawker Hunter jets. . . .

"Jesus Christ." My father saw the myriad headlights bearing down fast.

Rashid applied the brakes just as one of the Hawker Hunters roared overhead, not so teeny from down here, rattling the Land Rover, more monstrous than mechanical, a gigantic passing prehistoric bird that feeds on carrion, leaves nothing behind but shiny, empty skulls.

They were surrounded within seconds, my father and Rashid, by armored cars and trucks full of troops. Yanked from their Land Rover, guns stuck in their faces along with the blinding stabs of bright military flashlights, they were dragged stumbling and thrown at the feet of General Samir al-Rahal and the King. The King recognized my father and Rashid and laughed. He laughed so hard he had to sit down on the fender of a Jeep, holding his aching sides. He laughed the way he had laughed that first night out in the desert among the Bedouin with my father. General al-Rahal, baffled at first, soon could not resist a laugh himself. The troops followed suit until the merriment was, as my father said in a cable to Hodd Freeman the following week, "damn near universal." When the amusement had died down, and my father and Rashid were standing, my father pulled another bit of mystical hokum pokum from his back pocket.

"The Major and I have come to offer our services to the King."

Then again, as was the case before, he might have meant it. He probably did. He was given, in those days, I think, to melodramatic gestures. And the King, himself of course living right in the middle of a melodramatic gesture, responded with unabashed sentimentality. He embraced Major Rashid, he embraced my father, bestowing upon them each a kiss to each cheek.

As one, they climbed aboard their various vehicles and drove on to Hamra, there to reclaim the city, the palace, and the kingdom.

It was a little after midnight, August 24, 1958.

4

From my father's report, sent to Washington three days later: "Let us not underestimate the task that faced the King. Arrayed against him was an entire tank division, numbering, in all, twenty-eight tanks, any one of which, with a single well-aimed shot from its 75mm gun, could easily reduce an armored car to a mere semblance of its former self, a pile of contorted, burning black metal. No soldier could survive such an onslaught. The infantry on Anwar's side and the King's side were evenly matched, a wash. Artillery favored Anwar, since his gunners were far more experienced than the King's, having fought alongside King Hussein's Arab Legionnaires in a successful defense of Old Jerusalem during the 1948 war with Israel. The unknown factor was the so-called Air Force, the three Hawker Hunters flying overhead as the King's Army approached the hills of Hamra. Of what were they capable? It wasn't even clear to me what kind of bombs or rockets they had at their disposal. 'Don't worry, Mack,' the King kept telling me. 'They'll do fine.' General al-Rahal offered a much more realistic, I think, appraisal of the situation, and suitably bleak: 'If they don't, Your Majesty, we're fucked.' Or Arabic to that effect. Major Rashid was translating for me."

Dawn broke over Hamra's seven hilltops. It would be a daylight fight.

The first strike by the Hawker Hunters hit the Hotel Antioch. In three passes they had pretty much destroyed the top two floors. Body count: fifty dead, another seventy wounded, mostly soldiers and officers working with Anwar. The General himself was out inspecting the city when the airplanes streaked overhead and he heard the nearby deep concussive *thump-thump-thump* of bombs being dropped on his GHQ. His initial reaction was fairly calm, as if he were witnessing something so inexplicable it was hardly real, therefore harmless. But as the ground shook beneath his feet and fear flooded the eyes of the men around him, he came to understand that those were indeed the three supposedly defunct Hawker Hunters from Khudra. Unless, and this was a possibility that he clung to for the next hour, the nearby monarchy of Jordan had decided to aid the King and send air support.

Rashid dropped my father off at the American embassy, then drove to his own office ten blocks away. My father strode past the knots of now nervous soldiers and up to the Ambassador's office on the second floor, where he explained to Ambassador Muir, Chester Boyden, and Allen McCone what was happening. As he spoke, my father could hear dreamy, high-pitched gunfire and dull sonorous explosions coming from the direction of the Hotel Antioch. Windows rattled in their frames.

"Will the King succeed?" the Ambassador asked, agitated, wan, pacing.

My father shrugged. "Fifty-fifty."

"We should be helping him, goddamnit," the Ambassador suddenly exploded, kicking wildly at a chair, sending it crashing across the room.

This outburst was so uncharacteristic of the tall, professorial diplomat that my father worried for a second that he, too, like Milton before him, was cracking under the pressure and having some kind of nervous breakdown. Looking closer, however, he saw it wasn't true, saw, with admiration, that the man was simply royally pissed off. "Fucking Eisenhower Doctrine my fucking ass."

"Have you cabled Dulles?" my father asked.

"Goddamn right I cabled Dulles. Six goddamn times, proposing that here was a perfect opportunity to show the world what was meant by American friendship."

"What did he say?"

He thrust a cable into my father's hand. My father read it.

"Received and have mulled over your cables re present situation in Kurash. Firmly believe best course to be wait and see inasmuch as should on-the-ground circumstances dictate (as it appears they probably will) then our policy must accommodate new ruler Anwar to establish friendship. Any active military support shown now for current lost cause would vitiate new relationship with Anwar."

When I first read that cable, everything that happened afterward in Kurash, in 1958, suddenly made sense to me, the whole stinking debacle. My father should have known, or at least sensed, reading that cable in the Ambassador's office, what was to come.

Maybe he did.

"Mr. Ambassador, I think we should get all dependents into the compound now," my father said.

"I agree," said Chester Boyden.

The Ambassador nodded his assent. Boyden hurried off to get things organized. My father went down to his own office. Renee buzzed him in, smiled a smile borrowed from her good friend vodka, invisibly at her side. And yet even still the sorrow burned at the back of her eyes, a stubborn resistance to happiness of any kind, even the short-lived and chemically induced.

"How goes the war, Mack?" she chimed, so uncharacteristic a question, so uncharacteristically put, that it brought my father to a standstill, staring at her suspiciously.

"Are you all right?" he asked.

"Right as rain. Couldn't be better. How about you?"

"Fine. Anything new from Washington?"

"Nary a peep."

First the Ambassador, now Renee. Stress was luring alternate personalities out of everyone, it seemed. He wouldn't have been surprised if she suddenly started speaking in tongues.

"Where's Roy?"

"In his office."

Behind closed doors, his childish hand scooping Miltowns from the bowl on his desk and popping them into his mouth like so many M&M's. He looked up, a tad startled, when my father knocked abruptly and entered. "Any word from Sherif al-Hassan?"

"He's dead," Roy mumbled.

It wasn't clear to my father if this was a joke or not.

"He donned a disguise, a woman's long black robe and a veil, and scooted off to join the masses clogging downtown Hamra," Roy went on. "He figured he was safe, that he had assumed some kind of protective coloration, like a lizard, which, when you come to think of it, is kind of what he was."

"Roy, how many Miltowns have you taken?"

He thought about this, gave it his undivided attention, for what seemed like an hour.

"Several," he finally managed.

My father sighed and lit a cigarette.

"What he hadn't counted on was someone spotting his spiffy English shoes underneath the robe, his adamantly male shoes, I might add. A hue and cry went up, angry hands tore away the robe and veil, he was of course immediately recognized. He was then kicked to death. His genitals were cut off. His hands and feet were cut off. Body parts were distributed with much glee among the crowd. Children hacked off his head and kicked it around like a bloody fucking soccer ball."

Roy smiled weakly, leaned over, and threw up into his wastepaper basket.

"You saw all this?" my father asked.

Roy nodded, head still down, the back of his shirt drenched with perspiration. "He had called here, I told him to get out of his house, to meet me outside Oristibach's."

"It's not your fault, Roy."

"It never occurred to me that anyone would recognize him."

"The disguise was your idea?"

Again, Roy nodded. O Lord, my father thought, sitting back in his chair. Save us from overzealous intelligence officers. A *disguise,* for Christ fucking sake. In the middle of downtown fucking Hamra. Thank you, Camp Perry.

"When did the mob reappear?"

"Not too long ago. An hour, maybe. Radio Cairo's back on the air, declaring victory and encouraging everyone to go out and celebrate. Oh, Jesus, Mack, I'm sorry. I fucked up."

My father stood.

"Roy, take Hussein and get out to your house, grab the kids, grab Jean and Barbara, and bring them back here."

"There's a curfew."

"Fuck the curfew."

Next my father walked into Milton Gourlie's old office, where Sal sat with his M14 straddled across his lap, keeping an eye on Kumait, who looked as if he'd aged about ten years in the last twenty-four hours. My father nodded to Sal, Sal left, closing the door behind him, and took up a cautionary sentry's post outside, one ear cocked to the door, listening for trouble.

What trouble could Kumait cause, frail with remorse? My father sat across from him.

"You look tired, Mack."

"I am tired, Kumait."

"Is the King dead?" Resigned, though dreading it at the same time.

"No, he's not." My father tilted his head toward the sound of gunfire. "That's him."

An immediate and involuntary smile flickered across Kumait's face. His eyes lit up. "That's him? Really?"

"Really," my father said gently. "I think it best if you stay here for now."

"Whatever you think, Mack."

"If Anwar comes out on top of this thing, I can protect you in here. If the King comes out on top, he will want to see you, and I will have to deliver you."

"Oh, yes, I understand completely."

"When I told him, he wept."

Kumait lowered his head, burning with shame. "I never meant to hurt him. Does he know that?"

"I mentioned it, yes."

"I should have shot myself, back in my apartment. I'm such a coward."

"No." My father felt immense pity for him at that moment, this kind and gentle man who had robbed himself of any reason to live save habit, even though his betrayal was in fact a misunderstanding, an act on his part of incredible naiveté. "He'll forgive you," my father said.

He called Rashid's office, couldn't get through. The lines were down. He then climbed up to the roof of the embassy, squatted behind sandbags among the anxious Marine Guards, and gazed out over the rooftops of Hamra.

The Hotel Antioch was in flames. The Hawker Hunters had moved on to Hamzah Palace. They circled and swooped, loosing their miniature bombs, which tumbled end over end and exploded below among the palm dates and pine trees. Down on Al Said Street, three tanks hurried loudly past the embassy, on their way toward Jebel Hamra to aid their comrades. As they passed the intersection of Umal Street, some of General al-Rahal's infantry appeared, aimed a bazooka, and fired at almost point-black range, shredding the first tank's treads. The tank veered wildly to one side, turret swiveling blindly, machine guns firing. A second bazooka shell penetrated the steel cab, the hatch clanged open on top and soldiers spilled out in a cloud of smoke and fire, coughing uncontrollably, stanching wounds. Rifle fire cut them down as they appeared, helplessly tumbling from their burning tank to the ground. The two other tanks had ground to a halt, confused, but now their spotters found the King's men and machine-gun fire from the remaining tanks suddenly ripped into them as they retreated back into Umal Street. Three bodies remained behind, motionless on the street, asleep in bloody pools.

My father looked away. The Marine Guard next to him, eighteen at most, was transfixed by the sight below, his face drained, skin so pale it was translucent, like one of those see-through plastic models of the human body.

A grating whining noise pierced the momentary calm, and my father looked up to see one of the Hawker Hunters spinning out of control and trailing a plume of blue smoke. The plane fought the pull of gravity valiantly but finally could not resist and went screeching straight into the ground somewhere over by Feisel Square, followed by a huge silent explosion, dark flame and darker smoke, and then, seconds later, the sound of the explosion, shockingly loud, a solid blast of screaming heat that hit them hard on the embassy roof.

"Son of a bitch," the Marine Guard muttered, grinning idiotically.

Up on Jebel Hamra, Roy Sweetser came charging into his house where we were all crowded together once again in the living room, out of games, out of booze, out of anything but dread. He carried a gun, a pistol of some kind.

"Let's go," was all he said.

I was glad to see Hussein behind the wheel of the red Chevy. He gave me a wide and encouraging grin, crowned by his gold tooth. He too had a gun, lying on his lap. We piled in, crammed in, and then set out for the embassy. It was by now early afternoon. The mob was still absent. The two remaining Hawker Hunters screamed overhead and the armored cars moved in groups of three through the city, each group trailing two infantry platoons, stopping only when they met resistance, as they did for instance at the National Police Headquarters, or when one of

Anwar's tanks thundered into view and fired at them, at which point they dispersed frantically, the men running for cover, the armored cars seeking the shelter of buildings. I knew none of this, of course, at the time, ten years old in the backseat of the hot Chevy, Penny on my lap, my mother pressed close against me, Hussein steering us through streets frighteningly empty and silent.

"Are we going to die, Mom?" I inquired.

She snapped back, "No, we're not going to die."

As if such a thought were a failure of nerve on my part.

We traversed Jebel Hamra, began the descent into Hamra proper, and I saw for the first time the Hotel Antioch on fire, the flames congratulating themselves above the roof of Hamzah Palace on our left. As we moved into the maze of narrow city streets, we passed trolley cars abandoned on their tracks and row upon row of shops closed up tight behind metal padlocked grates. There was a terrible stink in the air, acrid, nauseating. It came from the fires crackling all around us. Hussein was a nervous wreck as he drove, probably because he alone fully appreciated what could happen if the wrong people pulled us out of the Chevy. I felt Penny's small bony body sitting on me, her damp limbs pressed against me, I stared at her sweaty blond hair falling in strands across the back of her neck, which was beaded with sweat from the heat in the car and maybe fear, although Penny never betrayed much behind her imperturbable blue-gray eyes; she was like her mother that way. Mrs. Sweetser sat leaning forward slightly and gazing over her husband's shoulder out the front windshield. Her hand rested upon his shoulder, both seeking comfort and giving it, and it strikes me now, forty years later, that this unconscious gesture, given and no doubt forgotten so long ago, a wife's hand on her husband's shoulder, contains all the beauty the world can offer.

It's way past midnight, there's an insectival symphony roaring outside the screen window of the guest room on the second floor of the Gourlies' Federal mansion on Dumbarton Avenue, in Georgetown, in Washington, D.C. I sit here surrounded by my research books and open file folders and pages and pages of notes.

I'd like to gather in a room all the people I've ever known and even fleetingly loved and never let them go.

Catch a falling star and put it in your pocket . . .

Perry Como singing to me from the little yellow Phillips record player . . .

Those men *tap-tap-tapping* their chisels into limestone in the field behind our house all day every day . . .

The damp swirl of blond hair on the nape of Penny's pale freckled neck, reflections of a burning city in the car window, Hussein's sweet cologne and his terrified hands grasping the red plastic steering wheel . . .

We entered Hamra Circle at nine o'clock, not time but place. Where once a proud statue of the King's grandfather Ali astride his prancing Arabian stallion had stood, a Centurion tank now rested, squat and ugly as a toad. Hussein drove very slowly and very respectfully. The tank, really like a living thing, seemed to prick up its hidden ears, as if it heard us, a suspicious intruder. Slowly the great turret swiveled until the barrel of its cannon was aimed directly at us. Mr. Sweetser sucked in his breath: "Christ Almighty." Hussein couldn't bring himself to look, he just kept driving, slowly, slowly, around the circle, around the tank. The turret rotated with us, gun barrel never wavering. We left Hamra Circle at one o'clock. The tank suspiciously watched us go.

A few minutes later we reached the embassy, the courtyard of which was packed with cars unloading dependents, women and children I knew from school and the American Club, my neighbors in our miniature Levittown in the desert. All around stood nervous Marine Guards in full battle gear, clasping their M14s, and there were many Desert Legionnaires in their *kaffiyehs* and British khaki, curved blades at their belts and automatic rifles in their huge sun-blackened hands. I could hear the two Hawker Hunters flying overhead, and when I looked up, craning my neck and squinting, and saw them, I reached up my hand and pinched my fingers together until I held one of them like a toy and moved my hand with it as it flew, as if I were flying it, as if I were a giant god and these things were my harmless toys, until my mother yanked me back to reality and into the embassy, the seething crowd of Americans camped out like refugees with really nice clothes. They had made milk shakes on the third floor, were distributing them among the clamoring kids when I arrived. I fought for, and got, chocolate. My mother told me firmly to stay put, then disappeared, reappearing later to tell me that my father wasn't in the embassy, he was "out," doing his "work."

For it had occurred to him and Rashid that occupation of the radio station might prove of importance, to which end, accompanied by Rashid's men and four Desert Legionnaires my father borrowed from the embassy, they had set out an hour earlier.

It was now five o'clock in the early evening of the second day of the revolt, August 24, 1958.

Allen Dulles, in his office in Washington, studied the overflight reports from the U2 he had ordered back in the air from its base in Turkey, this time to ascertain whether or not there was any troop movement on the borders of Jordan, Syria, or Iraq. There wasn't. Nor had Nasser moved any troops across the Sinai, nor had Israel dispatched any new troops to any of its borders. With a great deal of effort, everyone was controlling himself. Dulles glanced at his watch. Another Timex, by the way—symptomatic: the leaders of Little America were cheap, or unpretentious, or both. In Washington, it was nine o'clock.

Dulles also held in his hand a cable from my father. He read it for a third time, glanced up and through his own reflection in the window to the shadow of the Washington Monument on the Mall.

He called his brother on the secure line.

"According to my people in Hamra, this thing will be over in twenty-four hours." He heard John Foster tapping a pencil rapidly on his desk at the other end of the line.

"Any clearer indication of who might win?" John Foster asked.

"No. My people still say fifty-fifty, though I sense they think the King will prevail but are afraid to commit to that instinct, and I don't blame them."

"Muir says we should be doing more to help the King. He's gone all self-righteous on me. Remember Donald Muir?"

"Yes, I remember Donald. He's right, of course."

"Of course."

"Then why don't we, John Foster?" Allen Dulles fought to keep the anger out of his voice. "It's Hungary all over again."

"Don't be ridiculous, Allen. It's not Hungary. It's a teeny little country in the Middle East no one's even heard of. There are no natural resources at stake, no industry, nothing of strategic value whatsoever. Anyway, the President is adamant. He wants a summit conference with Khrushchev and absolutely nothing to jeopardize it."

They agreed to play tennis at the Chevy Chase Club that Saturday and hung up.

My father and Rashid, meanwhile, had managed to negotiate their way the half mile or so from Rashid's office, where my father and his four Legionnaires had gone to pick up Rashid, to Radio Hamra, a windowless vault bristling with antennae on rue de Fleuve. My father, squatting behind the Land Rover next to Rashid and peering at the too-quiet building, was reminded of the Tombs at Yale, homes to secret societies like Skull and

Bones, where many of his friends had whiled away their under-
graduate days. He'd always felt their moniker appropriate because
they were symbolically just that, tombs, places for the dead, or
else banks, places of money-worship, another kind of death. To
my father's credit, I'll give him this, he never tried to get into a
secret society while at Yale; he didn't even attend Tap Day. He is,
in his own way, Emersonian.

Speaking of Emerson, intrepid C.I.A. agent, disgruntled mole
within the local Communist Party, he too was dragged from his
home by General Anwar's increasingly efficient military police, as
were all known members of the Communist Party, and thrown
into the soccer stadium, which was now starting to resemble a
somber get-together of the Kurashian elite, or a particularly per-
verse TV game show in which each man present (they were
mostly men) is reunited with everyone he has ever hated. Ancient
grudges, usually of a political nature, divided prisoners into many
small clusters of glowering animosities. People forgot why they
were there, who put them there. They were in no way united by a
common enemy. The soldiers standing guard spent most of their
time breaking up fistfights among the prisoners, wild scuffles that
sent the dry dirt of the soccer field flying. Emerson suffered a broken nose and black eye at the hand of a retired Army officer who
still felt Kurash should have aligned itself with Germany during
World War II. This retired officer was in the stadium because he
belonged to a Fascist-Monarchist group called the White Eagle.
His goal in life was the expulsion of all non-Bedouin from
Kurash, or, that failing, their extermination.

I will not even attempt to explain how it is that my father,
Major Rashid, two lightly armed Kurashian intelligence officers,
and four Desert Legionnaires liberated the premises of Radio
Hamra, but they did. It took them several hours. Two of the
Legionnaires and one of the Kurashian intelligence officers, Mar-
wan Katib, were wounded, Katib fairly seriously, for he caught a
bullet in the larynx. My father had him rushed in the Land Rover

to Hamra Hospital, now running on generators, where he was successfully repaired. Just last year he retired after thirty years as deputy director of Arafat's secret Action Group, the PLO's deep-penetration intelligence arm, the only really important Palestinian intelligence officer never brought to ground by Mossad, an irony not lost upon the C.I.A., who had trained Katib. Standard Camp Perry training nomenclature now includes the cautionary phrase "Frankenstein Asset," meaning, of course, take care to create a monster you can control.

At seven-thirty that night, August 24, 1958, after a thirty-minute silence, Radio Hamra returned to the air with the following announcement, read in a halting manner by a man clearly exhausted and in no way trained in the art of broadcasting:

"My fellow Kurashians, please remain calm and in your homes until this mighty and noble battle for the soul of our country is over. Know that your beloved King is not only alive and safe, he is leading his faithful Army and Air Force into battle against General Anwar and his pack of traitors. May Allah be praised."

The voice, of course, belonged to Rashid. I suspect, given the high-flown rhetoric, that my father had a hand in the writing.

Renee, at her desk in the embassy, currently on a sober cycle, sat staring at the radio, computing the implications of what she'd just heard for a full minute before glancing across at Johnny Allen, who sat tilted back in a desk chair near the code vault reading an Archie comic book. Renee whispered, "They did it."

Johnny leisurely turned a page, smiling at the antics of his friends in Riverdale.

Clearing her throat, Renee spoke louder, clearer: "They did it."

Johnny looked up, quizzical.

"Mack did it. They got the radio station." There were tears in Renee's eyes. Pride burned where not long ago sadness reigned.

My mother and I and the Sweetser girls and Mrs. Sweetser and all the other women and children were sitting downstairs on the floor watching *King Creole* at the end of a swirling cone of dust-filled light projected from a clattering machine onto a sheet tacked white upon the wall. There was Elvis Presley, young and gawky and shy, walking down the wet streets of New Orleans past old men pushing carts and calling out "Crawfish!" I remember my father moving through the crowd to reach us, a happy smile on his face. "Everything's going to be okay," he said. And my mother responded with a proud smile, "Oh, Mack, I am so glad." They embraced, and what struck me as memorable were his clothes streaked with dirt, torn in places, his fingernails black, hands and arms covered with scratches, all the signs of a long, physical struggle the nature of which I could only guess at but which suggested to me a power, a forcefulness that set him apart from the other fathers. I waited for him to embrace me, too, but he didn't, not until my mother nudged him and he noticed I was crying. He leaned over and gave me an awkward hug, then stooped and looked me in the eye, wondering what to say, how to address my disconsolation. Finally, overwhelmed, he simply gave me a fatherly smile and said, "You did good, old chum."

5

Mrs. Gourlie died last night, in her sleep. I was shaving this morning when I heard Mr. Gourlie call down the stairs for Mary, an odd tone to his voice, scratchy, like a kid trying to be brave. I stuck my head out of the bathroom and saw him wavering over his ugly metal walking cane on the landing, dead center on the Persian rug, stooped and defeated. He saw me, blinked. "She's gone, Terryo." For a second I didn't know what he meant, I just stood there with the razor in my hand, lather all over my face, mute and stupid. "Could you go find Chipper and tell him? I don't have his phone number." That's when I finally realized what he was talking about, that his white-haired wife was dead, that Chipper's laughing, horse-faced, southern belle of a mother was dead. "Yes, sir," I said, snapping right to it, quickly rinsing off my face and hurrying out to my Taurus. In the face of tragedy, I've noticed, or even just an excess of emotion, My People respond with salutes and stiffened backs. We are at our best, our most communicative, when marshaling our organizational selves into subtle tribal rectitude. My near-military "Yes, sir" was my wailing on the coffin, my dancing New Orleans funeral parade. It brought tears to my eyes, and Mr. Gourlie's, the sheer force of which we both restrained, practically crippled by all we did not allow ourselves to express. I should have given him a hug, I suppose.

Chipper's little suburban house, out in Maryland, was locked up tight, windows covered with drapes, and was so still and quiet it was hard for me to believe someone might actually live in there.

I rang the doorbell, gazed back at Chipper's black London cab, damp beads of dew just starting to evaporate in the sun. I had never been a messenger of death before, and standing there waiting for Chipper I wondered suddenly what I would tell him, how I would phrase it, the news.

"Who is it?" Chipper's voice came from the other side of the door.

"It's me. Terry."

Several dozen bolts and chains were unfastened within; eventually the door swung open to reveal Chipper fresh as a daisy in maroon shorts and faded blue polo shirt, sipping what was surely freshly squeezed orange juice. Except for the rapid orbits of his dark pupils, there was nothing about him to suggest that his blood cells were at this point largely composed of cocaine. He bestowed upon me, as always, that huge grin of his, equal parts delight and mischief. It was his mother's gift, this ability to absolutely transfix you with a smile and make you feel poised on the edge of a great and glorious adventure. "Top of the morning to you, Terry. What brings you out to the boonies?"

It just tumbled out ungraciously. "Your mom died last night."

His smile made a few structural adjustments as his brain raced to find the right place to put this information. He stood there in a poised dazed stupor, glass of orange juice in hand, and then suddenly sprang into action, as I had done. "I'll meet you back at the house." With that, he disappeared inside. I walked to my Taurus wondering if in fact I'd see him again, or if he'd seek refuge from this news in the crack pipe down in the basement. As it turned out, he was already there when I got back to Dumbarton Avenue, his London cab parked in the narrow driveway that led to the garage. A garage, I saw for the first time, passing it on the way to the steps, the green gate with a creak, that had clearly started life as a carriage house. Why, except in grief, had I never noticed that? Chipper, I reflected, thinking of how fast he had gotten there, is a speed demon in more ways than one.

He quickly and quietly made arrangements, hushed at the old

black phone in the kitchen, while Mary brewed coffee and wept openly, the only one in the house capable of knowing what she felt, simple grief and abandonment, even though God knows she had suffered enough at the hand of the dearly departed.

"We'll have the service tomorrow, Terryster," Chipper told me, hanging up, conspiratorial even in his sadness. "St. James, around the corner."

Source of the tolling afternoon bells all those years, summer brick and boxwood heat . . .

Her body was removed by the funeral home this afternoon. I didn't look, I didn't see her carried one last time down the wide sweep of stairs, her silent farewell to the beautiful old house. . . .

I escaped and spent the afternoon out in the Research Library at Langley, lost in the events of August 1958, in Kurash, not long after Mrs. Gourlie and her husband had taken their young son, Chipper, and returned to the house on Dumbarton, never to leave again.

The cost of the little skirmish between the King and General Anwar? By morning, August 25, 1958, when the King walked in shock through the smoking ruins of Hamzah Palace, over three thousand military lives had been lost, as well as almost a thousand civilian lives, bystanders caught in the wrong place at the wrong time, men, women, and children. Among those killed was Rodney, felled, ridiculously, after the fighting was over, by a stray bullet fired from a celebrating gun as he escorted his string of precious sports cars back into Hamzah Palace. Another six thousand people were wounded. Hamra Hospital did its best, but it could not handle the overload and many of the wounded also later died. Besides Hamzah Palace, the Hotel Antioch, Government House, and the National Police Headquarters were almost completely destroyed. Nineteen tanks, twenty-three armored cars, thirty-two cannons, and one airplane never left the battlefield.

The King's mother took one look at the wreckage and wept, flinging herself to the ground and beating her head on the stones.

The King, sleepless for two days, jittery with caffeine and nicotine, sat stunned in the garden and gazed upon his grandfather Ali's fallen mosque.

General Anwar was captured fighting a last-ditch counterattack on Jebel Jerash. He was brought before the King, who had not moved from the shattered garden. The King started to speak but could not. He stared at Anwar. Anwar, pale with fatigue and failure and terror and shame, looked away. He was suddenly very small, as if he'd shrunk inside his tattered uniform, sheepish, a pretender. There was nothing left of the man of Nasserite vision except this dirty and shiftless old fool. Shock had aged him fast. The King, still speechless, waved dismissively, sadly, and the soldiers took Anwar away.

The King's soldiers released all prisoners held in the soccer stadium.

Professional broadcasters resumed their duties on Radio Hamra.

The King promoted General Samir al-Rahal to Army chief of staff. General al-Rahal immediately reshuffled the command structure, promoting Bedouin officers and discharging or demoting everyone else.

Soldiers who had fought with Anwar were herded into the soccer stadium and there awaited their fate. Irony rules.

As the sun went down that first night of victory, the King prayed in the ruins of his grandfather's mosque, bowing to Allah in thankfulness and misery.

Question: Who put the note in my father's Opel, twice?

I got back to the Gourlie house around five. Imagine my surprise when, entering the guest room, I saw a small canvas bag on the floor by the secretary and, stretched out on the other bed, fully clothed, hands behind head, eyes closed—my father. Napping. I sat on my bed and stared at him. Here he lay in exactly the same position on exactly the same bed as he had forty years ago, back in Washington to confer with Hodd Freeman and Dulles about the fate of the tiny kingdom of Kurash. A vein throbbed gently in his forearm, his mouth, pursed in sleep, collapsed around the occasional brief snore, snort.

"Dad." I spoke softly.

His eyes opened immediately, seeking focus, orientation. He saw me and smiled, closed his eyes again. "What time is it?"

"A little after five," I said. "When did you get here?"

"About an hour ago."

He had taken the Eastern shuttle down from Logan to National Airport, across the Potomac.

"It's called Ronald Reagan Airport now, did you know that?" he asked me. "What's wrong with these clowns, for Christsake, can't they leave well enough alone?"

He swung his legs to the floor, sat up, massaging his eyes. When he opened them, red-rimmed, he looked around at the room.

"I used to stay here, you know. Whenever I came back to the States for so-called consultations."

"I know. Is Mom coming down?"

He shook his head. "She can't. But she talked to Milton on the phone. I don't know what she said, but when he hung up he seemed more peaceful."

My father stood, positively talkative. "I always liked Lorraine. I'm going to miss her. Let's go get a drink."

The four of us—Chipper, myself, Mr. Gourlie, my father—swilled martinis in the study, listening to *My Fair Lady,* a scratchy old thirty-three, as it revolved on the turntable.

I have often walked
Down this street before . . .

When the record ended, we all listened to our ice cubes crack and expand.

"She loved those songs," Mr. Gourlie finally said.

We ate dinner together in the back dining room, Mary sniffling as she served, doting on my father. Chipper winked at me, knees jiggling wildly under the table. He did most of the talking, a running commentary on a wide variety of subjects, my father straining hard to follow the insane ellipses and synaptical contortions as Chipper held forth on everything from computers to space stations to the lost dance halls of Harlem. It was kind of like reading William Burroughs. My father's patient tilt of the head, his completely blank smile, was endearing. I liked him, at that moment, extending this courtesy to the babbling grown-up son of the man he had replaced as station chief in Hamra, Kurash, in 1958. There was loyalty to his friendship, and I admired that. "So we got the idea that if we downloaded the entire database and then simultaneously transferred it to the master computer and uploaded it back onto the Internet, we would in effect have created an information tape loop, an endlessly repeating closed form that, set to music, you know, something like Satie, or maybe Nine Inch Nails, could be a really terrific piece of electronic performance art. . . ." Chipper rambled on, eyes bright with invention and excitement, fingers flying from description to silverware to imaginary unruliness of the hair. Stoned out of his fucking mind. Periodic trips to the bathroom provided the only interruptions to his monologue. By coffee my father was bleary-eyed, and Mr. Gourlie had in fact passed out, upright and motionless in his seat, flawlessly polite even in sleep.

After dinner Chipper climbed into his London cab and roared away. Mr. Gourlie woke up and lumbered back into the study, where to my father's horror he turned on the TV and started watching *Married with Children*.

"Let's get the fuck out of here," my father muttered.

We walked aimlessly at first, along the back streets of Georgetown, past narrow brick rowhouses with their minuscule back gardens, until we found ourselves, as if by design, in front of our old house on P Street. It looked much the same. Lights glowed in the downstairs windows, and we could just see the bookcases in the living room my father had built for my mother many years ago. It was a nice night, warm, even a little muggy, but pleasant. We stood there staring at our former life, my father and I, without a word. Indeed, there was nothing to say, nothing we could muster, anyway, for there seemed a pain lurking there on the porch of our old house that neither of us could tolerate. I could feel my father slipping deeper and deeper into despair beside me as we walked away, and so I guided us toward Clyde's to get some booze to relieve his almost palpable existential dread. He seemed grateful when I told him where we were headed. We had passed Dumbarton Garden and were moving purposefully toward Wisconsin Avenue when it also occurred to me that if I could get my father drunk I might also get him to talk.

Clyde's was depopulated that night, a few businessmen having dinner at the tables, the bar empty except for a youngish couple, graduate students maybe, mesmerized by the inner workings of each other's eyes. They rarely moved, gazing having become their primary activity. I noticed her because, with her dark, wavy, shoulder-length hair and big friendly smile, she made me think of a forties movie girl, you know, someone sitting at the counter of Woolworth's waiting for the adventure to begin. My mother, straight out of Vassar, wearing fundamental red lipstick and smoking Chesterfields. Pretty much the way she looked when she met this anxious man sitting next to me, his lips with great discipline postponing ecstatic contact with the glass of bourbon now raised hoveringly upward, my father frozen, spiraling inward for a second, in a fit of aesthetic eudaemonism, Kierkegaardian self-torture. Then, released from his monkish meditation, he let the glass complete its journey, taking in the shuddering spirits, smacking his lips and sighing contentedly: "Ah."

This followed by a shy sidelong glance, a muffled giggle. "Damn that tastes good."

I sipped my Glenlivet, looking for an angle of attack.

"So Dad," I began. "You never told me you were expert in military assault techniques."

He gave me a baffled, then suspicious look. "What does that mean?"

I told him what I'd learned of his and Rashid's brilliant campaign at Hamra Radio Station. He allowed himself a toothy grin, nodded, sipped more bourbon. "Pretty good, eh?"

My turn to nod. "Pretty good. Did I detect your hand in the writing of Major Rashid's announcement?"

"You did." My father was feeling more cheerful by the second, whether because of the bourbon or the conversation I could not tell. "I know the language was a tad baroque, but I'd been reading *Seven Pillars of Wisdom*."

This surprised me. "You read T. E. Lawrence?"

"Sure. Loved it, too."

"What about *Travels in Arabia Deserta*?"

"Dougherty? You bet. Great book."

This literary father was new to me. All I'd ever seen him read were the comic strips in the morning paper.

"You and Major Rashid were close?" I asked, offhandedly as possible.

"We were good friends, yes."

"Were you at all shocked when you realized what Kumait and General Anwar had been up to?"

"Shocked? Yes, I was."

"Were you mad at Kumait?"

"At first, yes. But then I just felt sorry for him. He was in way over his head."

The time came when my father had to drive Kumait to Hamzah Palace, to the King. He brought his Opel to a stop at the front steps and waited for Kumait to depart and begin the long painful climb. But Kumait did not move. He lit a cigarette, his last, crumpled the pack, and carefully, thoughtfully put it away in a pocket of his wrinkled gray jacket. Outside, soldiers stood uneasy guard, their rifles at the ready. Staring straight ahead through the windshield, Kumait puffed in silence for a while, then turned to my father.

"I like your wife very much," he said.

"Thank you," my father responded, taken aback by the . . . was it a compliment? Or did it have nothing to do with him, only with his wife, my mother?

"What I mean is, she's looking for something, and those are always my favorite people. People on a journey. People on a quest."

"What is she looking for?" my father asked, genuinely curious.

"God, I suppose." Kumait gazed down at his glowing cigarette ash. "Or at least some manifestation of His presence."

"Magic, you mean. She always wants life to be more magical than it is."

"Miraculous, I think, is perhaps the more accurate word." Kumait stubbed out his cigarette in the overflowing ashtray. "Well. Good night, Mack. Thanks for the drive."

Gentle Kumait exited the car, started up the steps to the palace and his fate. My father, watching him go, suddenly wondered if he should attend him, escort him to the King and stay there as his advocate, or at least defender. No, he decided, that was not his place, this was something between Kumait and the King alone, Kurashian to Kurashian, friend to friend. He did not envy Kumait at this moment. In fact, he could think of nothing worse than having to face the King under these circumstances. If Kumait had told my father the truth, and my father tended to believe he had, than at least his conscience was clear, or should be: he had meant the King no harm. "On the other hand, we're held accountable for our stupidity and our moral ignorance," my father said, draining his bourbon and waving for the bartender to pour him another, a little jiggle of the right hand, thumb and pinkie finger held at acute angles, the motion of an airplane dipping its wings in greeting. I seditiously nursed my Glenlivet.

"What did you do after you dropped off Kumait?" I asked.

"Waited."

"For what?"

"To drive him home."

"What made you so sure the King wouldn't have him arrested or shot or something?"

"I wasn't sure. Not in the least. I was just hopeful. I liked Kumait, despite everything."

From what I can tell, it was hard *not* to like Kumait, now standing outside the door to the King's first-floor office, waiting for his knock to be answered. Captain Majali hovered by his side, dark circles under his eyes. Even he found it hard to dislike Kumait, the good captain who knew nothing of Kumait's sweetness. It's just that there was something benign about the man, about the sheer cliff of stiff, almost-white hair rising from his forehead, about his abstracted smile and nearsighted squint as he waited anxiously at the door.

"Come in," the King's voice said.

Captain Majali nodded at Kumait, opened the door for him. Kumait stepped into the room.

The King was sitting in an armchair, legs crossed, cigarette in hand, studying some papers on his lap.

The door closed behind Kumait.

The King looked up. He gazed at Kumait. No expression on his face. Almost as if he didn't recognize him. Then he glanced back at the papers on his lap, read aloud: " *Question:* 'So your plan was to act together, the Muslim Brotherhood and elements of the Army, led by Anwar.' *Answer:* 'Yes.' *Question:* 'But then Anwar moved without you? Is that it?' *Answer:* 'Yes.' " The King returned his gaze to Kumait. "Is this all true?"

"Yes, Your Majesty. Regrettably."

"You thought to convince me to abandon the West and return to my Muslim self, my Arab self, my devout Muslim, Nasserite nationalist self?"

"Not abandon the West, entirely." Kumait heard his words, and they sounded hopelessly false. "Merely balance its influence."

"That's a lie, Kumait. You wanted me to kick the bastards out."

The King had aged, he had hardened, in the last forty-eight hours. And he was right, although until now Kumait had not acknowledged it to himself. Kumait *did* want the King to throw the Americans out, along with what remained of the English, and, for good measure, the French, as well as the odd Dutchman and German. The Russians somehow did not seem so overbearing; they had yet to master the art of arrogant condescension that marked most Westerners in their dealings with all things Kurashian, all things Arab. This, Kumait realized, accounted for his almost orgiastic feelings of excitement at the sight of Oristibach's turned inside out, even the possibility that the fantastic goods of the West could be strewn upon the streets like so much rubbish. Yet Kumait knew enough about himself to know also that he adored the West, that he cared about Shelley and Wordsworth easily as much as he did about any eleventh-century desert poet, that he cherished the intellectual freedom of disinterested scholarship at least as much as the ethnocentricities of a smothering Islamic culture—

"Kumait?" It was the King, still waiting for an answer, a response.

Kumait was getting one of his headaches again, piercing pain stabbing at the base of his skull. He wanted to lie down and close his eyes.

"You're right, Your Majesty. I did want you to throw them out, but I didn't know that until just now."

The King stared at him, wondering. He turned his attention back to the papers on his lap, clearly the transcript of my father's and Rashid's interrogation of Kumait. He read in silence for a few minutes. Kumait looked about the room, walls singed black by fire, most pictures and furniture removed, no doubt damaged beyond repair. The glass panes in the French doors behind the reading King were either shattered or missing. A sweet breeze blew in from the garden, a scent of jasmine cutting briefly through the bitter stink of smoke. Finally the King looked up from his papers.

"I don't know what to do, Kumait," he said quietly. "If I can't trust you or Anwar, who can I trust? If I end up feeling that I can trust Mack Hooper, an American spy, more than I can trust you, what hope is there for any of us? What have we come to, Kumait?"

Kumait's legs were starting to hurt from standing somewhat at attention this whole time. There was only one other chair in the room, a plain wooden chair missing its back. Kumait gestured toward it. "May I, Your Majesty?"

The King waved his hand in consent. Kumait brought the chair closer and sat.

"First of all, I want you to know that I think now that all of us, except maybe you, suffer from self-hatred. That's certainly true of myself. We see ourselves from the point of view of the West and find ourselves lacking. The West is our temptation and our fall from grace, to use the Christian metaphors, which seems appropriate. We have been seduced, we have lost our innocence. Anwar was trying to get it back."

"An Arab point of view?"

"Precisely."

The King waited for more.

"With self-hatred, of course, comes a terrible nostalgia for the way things were, or at least the way we imagine things were, before, which is fairly unreliable and falls more into the category of myth than history. This nostalgia, the nostalgia of defeat, is dangerous, and breeds tyrants."

"Like Anwar?"

"Perhaps. Certainly like Nasser."

"But it draws so many people, millions of people." The King seemed dumbfounded by this illogicality.

"That's one reason it's so dangerous, Your Majesty. Poor people, rich people, educated people, uneducated people—it draws them all equally. The other reason this nostalgia is so dangerous is that it's terribly, terribly violent, as we have seen."

Here Kumait lapsed into silence, spent, expiated, exposed. It was the least he could do to honor the King he had betrayed. And he had betrayed him, that was clear to him now. He simply had not told the King the truth.

The King was tired. It was after midnight. "You may go, Kumait."

"Go?" Kumait repeated, startled. "Go where?"

"Home. To sleep. We'll talk again soon."

My father had fallen asleep in the Opel, dreaming of winter mornings in Hastings-on-Hudson, plumes of steamy breath leading him down to the railroad station. He used to walk there and back at the beginning and end of every day. It was the only exercise he got. Kumait's slamming closed the passenger door of the Opel woke him. He was still young then, and could make the transition to consciousness smoothly. He sat up, as if he'd just been resting his eyes for a moment.

"Home?"

"Yes, please, Mack," Kumait said, still in shock. "Home. That would be most kind."

My father looked down at his empty glass on the bar at Clyde's with a surprised and mournful expression. I nodded to the bartender and he poured my father another bourbon. His third. I was keeping count.

"Down the hatch," my father said.

And down it all went. He shivered, pleased, and motioned to the now-empty glass. "Another, please, barkeep."

His fourth. The bartender poured, retreated to a discreet distance, where he continued his tireless washing and drying of glasses at a small silver sink.

"So I drove Kumait home and that was that," my father concluded, not a slur in sight.

He sure can hold his liquor, my father. I'll give him that. It's a generational skill, I suspect, and as such indicative not of a strength but of a pathology. Or so I console myself.

"What happened to General Anwar?" I asked. "When last seen he was being marched off to jail." I knew, of course. I just wanted to hear it from my father. "Was he shot?"

"No, he was not. He stayed in jail for a few weeks, while we interrogated him, and then the King exiled him to Rome. He should have shot the son of a bitch."

"Really?"

"Really."

"You think the King was not harsh enough?"

"I think the King couldn't decide whether to shit or get off the toilet."

"What did Anwar say, when you interrogated him?"

"You haven't read it yet?"

"Not yet, no." Another lie.

My father absently patted his pockets for cigarettes denied him a long time ago, by my mother, for his own good. "He said nothing."

"Did he deny his connection to Egyptian Intelligence?"

"Of course."

"Even when confronted with the evidence Rashid had collected?"

"Yes. Mere coincidence, he maintained. We misconstrued what we heard in our surveillance tapes. He said he acted alone in the name of Allah and for the good of his country. He said his duty as a patriot compelled him to lead the rebellion. He said if the King had listened to him in the first place none of this would have been necessary. We interviewed him repeatedly over a ten-day period. Read it for yourself."

"I will."

After ten days in prison, General Anwar was put on a plane at Hamra airport and flown to Rome with his family, there to fritter away the rest of his days sipping coffee at the Café El Greco and taking daily constitutionals in the Borghese Gardens. At least, that was the plan. My father thought. They all thought. Back then in 1958 when his innocence had yet to be taken from him.

"Should've shot the son of a bitch," he said again, with some vehemence.

My father's eyes were now struggling to focus. The bourbon was at last having its effect.

"Dad?"

"What?"

"You keep patting your pockets. Do you want a cigarette? I can get you a pack. There's a machine back there, by the men's room."

My father considered this cruel and tempting offer. "Your mother would kill me."

"My mother barely even sees you anymore," I reminded him.

More consideration. He studied what was left of his bourbon. Looking up at me, he had a childish, wounded look on his face. "Why are you doing this?"

"Doing what?" I asked innocently.

He shook his head, denying me, or trying to clear it, I couldn't tell.

"Tell me, Dad." I leaned in closer. "Who was the woman? In Rome?"

"Who was she?"

"Yeah, who was she?"

"Emily."

"Emily what?"

"Emily none of your goddamn business."

"Where did you meet Emily? In Rome, or Hamra?"

"Neither. How about that?" He grinned, straightened, getting his bearings. "Gotcha there, didn't I?"

"Dad, tell me, does this Emily have anything to do with you and the King, what happened, or was she just . . . a girl?"

"Girl?"

"Lady, woman, whatever. You know what I mean."

"Just a girl."

I didn't believe him.

"Okay, Dad? Last question. What did happen, exactly, between you and the King? I'm thinking specifically of December 1958. What did you do?"

He stood from his stool, looked around near-empty Clyde's. "We used to come here for lunch sometimes, back in the early sixties. The K.G.B. liked to eat lunch here, too. We'd send beers to each other's tables. Christ, those bastards could drink." He took a deep, sad sigh. "Poor Lorraine Gourlie."

"Did you kill the King?" I asked.

He didn't even dignify that with a response. Or maybe he just didn't hear me. He turned without a word and departed from Clyde's, moving on steady feet out the door to M Street, leaving me to pay the bill.

6

For two weeks after reclaiming his rule, the King surprised everyone, including my father, by treating his near overthrow as if it had been a natural catastrophe, a hurricane or an earthquake, for which no one was personally responsible and for which no one in particular was to blame. His equanimity never failed him. He was gracious to everyone, punitive to no one. He had several large Bedouin tents pitched in a field not far from Hamzah Palace, and there lived with his mother while workers rebuilt the smashed palace. Here too he held all governmental meetings, sitting cross-legged on thick carpets under the heavy stretched black goatskins, just as his father had done, and his grandfather Ali before him. The temporary move seemed to reinvigorate the King. He rose early every morning, before light, prayed in solitude, then rode a horse out into the still-dark desert for over an hour. He cut down on his cigarettes, smoking only one pack a day. He reduced his Coca-Cola consumption by half, a mere six bottles a day. He met with Esmerelda, discreetly, in her apartment on Bayir Street, overlooking the flower market. They would make love in the afternoon; he would doze off, pleasantly relaxed, and when he awoke she would make them a pot of good English tea and they would sit on chairs just inside the French doors of the balcony, out of eyesight below, and there they would chat about nothing in particular, sip their Darjeeling, gaze happily down at the crowded, colorful stalls. I wonder: Did my father ever check out this Esmerelda Tweedy? I find only scattered and inconsequential references to her in the files at Langley, and she does not make even an appearance in the standard texts. In history, she's less than a footnote, and yet she surely played her part, one of those minor characters whose lives, I've always suspected, would tell us the most about what really happened, what it was really like, then, there, in this case Kurash in the year 1958—if we should ever bother to investigate. Instead, we tell the stories of kings.

Slowly Hamra, and the country, restored itself. With American money, investments cajoled out of Conrad Hilton by the State Department, Hotel Antioch was given a substantial face-lift, the sagging old dowager spruced up and modernized. The results, from my father's point of view, were loathsome: bright turquoise carpeting in the lobby, huge glistening chandeliers hanging overhead like leering, tawdry hookers draped in costume jewelry, the old and creaking wooden Otis elevators replaced by fast and silent metal coffins zooming ominously up and down. The worst damage was done in the bar, rattan and old paneling removed and replaced by obscenely large and nubbly armchairs and a wallpaper depicting happy water-skiers and slim women in large floppy hats strolling Parisian side streets, all in the style of the times, the kind of popularized, advertiser's *moderne* found on matchbooks, magazine covers, and menus. The new Army chief of staff, General Samir al-Rahal, thoroughly purged the armed forces, establishing Bedouin supremacy in all command positions. We American dependents returned to our homes and resumed our normal lives, the kids going back to the American Community School and learning next to nothing in hot airless rooms with a view of a disused construction site, the mothers dragging us to the pool at the American Club every weekend, there to deposit us while they retired to the shade of blue-striped beach umbrellas and lustily inhaled gin and tonics and Bloody Marys. Even the Hamra Go-Cart Club was soon operating again, with matches every Saturday, though for quite a while the green-and-red Kurashian flag on its white pole in the middle of the track was flown at half-mast in honor of Rodney, a little reminder, for those who allowed themselves to be reminded, that all was not necessarily well in the kingdom. Rodney's body, flown back to England at the King's expense, today lies buried in a sloping arboreal cemetery in Miller's Gate, Yorkshire.

The poor of Bakr resumed their anonymous lives, murmuring, squalid backdrop to the lives of those who really mattered, those who wrote history.

The Palestinian refugees in camps like the one my mother had visited settled back down on their haunches, eyes turned inward, dreaming of their lost orchards and clear babbling brooks, none of which had ever really existed. They cleaned their machine guns. They waited.

Dressing for Mrs. Gourlie's funeral, I showed my father the small lion she had given me. He sat on the edge of the bed contemplating it, recovering the memory: "Yeah, she's right, I got it for her in the *souk*. I think it was actually your mother who first spotted it. Lorraine gave it to you?"

"Yes," I said.

"I wonder why?" he mused, cradling the lion in his fingers.

"She also told me that there was a woman, a *girl,* in Rome."

"That's a red herring," he said. "Don't waste your time."

"Emily is a red herring?"

"Who's Emily?"

If you read through the transcripts of my father's and Major Rashid's interview with General Anwar, it becomes clear that what they're after is the Egyptian connection and, beyond that, in a hypothetical way, the Soviet-Egyptian connection. Major Rashid is also particularly interested in the goings-on of Syrian Intelligence, Baathists all, and the Israelis.

Question: When did you first form a relationship with Egyptian Intelligence?

Answer: I never formed a relationship with Egyptian Intelligence.

Question: How do you account for this photograph of yourself and Colonel Sonallah Qabbani of Egyptian Intelligence leaving a safe house?

Answer: Don't be childish. Sonallah is a friend of mine. We spend time together. We enjoy each other's company.

Question: In a safe house leased in his name and paid for by the Macador Travel Agency, Inc., a company with corporate headquarters in Bermuda?

Answer: He's a businessman, for godsake, Mack. For all I know he's got a dozen dummy companies. So he doesn't like paying taxes. Who does?

Question: General Anwar, please listen to this tape. (Tape is played.) Do you recognize your voice?

Answer: Of course I do.

Question: And the other voice?

Answer: Sonallah, naturally.

Question: And are you not discussing funds to be given to you by the Egyptians to fatten the pockets of your officers?

Answer: We are discussing ways to supplement the meager salaries of my men.

Question: By a foreign government.

Answer: I don't care where it comes from if my men need it. My job as senior officer is to make sure my army is alert and well taken care of, and that's what I was doing.

Question: You're denying reality, Anwar.

Answer: To the contrary, Major Rashid. I'm the only one around here who sees it. Tell me, do you consider yourself a patriot?

Question: Of course.

Answer: But you're working for a foreign government, as you put it, so how could you be a patriot?

Question: I'm not working for the Americans.

Answer: Yes, you are. They pay your salary. They decide the orders of the day. Mack Hooper isn't your compatriot. He's your boss. And it's not just you, Rashid. It's all of us, including the King. We all work for the Americans. They own us.

Imagine the awkward silence after that riposte. Did they all light cigarettes? I'll bet they did. I'll bet they ordered coffee, and that it was brought in, by a young boy who worked in a nearby café, on a small silver tray, in very small white cups, sweet and thick as sludge. Reading the transcript, I can almost see them shifting weight in their hard wooden seats, peeling their hot buttocks from the wood, sharing a moment dedicated to the plumes of white smoke exhaled into the light, more caffeine to excite their already frazzled synapses. My point being that I'll bet this interview, this shadow-world event the pulp imagination would call an "interrogation," was quite civilized from beginning to end. That's how it sounds, anyway, in transcript. I wish I had the tapes themselves to listen to, but they're long gone, or buried so deep within the walls of Langley that even Bob Easton can't find them, or won't.

Question: Help us.
Answer: Help you? How?
Question: We'd like to roll up all Egyptian and Soviet operations in this country.
Answer: And you expect me to help you do that?
Question: We're asking for your help.
Answer: Oh, I'd help if I could, but I don't know anything about such things. I'm an Army man. A military man. A soldier.
Question: Anwar, for godsake, tell us about the Syrians, at least. We know you met with them while visiting Damascus last month.
Answer: Of course I met with them. I was trying to see if I

could find a few extra weapons somewhere so that my men could actually be armed if and when they were ever unfortunate enough to go into combat.

And so on, hours of this, my father and Rashid laying down times and dates and names, Anwar never faltering in his pugnacious, combative testiness, a vain general until the end, a proud and stupid performance. Only toward the end of this marathon session, days and nights of questions and threats, did I find anything unexpected, anything revelatory or provocative.

Question: You and Kumait are old friends?
Answer: Yes, of course, you know that already.
Question: For the record, please, General.
Answer: Yes, Kumait and I are old friends.
Question: You met in university?
Answer: In Beirut, yes. A.U.B. 1938.
Question: You both attended Professor Earl Cartiford's seminar "The History of the Arab World"?
Answer: Yes.
Question: Professor Earl Cartiford was a Communist, wasn't he?
Answer: A Marxist, yes, I believe so. A Marxist from Philadelphia. A Marxist from Yale, your alma mater, I think, Mack.
Question: At that time you and Kumait formed certain opinions regarding the exploitation of the Arabs by Western powers?
Answer: At that time Kumait and I sat with other young dreamers from all over the Arab world and talked. That's all we did. Talk, talk, talk. I don't remember what we said. I remember the blue of the Mediterranean beyond the cypress trees and cedars; I remember the bougainvillea spilling over the white walls in spring; I remember the way the jasmine

smelled walking back to campus after a night in town smoking hashish and drinking cognac.

Question: You recognize these photographs?

Answer: Yes. Where did you get them?

Question: Is that you?

Answer: Yes, with more hair, as you can see.

Question: Is that Kumait?

Answer: Yes.

Question: These were taken in Beirut?

Answer: Yes.

Question: By whom?

Answer: Excuse me?

Question: Who took these photographs?

Answer: (Unintelligible . . .)

Question: Speak up, please.

Answer: I don't know. I don't remember.

Question: No memory at all?

Answer: None, I'm afraid.

History is what we choose to remember.

History is what is left to us after all the accidents.

Forty thousand volumes of classical Greek literature disappeared when the Arsenal annex to the great library of Alexandria burned to the ground in 47 B.C. Who knows what was lost? The truly great works, perhaps. Maybe Sophocles was a minor playwright, Plato a secondary and undistinguished philosopher.

If I had the original negatives of the black-and-white photographs taken of Kumait and General Anwar as young men in Beirut, and isolated and blew up, repeatedly, their eyes, would I find reflected in one of them the figure or face of the person holding the camera and taking their picture?

And would that tell me something?

7

St. James Church, around the corner from the Gourlie house on Dumbarton Avenue, was another brick edifice in the Federal style. Ivy climbed the walls, high dark doors opened to an aisle separating two rows of plain white pews, crowded that afternoon, the afternoon of Mrs. Gourlie's funeral service, with old spies. I stood at the back of the church, under the resounding organ, and gazed out over maybe four dozen white heads, a few of statesmen, a few of charity colleagues, but most belonging to C.I.A. men, now in their seventies, and their persevering wives. My father, himself, of course, white-haired, sat in the front pew with Milton Gourlie, who gazed upon the proceedings with a beneficent, addled smile, I suppose a kind of peacefulness, though maybe it was just shock, his grand beaked nose and Caesar's haircut making his profile look even more regal than usual, at least by American standards, someone who had done well in insurance and then signed the Declaration of Independence. Chipper sat on his other side, wearing a nice suit, face at rest, thoughtful, body in a posture of lanky composure, prep-school (Taft, in his case) cool having become, in his case, seemingly, a genetic factor. His eyes, however, were agog, living their own separate life, a curious, complex existence in no way confined by his cranium. To think this was the boy who, years after Kurash, when we were teenagers, proudly unpacked for me all his precious lead soldiers and invited me to join him in nostalgic tactical maneuvers on the painted wooden floor of the top-story rooms on Dumbarton Avenue, the crown of the old house, the brain of the old house, the imagination of the old house. I saw my father brush something from Milton Gourlie's lapel—dust? lint?—with an unconscious, almost female solicitousness. They had known each other a long, long time. I suppose it was inevitable that they would end up together someplace like this, at a funeral for one of their own, husband or wife or friend or colleague, here among their weakened if not infirm contemporaries. Many had entered the church aided by canes and aluminum walkers.

The priest, who had actually known Mrs. Gourlie well, she having attended this church every Sunday for forty years, stood and spoke, inarticulate and bashful in his elegant purple and black robe. Behind him lay Mrs. Gourlie's closed coffin, gleaming hardwoods, the best money could buy, no doubt.

"The souls of the just are in the hands of God . . ."

I noticed Chuck McGranahan, dainty, compact, sitting next to his redheaded wife, Margie, who was at least a foot taller and wore pearls. Mr. McGranahan had worked with Mr. Gourlie in Rome, in the late forties, making sure that Italy's first free elections in thirty-two years did not actually reflect the will of the people and propel the Italian Communist Party into power. They used to hang out together in the Grand Hotel bar on via del Corso in the days when trolley cars ran down the middle of the narrow boulevard now crammed with T-shirt stores. I saw Jonathan Eder, massive shoulder muscles crammed uncomfortably into a faded old blue suit, balding now, his blue eyes weak, the youthful freckles liver spots. He, too, had been part of that original Rome group, dispensing money, a small fortune in small bills, up and down the tired old boot of Italy, preaching to the villagers the ills of Communism and the virtues of the Christian Democrats. It's a miracle he wasn't shot.

In another pew I saw Hodd Freeman, my father's division chief when we were in Kurash, later deputy director of plans, that

hardy and lean Maine Yankee now frail and spindly, supported
by a cane, his curly golden hair sparse and thin, a baby's white
wisps. Next to him sat Jimmy Marshall, arthritic but still handsome, bent but deeply suntanned, dapper in a sparkling white
shirt, gold signet ring demure yet lordly on his crippled little finger. He served with my father in Kuwait, flying C.I.A. cargo
planes back and forth across the Middle East. It was he who
brought me my first bike, from London, in just such a cargo
plane, a big shiny red English bike. He was a former tight end for
UVA, a former Barnum and Bailey ringmaster, a former O.S.S.
bagman expert at slipping in and out of German-held territory, a
rider of trains, a solitudinous inhabitant of third-rate hotels near
dreary urban train stations, a walker in the black-and-white rain,
Auden's "marked man of romantic thrillers . . ."

> *Whose brow bears the brand of winter*
> *No priest can explain . . .*

And Auden should know. He would have made a wry and
witty poem of this convocation of old spies, demobbed intelligence officers, former *agents provocateurs,* cold war functionaries,
Ivy League bumblers and drunks who had once pulled the levers
of secret government in an age of high anxiety, circa 1958. Put
another way, these were the bastards who beat the bastards, unless
it was all just dumb luck. I doubt they felt anything but numbing
disbelief as they watched the Berlin Wall come crashing down on
TV, or when they were invited to join current C.I.A. officers on a
trip to Moscow and a tour of the K.G.B.'s now open files in
Lubyanka, on Dzerzhinsky Square. "I had a file as thick as a
phone book," my father told me last month, in Boston, before he
decided to clam up. "It was perhaps the strangest moment of my
life, seeing that file, flipping it open at random and seeing what I
was doing, what the Soviets thought I was doing, in Kurash in
1958."

"What did it say?"

"Well, of course, I can't go into the details."

"Of course. Were they right?"

"Fifty-fifty."

I have tried, needless to say, to get hold of that file, but the Russians at the Russian embassy assure me that all such files have been destroyed, and Bob Easton, when I asked him out at Langley one day what he knew, just gave me a funny look and said something like, "I'm a humble public relations guy. All I can tell you is the commissary's got raspberry Jell-O today, my personal favorite."

I saw Renee, without her dachshund, weeping quietly.

Chipper stood, addressed the congregation. He was calm, self-possessed, a good speaker. His eyes had stopped vibrating dangerously, they gazed steadily, and with humor, out at the assembled friends and relations of his mother.

"My mother, I'm sure, is very, very glad that you could all make it today," he said. "She loved a good party, as you know, and with this group under one roof a good party is pretty much guaranteed."

Chuckles rippled through the church.

Behind me, the door suddenly was flung open, admitting a burst of sunlight and hot air. I turned and saw a stout, crop-haired woman in her late forties maneuvering her way into the church, a child in tow, a boy, maybe eight, several large plastic bags dangling and crinkling from her other arm. She looked like an eccentric former country club matron now inexplicably homeless. Another woman entered right behind her, taller, thinner, a severe and admonitory lesbian if I ever saw one. The woman with the child moved closer to me, standing at my side, hushing the boy when he leaned back and asked her, "Which is the one that died?" It was only when his mother shot me an apologetic smile that I dimly recognized the pale blue eyes mottled with little flecks of green, the thin arch of the nose still visible beneath the additional weight.

"Penny?"

She cocked her head, appraised me, waiting for recognition, which, when it came, lit up her entire face, making me feel adored. "Terry?"

We were both whispering. She smiled and flung her arms around me and gave me a kiss. The other woman stood stoically close by, watching us sternly. Penny patted her son on the head. "Jason, this is Terry," she whispered. He gave me a blank, incurious look. To the other woman she whispered, "This is Terry Hooper." To me: "Terry, this is Edith. We're married." Edith allowed herself a terse smile, a quick, noncommittal nod.

"My mother was a deeply religious woman," Chipper was saying. "She believed in God, and His Son, Jesus Christ, and heaven, and hell, and she strove all her life to live accordingly, to worship and respect goodness and avoid and revile evil. I think all those who knew her at all well would agree she succeeded, and therefore it is with some confidence that I say she must be in heaven now. If so, she must also be very happy. I miss her already, I miss her terribly, and I know my father does too, but knowing she's in heaven, and happy, makes it possible for us to bear her loss, her leaving us. Because, after all, if she's in heaven, then she's also here, around us, in spirit. She'll live forever."

Did Chipper really believe this claptrap, or was it the cocaine talking, or grief, or demented irony, or simply exhaustion?

I glanced at Penny; she saw me and smiled. No indication of whether or not she found what he was saying as preposterous as I did.

I looked out at the backs of all the white-haired old heads and knew that I was looking at the end of something. Not just Mrs. Gourlie's life, but all of their lives, that specific midcentury American upper-middle-class Wasp East Coast thing, the mercantile remnant of the Puritans, I guess, the ruling class tossed up by the Civil War and westward expansion, a whole litany of crimes now lost within the comforts of civilization, harmless as a lullaby. As an historian and as a final participant, *I* felt nothing but regret. I do not suffer loss well. These people had started their factories in Lowell and their railroads in Baltimore; they had built their homes on the Upper East Side of Manhattan and Beacon Hill in Boston and the Main Line in Philadelphia and right here in Georgetown; they had built their rambling wooden summer-houses in places like York, Maine, and Martha's Vineyard; they had gone to Andover and Exeter and St. Paul's and Choate, Harvard and Yale and Princeton and Brown and Williams and Amherst; they had fought bravely and well in World War II and won; they had started the C.I.A. as a place of clarity and focus in confusing and tumultuous times. Their role in our national theater had all ended with their dark and unfortunate masterpiece, the Vietnam War. They were first dislodged, then replaced. Some among them found a precarious perch or hiding place here and there in the vast and intricate federal bureaucracy, but most never again wielded power, most saw their inherited wealth dwindle and disappear, most ended up in places like St. James Church, burying their dead and driving home to the suburbs in their Toyota Camrys, powerful now only in the heads of their children, the children of Little America, Chipper and Penny and myself. When we die, they'll vanish forever, the nominal grown-ups of Little America, their life-affirming Cocktail Hour, the smell of their boathouses opened each summer after a winter of hibernation, their songs spinning on heavy black plastic thirty-threes, songs of leisurely, expansive moonlight and seaside terraces . . .

What's new?
How is the world treating you?
You haven't changed a bit,
Lovely as ever, I must admit.
What's new?
How did that romance come through?
We haven't met since then.
Gee but it's nice to see you again.

It will all die with us.

Like the hieratic scratchings on the stones of el-Khirmeil my mother gazed upon in Kurash, in 1958, we will become enigmas.

Like little Kurash itself, invisible kingdom, we will disappear from all maps of the known world.

No one will remember why it was important that the chairs were upside down on the tables of the nightclub when Nat King Cole sat to have his photograph taken for the cover of his 1958 album *Cottage for Sale*.

No one will remember the day in late August 1958, in Washington, when Deputy Director of Plans Frank Wisner, after weeks of increasingly erratic behavior, finally broke down completely and had to be carted out from L Building by three burly hospital attendants and rushed in an ambulance to Sheppard Pratt, there to suffer six months of electroshock treatments. He was replaced by none other than Richard Bissell, Mr. U2, who in the course of things would suffer his own hour of despair and humiliation, running aground, several years later, in the Bay of Pigs.

No one will remember Frank Wisner *or* Richard Bissell.

"Blessed too are the sorrowing; they shall be consoled," the priest intoned.

If there is a heaven, who among these white-haired old people, so gentle in their retirement from Little America, would gain entrance?

If there is a hell, for what crimes would they be punished?

But of course there is no heaven, there is no hell, except what we know here on this earth, which is plenty if you ask me, more than enough of suffering and ecstasy for all.

The priest recited a final prayer, citing Corinthians, "For we walk by faith and not by sight"; the organ rumbled and coughed out a turgid "A Mighty Fortress Is Our God"; and we all filed from St. James Church as from a not-quite-successful wedding, exchanging affable nods, slightly embarrassed, eager to start drinking.

8

The next day, over lime Jell-O in the cafeteria at Langley, I casually asked Bob Easton how the C.I.A. would go about finding someone.

"Who?" he asked, studying the green quivering mass on his spoon.

"Anyone."

"What've you got?"

"A first name, Emily, a place, Rome, and a year, 1958."

"That's it?"

"That's it."

"What nationality?"

Good question. "American," I guessed. My working assumption was that my father would not have allowed himself to be intimate with anyone outside the C.I.A.

Bob studied me as but seconds before he had studied his Jell-O, as if I were an inanimate curiosity, colorful, perplexing. "I take it this is in relation to your research here."

"Sort of. Not really. It's more along the lines of a personal matter."

"Ah." As if that changed everything. "I see."

He gazed off at the crowded cafeteria, men and women of the C.I.A. chatting amiably beneath the unpleasant fluorescent lights. His colleagues. The atmosphere is collegial. I had come here once with my father in 1970, thirty years ago, to have lunch with the then–consul general and discuss the possibility of my becoming a career officer. We sat in a corner table I could see from where I now crouched above my Jell-O with Bob Easton. A solitary man in his fifties occupied it alone, reading the *Washington Post* and absently but meticulously picking at his food, what looked like a Cobb salad.

"That's Daryl Hamilton," Bob hissed in my ear, suddenly a leering snake, hypertrophic gossip.

He saw by my blank look I had no idea what he was talking about.

"The deputy director of operations," he added, a condescending footnote.

I looked back at the middle-aged man. Deputy director of operations is the number-three position in the C.I.A., not far below the Director. In the old days, under a slightly different title—deputy director of plans—it was Frank Wisner's job, until he was led screaming from the old building on the Mall. His successor, Richard Bissell, had enjoyed his office in this new building for less than a month before being dragged down by the Bay of Pigs. I wondered if Daryl Hamilton had the same office as Bissell. I wondered if there was some little mark that remained, an indication that Bissell had once paced the same floor, say a nick in the wall, evidence of Bissell's lost temper upon hearing that his Cubans had been stranded on the beach without air cover. More likely, any such indication of previous lives had probably been plastered smooth, repainted long ago, obliterating even the most obliquitous of Richard Bissell's memories.

He would recognize nothing but the view, and even that might have altered, more trees thickening the foreground, the glass walls of a nearby business park bifurcating the background, adding a gash, the scar of a gash, to the scene: ruminative Potomac undulating slowly southward.

After Mrs. Gourlie's funeral, we all adjourned to the house on Dumbarton, where Penny and I finally got a chance to talk, albeit under the watchful eye of her husband, Edith. Her son, Jason, clung to her knee while we sat in iron chairs out on the back flagstone patio, in the garden where Chipper, at his age, had chased wildly through the boxwoods looking for Easter eggs. My eyes wandered involuntarily up to Mrs. Gourlie's bedroom window. She was gone. She would never glance down here again. I was having difficulty with the fundamentals.

"So, you're gay," I blurted out.

Penny laughed, the same old Penny laugh, what Chipper used to call her "charwoman's chortle," gray distant eyes appraising me. "Yep, I am."

She turned to Jason, who was peering up at me from between her stout knees. "Jason, Terry and I grew up together. Why don't you say hi?"

Reluctantly, but obediently, Jason said, "Hi."

Not far away, Renee, drink in hand, pulled my father down to her and planted a big kiss on his cheek, leaving behind a smear of bright red lipstick, which she then proceeded to dab at ineffectively with a crumpled piece of Kleenex. Tears fell continuously, unconscious as a smile would have been on a more regular person.

Chuck McGranahan stood in the living room with Jonathan Eder and Jimmy Marshall; I could see them through the open French doors, all three assuming the posture of their former selves, loose-limbed, athletic, though bent now slightly at the knees, hair missing or white and soft, their familiar laughter rolling out to me like a kick in the gut, voices from a gone world I lived in more than they did, a world forty years old, obsolete, No Longer Real. O Penny, why could we not be sitting now on a bed in the shadows of a plain tree outside, adrift in the dusty silent heat of Constitution Square before the backpackers invaded? Why are you not naked except for your wristwatch, and just who the hell is this husband, Edith, anyway?

"It most likely can't be done."

I turned to see Bob Easton facing me, once again contemplating his Jell-O.

"What is Jell-O made of, exactly?" he asked. "Do you know?"

"No. Why can't it be done?"

"Well, because 1958 is a long time ago, and even then Rome was a large city, and it was no doubt full of Emilys."

"She would have worked for the American embassy. In some capacity. I suspect she worked for you guys."

He let out another little "Ah." Probed his half-eaten Jell-O.

"There must be some way of getting a list of Americans named Emily working for the C.I.A. in Rome in 1958."

"Records over twenty years old have a way of getting lost or shredded."

"Yeah, but some remain, right? Like that heap of inconsequential data you've given me upstairs."

He looked hurt. "Inconsequential?"

"Bob, I distinctly get the impression that not all vital records are included in what you've shown me."

"Everything I could find you've got." Miffed, guilty, he slurped his decaf, finally allowed, "I could look again. You never know. Emily?"

"Emily."

"Age?"

I pondered that one. "Young," I guessed. "In her twenties at the time."

"Righto. I'll see what I can do."

At one point during the reception following Mrs. Gourlie's funeral, Penny and Jason and Chipper and I escaped by climbing the stairs to the third floor, where we pushed open the door to Chipper's old bedroom and entered somewhat apprehensively. Much of course had been taken by Chipper to the basement of his paranoid suburban house in Maryland, but much remained, too, so much that I was somewhat shocked to see intact, unchanged, the bureau mirror covered with stickers from places like Gstaad and Lisbon and Beirut's long-gone King George Hotel. Penny opened a window to air the place out. Jason jumped up and down on one of the beds, springs creaking and dust rising in little explosive puffs. Chipper sneezed, rifled through drawers, came out with summer camp marksmanship medals and torn ticket stubs for the Beatles' concert at the Coliseum in November 1963. Chipper then discovered a white tin toy Jeep, two blue-uniformed men on the front seat, one driving, the other holding a red phone receiver in his hand, both wearing blue policeman's hats. There was a windshield, marked POLICE DEPT, that could fold down and rest on the hood. Jason was delighted, pushing the Jeep around on the floor, making growling noises.

"Keep it, son," Chipper said, feeling expansive, then sneezed again. "It's all yours."

"What do you say, Jason?" Penny prodded.

"Thank you."

"You're welcome, kiddo."

I surveyed the room, appreciated the Princeton banner on the wall, a copy of *A Separate Peace* on the shelf of the bedside table, unmoved since the last time I'd seen it, twenty years earlier. . . .

"Why don't you move back in, Chipper?" I suggested, only half joking. We could all be kids forever.

"*Au contraire,* Terryster, we're gonna have to sell the old girl."

"Sell the house?" I was horrified.

"Afraid so. Now that Mummy's gone, there's no reason to keep it anymore. It's too damn expensive to maintain."

"What about your father?" Penny asked.

"He has a rendezvous with a retirement home in Palm Beach."

I was too heartbroken to respond. The house on Dumbarton, gone forever? I couldn't imagine such a thing. I wondered what they could get for it, decided it was probably worth several million dollars, Chipper's share of which would go straight to crack cocaine. He was starting to come down from whatever high he'd been on all morning, I noticed. His eyes, red-rimmed and exhausted, had grown nervous, restless. He glanced once around the room. "Well, gotta go. See you in paradise, Terryster. Penny, you're looking great. Muff diving clearly agrees with you. Keep up the good work. *Ciao,* Jason."

He vanished like a genie.

Why didn't I say anything to him, why didn't I pull him aside and let him know that I thought he was killing himself, and that since I loved him I found this very distressing, and that I didn't want to be around him as long as he continued to play Russian roulette with his life? Why didn't I say that? I should have said that.

My father left, returned to Boston the very next day; having done his duty, he fled the sickroom stench of Mr. Gourlie's remaining days, the arduous corruption of the house itself, the many floors of memory and God knows what sadness when he climbed or descended the stairs past etchings of pastoral ruined Greece; he fled the proximity to Langley and his Other Life, our old place up on P Street, Clyde's and the ephemeral echoes of long-departed K.G.B. ribaldry. Who can blame him? Not me.

Before he went, he tried one last time to dissuade me from my seditious endeavor. Writing this book.

"The King is dead, the country doesn't even exist anymore, no one cares what happened in Kurash in 1958, you said so yourself."

"I'm a historian."

He gazed at me steadily. "You're writing my biography."

This infuriated me. "I'm exploring my autobiography. I was there too, remember? No, you probably don't. Well, let me tell you, I believe I have a few retrospective rights in this case, at least as many as you do."

"I signed an oath."

"I didn't. I didn't even sign a social contract. Far as I'm concerned, I can do anything I want."

He gave up, went downstairs and said goodbye to Mr. Gourlie, ensconced in front of *Oprah,* then took a taxi to Ronald Reagan, née National, Airport, and flew back to Boston.

The next morning Bob Easton came down to the Research

Library with a smug look on his face, and after much rocking back on his heels and jiggling of loose change, he handed me a piece of paper on which he had written, by hand, two names:

Emily Basquit Rothman
Emily Moody Crane

I looked up expectantly.

"These two ladies worked for our Rome station in 1958. I will not go into the exact details of what they did for us. Emily Basquit Rothman was, at the time, fifty years old. She has since deceased."

My heart sank. "And the other one?"

"Emily Moody Crane. She's still alive. She was, at the time, twenty-six years old."

"Where does she live?" I asked.

Bob Easton could keep the secret no longer. He announced with a grin: "Rome."

Five

1

I had asked the travel agent I consulted in Georgetown to book me a room at the Pensione Ruben, on via della Croce, which is where I had lived with my mother for six weeks in the winter of 1957, before we joined my father in Kurash, but I was informed it no longer exists, so I settled for a hotel on via Brunetti, near the Piazza del Popola. Its ancient wood-paneled Otis elevator, an elaborate Art Deco birdcage, creaked and clanked up to the third floor, strained, I imagined, by the weight of my duffel bag. Down a long dim hallway I walked to my small room. The mattress was sway-backed, and there was a view, if you craned out far enough, of via Brunetti, the red-striped awning of a nearby restaurant. I ate dinner there that night, my ears still thrumming faintly, disconcertingly, from the flight. *Spaghetti Carbonara,* two glasses of Chianti, *insalata verde, espresso.* I read the *International Herald Tribune,* then went out for a stroll along via del Corso. When I was a boy, trolley cars somehow insinuated themselves into the already crowded scene. They were gone now. I passed the Grand Hotel, where, in my mind, General Anwar opens his shutters for eternity, and soon reached via della Croce. Two blocks in, toward the Spanish Steps, I stopped in front of what used to be Pensione Ruben. I stared up at the smog-blackened stone walls, amazed that I had once stared down through that window, third from the corner, at this very spot where I now stood, forty years older and by no means wiser.

Despite my huge and inclusive chronological chart, my mind was cluttered with nothing but fragments. I could not attain

Overview. The Big Picture eluded me, despite my arsenal of information, my twenty-six standard schoolboy spiral notebooks filled with copious notes taken while I perused the yellowing declassified files granted me by the C.I.A. in the Research Library at Langley. Despite the dozens of books I have read. The interviews I have conducted.

The Pensione Ruben up there with its vanished white-clothed tables in the dining room, where Oxbridge intellectuals, academics, and high-minded journalists and their spouses read Joseph Campbell and *The White Goddess* while they ate clear delicious hot minestrone soup, breadsticks snapped with satisfying vigor, furled balls of fresh butter in silver dishes. . . .

High-pitched, giddy, singsong English voices passing my closed door every morning declaiming the Coliseum, the Forum, Roman Law, and various Caesars, my first inkling that behind or beyond the apparent and random chaos there might lie some order. . . .

Chronology.

Hamra, Kurash. 1958.

Late summer, a false autumn.

A period of subtle confusion, a confusion of the spirit, that caught everyone, especially the King, by surprise. Heat as thick and palpable as a heavy woolen cloak lay draped upon us all from early morning to dusk, when with darkness descended cooling relief. Carpets were spread out on the flat roofs of houses, and the men gathered there to smoke cigarettes and sip tea and discuss the day's events. Lively traffic clamored below in the streets, trolley cars rattled their way past the open sidewalk cafes on Feisel Square and Oristibach's on Al Kifah Avenue, which presently displayed seersucker summer clothes in its front windows, all worn by stoutly Caucasian mannequins frozen in unreal delight. From the gardens behind their high walls along Sarouja Street there floated a faint damp odor of recently watered dirt. The cinema lights burned bright purple and pink in the dark blue night, date palms outlined vividly against the lambent glow cast skyward by the city lamps. Every once in a while there was even a breeze, so light and quick it would often have passed before you realized it was there at all, leaving behind a memory of itself so tantalizing and vague you brought your hand to your cheek in mild, happy surprise, as if you'd been touched by a baby. I lay, those nights, near the open window, on the floor, listening to *Robin Hood* in the garden next door, the purposeful TV voices. My father was often out those nights, my mother alone downstairs, smoking cigarettes and reading novels or studying Islamic something. Eid and Ahmed had caught the bus home to their small rooms and large families, Eid in the Sukahr District, Ahmed in the warren's nest of shacks behind the Hotel Antioch. Our sentry outside stood slouched in his guardhouse, the red glow of his cigarette the only evidence that he existed. Kumait, under a form of house arrest, spent the nights working on a new manuscript, tentatively entitled *Guilt and Destiny.* Days he spent sleeping as best he could behind closed shutters, staggering through dreams too complex and horrifying to remember. He awoke each evening and got back to work more exhausted than he had been the night before, his fatigue growing exponentially, the dark circles under his eyes multiplying, deepening. If he leaned far enough out his window he could see the soldiers posted on the street below to ensure his benign captivity. He was allowed daily exercise, a walk around the block, and two meals a day at the Oasis Café across Nahas Street. His guards usually ate with him, in discreet proximity, at a separate table.

He had not seen the King again since their meeting the night the revolution had failed, the night my father drove him from Milton Gourlie's office up to Hamzah Palace. Incarcerated in his room, with nothing to do but read and write and think, a true scholar at last, he found himself pondering less and less the recent past, the series of now strangely vague events that had led him to betray his King. Instead, he began to question the entire enterprise of judging things Arab from a postcolonial point of view. Kumait, an intellectual Marxist of the thirties generation, asked himself if Arabs had been as brutally exploited by the West as they claimed, and the answer he came up with was no. Not enough to justify this whining, petulant, illogical bombast that spewed forth from the mouths of otherwise intelligent and cultivated people, like the various writers and artists who could be heard nightly on Radio Cairo. Intellectual honesty, critical distance, a forum's good manners, thorough historical grounding—these were still, in his opinion, what the Arabs needed most desperately, and they were all, and here the irony made him wince as he lit yet another late-night cigarette, these were all *Western* notions. As was Marxism itself, as Western as the internal combustion engine. You couldn't get more Western than a German-Jewish upper-middle-class industrial-urban intellectual-Idealist, rooted in the literature and morality of the Greeks, Romans, Hebrews, and Christians—especially the Christians. Marxism, an act of Jewish pique and pouting willful atheism, reeked of Christian piety: look to the poor to discover Good, or God. Marxism was, after all, an ideology so intense it had become a religion, and it celebrated the underaccomplished. True Believers were as monkish as Trappists, vengeful as Jesuits. . . .

All night long this went on, night after night, Kumait hunched above his desk, his reflection in the window mocking him, a sphere of lamplight mediated by drifting somnambulant cigarette smoke. Kumait struggling through an increasingly difficult deconstruction of all he had ever cherished.

O love, you could not know or do know the way I feel . . .

History is not the game, it's a brutal athlete, bigger than everyone else, faster and stronger than everyone else, dominant, terrifying. History does not play by the rules.

What, then, is the game? What do we call that within which even history is a participant?

He looked up from his notebook for a moment, considered

the deadly quiet of his smoke-filled room, the shelves of useless books, the photographs and reproductions of Kurashian antiquities tacked to the walls, once beautiful to him but now mere remnants of ancient violence.

Maybe I'm going crazy.

One night, that September, there was a knock on his door. Startled, Kumait rose and opened it. Outside stood my mother. She carried a neatly wrapped pastry box from Calude's in one hand, a thermos bottle in the other.

"Hi."

She entered brusquely, walking right past him, surveying the room in a glance—the unmade bed, the nicotine-befogged air, the pages of his new and possibly incoherent manuscript strewn about the floor. He saw it all with her and was momentarily appalled.

"Have you been eating?" she asked.

"Yes," he replied.

She cleared a space on the desk, opened the pastry box, pulled out a napoleon in wax paper, handed it to him. "Dessert, then."

He sat on the end of his bed and devoured the napoleon while she poured coffee from the thermos bottle into a cup and handed him that, too. He sipped, ate, until he was done, then lit a cigarette and enjoyed, however briefly, the feeling of being alive. She sat perched on his desk chair watching him with a worried smile on her face, hands folded in her lap, good Vassar girl on a rescue mission. Except, Kumait reflected, he could not be saved. He was one lost soul she could never recapture.

"How's Mack?" he asked.

"Fine. I don't know. Working too hard, I guess. I don't see him much."

He studied her carefully. She was lonely, he realized. She deflected his scrutiny by asking, "How are you, Kumait?"

"Surviving." This was followed by a macabre chuckle.

"Do they ever let you out of here?"

He explained his routine. "I'm lucky, Jean. In Syria, or Iraq, or Egypt, I'd be dead by now. So would Anwar. The King forgives too easily, I fear."

"Mack explained it to me. You meant no real harm, Kumait. The King knows that."

"People like me are dangerous. We blunder into corruption. We stumble innocently into deceit."

She glanced at the manuscript pages. "What are you working on?"

"I have no idea." He said this ruefully, with a slight shrug. "Gibberish, I'm afraid."

"About what?"

"Possible ways in which I have spent my life asking the wrong questions." Another death rattle of a chortle. "A list, I'm writing a list of all the self-accusations I can imagine, and believe me, it's a very long list indeed."

He hated the sound of self-pity in his voice and tried to change its timbre to offhanded joviality. "Intellectual doodlings, that's all, Jean. I'm fine. I'm kind of enjoying my internal exile. How are you? How's your son, Terry?"

That would be me.

"I think he's suffering from some kind of shock."

That would be correct, Mother. "Shock" would be a good choice of words. Qualified, perhaps, by "nausea," and "terror." God, I was beginning to think, is a monster.

Did I mention that from the rooftop of the Sweetsers' house, during the first few hours of Anwar's uprising, I saw soldiers, seemingly for sport, machine-gun several camels in a nearby limestone-littered field? And that these camels, when the bullets struck, buckled at their double-jointed knees, their spindly legs folding underneath them as they collapsed, confused, almost delicate, to the sand?

"Terry shouldn't be here, Jean," Kumait said. "You shouldn't be here, either. You both should be back home in Washington."

"No, this is good, I'm glad we're here. It's just difficult sometimes, that's all."

"Good in what way?" Kumait asked curiously.

My mother wasn't sure. "Well, the thing about Washington is, it's hard to remember, when you're there, that the rest of the world really exists, and how different it is. It's impossible to understand that everything is so . . . simultaneous."

He seemed pleased with her reply, for he clapped his hands and laughed and leaned intently forward. "Like Time?"

"Yes," she said, catching his point. "Like Time. Like el-Khirmeil, and the Crusaders' castle in Abirta."

"Good, good. Maybe this is what the Sufis mean by the 'mystical temperament'—the impulse to see that everything is happening simultaneously."

They sat for a while longer in comfortable silence, then she stood and gathered whatever dirty clothes she could find scattered about the apartment. "I'll have these cleaned for you."

At the door, she looked back at him. "I'll come and visit again, is that all right?"

"If it's acceptable to Mack, I would like it very much, yes."

She nodded and left, the bundle of laundry in her arms.

We should remember, too, General Anwar, Kumait's good friend, his old friend, his college pal and coconspirator, at that moment pushing open the heavy green shutters of his room in the Grand Hotel, in Rome, and looking down into the crowded and noisy via del Corso, his wife unpacking behind him, his children running excitedly in and out of the room.

And we should remember the King, alone in his tent, alone in his confusion. Not only did he not hate Kumait and Anwar, not only did he not wish them ill, he actively missed them, he could not imagine continuing without them. Though it made no sense, he wanted them back.

I saw in the files at Langley speculation on Roy Sweetser's part that Renee had climbed back on the wagon again, for she had become unspeakably nasty, short-tempered, even cruel, torturing in particular Johnny Allen, making him retransmit cables repeatedly, sending him back to the code book, calling him up in the middle of the night and making him drive to the office to make double goddamn sure he had locked the vault. . . .

Without its ever being discussed, one by one people stopped coming to the Hamra Go-Cart Club, including first the King, and then even my father. Soon the track was obliterated by vagrant tides of sand, then the gaudy pavilions, the garages, the go-carts themselves were nagged and choked and obscured. It was as if some pestilence had settled upon everyone's former good fortunes, a biblical plague equal to the fury of the locusts or a blue sky raining blood.

As indeed it had.

2

Back in my room on via Brunetti, I took a Valium and slept. That's not right. I lay still for eight hours with my eyes closed and my consciousness chemically interrupted. When I awoke, I felt, like Kumait forty years earlier, in his room on Nahas Street, in Kurash, more tired, not less. I dragged myself into the shower, shaved, had coffee in the little garden restaurant downstairs, then set out to find Emily Moody Crane.

My mother and Kumait were right, I think now, to seize simultaneity as a more accurate model by which to judge the world, accepting, as they did, the apparent and random chaos.

My mother, perpetually alone in a marriage made of desire and loneliness, wandering the streets of Rome with her mute ten-year-old son, me, both of us gaping at the gorgeous Italian mob out for its tribal evening stroll, a collective flirtation that boggled and intoxicated the mind of stern, self-denying Anglo-Saxons like us. We ate dinner at outdoor restaurants, where men would just walk up to my mother with big smiles, dapper in their gray flannel and white cotton and blue wool and burnished leather, gold watches gleaming on their fine-boned wrists. She kept them at a distance, the smiling men, yet could not resist thanking them with a grateful laugh, leaning back in her chair, elbow cocked, cigarette in hand, dark-haired New Rochelle girl tempted by the old, old stories. We bought ice creams, *gelati,* from street vendors, rode a carriage once through the dark Borghese Gardens. We waited.

To see my father.

Three days after arriving in Rome, General Anwar and his family flew to Cairo at President Nasser's personal invitation, where they took up what they assumed would be temporary residence, which turned out to be correct in ways they could never have imagined.

Sometimes I think history should be called cultural archaeology, and that I should write a book called *History of a Billboard*, or, here in Rome, *History of a Wall*, gently peeling back layer upon layer of advertisements, each the story of a time, the girl who stopped to light a cigarette in the rain, the young man who watched her, his heart exploding. . . .

The flower vendors were opening up along via del Corso, the streets had been freshly watered and were still damp, shiny. The smells of coffee seemed to convene from every open window. Could I enjoy the intoxicating light, the lighthearted step my feet so desperately wanted to assume? Oh, no. I was now worrying for the first time about my father's apparent slip, that "Emily" rolling so easily from his intoxicated inner self, at Clyde's, in Georgetown, the night before Mrs. Gourlie's funeral. Emily. A new sighting on the chronological curve, taking us . . . to Rome. Trouble is, trouble is, except for the slip of the tongue there was no indication whatsoever that my father was intoxicated, loose-lipped, in any way. He is, remember, like all of these guys, a boozer. He held his liquor well that night, in Clyde's. I had made note of that fact. So was he leading me, I wondered, freaked by the implications. If so, why? Can I trust him? His motives are unknown to me. He could easily be feeding me misinformation, throwing me off the trail, sending me on a wild goose chase. The metaphors multiplied, but not my understanding.

Kumait, meanwhile, back in late September of 1958, decided that he had to see the King again. He was suddenly desperate. He wanted to explain his latest thoughts on the whole issue of Arab identity, and began a series of frantic petitions to do so. He called, left messages. He heard nothing from the King. He called my father, who came to see him in his room. My father, skeptically, promised to do what he could. He kept his skepticism to himself, and in fact did raise the subject of Kumait the next time he met with the King, in the King's tent, about three weeks later. He handed him the briefcase full of cash, they sat together and drank tea, my father's legs as usual painfully falling asleep. Fuck appearances. He stretched his sore legs out straight, massaged them back to life, suffered the King's bemused chuckles.

"You'll never make a good Bedouin, Mack," he commented.

"I didn't know that was an option," my father retorted.

The King looked thoughtful. "You're right, I suppose it isn't an option, any more than it's an option for me to become a stock broker on Wall Street and live in . . ."

His knowledge of American geography failed him.

"New Jersey," my father said, coming to the rescue.

"New Jersey. How strange."

A hot evening breeze entered the tent hesitantly, invisible as Tinkerbell, flitted about from pillow to pillow, sniffing for sensory information, and then darted back out. It left behind a temptation to despair, dull heat, implacable and deadly.

"How's your mother, Your Majesty?" my father roused himself to ask.

"She's well, thank you, Mack. Do you realize she hasn't left her rooms in Hamzah Palace for over twenty years? I think being out here in a tent is fun for her. She sleeps better, she says. She thinks the stars talk to her in her sleep." The King assumed a more somber expression. "To tell you the truth, I'm worried she's becoming senile. Demented. She says if I would only listen to the stars, they would tell me exactly what to do, what decisions to make, like tarot cards."

"It's just a charming expression."

"No, she means it. Literally."

After a pause, my father asked him, "Would you like to have

an American doctor take a look at her? I could fly a specialist in. Or, if you'd prefer, we could get her to someplace really good in the States, like Johns Hopkins, or the Mayo Clinic. . . ."

The King nodded enthusiastically. "Could you arrange that?"

"Sure."

"Thank you."

"You're welcome."

Ritualistically, they each shook out a cigarette, the King lighting them both with his gold emblematic Ronson lighter. They puffed away in silence for a few minutes.

"Tell me about New Jersey, Mack."

"New Jersey? I don't know it very well. There's a lot of industry there, in places like Elizabeth it permanently stinks of sulfur, like rotten eggs. But there's also a lovely seashore with very nice vacation homes built at the turn of the century. I used to go there and stay with an uncle when I was young. Big houses, lots of porches, like Rhode Island. And then of course there's the famous Atlantic City. Have you heard of Atlantic City?"

The King shook his head. He was enjoying himself.

"Oh, well, you'd enjoy Atlantic City. It's a summer resort town. Right on the beach. Lots of crashing Atlantic waves. Cotton candy. Saltwater taffy. Ferris wheels and roller-coasters. A boardwalk where people stroll at night. Jazz bands play in large dance halls and outdoor pavilions. Fancy hotels."

"Are there any gangsters?"

"Oh, yeah. Lots of gangsters. They pretty much run the place. The Italians predominate, though the Jews and Irish get a good lick in every once in a while."

The King sat still, eyes half-closed, imagining all this, imagining most of all, perhaps, what it would be like to stroll along such a boardwalk with a girl like Esmerelda on his arm, sea breeze damp and cool on his face, surrounded by the loud and public night, unknown, anonymous, content. Free. He shook his head. He would never know.

My father finally broached the subject of Kumait. "Your Majesty, Kumait would very much like to see you."

"No."

"He feels terrible for his part in all this, you know that."

"No."

An awkward silence ensued.

"I miss our go-cart racings," the King finally said.

"So do I, Your Majesty."

"Everyone's too busy now. I agree with my critics, you Westerners are a very bad influence, but not in the ways they think. You work too hard. You are obsessed with work. There is no balance in your life. In that way, your influence is indeed dangerous."

"At the risk of sounding jingoistic, Your Majesty, our work ethic has served us pretty well, don't you think?"

"Yes," the King sighed. "I suppose it has. But be careful. It could also be your undoing."

As if, my father mused, he could do anything about it. Our work ethic is so deeply ingrained we're barely aware of its presence. My mother, frequently of late, insisted that work for him was an escape, and I'm inclined to agree. "Escape from what?" he demanded, indignant. "Your life," she said, not backing down. They were sitting on the edge of the tub again, water hissing from the shower, steam billowing into the small bathroom, sweat pouring down their faces. I was upstairs wondering why they spent so much time in the shower together, strangled by steam. My father was worried about . . . something. I could feel his worry drifting through the house, into every room, like poisonous, inquisitive fog, yellow and acrid, stinging my eyes, making me choke, making me extremely uneasy, much as the sight of insectile tanks probing the streets had made me uneasy, threatened a resurgence of my nausea. I returned to the cool tile floor, I clung to the voices of *Robin Hood* in the garden next door, I prayed *Dear God, I will be good I will be good I will be good. . . .*

"Escape from personality, escape from this house, escape from your family, escape from me," my mother was ranting in the bathroom downstairs.

"Jean, you're exaggerating, as usual," he responded, standing and departing with soggy dignity.

My mother sat on the edge of the slippery tub and screamed her frustration. I heard it, upstairs, and it startled me, scared me. Was she hurt? In pain? What was he doing to her?

He stuck his head back in the bathroom door and gave her a quizzical, condescending look. "Jesus Christ, Jean."

That's it. Then he was gone.

Back to the great black goatskin tent in the desert, back to the King.

"Mack, this girl I've been seeing, the English girl."

"Esmerelda?"

"Yes."

"What about her, Your Majesty?"

"I suppose you've checked her out?"

"Yes, I have."

"And she's okay?"

"Right as rain."

"Nothing I should know?"

"I'll bring her file over tomorrow."

"No, no, that seems too . . . that seems wrong. I don't want to spy on her. I just want to be sure she's not, you know . . ."

"Working for the Soviets, or Nasser, or the Muslim Brotherhood."

"Yes."

"She's not. She's a good, middle-class English girl with an interest in the arts."

"I know."

"She went to Slade for a while; that's a very good art school in London."

"She's told me all this, Mack."

"She's not political."

The King clapped his hands, and servants instantly appeared. He asked for more tea, then settled against the saddle that was serving as a back rest and fixed my father with one of his smiling, mischievous looks. "I like her."

"Esmerelda?"

"Yes."

"A lot?"

"Yes. Very much." The King explored a tooth with his tongue, absently. "I'm going to ask her to marry me."

My father was instantly, abjectly horrified. "Oh, no, Your Majesty, you can't."

"Why not?"

"Well, she's English."

"So?"

"You've already got enough problems in the Arab world vis-à-vis the West without going and *marrying* one of us." My father was agitated, to say the least. He leaned forward earnestly, beseeched the King. "Your own people will turn on you. The Palestinians will burn you in effigy. Nasser will have a field day. The only thing you could do that would be worse would be to marry a Jewish girl."

"Actually, Esmerelda's part Jewish, on her mother's side, or so she told me."

"Oh, God," my father groaned.

He stayed in the King's tent for the remainder of that night, trying to dissuade the King from marrying Esmerelda. The files in Langley are filled with his anguished cables sent to Washington over the next week or so. He was convinced that this single act of love, or passion, or obsession, or boredom, or loneliness, or whatever it was, would bring the King down. Not the Israelis, not Nasser, not the Arab Brotherhood, not the Communists, not Damascus or Baghdad, but a scrawny English girl with a quick smile and a lusty laugh. In one of the cables he actually raises the possibility of spiriting her out of the country, plopping her down in Rome with a lifelong annuity. The King, for his part, did not falter. Having made up his own mind, he now invited Esmerelda to spend the night with him in his tent. After dinner, he knelt before her and offered her a five-carat diamond Tiffany ring, purchased by his beloved grandfather Ali in 1927 while on a state visit to the United States and presented, upon his return, to his sixth and most recent wife, Narouza. Esmerelda's face, upon seeing the ring, the King supplicate before her in his underpants, went through many changes. At first, of course, she did not take it seriously, thinking the whole thing a joke. Then, realizing he was serious, she was in turn stunned, disbelieving, appalled, giddy, and, finally, deeply moved, weeping quietly as she let him slide the ring onto her finger, a perfect fit, and therefore, in the King's mind, an augury: this was meant to be. The enervation and lassitude that had so weighed him down over the past few weeks suddenly evaporated. He took her in his arms and held her as she cried, grinning from ear to ear. "I hope you don't mind, Your Majesty," she said, drying her tears, "if I still call you Your Majesty. O, you darling, darling Majesty." She collapsed in happy tears again, caressing his face, pulling him to her, yanking away his underpants and guiding him into her, spreading her legs so wide the muscles hurt, her legs almost straight back, offering herself completely to this gentle dark-skinned man now moaning with pleasure above her. She grabbed his balls with one hand and eased a finger of her other hand gently up his ass, heard him hiss and then felt him contract, buckle, and crash hard against her, pouring into her, thankful incomprehensible Arabic words breathed in her ear from his hot mouth as he slipped deep into darkness and rest, asleep immediately in her arms, her king, her husband. She couldn't wait to tell her mother in Sussex.

He told *his* mother the next night. She was, at first, not pleased. She sat in her own tent, puffing on his father's pipe, and stared at him.

"You told me to get married," he said, defending himself.

"Not to an English girl. Are you insane?" She angrily jabbed her temple with the stem of her pipe. "Who is this slut, anyway? What kind of family does she come from? No, no, no, this won't do, this won't do at all. Impossible. I won't discuss it. Good night."

He didn't move.

"Good night," she said again.

"I'm going to marry her," the King insisted.

"Why, why, why?" she wailed.

"She makes me feel good."

That was his way, I suspect, of saying Esmerelda made him happy, his way, probably, of saying he loved her, because from everything I've read he did indeed love her very much, which only makes what happened to them both later that much worse, that much more of a sick, sick crime. He even wrote a poem for her, in the manner of the ancient *qasida,* or ode, that he had been study-ing with Kumait long before the revolution, or rebellion, or power play, or assassination attempt, or whatever it was he had so recently lived through, had unalterably changed his life. I am aware of no extant copy.

3

Emily lived in Trastevere, across the Tiber from via del Corso, in what was once a working-class section of Rome. These days it's crammed with upscale restaurants and *espresso* bars and boutiques. On my way to Emily's apartment, I even passed, near the foot of Ponte Sisto, a health club. Her street, via Corsini, is a short, cobblestone cul-de-sac off via della Lungara that ends at the gates, closed the day I was there, to Gianicolo, a large, leafy park and botanical garden filled with tall cypresses. Emily's building, directly across from the gates, dates, I would guess, from the end of the last century, a handsome and solid bourgeois edifice five stories tall, faded terra-cotta in color, pots of bright geraniums blossoming on the balconies. Dozens of cats, lazily curled up among the flowers, watched me noncommittally as I pushed open the huge and heavy front door and entered. Emily's name was listed on a brass plaque inside. Fourth floor. There was no elevator. I climbed the marble stairs, rang the doorbell. Almost immediately the door was opened, revealing a handsome woman in her late thirties or early forties with long, dark brown hair parted in the middle. She wore a light gray sweatshirt, blue jeans, and sandals. In her left hand she held a cigarette. "Can I help you?"

She spoke English with a slight Italian accent. My nationality betrays itself, I guess.

"My name is Terry Hooper, and I was looking for Emily Moody Crane. Is she here?"

"Emily is my mother," the woman replied. "Are you a friend of hers?"

"No, not exactly. I'm an historian, from California, and I was hoping to interview your mother for a book I'm writing."

My interlocutor found this, for some reason, deeply suspicious. "A book? What kind of a book?"

"A history of American foreign policy in the Middle East during the cold war." I ventured.

"Oh." As if that explained everything. "I see."

Her cigarette had now burned down to a precipitous ash. Glancing around for an ashtray, she waved me in, disappeared down a long hallway.

I followed her past a wall of books into a living room looking over the botanical garden across the street. Here more books lined the walls. There was a desk under one window, an old Olivetti portable resting on top, with a sheaf of paper rolled into it, half-covered with writing.

"My name is Melissa," she offered.

"Nice to meet you, Melissa."

She found an overstuffed ashtray, jammed her cigarette in among the butts, brushed back a loose strand of hair, where I now saw faint evidence of gray, which for some reason I thought very sexy. She motioned me to a couch, Danish modern, a relic of the fifties, then took the desk chair for herself. She studied me.

"Is your mother here?" I asked.

"No." Melissa gently shook her head.

"When are you expecting her back?"

A small shrug. "I'm not sure. It could be a few weeks, maybe a month."

"I've come all the way from America to see her."

No response.

"Could you tell me where she is?"

"She's on holiday."

This was not going well. I changed the subject, nodding to the Olivetti. "You're a writer?"

"A journalist. Freelance."

"You don't use a computer?"

"Evidently not."

I felt like an idiot. Her appraising brown eyes watched me carefully, like the cat I now noticed sitting motionless on the windowsill.

"What kind of questions do you want to ask my mother?"

"Well, I'm not sure, to be honest. Her name has come up several times in my research, but I can't quite figure out how she connects to my subject. As much as anything else, I'm intrigued. You wouldn't happen to know what she was doing in 1958, would you?"

Not a flicker. "I wasn't born yet in 1958."

"But surely she's said something over the years that would give you an idea?" I persisted.

"She lived here, I believe, in Rome."

"My information is that she worked for the American embassy."

"Perhaps. She was a translator."

"Did she travel much, do you know?"

"I have no idea," Melissa said. "I've never asked."

I took a deep breath. "Was she ever in Kurash, around that time?"

"Kurash?"

"A small country, in the Middle East, near Jordan. It doesn't exist anymore. Did your mother ever mention being there."

"In 1958?"

"Yes."

Melissa's eyes lowered from mine, found a corner of a rug snagged, straightened it with her toe. "I don't think so, no."

The sun coming though the window behind Melissa filled the room with a beautiful light, framing her beautiful face. I stood and appraised a collection of photographs on one of the bookshelves, a laughing dark-haired woman standing next to a succession of Italian authors, Calvino, Moravia, Giorgio Bassani. . . .

I pointed. "Is that your mother?"

"Yes."

In some of the photographs Emily was a young woman, maybe early thirties, lithe and tanned in a summer dress, hand resting gently on a writer's arm, a drink in her hand, or a cigarette. In others she was middle-aged, the same age as Melissa, and just as beautiful, though more fair-skinned, her shoulders freckled, her eyes a paler shade than her daughter's, perhaps a dark hazel, or slate-gray. In one photograph she looked close to her present age, sixty-seven, still attractive, hair white and cut short.

"Are these writers she has translated?" I asked Melissa.

"Yes."

"Into English?"

"Yes."

Which meant that I'd read several of Emily's translations over the years. "She's very beautiful."

"Yes, she is."

Skimming the books on the bookshelves, I suddenly came to a great grinding halt at *Travels in Arabia Deserta*. I reached out, fingers trembling, and brought the volume down from the shelf. It was an old Penguin paperback, identical to my father's. I opened the frail, brittle pages. There was no name written on the title page, but inside, as I flipped through the book, I saw faint pencil marks in the margins and certain words here and there underlined.

I turned to Melissa with the book in my hand. "Is this your mother's?"

She looked. "Yes, I should think so. All these books are hers."

"I know this is a weird question, but may I keep it?"

"It's not mine to give to you." She stood, still holding the cat, and with her free hand retrieved *Travels in Arabia Deserta*. "You should go."

"You won't tell me where she is?"

"No."

She escorted me silently to the front door.

"Melissa, please, I just want to talk to her."

Melissa opened the front door, hesitated.

"Please," I begged.

Still, she hesitated.

"Melissa, there's a mystery in my life I'm trying to solve, and only your mother can help me solve it."

"What mystery?" she asked.

"Who is my father?" I said.

She recoiled, blushed, as if I'd caught her out in a terrible secret. At the same time, for the first time, I saw in her eyes a genuine curiosity about me. I pressed on.

"My father lived a secret life, back in the fifties, and I'm pretty sure your mother was part of it, or at least knows something about it."

"They were lovers?"

"I don't know. Maybe."

"Portofino," she said, very quietly. "She's in Portofino."

She gently pushed me out onto the stairwell landing.

"Where in Portofino?" I asked.

"She has an apartment there."

Then she handed me *Travels in Arabia Deserta,* threw me a surprisingly shy smile, and closed the door. I hurried to my hotel, grabbed my stuff, sped to the train station, where I bought a postcard, an aerial view of the Colosseum, on which I scribbled, "Off to see Emily. Love, Terry." This I sent to my father, just to keep him on his toes. Then I boarded the train to Genoa, the nearest stop to Portofino. I had with me, of course, the cumbersome duffel bag, to which I had added Emily's copy of *Travels in Arabia Deserta.* I was taking no chances with my traveling archives. After a struggle, I got the duffel bag onto the overhead rack, then sat near a window and gazed out at the busy station, all the good-looking Italians intent on arriving and departing, a swirling, graceful chaos beneath the high, high web of steel, everyone waving, hugging, weeping, plucking, shaking, sucking cigarettes,

slurping *espresso.* An elderly couple joined me in the compartment, smiled, nodded, sat, busied themselves with their newspapers. A young student with many rings pierced through many
facial punctures stuck his head into the compartment, surveyed
the scene, found it wanting, and left, the sliding door clattering
closed behind him. Soon the train was pulling away from the station and chugging through the slums of Rome, past bare-legged
boys playing soccer on steaming rubbish heaps. I stood, opened
my duffel bag and brought down some relevant materials,
watched curiously but circumspectly by the elderly couple.

Emily's Penguin edition of *Travels in Arabia Deserta,* the same
as my father's. Was that a coincidence? How could that possibly
be a coincidence? What were the odds? On the other hand,
Travels in Arabia Deserta is one of the classics, along with
T. E. Lawrence's *Seven Pillars of Wisdom* and Wilfred Thesiger's
Arabian Sands, that most people at least glance at when posted to
the Middle East. I looked more closely at the penciled notations
inside, underlined words and little *x*'s in the margin, but also,
here and there, a handwritten word or phrase: "marble," "confusion," ". . . shade of the date trees . . ."

I set the paperback aside and consulted one of my spiral notebooks. It was crammed with my final jottings taken while viewing
the declassified files at Langley, in particular my father's cables
from the weeks of October and November, 1958, where he
described, in some detail, the frequent all-night sessions in the
tent of black goatskins, all his futile attempts to talk the King out
of marrying Esmerelda. Despite the wry, almost comic tone my
father favored in his cables— ". . . mentioning to the King once
again that this proposed marriage was indeed a slippery slope
down which he could easily spend the rest of his no doubt short-
ened life sliding, sliding . . ." —you can hear his fear, the worry
that I had sensed filling up our house like a greasy fog. He
becomes more and more frantic as the date set for the wedding,
November 23, approaches. "Perhaps if the King were to be invited
to the United States as a guest of the President and distracted by

Yankee pomp and circumstance in all its devilish cunning he might forget or grow bored with his matrimonial fantasies. . . ." And then, two days later: "It occurs to me that the King might have traded in his depression for a death wish. Could you have the resident witch doctors noodle that thought around?"

For a description of the wedding itself, the wedding my father, despite his best efforts, could not prevent, I refer you to chapter twelve of Thomas Polmar's *Heartbreak Arabia.* Polmar was an English journalist, at the time writing about the Middle East for *The Spectator.* His travels deposited him in Hamra the week of the King's wedding. He checked into the Hotel Antioch, finagled himself an invitation, probably through his embassy's press officer, and showed up three hours before the event to make sure he got a good view. He did.

The wedding was held in the Museum of Kurashian Antiquities, an odd choice until you remember that this was one of the few government buildings that had not been destroyed by shelling during what was now being called The Events of August 1958, that is to say, General Anwar's recent attempt at insurrection and betrayal. Over three hundred people attended, including members of the diplomatic community, ranking Kurashian and Palestinian families, heads of all the Bedouin tribes, the military leadership, including General al-Rahal and Captain Majali, and various and sundry visitors, among them Thomas Polmar. Dressed in tuxedoes, tribal robes, formal dresses imported from New York and Paris, the guests mingled among the broken Roman columns and Nabataean pots and lamps and wind-worn late-Hellenistic sculptures of Zeus and Nike. Outside, soldiers carrying machine guns warily guarded the premises. Polmar could see them through a window from where he stood. It made him nervous, this show of force, or so he let his newspaper readers believe. He comes across as a brave man for even attending the wedding, which I think is overstating the case, but then again he was a journalist. What surprised him was that once the King appeared, wearing his full military uniform and Desert Legionnaire *kaffiyeh,* the event turned out to be less a wedding than a ceremonial presentation, a proud and public gesture on the part of the King to let everyone know that he wasn't just marrying this English girl, he was *marrying her.* She was his wife, the Queen of Kurash. The King, so touchingly short, stood beaming out at the hushed assembly of dignitaries, then nodded off-stage, and his mother appeared, looking like a stuffed bird, awkward in her ten-year-old sensible British matron's dark purple suit and black low-heeled pumps. She tottered stolidly to his side, lifting her nearsighted gaze to the crowd, clutching a shiny Gucci purse. Next came Mohammed Rassaq, chief cleric of the Khalidi Mosque, an old friend of the family's, who bleakly and dutifully announced that a marriage contract had been signed by the two parties, that Esmerelda had converted to Islam, that both families were content with the vows, and he beseeched Allah to bless this union. At which point Esmerelda, a full foot taller than the King, appeared from the wings, a broad and happy smile lighting up her face, dressed, as Polmar noted, "like a toney schoolgirl on her way to visit the Queen Mother: high heels, elegant black dress, a single string of pearls." With her came a pink-faced and utterly bewildered couple in their mid-forties, very English, Esmerelda's disoriented parents, all the way from Sussex. The King took Esmerelda's hand and spoke. "I feel I have found the woman with whom I wish to spend the rest of my life, the woman I want as my queen and the mother of my son, a future king of Kurash. She is kind and wise and beautiful. She will serve me faithfully, I know. My mother has already taken her to her heart and loves her as a daughter." At this point the King's mother squirmed uneasily but maintained her fixed, deathlike smile. The King went on: "I wanted all of you, my friends and colleagues, to meet Esmerelda today, to welcome her, to make her feel welcome. You honor me by honoring her. There's plenty of food in the Edomite Room behind us. Please enjoy yourselves. And thank you for coming." Oddly, after a moment's dazzled pause, thunderous applause greeted this modest speech, its very modesty that which endeared the King to everyone there, even the Arabs and Palestinians who, on principle, hated Esmerelda and this union. My father, standing with my mother not far from Polmar, realized, he said in a cable sent to Washington the next day, "that the full purpose of this wedding reception, which is what it was, the wedding itself, I now know, having been a simple signing of a contract, privately held the day before—the full purpose of this public get-together was for the King to make clear to all of us that he wanted this marriage, and Esmerelda, treated with respect. He was laying down the law." Tables laden with freshly slaughtered and roasted lamb waited for everyone, as promised, in the Edomite Room. Several hours later, the King and Esmerelda left the Museum of Antiquities and drove in an open Cadillac, gift of the United States, through the streets of Hamra. Crowds lined the sidewalks three deep, some cheering their support and enthusiasm, some simply drawn by the circuslike atmosphere, celebrations, as we all know, having a life of their own. That night, out by the tents near the burnt ruins of Hamzah Palace, volley after volley of gunshots could be heard fired aloft by celebrating Desert Legionnaires. Their king was married. Their king was happy.

Their king was vilified that very night on Radio Cairo as "the sexual slave of Western hegemony, so eager for filthy Anglo-Saxon pleasures that he has begged a whore to be his wife. The moment she accepted, this king lost all claim to his throne and our affections, much as his new wife's empty and withered breasts long ago lost all claim to beauty."

And so forth.

Italy clattered by my window, the train jounced and jiggled reassuringly. The couple across from me, who reminded me of Esmerelda's parents, had fallen asleep, their heads leaning together in open-mouthed support.

Kumait did not attend the wedding celebration. The King, though he still missed him, though he had in fact forgiven him, did not invite him, and so Kumait spent that afternoon sitting in his rooms on Nahas Street, trying to concentrate on *Guilt and Destiny,* which he had retitled *The Oldest Rose,* from an anonymous eleventh-century desert poem.

> *Across the sands of time we find*
> *the oldest rose in the shade . . .*

It grew late. Darkness pressed at the windowpanes. Kumait heard the gunshots in the hills. Startled, he feared another insurrection had started, then realized it was a celebration instead, the exact opposite, Allah be praised. Kumait stood from his desk and walked back and forth, back and forth, his reflection at regular intervals stepping into the opaque glass of the windows and joining him. Would the King ever release him? Would the King ever allow him to teach again, or help him with speeches, in any way advise him? No, the King would not—that was pretty much the simple truth of things, and now, for the first time, Kumait forced himself to face the full brunt of the fact that, in all likelihood, he was looking at the end of his life as he knew it. He might as well have pulled the trigger the day my father and Rashid had come for him here in these same rooms. He wished he had.

Why didn't you?

I'm a coward.

When the train reached Genoa, I disembarked, lugging my duffel bag behind me, and found a magazine and newspaper stand selling tourist postcards. While sipping *espresso* at a nearby stand-up bar, leaning on the zinc counter, I wrote again to my father. "Dear Dad, I'm now in Genoa, home of Christopher Columbus. That's the house where he was born, on the other side, in the photograph. Nice, huh? I'm about to talk with Emily. Looking forward to meeting her. Love, Terry." I dropped the postcard in a mailbox, left the train station, and took a taxi to Portofino.

O love, you could not know or do know the way I feel . . .

Kumait returned to his manuscript.

The King and Esmerelda slept contentedly in each other's arms.

My father asked my mother to dance, that night, late, in the living room below. He was experiencing personally the inertia of history and, in ghoulish response, thought, What the fuck, I might as well dance. He liked to dance, to guide my mother from invisible square to invisible square. Don't forget, he's erotically challenged. This was a big deal for him, like going to an orgy. My mother, I'm sure, responded in kind, pleased to be asked. In his arms, she had to admit, she was as light and graceful as a geisha girl. She chose the song, accepted his grace.

> *Fly me to the moon*
> *and let me play among the stars;*
> *Let me see what spring is like*
> *on Jupiter and Mars . . .*

Let's leave them there, for now, dancing in each other's arms, long ago, in Hamra, in Kurash, when they were young and I was still a boy, lying in bed upstairs, loving them so much I thought my heart would explode.

> *In other words:*
> *hold my hand!*
> *In other words:*
> *darling kiss me!*

4

$\mathbb{1}$ n the late fall and winter of 1958, in Kurash, the Americans made a series of mistakes, policy misjudgments, their first serious miscalculations, really, that led to the undoing of their relationship, my father's relationship, with the King. It must have been hubris, hubris and laziness, maybe, the thoughtless conviction that when things are going well they will, left to their own devices, continue to go well, as if optimism, like history, were run by the laws of inertia. My father knew better, but no one listened to him. Maybe he lacked bureaucratic clout, or maybe cautious skepticism was just too foreign a concept to those gung-ho types in their drip-dry shirts who by God were going to get things done around here. Whatever the reason, my father soon found himself in the awkward position of trying to ignore or get around almost every order or request that came his way from Washington. Copies of some of these cables were lying around the files in Langley, and they are indeed fairly mind-boggling. Would it be possible, Hodd Freeman inquired, to raise in Kurash a secret Army that could then be sent as saboteurs into Egypt? Could not the Kurashians form a clandestine pact with the Israelis, guaranteeing that neither will attack the other in case of a new Middle East war? Could not the Kurashians and the Israelis then act together, infiltrating not only Egypt but Baathist Syria as well, kick up a real shit storm, then get out? Then, in October, Dulles (Allen) cabled, asking if we could not add a few additional listening stations along the northern border. My father, knowing the Kurashians would object, prevaricated. Dulles (Allen) cabled again, insisting that we add a few additional listening stations along the northern border.

My father dutifully, reluctantly, added a few additional listening posts along the northern border.

He did not tell the King what he was doing. He just did it, hoping no one would notice. Of course, someone did notice. Major Rashid noticed, or rather, the agent he had adjoined to the listening station mission noticed, and reported what he noticed to Rashid, who for the moment said nothing to anyone, especially my father, about what he now knew. He simply noted the information, filed it away. It is safe to assume, I think, that Rashid did not want my father to know that he, Rashid, had his own agent in place along the northern border reporting directly to him.

Dulles (John Foster) no doubt viewed Kurash as a client state, and therefore beholden to us, and therefore obliged to look the other way when we simply did what we wanted to do.

Like build a few additional listening stations along the northern border.

And an airstrip for the U2, enabling us to launch flights from somewhere other than Turkey, so that we could fly farther and more completely over the vast stretches of the eastern Soviet Union, *click-click-clicking* away with our amazing Land cameras, developed especially for C.I.A. wunderkind Richard Bissell, capturing crystal-clear images of everything from steaming Siberian sheep turds to nonexistent missile bays.

And a pencil factory with certain American partners who, with our embassy's help, soon squeezed out certain Kurashian partners, so that the much-heralded bilateral business venture became quite unilateral; that is to say, we got the money, not them.

When restoration work on Hamzah Palace was completed, the King was escorted from room to room by the anxious architect and the nervous, hand-wringing builder, both, by the way, decidedly Kurashian. They had, in a relatively short amount of time, worked wonders. If anything, the palace had improved, the rooms less cluttered with the kind of tacky and garish detail pretending to European grandeur that the King's grandfather had favored. The architect and builder had somehow managed to incorporate into their work distinctly Arabic features such as arched doorways and bright mosaic patterns. When the King reached the garden in back, so lovingly returned to its former self that even Yusuf was there, puttering about among the date palms and oleanders with his hose, when the King saw his grandfather's little mosque so perfectly re-created, he had to fight back tears. He embraced the architect, he embraced the builder, and thanked them from the bottom of his heart, in the name of all his family, the Hashemites of old, sons of Muhammad the Prophet. They both left the palace in a daze, blessed. The King later awarded them medals, struck especially for the occasion.

So there he was, standing in the garden, contemplating his good fortune, smoking only the third cigarette of the day, a dull empty ache down in his loins bringing him a smile, reminding him of Esmerelda and her sublime antics in bed that morning, when Laith Saleh, the Kurashian partner in the new pencil factory, who had showed him around so proudly a mere two months earlier, now appeared in a state of hyperkinetic agitation, his long sallow face, a face from the south, the King guessed, scrunched up in despair, sweating, flushed.

"Your Majesty, I've been robbed," he began, pacing. "*We've* been robbed."

Out it all came. The sudden demand ("This morning, Your Majesty!") for repayment of the low-interest loans floated him by his American partners and the American government, the appearance of sullen inquisitors from the American embassy at his factory ("This afternoon, Your Majesty!") when he had not been able to make immediate restitution. "Where in the world am I supposed to get such money, at such short notice? Our signed agreement states quite clearly that I have a full five years to repay these loans, Your Majesty." But the worst moment came when the poor man realized that all those pencils he was so lovingly making were now no longer destined for the stationery stores of Italy and France, as he had thought, but for the PXs of American bases in the Far East.

Which he personally found offensive, for these were artistic pencils, destined for the subtle hands of fine and noble customers, not thick-wristed louts in khaki uniforms whose highest intellectual achievement was the making of lists! He was shaking with rage. The King sent him away with a pat on the back, then called my father.

Within an hour, my father was at the palace, sitting in the King's new study, which still smelled of fresh plaster and paint. They sat together, sipped Turkish coffee. After a few pleasantries, the King brought up the pencil factory, the Kurashian partner's consternation, and so forth. My father had no idea what the King was talking about, and said so. The King repeated in greater detail what Saleh had told him. My father was baffled. Could any of this be true? If so, why? What was going on? He promised the King he'd look into it.

He drove back to the embassy in the Opel and walked straight to Tad Greenway's office. Tad, as the economics officer, was in charge of all redevelopment projects.

"What's up with the pencil factory?" he asked.

"Pencil factory?" Tad shuffled through the miasma of papers on his desk. "There's a problem with the pencil factory?"

"Something about loans being recalled."

"Oh, that." Tad looked miserable, could not meet my father's eyes. "I was ordered this morning to recall the loan, that's what's going on."

"Ordered by whom?"

Tad showed him the cable. "The undersecretary of state for Middle Eastern affairs, that's who. A right arsehole, by the way."

My father read the cable aloud: "It seems wiser to us upon reflection to demand immediate repayment because of certain information recently brought to our attention regarding the fiscal solvency and responsibility of our Kurashian partner, Mr. Laith Saleh."

"What are they talking about?" my father asked.

"I don't know."

"Did you guys or did you not have a five-year agreement with Saleh?"

"We did."

"I'll be back."

My father retreated to his office, sent a cable to a friend on the Middle Eastern desk in the Quonset huts along the Washington Mall, received, within hours, a reply, which he studied carefully, handed Renee to shred. He returned to Tad's office.

"The undersecretary of state for Middle Eastern affairs is a first cousin of the principal American investor in the pencil factory."

"No shit." Tad whistled, impressed.

"The principal American investor would seem to have a cash-flow problem at the moment. The principal American investor, to solve his cash-flow problem, has made a side deal with the Pentagon to supply our military bases in the Philippines with all the pencils they need at considerable discount. The principal American investor and the Pentagon procurer for the Far East were roommates at Princeton."

Tad gazed at my father in wonderment.

"You guys are good," he finally offered.

Back in his office, my father drafted a cable to the undersecretary of state for Middle Eastern affairs, notifying him that Mr. Laith Saleh and his pencil factory were, unfortunately, deeply involved in a top-secret C.I.A. operation and that therefore both Mr. Saleh and his factory were off limits, that unless the undersecretary of state wanted to hear from the National Security Council, he should cease and desist with his premature loan repayment. My father then sent an identical telegram to the principal American investor. My father then called the King, who had returned to bed with Esmerelda. It was an open line, so he was circumspect. "Your Majesty, that little problem involving pencils we discussed? It's not a problem anymore. Everything is back to normal."

"Excellent, Mack," the King exclaimed, pleased. "Thank you."

"Give my best to Esmerelda."

"I will."

Worry, the steam from the bathroom that had become the fog that had invaded our house, clung to everything, furniture, banister, and lamps, in weird tatters, half-present, half-real, half-seen, like torn banners in another kind of battle raging in the world I could not tolerate.

Johnny Allen got a girl from the French embassy pregnant. My father had to take care of that, too.

Roy and Barbara Sweetser decided to redecorate their house using an intensely Arabic motif. When they were done, they had a cocktail party to celebrate. They invited my parents. My mother and father arrived to find themselves inside an ersatz *souk,* the only light coming from cloying scented candles. They sat on pillows, on the floor, downing martinis, listening to Chet Baker on the record player, arguing about nuclear disarmament (the men con, the women pro) and civil rights (all pro except Mr. Sweetser, who felt things weren't too bad as they were, all things considered, which really pissed my mother off, and led her to an early and indignant departure, dragging my father with her). The Sweetsers, excited by the commotion, by their new decor, by Chet Baker, made love right there on the pillows, in the scented candlelight.

Renee came to dinner and drank so much she fell facedown in her soup. Misery, in grown-ups, I was beginning to sense, knows no bounds.

One Monday morning that November, at the weekly staff meeting, Ambassador Muir mentioned, in passing, that the statue of Abraham Lincoln should be constructed in a prominent spot, not some godforsaken backwater alley. His own suggestion was to have it built right smack in the middle of Circle Two on Jebel Hamra, of bronze, he imagined it, gleaming, solemn, inspirational for all the thousands of Arabs screeching daily around the circle in their exhaust-spewing cars and trucks.

"This is, after all, the whole point of building a statue of Abraham Lincoln," he went on. "To inspire people, to let them know that we have leaders to admire greater in stature than any Lenin or Stalin."

My father looked around the table. No one else had flinched. No one else seemed even slightly puzzled by this turn in the conversation. So it was left to him to raise his hand and ask the Ambassador, "What statue of Abraham Lincoln?"

The Ambassador peered at him, adjusted his wire-rimmed glasses. "Ah. I presumed you knew."

"I'm sorry, I don't."

"Well, a directive went out last week to all third-world ambassadors, instructing us to have built in our respective capital cities a highly visible and aesthetically pleasing statue of Abraham Lincoln."

"A directive from where?"

"The State Department. The highest level."

"The secretary of state?"

"Precisely. And just between those of us here, this comes with the President's full endorsement."

My father had to ask. "Am I the only one who thinks that's an insane idea?"

Much shuffling of papers, a sudden interest in just-remembered notes, preoccupied scribbling on yellow legal pads.

"You object, Mack?" the Ambassador asked.

"You bet I do, yes."

"Might I ask why?"

"Because the last thing we should be doing in this country is building monumental statues to ourselves." He was finding it hard to contain his anger.

Chester Boyden spoke up. "The point, as the Ambassador mentioned, is to inspire people locally."

"Inspire them to what?"

Chester grimaced. As far as he was concerned, that was a curve ball.

"We need everyone to get behind this, Mack," Jeffrey Blake said. "It's a strong idea. Sends a clear and direct message."

"What message?"

"Excuse me?"

"What is this clear and direct message? I sure the hell don't get it."

"The feeling at Washington is that a statue of Abraham Lincoln would project a positive image of America, which God knows we could use these days."

Chuckles all around.

"But nobody in Kurash has any idea who Abraham Lincoln is," my father countered, driving a nail into that particular argument.

Now there was a general and uneasy shifting of weight at the table, everyone apparently seeking new purchase on his sweaty wooden chair. The mood had turned truculent, resentful.

My father continued.

"All the average Kurashian will see is a huge and incomprehensible statue of an American, built by Americans, to glorify all things American, which I predict will quickly turn the average Kurashian even further against us. Furthermore, I'll bet you my wife that the King would not sanction such a thing. He, thankfully, is not an idiot."

He'd gone too far, and he knew it.

The Ambassador glanced around the table. Sensing consent,

he brought the discussion to a close. "I appreciate your thoughts, Mack, but this is pretty much a done deal. Now, let's turn to the redevelopment projects. Tad?"

Later that same day, back in his office, my father received the following cable: "Current intelligence suggests Soviets infiltrating Kurashian high command. DDP wants American asset placed at senior level immediately."

My father stood up from his desk and crossed to the window, that view he turned to when he needed to think: scraggly palm trees, rooftops, a minaret looking like a slender rocket ship about to be launched, much as, he reflected, the prayers within were launched by the faithful to heaven.

God help us, he sighed.

5

In 1957, before my mother and I joined my father in Kurash, we had spent a weekend in Portofino, which was then a sleepy, sun-washed haven for wandering yachts, with only two or three little restaurants. A few villas belonging to what we would now call the rich and famous—David Niven was one of them—were tucked discreetly into the deciduous hillside. Today Portofino is clogged with discotheques and boutiques, huge Mercedes wallow through the narrow street, Jet Skis whine like mosquitoes across the harbor jammed solid with bristling, top-heavy motorboats. I managed to find a room in a moderately priced hotel three blocks from the water. I immediately looked up Emily Moody Crane in the telephone book. She wasn't listed. I went down to the lobby, bought a postcard of Portofino, wrote another brief message—"On the trail of Emily"—and handed it to the desk clerk to mail. I also asked him for directions to the local police. He seemed stricken.

"Is anything wrong, signore?"

"Oh, no, no. Everything's fine."

The police were cordial, mildly curious. A Captain Giorgio Battiato welcomed me to his office, got me seated, offered me coffee, asked if I minded if he smoked, and when I said I didn't, lit up a Marlboro and studied me with kindly, forgiving eyes. Leaning forward, assuming what I hoped was an innocent, anxious attitude, I explained to Captain Battiato that I was looking for my very eccentric aunt, Emily Moody Crane, related on my mother's side. I told him that Aunt Emily had recently decamped from New Rochelle without a word of explanation to anyone, and that I was here only because we had received a series of cryptic postcards postmarked Portofino. I told Captain Battiato I was worried for Aunt Emily's safety, inasmuch as she had a habit of forgetting, at odd moments, who and where she was. "Like ex-President Reagan," I added, for verisimilitude.

Looking deeply concerned, Captain Battiato leaned back and drummed his fingers on the desk, considering various unknown possibilities. Was it a crime in Italy to lie to state officials? I wondered.

He told me, in hesitant English, to return to my hotel, that he would see what he could do, and that he'd be in touch. I thanked him and left.

I fully expected, the next time I saw him, to be arrested.

However, I had no choice but to wait, and while I waited I reviewed again my chronological chart, unfurled from the duffel bag and pinned to the wall of my hotel room. There were still significant gaps, especially in the crucial months of November and December 1958. Only inference could fill them. For example, I knew from the Langley files that on December 8, 1958, my father, reluctantly following orders from Washington to infiltrate the Kurashian Army Command, had sent Roy Sweetser to meet with Colonel Fawaz Mahmoud, General al-Rahal's second-in-command, and that Roy had proposed to him a working relationship. After meeting with Roy Sweetser, Colonel Mahmoud, the confused and frightened former tank commander, drove aimlessly around Hamra for several hours, trying to understand what had just happened to him. It seemed incredible, but it also seemed true, that a foreign government had asked him to spy on his own country. That he was being asked by what, in cold war terms, amounted to his country's parent state simply made the whole thing that much more complicated. I have seen pictures of him, standing behind the others, his superiors, a squat, barrel-chested man in his mid-thirties, mustached, rigid, faintly embarrassed. My father had picked the wrong man to approach, he was mistaken about what he took to be Mahmoud's neediness and vulnerability. That was simply Mahmoud's social awkwardness, a private man's bumbling presence in a public world, a look in his eye that said, Help, please get me out of here. You can see it in the photographs. But he didn't mean it. He was not ambitious. He needed nothing except solitude and maybe the simple comforts of his tank and crew on night maneuvers in the Syrian desert, his wife's obedience, his son's respect. So after driving around Hamra for a while, wondering what the hell he should do, he finally did the obvious, the right thing to do, and drove to the modern white limestone building downtown, asked to see Major Rashid, and then, when they were alone in Rashid's office with its plate-glass window and view of downtown Hamra and portrait of their young and smiling King, told him what had happened.

My father was summoned that night to Hamzah Palace. We were halfway through dinner when the call came. He left his meal unfinished on the table, shot my mother a guilt-ridden, apologetic look, and hurried out to the Opel. We heard the car sputter away down the street. For a moment, my mother sat perfectly still, her face a study in martyrdom, and then, with a great, surprising effort, she turned to me an utterly false smile and suggested we play Monopoly after dinner. Which we did, in the living room, on the floor, amid the stacks of her novels, sustained by Ella Fitzgerald, in a frenzy of forced cheerfulness.

My father, for his part, left his guilt behind at the front door. By the time he reached Hamzah Palace he was focused, alert, looking forward to another evening of holding the King's hand. Soldiers waved him through the gates, he parked and was escorted into the refurbished study that still smelled, faintly, of fresh paint. He sat and waited. Fifteen, twenty minutes went by. He smoked a cigarette, then another. He looked at his watch. He had been waiting for half an hour. He stood, went to the door, looked out into the dim hallway. There was a guard standing there, armed, who gave my father a friendly smile, but he spoke no English, and anyway, he had no authority, so my father returned to the study and waited some more. A full hour had passed, and he was just about to leave, figuring there must have been some mistake, or the King and Esmerelda were back in each other's arms, when the door across the room opened and the King abruptly entered. He did not apologize. He did not look directly at my father. He strode straight to his desk, sat down, his face working hard to find full expression for what he felt, the rage and betrayal and loss of faith in my father roiling and finally exploding, his voice, usually gentle, now strident, high-pitched, strangled. "He hauled me over the coals," is the way my father put it in a cable sent later that night.

"You ask my own officers to work for you?" The King was red-faced, furious. "To *betray* me?"

Oh, Christ, my father thought. Colonel Mahmoud.

Mistake #1.

"I thought we were friends," the King practically shouted. "I thought I could trust you."

"Your Majesty—"

"No. Don't say anything. You'll only make it worse. Goddamnit, Mack, how could you?"

My father said nothing, as ordered. The King finally looked him in the face, and his eyes were full of something my father had never seen there before: suspicion.

"You build three new listening posts and don't tell me?" he asked softly.

Rashid, my father thought. Fuck.

Mistake #2.

"This afternoon your Ambassador pays me a call. I treat him with dignity, with respect, and what does he do? He *informs* me that the United States intends to purchase the empty land in the middle of Jebel Hamra to build a statue of Abraham Lincoln. He *informs* me. That's the word he used."

Mistake #3.

My father lit a cigarette, shook his head sympathetically, affected an ironic despair. "You told him to go fuck himself, I hope."

"Stop it, Mack. Don't pretend anymore that you're different from them, that you and I must work together to keep them off my back. You *are* them, Mack. You're more them than they are."

The King rose to his feet and walked quickly from the study, neither saying goodbye nor closing the door behind him. My father waited for a while, then realized that the King wasn't coming back, that he had been dismissed. He drove to the embassy and drafted his cable to Washington.

O love

I know from a footnote in Thomas Polmar's *Heartbreak Arabia,* that on December 12, 1958, Roy Sweetser was "arrested at his home on Kaftoun Street by Major Rashid of Kurashian Intelligence and escorted to Kifah Prison. The United States government protested vehemently, and three days later, after a secret military trial, in which Mr. Sweetser was summarily judged guilty of espionage, he was escorted to the Hamra airport and sent back to Washington. It is only fair to assume that the King would have found this entire episode particularly egregious, since Kurash was America's putative ally."

Everything my father feared was coming to pass.

On December 10, the King closed all C.I.A. listening posts along his northern border and expelled the American technicians and the entire support staff, fifty-two people in all.

On December 11, the King demanded that the American Ambassador, Donald Muir, be immediately recalled and replaced with someone more understanding of Arab issues. The State Department sent out Randall H. Keeney, an old Middle East hand and former Ambassador to Saudi Arabia.

On December 12, the King released all political prisoners from Kifah Prison.

On December 13, the King invited the Russian Ambassador,

Pyotr Petrovitch, and his K.G.B. chief, Sergei Prokov, to dinner at Hamzah Palace.

On December 15, the King paid a surprise visit to Kumait in his apartment. A C.I.A. bug inexplicably malfunctioned and therefore the text of this conversation was garbled and unintelligible.

The King was pissed.

On December 16, no longer under house arrest, Kumait began reporting daily to Hamzah Palace to "advise" the King.

On December 17, the King made a short telephone call, monitored by the C.I.A. tap, to General Anwar, currently in exile in Egypt, to say he "forgave him."

During this period the King would not speak to or receive my father or, for that matter, anyone else from the American embassy. During this period, the King refused to accept any more financial assistance from the United States, including the monthly briefcase full of cash, which led Allen Dulles to call John Foster Dulles and say, grimly: "If he's not taking the money from us, then he's taking it from someone else." They both knew what that meant. John Foster had that very morning been diagnosed with inoperable colon cancer, but he did not tell his brother, he kept it to himself.

On December 18, on Radio Cairo, the King was praised for his courage in facing down the American bloodsuckers and he was lauded for his decision to stand with Nasser in defiance of American Imperialism.

On December 19, Kumait closed his notebook, finished with *The Oldest Rose*. It was incomplete, but he did not have time for scholarship anymore; *The Oldest Rose* would remain incomplete, a mere six chapters long. What had struck him most, reading back over what he had written, was how little history it contained and how much, too much, autobiography. He stretched his tired body. Then, for the first time in months, he tidied up his room. *The Oldest Rose*, he reflected, would not have been the story of

Kurash, but rather the story of his journey through Kurash's recent history, the story of his generation's bumpy ride through the postcolonial confusion that was not yet, it must be remembered, quite over. Kumait picked up his scattered books, stuck them firmly, dismissively, back into the bookcases, as if he were putting away forever his old affections.

He would be a modern man.

On December 20, Allen Dulles and John Foster Dulles met in Georgetown for lunch, in a little French place they liked on Wisconsin Avenue, then wandered through the Better Mousetrap looking for Christmas presents. Both wrapped in dark overcoats and muffled in plaid scarves, they looked like two aging funeral directors, which I suppose, come to think of it, is pretty much what they were.

"The little king," Allen sighed.

"Has the K.G.B. drugged him?" John Foster inquired hopefully.

"No, I think his derangement is his own doing."

It would never have occurred to either Allen or John Foster to plead guilty for pushing in the wrong direction at the wrong time. *Mea culpa* was not in their vocabulary.

John Foster lifted up a laminated place mat decorated with a Currier & Ives print, ice skaters on a cold day, leafless trees, and snow.

"Do you think Clover would like a set for Christmas?"

"I'm sure she would."

John Foster bought eight. They moved on.

"I don't like the idea of our little king meeting with the Soviets at all," John Foster said. "I mean, we're paying for the date, and he's off flirting with another girl."

Allen strolled placidly at his side, stopped to examine a very nice casserole pot, made in Sweden. "I'm afraid it gets worse."

"How could it possibly get worse?" his brother exclaimed, alarmed.

"Last night he secretly flew to Cairo and met with Nasser."

John Foster came to a stop in the middle of the Better Mouse-trap. "How do you know that?"

"I know it."

John Foster looked to see if Allen was joking, and when he saw he wasn't, revealed the flinty soul of his true Presbyterian self. "Fuck it. Burn him."

They continued with their Christmas shopping, moving on to Saville Bookshop, where Allen bought John Foster a nice edition of Churchill's *History of the English-Speaking Peoples*. Remember, if this seems callous, that these two men could devote no more than ten minutes to the King and his small country, now vanished. Even as they strolled among the crowded bookshelves of Saville, they had turned to other, pressing problems in Lebanon, Yemen, Saudi Arabia, Eastern Europe, Korea, Central America.

My questions are: How did Allen Dulles know the King had secretly flown to Cairo and met with Nasser? Did they in fact meet? I can find no verification that they did. And if they did meet, what did they talk about? What would the King say to the man who only five months earlier had ordered his assassination? What was the King *doing*?

I sat pondering these questions at the small hotel bar in Portofino, a polished counter and four stools. I was sipping my second Campari soda when Captain Battiato appeared, all smiles.

"We've found your aunt Emily," he announced.

6

I have since wondered why Emily Moody Crane agreed to see me. Was she merely curious to meet this unknown relative of hers? Had she sensed, or even been waiting, all these years, for my arrival, or the arrival of someone like me? Maybe she talked to me, once she saw me, because she took pity on me, or maybe it was to unburden herself of her part in this story, her secret role. Whatever the reason, she did not give me away to Captain Battiato, who had tracked her down to a rented apartment by the harbor. She did not condemn me to him as a liar, she did not tell him that she lived in Rome and had for close to forty years, which she could easily have proven. Did he not wonder at my New Rochelle aunt's fluent Italian? At any rate, she had asked him to speedily escort me to her building, which he did, a turn-of-the-century three-story house now divided into three apartments, one to a floor. We entered the *loggia,* creaked our way upward in another one of those ancient elevators of which the Italians are so fond, and rang her doorbell. It was opened by a woman in her mid-sixties, long and lanky, white hair worn in a ponytail. Emily. She had somewhat brutal green eyes, very honest, direct, giving me a once-over as she greeted Captain Battiato. He ceremoniously presented me, her long-lost . . . nephew, was it? I had gone completely blank. Emily thanked Captain Battiato. He gave me a wink, shook my hand, and departed. Emily looked me over again, this time more slowly, more carefully. There was something tough in her attitude, something not to be fooled with—it immediately forced an apology from me.

"I'm so sorry," I stammered. "I didn't know how else to find you."

"Who are you?" she asked.

"Terry Hooper. Mack Hooper's son."

"Jesus fucking Christ." She said this softly, leaned closer, looking for resemblances, then, without another word, retreated into her apartment.

"Shut the door behind you, please," she called back.

I did, then followed her down a short hallway. "I met your daughter in Rome. She told me you were here, but not where, exactly."

"Melissa told you I was here?"

Had I betrayed a confidence? I suspected so. "Well, I kind of browbeat it out of her."

"Bullshit. Nobody can browbeat anything out of Melissa."

We entered a small living room, clean white walls, bare of adornment, tile floor, a couch and a few chairs covered with a colorful material, floral in design, more South Seas than Italian. The lamps, however, were very Italian, modern, slender, angular, black.

"Sit down." She motioned to the couch.

I sat.

"Drink?" she demanded.

"No thanks."

"Well, I'm sure the hell having one."

She poured herself a whiskey at a small bar in the corner, then sat down in one of the armchairs and faced me. She took a good, hard pull on her drink, smacked her lips. "Terry Hooper."

"Yes."

"How's your father?"

"Fine. He lives in Boston. Charlestown, to be exact."

"Your mother?"

"Nearby. In Cambridge."

She seemed surprised. "They're divorced?"

"Not exactly. It's hard to explain. I don't understand it myself.

They live apart, but they see each other. They go to concerts, the museum."

"How fucking artsy. And how fucking like them." She treated herself to another substantial sip of whiskey. "They're well? I mean, physically? All working parts in good order?"

"Yes." I found myself looking around for wood to knock, settled for the arm of the couch.

"Good. I'm glad. I liked them very much."

"Where is it, exactly, that you knew them?" I finally allowed myself to ask.

She said nothing, just sat there quietly gazing at me, then slowly roused herself. "You don't know who I am?"

"No, I'm sorry, I don't."

"How did you find me, then? How did you know even to look for me?"

I told her about Mrs. Gourlie mentioning her existence, and Rome, and my father letting it slip, if that's what he did, and Bob Easton and the C.I.A. computer. A few fragments, connected together, a name—her name.

"That's it? My name?"

"Well, there's this."

I handed her my father's copy of *Travels in Arabia Deserta*. She seemed to start a little when she saw it, took it gingerly, warily.

"Open it," I said.

She opened the paperback and pulled out the single sheet of paper, read aloud: *"O love, you could not know or do know the way I feel thinking of you . . ."* She stopped.

"Go on," I said, more gently.

"*. . . as I stare out this window at the gravel driveway, the high garden wall, the palm trees and flat-roofed houses of the city . . .*"

She carefully folded the piece of paper, placed it back in the book, closed the book, and then, reluctantly now, it seemed to me, handed the book back to me.

"So?"

I showed her the other copy of *Travels in Arabia Deserta*.

"I found this in your apartment in Rome. Melissa let me borrow it."

"How *very* kind of Melissa," she muttered darkly.

I opened the book, pointed to the penciled comments scribbled in the margins.

"It's the same handwriting as the letter," I said.

She nodded, absently, staring at the book.

"A woman's handwriting, I would guess," I said.

"So it would seem."

"Yours?" I asked.

"Yes," she finally answered. "Mine."

"Emily, were you and my father lovers?"

"Lovers?" She asked me this as if she hadn't heard me right.

I nodded, starting to feel a tad embarrassed. I do believe I was blushing. But I don't think Emily noticed.

"*Lovers?* Your father and me?" She burst into laughter. "Is that what you think? Is that why you're here? Is that why you tracked me down?"

I'm sure I was bright red by now.

"Well, not just that, other things too."

"What? Do tell."

"I'm writing a book about my father, sort of. I'm a historian and I'm interested in Americans in the Middle East in the fifties, the ways in which we fought the cold war, the ways in which we lived overseas. Pax Americana, I guess."

"You know, I take it, what it is your father did?"

"You mean his work?"

She nodded.

"For the C.I.A.?"

She smiled sadly.

"Yes," I said. "I know."

We both contemplated the reverberations of that response. I

reconsidered, as I sensed she wanted me to. "Actually, I don't have a clue what he really did. That's why I'm here."

"To find out?"

"Yes."

"From me? Whoever I am?"

"Yes."

"You really want to know, Terry?"

"Yes."

She stood, moved to the bar, poured herself another whiskey. "Let me get this straight. You're spying on your own father? Is that right?"

"I'm just trying to figure out what happened."

"You sure you don't want a drink?"

"No, thanks."

"You're not much like him at all, then, are you?" She motioned with her chin to her drink as she returned to the armchair. "He was a drinker."

"Everyone was a drinker, as far as I can tell."

She laughed that laugh again, kind of bawdy, deep from the chest. "True enough."

"Drinkers and smokers and pill poppers."

"True, true, and true," she said, still laughing.

Emily Moody Crane, it suddenly seemed clear to me, had once been a very attractive woman, perhaps even beautiful, in a gangly, long-faced English kind of way. Her lusty, open laugh, the merry sparkle of her green eyes, the restless body, her blunt, strong hands clasping her glass of whiskey—though sixty-something, she radiated an aura vaguely promiscuous, a toss of the head and a challenge to follow her someplace exciting and dangerous.

"So, will you tell me?" I asked.

"What?"

"What I need to know?"

This seemed to irritate her. "More specific, please."

"Did you know my father in 1958?"

"Yes."

"How old were you at the time, if I may ask."

"You may not." She swirled the liquid amber in her glass. "Twenty-five."

"And how did you know my father?"

"I worked for him."

This threw me. "I thought you worked for the C.I.A. station in Rome, as a translator?"

"I did. That was before Kurash."

"You went to Kurash?"

"Yes."

"From Rome?"

"Yes."

"In 1958?"

"Yes."

"To work for my father?"

"Yes."

"I'm sorry, I'm confused. In what capacity?"

"A Happy Helper capacity. A Young Woman's Adventure capacity. A Stupid and Cruel capacity."

"You worked with him in the embassy?"

"No." She leaned forward, intent, her green eyes focused by the two whiskeys. "I worked with him outside of the embassy. My cryptonym was Esmerelda."

I stared, flabbergasted, at this white-haired ex-beauty with her flinty, bony English pride. She was Esmerelda? Was this possible? I scrutinized her closely, saw nothing but truthfulness shining from her unhappy face. She was about the right age, with the right features. And she was, of course, English. I remembered that after the King was assassinated, in early 1959, his widowed bride Esmerelda had returned to Europe, never to be heard from again.

The pieces tumbled into place. Astonishing, brilliant, and horrible.

"You were brought in from Rome by the C.I.A.?"

"Yes."

"Working directly for my father?"

"Yes."

"And it was arranged, by my father, that you would meet the King?"

"Yes. At the Go-Cart Club."

"And you took care of the rest."

"God help me, yes."

"What exactly was your assignment?"

"Spend time with him. Report on his activities, his moods, his thoughts."

"Was marrying him always in the plan?"

"No, of course not. We weren't expecting that at all."

"Why did you accept?"

"Because by that time I was in love with him. Your father was furious at me."

"Did you stop spying on him then? After you were married?"

She hesitated. Something inside her was crumbling away, letting go. I could see it in her face. "No," she said, very quietly.

The thought occurred to me: "Was it you who told my father the King had slipped off to meet secretly with Nasser?"

Again, the quiet voice, low, a child's confession. "Once the King and I were married, your father of course wanted me to continue letting him know anything I learned."

Emily said.

Esmerelda said.

"I told him, at first, to bugger off. I was the man's wife. Leave me alone. But when the King told me he was flying to Cairo to meet with General Anwar and President Nasser, and that they were going to sign some kind of cooperation treaty, I passed it on to your father."

Emily said.

Esmerelda said.

"How?" I asked.

"With this," she said, pulling the brittle piece of yellow paper from my father's copy of *Travels in Arabia Deserta* and pointing to the note: *O love . . .*

I stared at the straggling, faded words. "I don't understand."

"Each letter indicates a certain number, for example, 'a' indicates 'three,' which in turn indicates a certain word in the text, 'three' the third word, or 'nine' the ninth word, and so forth."

"The text being this?" I held up *Travels in Arabia Deserta.*

"Correct."

"Which is why you each had a copy?"

"Correct."

"How did either of you know which page or sentence in the book the numbers referred to?"

"We arranged it beforehand. Each week, a different page."

When the operation had started, in February, Renee used to drive past Esmerelda's apartment every day on her way to work, glancing up at her bedroom window. If there was a red dress hanging in the open window, Esmerelda was calling for an emergency drop-off. They continued this call system after Esmerelda married the King, Renee now swinging by Hamzah Palace on her way to work. On the day in question, she was startled to see a bright red dress hanging inside Esmerelda's room in the palace. Renee sped her way down to the embassy and informed my father. At noon that same day, Esmerelda had herself driven to Oristibach's Department Store in downtown Hamra. The car waited for her while she went up to the second floor escorted by several bodyguards, who left her alone only when she went into a changing room to try on a pleasant if somewhat conservative blue blouse. While in the changing room, door bolted closed, she removed an envelope from her purse and Scotch-taped it to the bottom of a chair placed there for customers' convenience. The changing room was, in espionage parlance, Esmerelda's "dead drop." She left Oristibach's after purchasing the blouse. Fifteen minutes later my mother wandered into Oristibach's and up to the second floor. She too stepped into the changing room, she with a skirt in her hand. She removed the envelope from underneath the chair and put it in her purse. She did not buy the skirt, thanked the salesclerk, took the elevator down to the first floor, and left Oristibach's.

My mother.

No doubt excited to at least be *doing* something.

Picture a small city in the desert forty years ago, call it Hamra, put a trolley line down the main boulevard, Al Kifah Street, add some silver-topped café tables under the arcades, men crowded there in *kaffiyehs,* soothing their worry beads, sipping the small cups of hot, sweet, Turkish coffee. Picture the way the sun, which is setting, casts long shadows across the windows of Oristibach's Department Store, explodes brilliantly in the windows on the other side of the avenue. The men, as one, slide on their dark glasses. Picture a dusty and somewhat battered red Opel moving cautiously through the insane traffic, buses and trucks and cars jammed every which way and all tooting their exasperated horns. Look closer, there—a man gets out of the Opel, parked at the curb now, and approaches one of the outdoor cafés. He stops, seemingly on a whim, and buys, from a man inside the shady sanctuary of his kiosk, a newspaper, the *International Herald Tribune.* He then continues on to the café, sits at a table, where my mother is waiting for him. They exhange hellos, a kiss. He orders a beer, lights a cigarette, a Chesterfield. She asks if she can see the newspaper, takes it, glances through it, folds it up, hands it back to him. They chat, pleasantly, at ease with each other, enviably so, if you ask me. The man knows that in a few minutes he will have to leave, but for now he is content to thank the waiter for his beer and take a first long, grateful gulp, enjoying the cold, cold rush down his throat and the gorgeous amber light falling upon the city at this hour. Then, almost reluctantly, he stands, drains his beer, takes the newspaper, kisses my mother goodbye, returns to the Opel, and drives back to work. In his office, alone, he opens the *Herald Tribune,* inside of which is folded Esmerelda's envelope. He pulls out the paper, reads, scrawled in her girlish hand: "O love, you could not know or do know the way I feel thinking of you as I stare out this window at the gravel driveway, the high garden wall, the palm trees and flat-roofed houses of the city . . ." Taking a Penguin paperback down from a shelf, he sits at his desk and ponders for a while certain correspondences, the transliteration of fragments. This is what he does, this is his job. He encourages people to see larger loyalties within their quotidian existence and then write him secret love letters betraying those living by other larger loyalties or, for that matter, by smaller loyalties, older loyalties. He lives by a code of sorts, a knight who knows he must bring home from battle not the shields of fallen enemies but sacred information, sacred because it can then be used to forecast and manipulate the fortunes of others, surely a godlike power if ever there was one. To know our secrets is his Holy Grail. He's an intelligence officer. He's a spy. He's my father.

"Why, if you really loved the King, would you betray him like that after you were married?" I asked Emily.

"I don't know," she said. "I've spent forty years asking myself that question." She shrugged. "Duty?"

"Emily—is your real name Emily?"

"Yes."

"Emily, did my father kill the King?"

"I don't know."

She pushed herself up from the armchair and finished off the whiskey bottle, no longer even bothering to ask me if I wanted any.

"The King *was* shot, right?" I asked.

"Yes. He was assassinated, in the garden behind Hamzah Palace. I was upstairs, reading. Your father was standing right next to him."

"Who assassinated him?"

"No idea."

Before leaving, I asked her one more question.

"Is Melissa the King's daughter?"

"Very good, Terry. Very, very good. Son of Spy. It's in the blood. It's in the bloody blood."

"Does she know?"

"Not bloody likely."

"I'm sorry, Emily, but I'm going to have to tell her."

"Figures. You kids all stick together."

"Good night."

She didn't answer. I left her sitting there in the bright arm-chair, as if folded within the palms of a forgiving flower, and walked slowly back to my hotel in a soft October rain.

7

What do we know?

Nothing but fragments.

What kind of man befriends another man, really befriends him, even as he's fucking him up the ass?

We know nothing but fragments, and yet we need to know the whole story, we need an ending, we'll even invent an ending if we have to, which is how history becomes myth.

Here and there, in the construction of history, you have to fill in the blanks, connect the dots, the fragments. Plausible reality must suffice, otherwise passive opposition will out—passive opposition being the notion, in C.I.A. jargon, that ninety-five percent of operational failures are due to incredibly small pieces of bad luck. I do not apologize.

As my father would say, I'm just doing my job.

No wonder Melissa did a double take when I told her I thought my father and her mother might have been lovers. She suddenly found herself confronting the hypothetical identity of her own long-lost father, and for a few seconds thought that I might be her brother. Her helping me, just that barest hint of a clue—"Portofino"—was a sister's gift, hesitant and hopeful. I did not have the strength to tell her yet what I now knew, the more complicated truth, so I flew back from Rome to Washington without calling her. In Washington, I stayed with Penny and her husband, Edith, and their adopted son, Jason, avoiding the sadness of the Gourlies' house on Dumbarton.

I called Renee. She answered on the third ring.

"Where the hell have you been?" She sounded really pissed off, as if I'd stood her up on a date, left her lonely and embarrassed in a restaurant or standing aimless in front of a theater. "I want to talk to you."

"I'll be right over," I said.

She was waiting for me at the door of her apartment, struggling to restrain Bertie as he tried to lunge at me in frenzied affection.

"Sit down," Renee ordered.

Bertie reluctantly settled, all guilty eyebrows and sidelong glances.

"You, too," she scolded me.

I sat down on the couch.

"I know about Emily," I said. "Or Esmerelda."

"Do you now?"

"Yes. I talked to her, in Italy. Portofino," I added, to be exact. "She told me everything except whether or not my father killed the King. She said she didn't know. I believe her. But I think you know, don't you, Renee?"

She gave me a very dirty look, lit a Salem, jabbed her gnarled finger at me as she spoke.

"I am sick and tired of having to watch people like you hound people like your father without my being able to say anything simply because decades ago I signed some goddamn oath. I've been looking for you because I've decided I'm going to tell you the truth."

She took a moment to suck angrily on her Salem.

"Secrecy is a double-edged sword, Terry. It's true that you can get away with murder, sometimes literally, simply by saying, 'Sorry, it's off-limits, top secret.' On the other hand, sometimes, because you have to keep a secret, you can't explain what's really going on, you can't tell the truth. That's what happened to Eisenhower during the so-called 'Missile Gap.' There was no Missile Gap. The U2 plainly showed that we had nothing to fear militarily from the Soviets. We were way ahead. But Eisenhower couldn't say that because he couldn't reveal his source: the U2. So all those right-wing lunatics and military suppliers, what Eisenhower later called the 'military-industrial complex,' were free to create a phantom crisis."

Renee leaned back in her chair, collected herself. "You want to know what happened?"

"Yes."

"I'll tell you what happened."

On the evening of December 22, 1958, around midnight, my father sat, benumbed, jet-lagged, in Hodd Freeman's office, admiring his suggestion of a view of the Mall and its sparkling Christmas lights.

She said.

Renee said.

We had not yet succumbed, as a nation, as a culture, to overhead fluorescent lights, and so lamps set the scene, gooseneck desk lamps, green-shaded library lamps, nautically minded table lamps, warm puddles of light between which three gloomy-faced men had gathered: a frail, etiolated Hodd Freeman; the new DDP Richard Bissell, tall, stooped, infinitely bemused, and quite possibly, it had occurred to my father, insane; and my father himself, afraid he might, at any moment, faint. He had been summoned back to Washington by Hodd only forty-two hours earlier, flying from Hamra direct to Rome, and from there to London, and from there to National, now Ronald Reagan, Airport. He's here, he's been told, to discuss the "Kurash situation," which is receiving "serious attention" at the "highest possible levels." This from Richard Bissell, now gazing intently at my father with what seemed to be almost scientific interest. "So, Mack, before we go any further, let's just say how proud we are of the work you've done in Kurash. Single-handedly, I might add."

"Thank you," my father muttered, susceptible, as always, to flattery.

"You staying with the Gourlies?" Hodd asked.

"Yes."

"Who's holding the fort in Hamra?" Bissell asked curiously.

"Jean," my father said, referring, of course, to my mother.

Hodd gave my father one of his happy, flickering half smiles, pleased and amused by this affront to orthodoxy. Station chief flies home to Washington for consultations and leaves his *wife* in charge. Bissell, on the other hand, seemed not to have heard. He continued staring at my father in that disconcerting way of his, as if my father were a specimen. It should be noted, for the record, that during the two days my father was gone from Hamra, my mother, with the help of Renee and Johnny Allen, acquitted herself honorably.

"Our little king has become a problem, Mack," is how Bissell got the conversation back on track.

This was the first time my father had heard the expression. "Our little king." He found it irritating in all possible ways, implying, as it did, that the King was "ours," implying, as it did, that the King was, in stature, small, childish, politically insignificant, a toy to be played with, or condescended to.

"The King is quite pissed with us at the moment," my father said. "Can't say I blame him."

Bissell nodded, not really listening.

"Last thing we need is more Communists in the Middle East," he noted. "I mean, we've got Nasser, we've got the Syrians—"

My father tried interrupting. "They're Baathists, Richard—"

"Same damn thing and you know it." Bissell wasn't interested in subtle distinctions. "We've got Abdul Karim Kareem in Iraq, and now . . ."

"Our little king," my father finished for him.

"Exactly," Bissell said, without irony.

And stood. "Dulles is waiting. Let's go."

My father and Hodd followed Bissell through a series of non-descript gray hallways cluttered with cardboard boxes of files until they reached Dulles's office, door open, the Great White Case Officer himself in plain view inside, behind his desk, sitting remarkably upright, lips pursed in concentration as he gazed down through steel-rimmed glasses at a pile of reports before him. He glanced up, saw Bissell, Hodd, and my father, waved them in, stretching out a hand to my father as they entered. "Good to see you, Mack."

He said it earnestly, and, as far as my father could tell, honestly, though they had only met a few times in the past, and then always briefly and in passing, in my father's memory mainly a rushed exchange of pleasantries, a stout man in a fine gray suit hurrying by and flinging back a quick "Hello." My father was surprised Dulles knew his nickname, "Mack," then realized that of course Hodd or Bissell would have told him.

"Sit down, everyone. Let's get right to it."

Dulles settled back behind his desk, shared with them a story. He had attended a meeting that very morning with the National Security Council, at which several members had asked him bluntly, "Why don't we just get rid of this little king?"

"Nudge him aside?" Dulles had asked. "We're not in control of the political process over there. The man's a hereditary tribal leader, his family has ruled various parts of the Middle East for centuries, he's related to a Prophet, for Christsake."

"No, no, Allen, we mean *get rid of him*," one of the President's men then said, leaning forward intently. "Wouldn't that be the simplest thing to do?"

Dulles had, according to his own description, flushed red and leaned right back into the idiot's startled face. "I want one thing to be understood by you and everyone else in this room. We do not assassinate our opponents. That is not in our nature; it is not part of our character. Never again are you to discuss murder with me, is that clear?"

Dulles finished his story, shared a commiserating shake of the head—sad, disgusted—with Hodd and Bissell. My father was starting to feel as if he were watching a puppet show in a language he didn't understand.

"Mack feels we should give the King a little room to breathe," Hodd said, turning to the subject at hand.

Dulles nodded, as if giving that thought due consideration, which he wasn't.

He turned to my father. "But Mack, you say he flew to Cairo, met with Nasser."

"It appears so, yes, sir."

"I don't like that at all, do you?"

"No, I don't. But I think the best solution is to let me talk to him, to rely on my relationship with him to calm things down. And don't forget, like his father, and his grandfather before him, he hates Communism."

"Hmmm. Give him time?"

"Yes, sir."

Dulles cracked his neck, stared out his window. "I think not, though I appreciate your point of view, Mack."

"I'm sure we can find a way to rein him back in," Hodd offered.

"I'm sure you can," Dulles said, and stood.

The meeting, apparently, was over. My father felt, if anything, even thicker. Why had they bothered to bring him all the way back to Washington? To tell him to "rein in" the King, whatever the hell that meant?

"Thanks for stopping by, Mack," Dulles said, as if my father had simply wandered down the hallway for a chat, not flown five thousand miles from a far-off desert kingdom. "Hodd will fix you up."

They shook hands goodbye, and then my father found himself being led by Bissell and Hodd into yet another Quonset hut and introduced to someone named Patrick Nitze, whom he had never seen or heard of before. In his early thirties, wearing a tweed jacket and gray flannels, his face scarred by adolescent acne, Nitze showed them into a room, locked the door behind him, pointed

sat at forty years later. There was no blaring TV in 1958 to inter-
fere with either conversation or solitary rumination, only a jukebox, playing Frank Sinatra's "I've Got You Under My Skin." With
the box from Garfinkel's placed gingerly on the counter between
them, my father and Hodd ordered the first of many malt
whiskeys. The next thing my father knew, he had a terrible hangover and Hussein was driving him to the embassy in the red
Chevy.

"I had stayed late, waiting for him," Renee said, speaking from
the past that had come alive for us both in her small apartment on
Wisconsin Avenue. "I was still on the wagon and I think envious
of his lingering hangover. Crazy, huh?"

"That's when he told you all this?"

She nodded.

"Then what?"

"He put the Garfinkel's box in the office safe and swallowed a
handful of aspirin. I dropped him off at your house."

In her clattering Renault.

From my window, I saw her drive away, saw him carry his
suitcase to our front door, heard him enter. Daddy was back. I
ran downstairs. He said, "Hey, chum," but was too tired and
depressed to do much more than that, so I sat nearby as quietly
and unobtrusively as possible while he relaxed with my mother in
the living room by the Christmas tree, drinking a drink, then
another, then another, his mood improving all the while until
finally he scooped me up with a monster's roar and carried me to
bed, more than I could do when my son was ten. He tucked me
in and kissed me, smelling of gin (he had switched to martinis
mid-Atlantic) and scratched my face with his unshaved cheek and
turned off the light and returned downstairs to my mother. I later
heard them, once again, in the bathroom, the shower running,
steam leaking out from under the door and filling the house with
the sticky, muggy sweat of anxiety and dread.

It was Christmas Eve.

to a Garfinkel's gift-wrapped box on a gray metal table. Garfinkel's was a prominent downtown Washington department store
in those days, the last days, the dwindling days, of 1958. The room
had no windows. The place was cold and stale.

"That's it," Nitze said, his voice strangely neutral, pointing at
the box.

They all stared at the box.

"Pat's the head of the DDP's technical services division," Bissell said. Nitze nodded hello to my father.

"He's prepared a little treat for you," Bissell went on. "He'll
explain everything, won't you, Pat? Well, I'm off. Good luck,
Mack."

Nitze let him out of the room, locking the door again when he
was gone. My father was looking to Hodd for information, a clue
as to what was going to happen next, but Hodd had retreated into
his own private universe and would not meet his eyes. Nitze
stepped to the table, untied the ribbon, opened the box, and with
a pen he pulled from his pocket lifted back a sheaf of tissue paper.
My father and Hodd stepped closer, peering inside. What they
saw was a plain, white handkerchief.

"Just give it to him as a gift and let chemistry take care of
the rest," Nitze said. "Don't touch it yourself. Give it to him in
the box and walk away."

Nitze, with his pen, prodded the tissue back down, closed the
box, tied the ribbon in an expert, graceful bow, and handed the
box to my father. "Have fun."

He unlocked the door, escorted them out, waved goodbye
from the door to his Quonset hut as my father and Hodd headed
back to Hodd's office.

"I've got you on a flight out of National tonight. How's Milton holding up? I worry about him. He shouldn't have quit the
Glue Factory. We'd have found a place for him."

It was about now that my father's mind started reeling, and he
wondered if he had heard all this right. Had Bissell and Hodd and
that man Pat Nitze said what he thought they'd said, or hadn't

said, or implied? When is an implication an order? *Was* it an order?

"You bet it was," Renee snapped, then whirled on Bertie, who had craftily slithered closer to me while Renee was talking and was now humping my leg, a glazed, lolling grin on his dachshund face. "Get *down,* goddamnit."

She dragged Bertie off me.

"I'm confused. What was all that business with Dulles and the National Security Council? 'This is not our nature, this is not part of our character'?"

"The Regular Spiel," Renee muttered darkly.

"The what?"

"The Regular Spiel. We don't, we never, it's not in our nature, how dare you . . . The Regular Spiel. Nothing must be *said.* Nothing must be *written down.* Nothing must be in any way *acknowledged.*"

"But still, somehow, orders are given."

"Yep."

"Can it be, Renee, is it really possible, that in the same world I inhabit my father was given a *poisoned handkerchief* to kill the King of Kurash?"

"Two years later, in 1960, the morons your father and I used to work for tried to kill the Iraqi dictator General Abdul Karim Kareem with exactly the same kind of poisoned handkerchief."

"Did it work?" I asked, gruesomely curious.

"Never got a chance to find out. His own countrymen got to him first. He was executed by a firing squad."

Still, there it is—a poisoned handkerchief.

"But the King was shot," I said.

"We'll get to that in a minute."

For now let us rejoin my father as he placed his hand on Hodd's sleeve and pulled him out to a dark, grassy area between Quonset huts. On the other side of a green fence, in the distance, probing the starry night, he could see the spotlit slender top of the Washington Monument.

"Hodd, what the fuck is this?" My father poked a finger at the gift-wrapped box from Garfinkel's.

"The means to an end."

My father looked closely at Hodd, who shrugged.

"Tell him it's a gift. He likes you. He'll accept."

"What are we talking about here, Hodd?" My father was trying to stay calm, but in fact he was starting to feel something like panic, he had now reached that dream state where every step seems taken through heavy, foot-dragging sand. He fought to control his voice. "This is nuts."

Hodd shrugged again and lit a cigarette.

"You've signed off on this?" my father persisted.

"I'm not stopping you, am I?"

"And Bissell?"

"Quote *incapacitation* unquote is quote *highly desirable* unquote."

"Bissell said that?"

Hodd nodded.

"What about Dulles?"

"It all starts upstairs, Mack."

"The President?"

"Let's go inside. I'm getting cold."

Hodd tossed his cigarette away and entered the Quonset hut. My father caught up with him, clutching the gaily wrapped package.

"It won't work."

"Sure it will."

"It'll get out, Hodd. You can't keep something like that secret."

"We can try, can't we?"

"Even if it works, someone worse will end up running the country, you know that."

"We were thinking of General Samir al-Rahal. He's not so bad. Come on, let's go get a drink. I sure could use one."

They repaired to Clyde's, sat at the same bar my father and I

What had my mother said to my father sitting in the bathroom choking on steam?

"I don't remember, sweetheart," she replied when I asked her,
on the phone in Penny's kitchen, back from Renee's that same
night.

From where I was standing I could see Penny and Edith sitting
on the couch in the living room, Jason between them, a blanket
covering them all, everyone laughing at the Simpsons on TV.
Edith's right hand idly, lovingly massaged Penny's neck. Jason
leaned his head on Edith's shoulder.

"You don't remember?" I asked my mother. "Or you're pretending you don't remember so you don't have to tell me?"

"The latter."

"Did you tell him not to do it?"

"Do what?"

"Kill the King?"

"With a poison handkerchief?"

"Yes."

"Do you know how ridiculous that sounds?"

"Of course I know how ridiculous that sounds," I said. "It also
seems to be true."

"I wouldn't know about that."

"Mother, I have a new theory. My new theory is that the reason you left Dad—"

"I didn't leave your father—"

"The reason you left Dad is that you're getting back at him for
having a crush on Emily."

"Who?"

"Esmerelda."

"Who's she?"

"You deny it? How can you?"

"Darling, shouldn't you be getting back to your adorable wife
and that darling house in Santa Monica?"

She may have been right, of course. Could be I was over the

edge. God knows I was suffering from jet lag as brutal as my father's, a hectic buzzing confusion that had been with me since I left Rome the night before in the hands of some hotshot Italian pilot gleefully lifting his Alitalia 747 into an opaque and terrifying fog. Like Sherlock Holmes in awful pursuit of his morphine nightmare Moriarty, I no doubt had let the search for my real father overwhelm me. I was aware of that. Critical distance had not completely abandoned me. I was even aware that perhaps it was too easy for me to demand moral rectitude of my father, in 1958, because he was, after all, at the time, in 1958, working in a world of mind-boggling uncertainties, or, put another way, such iron-clad certainties—Free World vs. Iron Curtain, God vs. godlessness, Democracy vs. Totalitarianism—that what seems now a questionable act might have been, at the time, an unpleasant necessity.

On December 26, 1958, a Thursday, two days after my father sat on the edge of the tub in the downstairs bathroom of our house in Hamra and had an unknown conversation with my mother, he awoke with a sharp pain in his stomach, a stabbing pain that signaled, though he did not yet know it, the beginnings of his bleeding ulcer. It would take him another six months to figure that one out, back here in Washington, in our house on P Street, crapping blood and being rushed to the hospital. His blood count was so low the doctors were afraid his heart would stop. They strapped him up to two IVs, both arms punctured, then cut him open and repaired the ruptured artery. But as I say, that was 1959. In 1958, he still had no scar running the length of his belly.

He drove to the embassy.

"I was, as usual, already there, waiting for him," Renee said, reaching down and stroking Bertie gently behind the ears. "Faithful Renee."

My father paused gloomily on the threshold of his tiny office with its bleak view.

"I suggested he move into Milton's old office." Renee gave me a baleful look. "As if a change of scenery could solve what ailed him. God, I was stupid sometimes."

Little paroxysms of pain evidenced themselves in his lower intestines. Without a word, he entered his own office and shut the door, alone with his misery, his decision.

Should he kill the King, as ordered?

Was he a good man, or a bad man?

"An hour later he came out of his office and walked straight to the safe and took out the Garfinkel's box." Renee looked me right in the eye as she told me this. "He asked me for a pair of scissors. Using the scissors as tongs, he lifted out the handkerchief and dropped it into an ashtray on my desk. Then he lit it with his Zippo and we went and stood over by the open window while it burned. We threw the ashes away."

"How did he explain not delivering the handkerchief to Hodd Freeman and Bissell?" I asked.

"He didn't have to explain it."

"Why not?"

"Because he did deliver a handkerchief, and he told them so."

"What handkerchief?"

"Another handkerchief, a perfectly normal handkerchief."

"How did he explain the fact that the King didn't sniff it and keel over?"

"He just said it must not have worked, that's all. Something wrong with the poison. Back to the drawing boards, Mr. Nitze."

"I'm confused. Why bother giving the King a substitute handkerchief? Why not simply tell Hodd Freeman the real one failed?"

"Cover story, Terry. You've always got to have a cover story. Your father didn't kill anybody."

This is Renee's story.

Her ending.

On December 31, 1958, my father was called forth by the King, a ringing telephone in our house a little after one in the morning. They had not spoken for almost a month. When my father arrived at Hamzah Palace, he was surprised to find the King alone with Esmerelda. No General Samir al-Rahal, no Major Rashid, no Kumait. Esmerelda lounged on a couch, barefoot, sipping Coke and reading *Dr. Zhivago*. Coming from a huge birch RCA console record player were the plaintive sounds of Ricky Nelson singing "Poor Little Fool." It was like walking into a teenage girl's bedroom, and there, in the midst of all this Western female dreaminess, sat the King, looking miserable.

"There you are, Mack," he exclaimed, seeing my father and springing to his feet.

Esmerelda let her eyes drift from her book lazily to my father.

He nodded. "Good evening, Your Highness."

"My what?" She laughed. "Esmerelda will do, thank you very much."

The King was pacing, agitated. The dark circles under his eyes were even darker than the last time my father had seen him. "I've called Kumait, Mack. He'll be joining us."

"How is he?"

"Fine, fine," the King declared absently. "He's helping me with my speech."

"Speech?"

"Yes. I've decided to give a speech tomorrow on Radio Hamra. Not only to the people of Kurash, but also to the rest of the Arab world. It's important that they all understand what I'm thinking."

"And what are you thinking, Your Majesty?"

"I haven't told you?"

"We haven't spoken in a while."

"I'm sorry, Mack. I've been so busy. There's so much to do."

"Your Majesty, could we talk alone for a moment?" my father asked.

Esmerelda, without looking up from her book, stuck her tongue out at my father.

"Yes, of course, let's go outside," the King said.

And so they came to sit in the dark garden, on a bench, admiring the shadows of Yusuf's handiwork, rich green foliage damp and sweet in the dry desert air. Fig trees, date trees, eucalyptus trees, olive trees, lemon trees, and the occasional spindly awkward palm tree surrounded them, arboreal sanctuary for their frazzled friendship. They said nothing for a brief while, smoking cigarettes, enjoying the night. Finally the King spoke.

"You're well?"

"I've been better."

"Jean, and Terry?"

"They're good, thanks."

"I am sorry, Mack." The King really did look guilty.

My father shrugged, studied the glowing red ash of his cigarette.

"Something happened inside me," the King said. "Something tumbled into place that's very hard to explain but which I know is guiding me onto the right path."

"You feel confident, about this being the right path?"

"Oh, yes, very confident."

"How do you know?"

"I've consulted Allah."

My father turned on him, appalled. "God told you to do this?"

"He let me know, in prayer, that my father, blessed be his name, would have approved, and that my grandfather, blessed be his name, would also have approved."

Hard to argue with a man who thinks he's getting instructions directly from heaven, my father reflected. The King looked so small and vulnerable on that bench in the garden that as always my father felt the urge to put his arm around him and reassure him, to protect him. Twenty-three years old and he already had the face of a tired, bewildered middle-aged man. For the first time, my father realized that the look of gentleness, of shyness, in the King's eyes, reflected also some kind of deep, unspoken sadness, and because of his youth it seemed a child's sadness, lost and needy, gazing out through the mask of this seemingly middle-aged monarch sitting on the bench next to him.

"You've been using me, Mack," the King said quietly.

My father chose not to deny it, to say nothing.

"I don't mean you, personally, I mean the United States. You I've always trusted."

Surely my father winced inwardly at this declaration of faith. After all, Esmerelda was close by, upstairs, a mocking denial of all the King believed regarding my father, personally.

"I have so much to learn," the King said, a kind of sigh. "I wish I were smarter."

"You're plenty smart, Your Majesty."

"Listen, Mack, just so you know, *I* know that Anwar would betray me again, *I* know that Nasser would use me as easily as the United States did, *I* know that the Soviets have met with as much success in Cairo as they have failure here."

"As I said, you're plenty smart."

"But I have no choice, given our history, given the West's unrelenting support for Israel, given the striving now gaining strength to create an *Arab* world, truly a world of my people, by my people, for my people—I have no choice, Mack. I must stand with Nasser."

"And the Soviets."

"If need be."

"They'll swallow you."

"I don't think so."

My father leaned closer, touched him on the elbow, with the concern of a father. "They'll get rid of you."

"Kill me?"

"If necessary."

"Why would the Soviets do that if I'm not a threat to them?"

"I don't mean the Soviets."

The King tried to read my father's eyes in the darkness. "The Americans?"

My father, again, for a long moment, said nothing. Silence, in this case, being affirmation. Then he straightened and gazed back out to the garden.

"Your best chance is with us," he said. "That's what I told you that first night we met, remember? When you took me out into the desert, and we ate dinner in the tent?"

"Sheep's eyes." The King chuckled.

"Yes." My father smiled. "Sheep's eyes."

Their eyes met, locked, broke apart.

"I told you then, and I'm telling you now, no matter what our flaws, no matter what our monstrosities, we will do you less harm than the Soviets, than Nasser, because we will never completely take away your freedom."

The King thought, shook his head slightly, and then said, for the third time that night: "I'm sorry."

"So am I," my father replied.

At that point Kumait joined them, shyly appearing on the terrace and squinting nearsightedly into the darkness. "Your Majesty?"

"I'm here, Kumait. With Mack."

"With Mack?" Kumait approached, saw the King, saw my father, smiled broadly. "Hello, Mack. How are you?"

"Tip-top, Kumait."

"And Mrs. Hooper?" he asked anxiously.

"I think Jean misses your excursions, to be honest."

Kumait looked uneasy. "Ah." Then: "Please give her my best."

"I will."

Kumait's graciousness made it almost impossible for my father to stay mad at him for very long. Then my father remembered the Garfinkel's box wedged into his inside jacket pocket. The charade must continue, if he was to have his way, if he was to inhabit his lie, his cover story. So now he reached into his pocket and pulled forth the nicely wrapped box and held it out to the King.

"While I was in Washington, I got this for you."

The King, delighted, a child at Christmas, accepted the box.

"It's nothing, it's stupid," my father quickly said. "When I told Jean what it was, she laughed at me."

"You went to a store and bought this for me?" the King asked, clearly touched.

My father nodded.

"Garfinkel's?" he asked, reading the lettering on the wrapping.

"It's a big department store, an old one, downtown."

The King fingered the lovely box. "Jewish?"

"Most likely. They've done very well in retail."

"Yes, yes. As they have here. Oristibach's is world-class, don't you think?"

"It is, yes."

"And now they will do very well in the desert. They will grow things where nothing has ever grown before. They will build universities to rival those in England and Germany and the United States. They will destroy our armies in battle, humiliate us, all of us—Nasser most especially, because he understands them the least. They are an admirable people."

He carefully unwrapped the box, opened it, pulled out the handkerchief, glowing with pleasure. Lifting it as if it were a precious diamond, he grinned. "Thank you, Mack."

He surprised my father, and maybe himself, by reaching out to embrace him, and as they fumbled awkwardly in each other's arms, trying to make sense of this improvised and deeply felt dance, the King dropped the handkerchief. Kumait leaned down to retrieve it. There was a quick, muffled report, a sound my father and the King recognized simultaneously. A gunshot. They exchanged this knowledge in a look. That's all the time they had. Then the bullet struck the King above his left lobe, jerking his head to the right, a hole exploding in his skull, bone splinters and blood and brain matter spraying out like a leaking fire hydrant. He was already dead.

On the outskirts of Little America.

December 31, 1958.

Three a.m.

New Year's Eve.

8

On that hot summer morning in Georgetown, in 1957, more than a year before the death of the King, when the front door of our stucco house on P Street opened wide and I stepped out with my mother and my father, playing Spy, the great good fun was being able to feel, while playing, that everything in life holds some significance, that even such a simple task as walking into People's Drug Store holds the suggestion of meaning. Reality is a mosaic of clues to be deciphered and interpreted. That's not just a frizzy-haired lady behind the counter, that's a plant, a tail, watching you. Speak openly and the microphone concealed within the sugar jar will record everything you say. It's exhilarating, the pure positive charge of paranoia, which sometimes I think is all we've got left to grant us a universe with plot, now that religion has abandoned us. While the rest of us sank further and further into a miasma of rootlessness all through the fifties and sixties, my father and his cohorts were living in a world bursting with signification. Everything made sense, at least hypothetically. Line up the clues, get your fragments in order, and there it is—a story, unearthed, revealed, by you. The Truth. What's Really Going On.

Was my father a good man, or a bad man?

I don't know.

Did he betray the King?

Yes.

Did he kill the King?

I wonder now if these are the appropriate questions . . .

Question: As a servant of the United States government, if my father failed to discharge his orders and pass to the King a contaminated handkerchief, was he not, in fact, a bad man? Would a good man, by that definition, not have done his duty and got rid of the twenty-three-year-old monarch?

Question: As an employee of the Central Intelligence Agency, did my father ever really have a friendship with the King to betray, or was the only betrayal possible for him a betrayal of the Central Intelligence Agency, which in a way is exactly what he did by passing to the King a noncontaminated handkerchief?

Of course, as my father said to me a long time ago, we never know the whole story, not one of us really ever knows everything. So the plot remains arbitrary, the meaning an illusion, the intelligence officer's world as chaotic, finally, as our own. Perhaps more so, because for one fleeting moment he allows himself to think he's . . . almost . . . got the . . . answer.

When I left Renee the night she told me *her* story, *her* ending, as I bent down to kiss her goodbye, she suddenly grabbed me, her fingers digging into my shoulders like claws. I could hear her, breathing hard beside me, but she said nothing, just held me like that, then just as suddenly let me go, whispering, "Good night, dear boy." I drove back to Penny's, wondering what that had been all about. Standing in Penny's kitchen, I called my mother, challenged her, learned nothing. The next day I telephoned Bob Easton at Langley and asked him if I could come back out and look again at the declassified files.

"Why not?" he said, cheerful as the prep school coach he so resembled.

I spent five ten-hour days in the Research Library at Langley, going back through reams of paper, trying to find half-remembered fragments of fragments, scraps I had already read without seeing their place in a pattern. When I felt I could learn no more, I said goodbye and thanked Bob Easton, I said goodbye and thanked Penny and Edith and Jason. I left Washington and drove slowly north in my rented blue Taurus, listening to the radio and, I guess, thinking. When I got to Boston it was almost ten, a cool New England night. I drove straight to Charlestown, parked, walked past the old Navy Yard to my father's condo. I looked up at his lighted window. An occasional shadow passed back and forth. My father, no doubt.

Who did not poison the King.

I sat down on a low stone wall bordering the brick walkway, gazed out over Boston Harbor, boats asleep in the lulling liquid darkness, the only sound a quiet slap of wavelets and jingle of rigging against aluminum masts.

If my father did not poison the King, does that mean he didn't kill him?

In a cable sent to Washington on January 1, 1959, the morning after the King's assassination, my father reports that "so far we have unearthed not a single clue as to the shooter's identity. Major Rashid and I found the hillock outside the garden from which the shot was taken, footprints and cigarette butts and a single spent shell, but that's it so far, no condemnatory evidence or witnesses. Rashid is sure Nasser is responsible. Lacking any other facts to the contrary, I tend to agree with him. I should add that Major Rashid is distraught at the King's death, as indeed is the whole country, and that I worry about him. His hands shake and he constantly looks away from me, embarrassed by his unbidden tears."

In a cable sent the next day, January 2, my father mentions that "our station driver, Hussein, has vanished, and with him our Chevy." He chalks it up to thievery, and requests a new Chevrolet, which by then would have been a 1959 model, with its swooping gull wings for fins, one of my personal favorites, especially in aquamarine.

Checking through Hussein's file, compiled when he first applied for the job as station driver in 1956, two years before my father arrived in Hamra, I found that Hussein served for three years in the Kurashian Army and that he was a sharpshooter. I also found a note, initialed RS—Roy Sweetser?—indicating an unconfirmed report that Hussein, a deeply devout Muslim, belonged to the then-outlawed Muslim Brotherhood. "This is not considered evidentiary, given the source. Furthermore, even if true, it would in no way disqualify him for the job. Though outlawed, I do not consider the Muslim Brotherhood a serious threat in any way to American interests."

Good call, Roy.

According to a newspaper article clipped from the English-speaking *Kurashian Times* and marked "Background Information," published six days before the King's assassination, "Jamil al-Amir, one of Amarak's leading businessmen, spoke to a gathering of concerned Kurashians today at the Hamra Rotary Club luncheon in the old Government Building on Al Kifah Street. His economic forecast for the coming fiscal year was surprisingly upbeat. He did caution, however, against placing 'too much faith in the ability of His Majesty to make good in three months promises made today,' instead urging his listeners to 'create business channels independent of the current monarchy.' Hamzah Palace had no comment."

Current monarchy?

Jamil al-Amir, it must be remembered, was a member of the Islamic Action Front of the Muslim Brotherhood. When last seen speeding away in his Mercedes from his country house near Lake Ramadi, in the marshlands of southeast Kurash, fleeing the arresting agencies of General Anwar's revolution, he swore vengeance on Kumait, who he assumed had betrayed the Muslim Brotherhood to General Anwar and the Socialist Nasserites.

Kumait, at Jamil al-Amir's insistence, had been drummed out of the Muslim Brotherhood soon after the King defeated General Anwar and released all political prisoners from the soccer stadium. Jamil had accused him, in his absence (he was still under house arrest) of "murderous betrayal." Kumait protested his inno-cence in a letter to the executive committee, but no one, certainly not al-Amir, believed him.

Kumait was standing right next to the King when the King was shot.

Kumait was standing between the King and the barren hillock beyond the garden wall from which the assassin fired.

The assassin fired.

At the same moment, Kumait stooped to retrieve the fallen handkerchief.

The bullet, destined for Kumait, hit the King and killed him instantaneously.

Hussein, who frequently drove my father in the Chevy to Hamzah Palace, and who would therefore have been familiar with the lay of the land, disappeared twenty-four hours later.

"Enjoying the view?"

I looked up, startled. It was my father, standing in the light cast by the glass door to his building.

"I glanced out my window for a reassuring vista and what did I see? My one and only son sitting down here desolate as Eeyore."

He came and sat next to me on the low wall.

"Thanks for the postcards," he said, with what I took to be a smile. "Did you find Emily?"

"You mean Esmerelda?"

"Yes, I guess I do."

"I found her."

"She told you everything?"

"She told me a lot. Is it true?"

"Probably. How is she?"

"Guilt-ridden, I'd say, despite the forty years."

My father nodded. "She was really a beautiful girl back then. A real spark."

"I could tell," I said.

"I'm not sure I really care about any of it anymore," he said softly, to the night more than to me. "You were right. It's a gone world."

"Yes, it is."

He looked at me. "Were you going to sit out here all night?"

"I've got a midnight flight back home. I just wanted to say goodbye."

We stood.

"Are you happier?" he asked me. "Did you learn whatever it is you wanted to learn?"

"I certainly wouldn't use 'happy' to describe my state of mind at the moment. Did I learn what I wanted to learn? I don't know. Maybe. More than anything, I'm tired."

And I missed my wife, whom once again I want to praise in the strongest possible terms for her striking good looks and wise, generous spirit, letting me wander the ends of the earth all these months without complaint.

I decided it was time and faced my father.

"Dad, Hussein the driver killed the King, didn't he?"

For the first and only time in my life I saw my father startled, completely taken aback. He covered, fast.

"It's possible," he acknowledged, speculatively, calmly. "He had ties to the Muslim Brotherhood we should have investigated but didn't."

Hussein the lowly driver, the man no one would notice, the man no one thought could possibly be important.

"Actually, Dad, I was thinking more along the lines of maybe you got Hussein to pull the trigger and then spirited him out of the country."

My father's sagging defeat, a sudden slouch of his shoulders, told me I had scored a direct hit. It made my stomach turn over, and for a second I was afraid I might throw up.

"Hussein missed Kumait and hit the King," my father countered.

"No, I don't think so. I don't think he was ever supposed to kill

Kumait. That was just the cover story. He was supposed to kill the King, which he did. But if he were ever caught, it could never be traced back to you, unlike that idiotic poisoned handkerchief. He'd say he did it for Jamil al-Amir, for the Islamic Action Front of the Muslim Brotherhood, that he'd been aiming for Kumait, in revenge for Kumait's supposed betrayal of the Muslim Brotherhood, only he'd missed, being a little rusty, and hit the King instead. And he'd say it convincingly, since he thought it was true. Al-Amir recruited him. Al-Amir worked for you. Al-Amir was Thoreau."

My father said nothing. He was very small beside me now.

"Renee almost convinced me otherwise. You can tell her for me, she's good."

Still, he said nothing. He glanced away.

"Goodbye, Dad."

Were those tears in his eyes?

"Goodbye, son."

We did not embrace. He turned and walked back into his building, up to his condo and his view of Boston Harbor. I returned to my blue Taurus and drove out to Logan Airport, where I caught the red-eye back to L.A.

Consider the fragments . . .

By mid-1959 it had become apparent to all concerned that Kurash would not survive the King's death. For a while General Samir al-Rahal, Army chief of staff, tried to rule, calling himself a Royal Prefect, but he was soon ousted by his own junior officers, young Baathists who, with Egyptian and Syrian backing, arrested and executed just about everyone they could get their hands on, certainly all leading Bedouin officers and the entire Islamic Action Front of the Muslim Brotherhood, including Jamil al-Amir, aka Thoreau, my candidate for the man behind the seemingly inadvertent assassination of the King. Executions took place at night, in the desert thirty miles outside Hamra. General Anwar returned with his family from Cairo and set himself up in

Hamzah Palace, sleeping in the King's bed. The King's mother was smuggled out of the country by the C.I.A. and relocated to Beirut, where she lived another four years before dying of lung cancer. Esmerelda, as we've seen, pulled a vanishing act, back to Rome. Her daughter, Melissa, was born in San Giacomo Hospital eight months into 1959. Last week I sent a letter to Melissa at her mother's address in Rome, telling her what I know, about her father, but I have no idea if she ever got it. She appears to me, sometimes, in my dreams.

By 1960, Kurash was close to anarchy, General Anwar having been arrested and shot by a resurgent Muslim Brotherhood, bearded conservative *imams* eager to have things their way. Terrified women all across Kurash disappeared behind veils. Those who refused were viciously beaten in the streets by wild-eyed divinity students, young men hopped up on visionary horseshit. Soon the countryside had drifted apart from Hamra, ruled by provincial tribal chieftains all at war with each other for obscure reasons dating back thousands of years. Israel moved its armies to their border nearest Kurash, threatening to intervene, and, in the process, implicitly, take over. Spurred on by this threat, supported by Nasser, Iraq and Syria sent in their tanks and infantry on the night of August 12, 1963. Within three days they had squelched all resistance, and within a month they had divided the spoils, the northeastern portions of Kurash going to Syria, the rest, including Hamra and the southern marshlands, merging with Iraq. Kurash was gone.

Kumait made it out, first to Beirut, then to Cyprus, where he died in exile of natural causes in 1975. *The Oldest Rose,* all six chapters, was published posthumously.

Major Rashid was brought out by the Americans. He lived near Dupont Circle in Washington for a few years, working for the C.I.A. as an analyst in its Middle East division, then quit to manage a rug business in Arlington, whose principal clients were exiled and nostalgic Kurashians, Palestinians, Iraqis, Syrians,

Egyptians, Saudi Arabians. They came not so much for the rugs as for the conversations and small white cups of Turkish coffee.

John Foster Dulles died of colon cancer in 1959.

Allen Dulles retired as Director of the C.I.A. in November 1961, his career cut short by the Bay of Pigs debacle that April.

Question: Who took the photographs of Kumait and Anwar when they were students at A.U.B. in the thirties?

Question: Did my father ever meet with Abdul Kilani, the member of the Kurashian Communist Party introduced to him in the Hotel Antioch bar by MI6's Leslie Smythe-Jones? There is no record in the C.I.A. files I studied of such a meeting. But why wouldn't my father have followed up Smythe-Jones's introduction? Remember, Smythe-Jones later urged my father, quite strongly, at the American Club, to call Abdul. He even gave my father Kilani's telephone number.

Question: Is it pure coincidence that Abdul Kilani was a young professor and neophyte Communist at A.U.B. in the late thirties, the same time Kumait and Anwar were students there?

Question: Who took those photographs of Kuwait and Anwar, in Beirut, in the late thirties?

The only time I've seen what was once Hamra, Kurash, since leaving forty years ago, was during the Gulf War, when, to bolster our morale, to make it quite clear how much of a monster we were going up against in Saddam Hussein, CNN broadcast footage of his most recent use of biological toxins against his own people. There I was, in my kitchen in Santa Monica, boiling water for the pasta, when Hamra appeared on my TV screen, only now it was called something else, another name, I can't remember what. With gruesome attentiveness, the camera wandered from pile of corpses to pile of corpses, what was left of the gentle citizens of Hamra, now, finally, really dead. Dead mothers curled up, their dead babies in their arms, their dead fathers and husbands holding them both, as if they could ever, in this life, protect them. My wife glanced away, but I said, "No, look, there's Feisel Square, there's Al Kifah Street, that's the store where I got my British soldiers." British soldiers still with me, marching across my mantelpiece in the living room.

Hamzah Palace, now some kind of school, or prison . . .

Hotel Antioch, now called Hotel Saddam Hussein . . .

The dead so unruffled, so untouched, they looked as if they were sleeping . . .

In a drawer of his desk my father keeps several black-and-white photographs that I have studied as closely as rabbinical students have studied the Talmud. In one photograph my father can be seen shaking hands with Allen Dulles in what looks like an airport waiting room, at night. Indeed, there is a clock on the wall over their shoulders that reads 12:00, and across the photograph an inscription has been scrawled: "To my midnight friend, with genuine regard, Allen Dulles." In another photograph, the saddest photograph I have ever seen, the King sits in the garden of Hamzah Palace playing chess with General Anwar. The King is concentrating hard on his next move, probably no more than nineteen years old, surely no more than five feet five inches tall, and he is being watched laconically by the man already, no doubt, plotting his downfall. The third photograph that holds me most avidly is of a group of men, the King and my father among them, racing around the track of the Hamra Go-Cart Club in their speedy, tiny, toylike go-carts. One night, upon closer examination, staring at this photograph through a magnifying glass, I realized with a start that the solitary figure of a boy in shorts watching from the sidelines is me.

When my father was rotated back to Washington in 1959, when we returned to our stucco house on P Street, he was rewarded for "valiant service" in Kurash with an Intelligence Medal, the highest award offered by the C.I.A., pinned to his suit lapel one October afternoon by Allen Dulles. In attendance were my mother, polite but stony-faced; Renee, weeping uncontrollably; Milton and Lorraine Gourlie; Roy and Barbara Sweetser; Hodd Freeman; Richard Bissell; and a few other close C.I.A. friends. After the presentation, at which Dulles spoke of my father's "modest, indeed self-effacing courage," white wine and cheese bits skewered by toothpicks were served. My father was warmly congratulated by all those present. As they congregated around him, a short, almost nondescript man none of them had ever seen before inconspicuously relieved my father of his Intelligence Medal and carried it off to another room, where he put it in a safe, where it joined the company of all the other Intelligence Medals passed out since the beginning of time. Because my father could never admit to working for the C.I.A., he could not possibly have been given a medal by the C.I.A. Officially, you see, he did not exist. The medal stayed in that safe until he retired. He keeps it now in the same desk drawer as the black-and-white photographs.

"All is forgotten, all is forgiven," I've heard him mutter.

He too has learned his history.

Acknowledgments

The poem "Resurrection and Ashes," quoted on page 71, is by Al Almad Sa'id, aka Adonis, and appears in *Modern Arab Poets, 1950–1975,* translated and edited by Issa J. Boullata (Three Continents Press, 1976).

The translation of the Muslim call to prayer and the translation of the Koran quoted on pages 86–91 are taken from *Islam* by Alfred Guillaume (Penguin Books, 1954).

The translation of the line "Fate proceeds on its way, and both doctor and patient depart . . ."—which appears on page 174—is from a poem by the Iraqi poet Al-Sherif Al-Radi. For this translation, as well as wealth of information about Arabic prosody, I am indebted to A. J. Arberry's *Arabic Poetry* (Cambridge University Press, 1965).

The notion of the "regular spiel" I first discovered in Thomas Powers's biography of Richard Helms, *The Man Who Kept the Secrets* (Alfred A. Knopf, 1979), there attributed to an unidentified C.I.A officer.

A NOTE ON THE TYPE

This book was set in Adobe Garamond. Designed for the Adobe Corporation by Robert Slimbach, the fonts are based on types first cut by Claude Garamond (c. 1480–1561). Garamond was a pupil of Geoffroy Tory and is believed to have followed the Venetian models, although he introduced a number of important differences, and it is to him that we owe the letter we now know as "old style." He gave to his letters a certain elegance and feeling of movement that won their creator an immediate reputation and the patronage of Francis I of France.

Composed by Creative Graphics,
Allentown, Pennsylvania
Printed and bound by Quebecor Graphics,
Fairfield, Pennsylvania
Designed by Virginia Tan